— BOOK 3 —
TARAN EMPIRE SAGA

EMPIRE
DEFIED

A K DUBOFF

Published by Dawnrunner Press
Cover Copyright © 2022 A.K. DuBoff

ISBN-10: 1954344287
ISBN-13: 978-1954344280
Copyright Registration Number: TXu002316470

0 9 8 7 6 5 4 3 2 1

Produced in the United States of America

TABLE OF CONTENTS

THE CADICLE UNIVERSE

Tarans are the predominant race in the Cadicle Universe; humans are a Taran genetic offshoot. Most of the Taran sphere falls within the purview of the Taran Empire, governed from the planet Tararia by a council of High Dynasty families. Earth is one of several rogue colonies on the outskirts of the Empire, separated so long ago that they have forgotten their Taran ancestry.

The Tararian Guard is the primary military force for the Taran Empire. Its counterpart, the Tararian Selective Service, includes a specialty branch with Agents gifted in telekinetic and telepathic abilities. The TSS is headquartered at a base inside Earth's moon, and its iconic Agents are known in Earth lore as the mysterious 'men in black'.

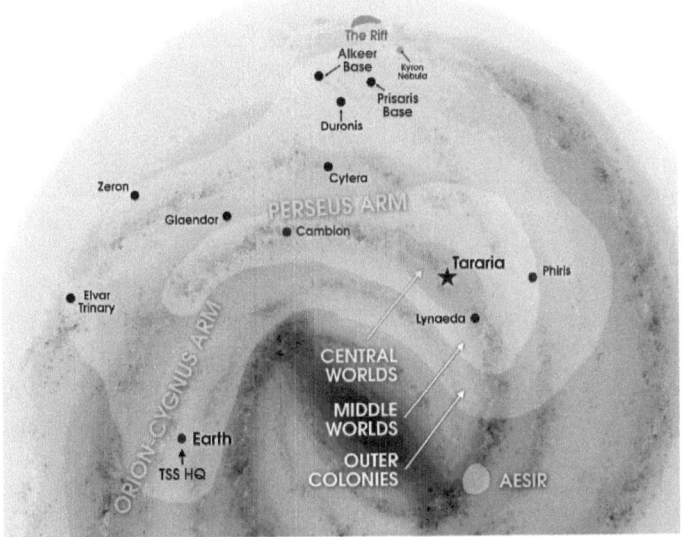

KEY TERMS, CAST & LOCATIONS

KEY TERMS

Taran – The race of all people in the Taran Empire; synonymous with human

Aesen – The foundational energy of the universe; pure energy capable of being shaped into any form

Erebus – The nickname for a race of high-dimensional aliens with exceptionally strong control of aesen energy

Jump – Faster-than-light travel through subspace using the SiNavTech beacon network

Beacon Network – The navigation method for subspace jumps, maintained by SiNavTech

Independent Jump Drive – A jump drive that does not rely on the SiNavTech beacon network for navigation

High Dynasties – The seven ruling families of the Taran Empire, collectively a governing council

Lower Dynasties – Influential families throughout the Taran worlds, second only in power to the High Dynasties

ORGANIZATIONS

Tararian Guard – The primary military force for the Taran Empire

Tararian Selective Service (TSS) – A quasi-military

organization with Agents specializing in telekinesis; a complement to the Tararian Guard

Taran United Force (TUF) – A new unified branch of the Taran military

Coalition – A shadow faction operating in the shadows of the Taran Empire, known to have multiple arms including the Alliance and SPEAR

Priesthood – The former governing body of the Taran Empire

Aesir – A reclusive group of technologically advanced Tarans

CAST

TSS

Jason Sietinen – TSS Primus Elite Agent; son of Wil and Saera; twin brother to Raena

Wil Sietinen – TSS High Commander; Jason's father

Saera Alexri – TSS Lead Agent and head of Primus Division; Jason's mother

Michael Andres – Primus Elite Agent / Head of TSS Operations and lead Primus Division trainer; Wil's close friend

Lexi Karis – Head of Civilian Training; Jason's partner

Coalition

Magdalena Steyn – Suspected leader within the Alliance/Coalition

Tararian Guard

Jakob Mathaen – Admiral of the Tararian Guard

Taran United Force (TUF)

Kira Elsar – Head of the recently formed TUF; former Major in the Tararian Guard

Leon Caletti – Civilian consultant, geneticist/scientist; Kira's fiancé

Taran Government

Raena Sietinen – Sietinen Dynasty heiress; twin sister to Jason; Ryan's wife

Ryan Dainetris – Head of the Dainetris Dynasty; Raena's husband

Cris Sietinen – Head of the Sietinen Dynasty and SiNavTech executive; Wil's father

Kate Vaenetri – Cris' wife and Wil's mother; member of the Vaenetri Dynasty

Celine Monsari – Head of the Monsari Dynasty and MPS executive

Other Key Characters

Dahl – Oracle with the Aesir; Wil's main point-of-contact and longtime friend

Darin Suro – Sole survivor of the *Andvari*

Melisa – Lexi's friend, who disappeared after joining the Alliance

Ships

Conquest – TSS flagship with a unique telekinetic energy weapon

LOCATIONS

TSS Headquarters – Base inside Earth's moon

Earth – A 'lost colony' of the Taran Empire, located in the remote Outer Colonies

Tararia – The capital planet of the Taran Empire

Duronis – A developed planet in the Outer Colonies, base of operations for the Alliance

Lynaeda – Technologically advanced central world, specializing in AI and cybernetics

CHAPTER 1

JASON SIETINEN'S HEARTRATE accelerated with anticipation. They'd been waiting for a turning point in the Coalition investigation for months, and now his team was only moments away from what might be their breakthrough discovery.

He brought up a telekinetic shield around himself as he stepped off his team's transport ship into the hidden facility. *We might finally get answers about what they've been doing in the shadows.*

His investigative team had received a tip about the lab they were about to enter. Located on an asteroid, it was the kind of place that could easily go undetected for years. Though the facility appeared to be powered down based on the remote scans, it was also possible that it utilized shielding to hide the real activity within.

"I don't know what we're going to find in there, so stay sharp," he told his team.

Two Agents took the lead ahead of him, and the three of them were followed by a dozen Militia soldiers. Though the place was supposed to be empty, he wanted enough people on their side to respond to any hidden resistance they might encounter.

Stale air assaulted his nostrils as he entered the bunker. A thin film of dust had settled on the surfaces, suggesting that the place was, indeed, abandoned. However, he noted that there was still artificial gravity—though thirty percent below standard levels—so the power reserves were intact. This had been a planned shuttering of the facility, possibly with the intent to return at some point in the future.

Jason scanned the metal-clad corridor walls as he stepped through the confined space, looking and telekinetically sensing for any signs of traps. Though they'd already disabled the occupancy alarm sensors, there would likely also be triggers on the computer network. Fortunately, he'd brought tech specialists along on the mission.

The corridor opened into a lab space with terminals around the outer perimeter, a medical bed, and an enclosed chamber along the back wall. He recognized the pod as being used for inducing stasis, though there were no signs of a person currently being held in suspended animation.

"What the fok went on here?" one of the Militia officers whispered.

Jason's private thoughts echoed the question. *This looks like a lab for medical experimentation.*

As soon as the TSS had learned that people with abilities were specifically being pursued, Jason had feared that it was for those ends. Gifted people had been targets for as far back as anyone could remember. It was entirely possible that someone had continued the Priesthood's line of research. To what ends remained to be seen.

"We need to get into the computer system to see if there are clues about who was working in here." Jason motioned to the Militia tech specialist on the team, Anya, to take the lead.

She approached the main console and tapped the screen; it didn't respond to her touch. "Looks like we'll need to get the main power on first."

One of the Militia soldiers located and opened the control panel, and Anya brought over her tablet to begin trying to crack the system's security.

"Bomax, this is sophisticated encryption," she muttered. "Things this good aren't normally in criminal syndicates."

"What kind of organizations, then?" Jason asked.

"Business. Government. Definitely good funding to hire top programmers for custom code."

He nodded. That would fit with a Priesthood connection. It also didn't rule out Monsari or one of their subsidiaries.

"I'll make a copy of the code and see if I can track down who did it." She frowned. "Once I'm in, that is."

After another minute, her expression brightened. "All right! Got it."

A moment later, the lights flicked on in a satisfying display of victory.

"Well done. Now, let's see what secrets they left behind," Jason said.

"My pleasure." Anya switched her setup back to the computer console.

This time, when she tapped on the console, the screen illuminated with a login prompt. Anya made several inputs on her tablet to begin bypassing the safeguards.

"This could take several minutes," she said.

Jason took the time to examine the room in more detail. There weren't any identifying marks on the computer terminals, and the rest of the furnishings were too generic to offer significant insights.

The stasis pod setup at the back was by far the most intriguing. He didn't know much about the technology aside from it was rare and expensive. Whoever'd installed it here had deep financial backing. The rarity meant that the investigation pool was narrower, but most likely it had been procured through illegal means with well-covered tracks. The apparatus itself had no clear exterior markings, like the rest of the equipment in the room.

What were they doing in here? With any luck, they could pull log data to see when the device had last been used to put someone in stasis.

"Sir, I'm in!" Anya called out.

Jason returned to the access console. The screen had changed to a file directory.

"What are we dealing with?" he asked.

"It's a pretty basic system, actually. There's not a lot of computing power here. I think this terminal's primary purpose was to control that stasis unit."

"Are there any records of its use?"

She shook her head. "No, I don't think we're going to get a lot out of this. The records have been sanitized."

"Auto-wiped on access?" Jason asked.

"No, there's just nothing left here. If there *was* sensitive data, it was purged a long time ago."

Jason's heart dropped. "What else is in the directory?"

Anya flipped through the information. "Looks like a mixture of genetic records and research notes."

"That sounds encouraging." Jason moved to look over her shoulder at the screen.

She shook her head. "No, these are dummy files." Her gaze scrolled over the information as she drilled deeper into the properties. "It was expert work, but these are fabricated data sets. The kind of thing someone would leave behind so looters would *think* that they'd found something useful without actually getting anything at all."

"How can you tell?"

She smiled. "The file sequencing doesn't match up with the database—a little trick I picked up for on-the-fly validation. See here?" Jason followed Anya's finger as she pointed to several key locations in the metadata. "The files themselves look complete, but they were added into the directory more recently than their creation dates, despite what it says at first glance."

He confirmed the observation. "Well spotted."

"When you're at this long enough, it's easy to notice a forgery."

"Does that mean that there's nothing here to find?"

"Perhaps. Or, this console was configured as a decoy so intruders wouldn't go looking for the real repository."

Jason nodded. "I guess we'll have to keep looking, then. Copy what you can, just in case there's something useful buried in it."

Disappointment was a common experience. They'd been on the Coalition's trail for the past two months, with frustrating results. The organization had gone into the shadows again after the widespread attacks on Duronis and the other Outer Colony worlds preceding the incident on Quel. Jason hated that their investigation had been guided by vague tips since then, but he kept telling himself that the momentum was about to shift to their favor.

We just need a lucky break. But what? He was getting worn out.

Chasing stale leads was demoralizing business, with each new trail invariably leading to disappointment. Some of the information may have been good if it had been timelier, but so much could change in a short span that even a slight delay meant the difference between catching someone in the act or finding an empty room.

The intel pointing toward this particular facility was old news—an informant relaying a sighting from months back. Though Jason didn't expect to find anyone still in the place, he had hoped that there might be an indication of where its occupants may have gone or with whom they might be working.

It seemed like there must be more to the facility. The exterior scans had indicated a larger structure; yet, there was no clear place to go from this room, aside from the door they had entered through. A deeper telekinetic probing might be in order.

"Over here!" Ron, one of the other Agents shouted. He was a Primus Agent a few years older than Jason, recruited to the Coalition task force because of his investigative background.

Jason ran over to him.

Ron was standing in front of a passageway, which had been hidden behind a cabinet. "Hey, I found a secret tunnel!" He grinned, bringing an extra shine to his bioluminescent hazel eyes.

Great minds. Jason smiled back. "Now we're making progress."

It made sense that the outer lab would be a decoy facility. Though the asteroid was a remote site to begin with, anyone with something to hide wouldn't make the valuable secrets readily accessible to anyone who happened to stumble upon it. This corridor might lead to the heart of the place—which may hold genuine records.

Jason sent out a telekinetic assessment to check for potential hazards. He didn't detect any cause for concern, so he proceeded inside.

The tunnel curved around then down. Jason maintained an extrasensory probe to get a feel for the space, determining that the pathway led to an open area one story below. There was a strong electromagnetic signature coming from behind the walls, which were covered in a plastic-like substance but had the appearance of roughly carved stone. Most likely, the entire facility had been carved into the asteroid and then coated in the material to seal it after the environmental mechanics were installed.

He paused at the base of the ramp where the tunnel opened into a larger chamber. Dim lights cast a soft, yellow glow throughout the room, which brightened with his approach. The space was significantly larger than the lab above, equipped with numerous workstations and large pieces of equipment. Many of the devices were unfamiliar to him and their purposes weren't readily apparent.

What was clear, though, was that the lab had been abandoned for quite some time. Like above, dust had settled over the items in the room despite the air handling system still being active.

"What have we here?" Ron commented as he came up behind Jason.

"The secret lair." Jason surveyed the room. "With any luck, we'll find some answers here."

He stepped forward while maintaining an extrasensory probe. There were definitely strange energy signatures from behind the walls, though he couldn't tell if it was due to poorly shielded environmental generation equipment or something else.

"Don't touch anything," Jason warned as the others came in through the tunnel.

"A trap?" Ron asked.

"Maybe." Jason approached one of the consoles.

The largest energy signature was coming from behind the station. Explosives might be rigged to ignite with activation of the console.

"Anya, can you take a look at this with me?" Jason requested.

The tech specialist hurried over with her interface equipment. "Your instructions, sir?"

Jason expanded his telekinetic shield to encompass Anya and the others in the room. "Is there any way to tell if a system has an intrusion detection trigger?"

"That's tricky, since you'd need to intrude in order to get a direct interface to learn anything meaningful."

"I was afraid you'd say that."

"Is there any reason to suspect such a trigger?"

"There's something hidden in here. It might be innocuous, but I'd rather be cautious."

"I feel it, too," Ron concurred.

The console in question was next to a large transparent box just over two meters long and one meter tall. Various piping systems and electronic cords were attached to the exterior and hookups inside. A quick visual check confirmed that the electronic conduits connected the tank and the console.

"I'm guessing this isn't an aquarium," Jason joked.

"No, it's a cloning tank," Gina, the third Agent on the team, said.

He gaped at her. "It is?"

She nodded, walking over to the tank to examine it closer. "I've watched a lot of videos from the cleanup efforts after the Bakzen War. They had massive warehouses full of these things."

Jason had reserved his study of the war records to the space battle tactics. He'd heard enough about the ground-level footage to avoid seeking out anything that wasn't required viewing in his courses. "Then we have confirmation that someone has been engaging in illegal research."

Gina continued looking over the device. "It's Taran manufacture, not Bakzen."

All of the evidence was pointing toward the Priesthood's covert genetics and cloning research. *Did some of them escape?*

Jason had discussed the possibility with his father. The decisive assault on the Priesthood had been thorough, but it hadn't been a guaranteed sweep of all the organization's members. Nonetheless, the TSS had spent years tracking down Priests from bases on remote worlds, and every single person they'd found had suffered a mental break from the attack. No one in that state would be capable of performing advanced scientific work or planning a devious plot against the Empire.

That left several possibilities. Someone might be emulating the work of the Priesthood. Or, some of the Priests may have escaped the mass break. Jason wasn't sure which option was more disturbing.

"All right, we have a cloning tank and control interface. How might that be rigged to deter intruders?" Jason asked.

"Hypothetically," Anya began, "if I wanted to hide the details about illegal research projects, I'd let someone get deep enough into my lab where there was no easy escape and then set the whole thing to blow up as soon as they thought they'd found something useful."

He found her cheerful tone oddly amusing, given the subject matter. "That's a problem for us. How would that trigger be set, and how do we disable it?"

"Identify the connection and sever it. I would suggest doing so without any direct interface with the system."

"Good thing we have Agents here, then." He nodded to his two black-clad companions to begin a deep telekinetic assessment of the equipment.

Jason delved inside the console using his mind's eye, tracing the interior components. The portions heading to the tank were of lesser concern, so he focused on the parts that extended backward behind the wall. One of those wires led toward the unidentified energy signature he'd first detected upon entering the room.

He felt his way to the source of the energy signature. It appeared to be the central point of a cascading explosive relay, as he'd feared. By his assessment, the explosives were set to trigger when the console activated.

Jason exchanged glances with the other Agents. "Did you sense that trigger, too?"

"Yep," Gina agreed.

Ron nodded. "I'm not sure how to defuse it. My concern is that if we sever the connection, it'll go off."

"That was my first thought," Jason agreed.

"What if we transitioned all of the explosives into subspace?" Gina suggested.

"I like that idea." Jason began thinking through how that would work. He'd need to trace the entire interconnected system and create a shaped spatial distortion around it without disrupting the other structural or environmental control equipment in the vicinity. Challenging, but not impossible.

The entire facility—if not the whole asteroid—could explode if the transition didn't go smoothly. He might be able to survive such an event with a shield around himself, but tracking the procedure as well as the entire TSS team would add unnecessary complexity. He needed to limit the variables.

"All right, everyone but Anya fall back to the shuttle,"

Jason instructed.

"*Sir?*" Ron asked telepathically. "*Are you sure you don't want Gina and I to stick around?*"

"*Thank you, but I'd rather know the team is safe.*" He wouldn't have Anya stay with him, either, if he knew enough about electronic infiltration to handle it himself. Perhaps he was being overly cautious, but after what happened on Quel, he was reluctant to take any chances.

"We'll be standing by," Ron replied aloud and nodded to the rest of the team.

The group retreated up the ramp.

Jason maintained a telepathic link with the two Agents and confirmed when they were on the transport shuttle.

"Okay, let's do this," he said to Anya.

Jason bolstered the telekinetic shield around himself and Anya, which should withstand any blast they might trigger. He made it larger than necessary to trap extra air in the event it became their only protection from the vacuum of space.

Next, he began reaching out telekinetically to grasp the wiring and explosive packs. He traced the entire system and added each component into his hold, giving it a light energetic charge.

When the entire network was in his grasp, he began drawing energy to create a spatial distortion around the items. He sensed the dimensional veil growing thinner in those areas. Creating such an intricate shape with such precision took most of his concentration. The actual quantity of material was well within his comfort level for a casual exercise, but its configuration was significantly more complex than his usual tasks.

Almost there. Just a little at a time. He started to ease the components into subspace, where he could release them into the ether outside physical reality.

Heat and cascading chaos filled Jason's senses. The explosives were destabilizing. They weren't yet all the way into subspace, so an explosion would likely take out this entire portion of the asteroid.

Shite! Jason shifted his hold on the items. Slow and steady wasn't going to do it. He needed to act now.

In one final push, he forced the entire assembly into subspace. The sudden surge of energy triggered the blast. He instantaneously released the subspace distortion, narrowly preventing the explosion from coming through.

He breathed out. *That was close.*

Before he could relax, he realized his mistake. A variable that he hadn't considered beforehand was that the removal of the charges and connected circuitry had left a void in the wall's structure. On a planet with a habitable atmosphere, there wouldn't have been an issue, but the extreme conditions on the asteroid were another matter.

Hairline cracks began to form in the wall.

Oh no! Jason frantically began rearranging the material within the walls and fused it together in an attempt to regain the structural stability. Even so, there were breaches forming on the inside surface, posing a risk for maintaining the atmosphere within the chamber.

He telekinetically traced each of the cracks and sealed them, racing to stay ahead of potential breaches. Just as he fixed one crack, a new one would form. He was beginning to think it would all be lost when the rate of collapse began to slow. At last, as he made the repairs, no new cracks formed. Once complete, there was no evidence that there had ever been a separation in the sheeting.

Relieved, he eased off his telekinetic hold, checking for any weak points. It seemed stable, so he pulled back more, then released completely.

Jason kept the shield up for another minute, just in case. "Okay, I think that did it."

Anya smiled, unaware how close they'd come to disaster. "Yay, we didn't die!"

"Wasn't ever an option. I have too much to live for." He thought of Lexi waiting for him back at TSS Headquarters. *Life is just getting started.*

"Are we good to go with this, then?" Anya asked, motioning to the console.

"Yes. Go for it." Jason then sent a telepathic message to the rest of his team. *"We're in. Facility secured."*

Anya hooked up her interface equipment.

Please find something good in here. Jason paced behind Anya while he waited for her report. *"Bring the rest of the team back in,"* he instructed Ron telepathically. *"There's a lot to catalog. I think we're past the dangerous part."*

"You 'think'?" The other Agent feigned concern; they'd been working together for long enough now that the trust was there.

"Only the tiniest chance of getting lost in the void."

"Wouldn't be any fun without some unknowns," the other Agent replied. *"On our way back."*

Anya was still working at the console as Jason concluded the telepathic discussion.

"Ah, shite!" she muttered under her breath. Her fingers raced over the touch-surface console.

Jason was about to ask her what was wrong, but her furrowed brow made it clear that she was concentrating on the task at hand. Her shaking head and frustrated groans didn't bode well.

Data scrolled across the screen, deleting and pixelating in a disconcerting fashion. Jason hoped the situation wasn't as bad as it appeared.

Is the database corrupting? Perhaps there was one last failsafe they hadn't anticipated.

After a minute of frantic typing, Anya stopped, resting her palms on the front edge of the console as she leaned against it. She sighed.

"Bad news?" he asked.

She nodded. "Sorry, sir. There was an auto-incinerator program."

Jason let out a long breath and nodded. While the system wasn't literally on fire, it may as well be. Such digital security traps could wipe out an entire database in a matter of seconds. *Shite, another dead end.*

He tried to keep the disappointment from showing in his expression. "Document the equipment and take anything the digital forensics team might be able to analyze."

"Yes, sir. We'll see if we can piece any of it back together at Headquarters," Anya replied.

"All right. I guess that's it, then. Pack it up." It wasn't the outcome he'd hoped for, but it had yielded new information, in a way; they had confirmed that *someone* was, in fact, conducting illegal experimentations. *A criminal is out there. I won't stop until we find them.*

CHAPTER 2

NEVER WOULD LEXI Karis have guessed that she'd one day hold an official position within the TSS, but now she couldn't imagine following any other career path.

She smiled to herself as she looked over her outline for the new civilian training program. It was hope for a more united future, bringing together Gifted people from across the Taran worlds. Unfortunately, she only had three weeks left to get the details for the full program curriculum worked out with the education specialists within the TSS.

Lexi stretched her arms above her head and leaned back in her desk chair, passing her gaze over the bare walls of the room. Her small office in the Command Wing of TSS Headquarters was comfortable, but it didn't foster a creative mindset. With a frown, she decided that it was past time she started to decorate it with some personal touches.

What did I *want to know when I was first exploring my abilities?* She'd been asking herself that question a lot over the past several months.

The TSS had offered her the Director of Civilian Training

position precisely because she could provide a layperson's perspective. Though she'd had more telepathic and telekinetic training than most non-military people, it had been far from the structured lessons typically found within the TSS. The new civilian training program needed a different approach than the strategies to condition soldiers. Despite the TSS making efforts toward demilitarization in the decades since the end of the Bakzen War, Agent training remained focused on attributes that supported a role within a chain-of-command structure. Working with free citizens would require much greater flexibility and different areas of emphasis.

Nonetheless, aspects of the TSS' culture were important to preserve. The organization cherished a person's attitude and accomplishments over birthright, which lent itself to bringing people together over a shared sense of purpose despite radically different backgrounds. The TSS also taught respect for others' privacy even when a person possessed abilities capable of bypassing conventional defenses. Imparting that same ethical code of respect to the new trainees would be critical to the program's success.

Lexi's efforts to structure the training curriculum had thus far been focused on teaching practical skills, and she knew that she'd need to layer in those important cultural elements. But *when* and *how*?

After several more frustrating attempts to get in the mental work zone, she concluded that it wasn't going to happen by force. *Tomorrow. Tomorrow will be the day.*

She slipped on her jacket and slid her handheld into the pocket designed to hold the device. She was still getting used to wearing an official uniform.

If there was anything she'd learned about the TSS over the past few months, it was that they took symbolism seriously.

After a heated debate, they'd settled on a deep shade of teal as the uniform indicator for Gifted civilian trainees.

There'd then been another lengthy discussion about how to apply that color scheme to an outfit. Lexi had argued that the monochromatic uniforms for the TSS' other trainee classes didn't translate well to the civilian realm, so they'd eventually settled on black pants, teal base-layer shirts, and black jackets with teal accents, cut in the style of Initiate attire. The resulting outfit struck the desired balance between recognizability and comfort, which would be important for attracting trainees to the new program.

As an instructor, Lexi's uniform included a slim, silver-hued band around the end of her jacket's sleeves and around the collar. Though subtle, it served its purpose.

She ventured from her office into the side corridor of the Command Wing and then out into the main hallway, which took her past the Lead Agent's office. She'd hoped to slip out undetected, but Saera waved to Lexi as she passed by, motioning her inside.

One guess what this is about. Lexi took a long breath and entered the office. "Hey, how are you?"

"All right. Lots going on," Saera replied. "I was hoping to get an update on the program...?"

Yep, no surprise there. Lexi forced a smile. "It's coming together. I'm sorry it's taking this long."

"It's a big project. We are getting a little tight on time, however."

Lexi shifted on her feet. "I know. I feel like I've let you down."

"Not at all. I didn't expect this to be an easy or quick task."

"Still, I know it's taken longer than you anticipated."

Saera folded her hands on her desktop. "There were complications I didn't foresee, yes."

"Like just how difficult it is to go about training civilians in potentially dangerous abilities without knowing how they'll use those new skills."

"Yes, it's a risk. And we do need to mitigate those risk factors."

"Except you can't separate the two," Lexi countered. "That's the heart of the issue I keep going over with the consultants. I don't mean to stall. It's just that the TSS places so much emphasis on selecting the *right* people to invest in, but the inherent nature of having a civilian training program is to make it open to just about anyone. It's difficult to reconcile those two points."

Saera nodded. "I appreciate the challenge of your position. However, we do have a particular code to uphold. We need to be careful about what we teach."

"Sure, and I get that. If I'm being honest, though, no one is going to care about the training initiative if we don't teach them anything beyond what they could learn from a random 'instructor' off the street who's picked up enough skills to look like they know what they're doing."

"There's a sweet spot to be found."

What a very diplomatic way of putting it. Lexi raised an eyebrow. She tried to think of a response that wouldn't come across as sarcastic. "Didn't you bring me into this position because I think about things differently?"

"Yes."

"So, here's my outsider's opinion. What you're proposing isn't going to resonate with the average civilian."

"What do you mean?"

"These are people who've had to downplay their abilities for most of their lives. They'll want quick wins to show why it's worthwhile to put in the time and effort to become competent with the more advanced skills."

"Nonetheless, teaching unvetted individuals potentially dangerous skills, which could be used to harm others, would be at odds with our duty to the Taran people."

Lexi crossed her arms. "I think we need to give the students the benefit of the doubt."

"In what way?"

"By going into this program with the intention of teaching students everything they might want to know and then evaluating them and terminating training with anyone exhibiting worrisome behavior. I suggest that we begin by establishing an ethical foundation coupled with basic mental guarding and telepathy, then move on to practical skills like personal shields and object levitation."

"That sounds like a reasonable high-level approach," Saera said. "I'd like to see how that translates into a detailed lesson plan for the multi-term course of study."

A totally reasonable request, except that I'm nowhere near where I should be with this. Lexi looked down. "I just need to finalize some things. I'll have it to you by the end of the week." It was a bold promise, considering that she, in fact, had no *clue* what to do.

"Okay. I look forward to reviewing it."

Shite, it's going to be some late nights. Lexi was about to go when she added, "I do hear what you're saying, and I'm working on strategies to mitigate the risks. There are a lot of opportunities for intervention if we identify a problem student. Keep in mind that many of these people have received *no* training at all. They don't even know how to tap into their abilities."

Saera nodded thoughtfully. "A little thought-gleaning, at most?"

"Right. Aspects of telepathy are fairly intuitive, but a lot of people have difficulty getting started with telekinesis. Aside from the occasional prodigy, it takes a lot of practice to learn how to visualize what you want to happen." Lexi thought back to her own education and the challenge of unlocking those early skills.

"We often talk about it in the TSS as envisioning a magical aura."

Lexi raised an eyebrow. "How very scientific."

"But it sort of is like that, isn't it? Each person sees the manifestation of the energy in different ways. A glow or electric sparks. It makes it a lot easier to control what you're doing when you picture it like that."

"Yeah, I guess I do the same," she realized.

"I've found it's helpful to establish a shared vocabulary with students so you can better guide them when they get stuck."

"Yeah, that makes sense. Okay, so the first class needs to be about getting on the same page—terminology and ethics."

"An excellent place to start."

"I think I know what I need to do now."

Saera smiled. "Good. I know this initiative will be a success."

"I hope so. I've gotta give you a reason to let me stick around."

"You'll always have a place here."

Because of Jason, but I want to be here in my own right. Lexi nodded. "Thank you, I appreciate it."

"You won't be the only civilian around here for long, Lexi." Saera brought up a list of names on the holodisplay. The information began scrolling through hundreds, possibly thousands, of entries.

"What's this?" Lexi asked.

"Applicants. These are all civilians who've expressed interest in the new training program... since we began advertising yesterday."

Lexi choked. "This many? In a *day*?"

"High demand." Saera tapped her fingers on her desk. "We were expecting a positive response, but not this."

"Well, the curriculum will be scalable," Lexi said. "But we're going to need more instructors."

"A *lot* more."

"We don't need to get everyone in right away. Once we get started, we can have more advanced students start mentoring the newcomers."

"Like how we do in other areas within the TSS."

"Exactly."

Saera nodded. "Eventually, we'd like to expand the program's reach. You worked in recruitment when you were with the Alliance, right?"

Lexi's heart skipped a beat at the mention of the organization. "Tangentially. It was more like marketing—written communications."

"Perfect. Would you be willing to help craft the messaging for future student and instructor recruitment?"

Stars! Where am I going to find the time for even more work? Nonetheless, Lexi couldn't turn down the request. "Sure, I'd be happy to."

Saera gave her an evaluative look, as if weighing her true feelings on the matter. "Okay."

Lexi met her gaze, unwilling to show any sign of doubt. "I should get back to work."

"I'll see you later."

Lexi saw herself out from the Lead Agent's office. Rather

than resuming her path to her quarters, she turned back toward her office and let out a long breath. *I never thought I'd work on recruitment messaging again!*

Moreover, she never dreamed that her experience in the Alliance would be applicable to anything in her subsequent life. As it turned out, she *had*, in fact, done some real work while she was in the organization, and it was quite useful preparation for her current role. She'd entered into this TSS position with a 'fake it until you make it' mentality, feeling out of her depth in the leadership position. However, the more she got into it, she realized that she *did* bring an informed perspective and could offer genuine guidance to her team. It had been an exhilarating realization. Not only could she believe in this work, but she might actually be good at it, too.

All the pieces are coming together. I've found my place here. Maybe I can help others do the same. With new determination, she picked up the pace toward her office. She had a lot of work to do.

— — —

The velvety black of space stretched out before Wil, a limitless expanse to explore. Somewhere, hidden beneath the visible layers of physical reality were secrets woven into the cosmic pattern.

For the past two months, he'd been spending more time roaming the expanse with his consciousness in an attempt to uncover the hidden meanings. The Aesir insisted that he possessed an ability to read the patterns, yet he'd been unable to see the web of truth since his glimpse into the nexus decades before. Wil wanted to honor Dahl's wishes and become a visionary leader like the old Oracle and his companions hoped he would be, but he didn't know *how* to gain those insights.

His astral projection voyages were a pleasure—an unburdened and free exploration of star systems that would be difficult to access in most ships—but the exercise had yet to yield the results he'd attempted to achieve.

Since reading the cosmic pattern was still beyond his reach, Wil had instead chosen to focus his efforts on inspecting the worlds where the new planetary shields had been installed. The innovative technology, which drew on theoretical designs from the Aesir's data Archive as well as the efficiencies of the Erebus' power core design, offered a significant security upgrade over standard shields. In most cases, cosmic radiation and meteor strikes were the biggest concern. Defending against a transdimensional alien attack was another matter.

The installations had been progressing without incident. The inhabitants of the test worlds had welcomed the upgrades with open arms, to Wil's simultaneous relief and apprehension. He still had significant misgivings about the reliability of the new technology, despite their extensive testing, and he was concerned about the Taran worlds becoming reliant on the systems.

His latest roam among the stars took him to Veraria, which was in the final stage of installation. He gazed at the massive shield generators being placed in orbit to bolster the ground-level infrastructure. From his vantage at the outskirts of physical reality, the global construction project was like watching a miniature model being assembled under a magnifying glass—the massive scale completely lost.

It reminded him how much the Taran people had accomplished. Their power might appear insignificant compared to the likes of the Erebus, yet his people had learned to accomplish things together that could never be possible as individuals.

There is hope for us, he mused. *We need to remember what incredible feats are possible when we unite.*

The separatists in the Outer Colonies needed that reminder. While Wil supported autonomy and choice among the Taran people, the worlds insisting that they wanted to go it alone had long since outsourced the necessary skills to sustain a long-term society. They had every right to transition away from central Taran rule, but it would need to be an incremental and planned process to have a genuine chance at success. The clean break promoted in the media commentary was nothing other than rash and shortsighted.

He fought back the swell of annoyance. *Power-hungry opportunists are taking advantage of well-meaning people. We need to win them over through kindness, not force.* The political tiptoeing was exhausting.

With a renewed wave of consternation, he realized that he wasn't focusing on reading the cosmic patterns like he was supposed to be. Granted, the other matters on his mind were important, but he needed to set those worries aside if he was going to see the bigger picture.

Wil tried to force the other thoughts aside, opening his mind to the energy patterns just beyond his present reach. *Read the patterns. All the mysteries will be unlocked.*

The sarcasm in his mental tone wasn't a great indication that this would be the day for a breakthrough.

"Wil."

Saera's voice called to him from the distance across the void. Her presence beckoned him.

Almost relieved for the interruption, Wil paused his search for universal truth, retracing the thread tethering him to his physical self.

He took a sharp, deep breath as his eyes shot open. He stretched out his limbs, cramped from sitting cross-legged on the floor for an extended time.

Saera was standing in the doorway of his office, watching him. "I'm sorry, I didn't mean to disturb you."

"That's okay. I wasn't making much progress."

"Maybe you're overthinking it," she said, stepping inside and closing the door.

"No doubt." He stood up and stretched. "I haven't seen any pattern, or whatever it is the Aesir expect me to see."

"Have you tried locating the nexus?"

"Yes, multiple times." He sighed. "I don't know where it is. It seems like I should have come across it by now with all the astral roaming, but I haven't felt so much as a tug directing me to its location."

Saera crossed her arms. "Strange. For someplace allegedly so powerful, you'd think it would have a distinctive signature."

"Right!" Wil shook his head. "I've tried everything. I'm at a loss for where to go from here."

She leaned against the back of the couch in the center of the room. "I think you need to go back to basics."

"Meaning?"

"Well, how did you see the pattern when you first visited the nexus?"

"I let myself go."

"And are you doing that now?"

"Not entirely," he admitted.

She gave him a knowing smile. "Then that might be what you have to do."

"Letting go completely is how people get lost."

"Only if you don't know how to find your way back. You do." She tilted her head. "You told me after you came home from visiting the nexus that you'd never felt so free. Maybe you just need to recapture that feeling."

He nodded, recognizing the truth in her assessment. "Except, back then, I didn't know what was lurking in the unseen realms. Being out there is different now."

"I wouldn't want to get too close to the Erebus, either."

He winced. *Everyone is counting on me to deliver answers, and I've gotten nowhere.*

Saera knew him well enough to read the subtle guilt in his expression. "I'm sorry so much falls to you, Wil. Again. It's not fair."

"Fairness is hardly the issue. Someone needs to take responsibility."

She nodded and looked down for a few moments before meeting his gaze again. "I don't expect the cosmic pattern to show us all the secrets, but I do believe it can reveal important information about the Erebus and their place in the universe. That could make all the difference in how we respond."

"I know."

"And you can do that."

He took a long breath and let it out. "The last time I saw the cosmic web, the events that followed broke me. It took a long time to come back from that."

"You're not the same person you were then." Saera reached out and took his hand.

"Stronger and smarter now, am I?"

She smiled. "I was going more for thoughtful and patient. You have an experienced perspective, and we need that kind of insight."

"I'll try."

"I believe in you."

An alert chirped on Wil's desk. "Duty calls."

Saera patted his shoulder. "I should get back to it, too."

Wil walked over to his desk to check the message. One glance at the screen and his heart dropped. *Ah, shite.*

— — —

When Raena Sietinen began her investigation into the revered ancient sites on Earth, she never would have guessed where that search would lead. A smile spread across her face as she studied the map depicting what could only be described as a global network—advanced technology from a bygone era, buried and forgotten.

"What does it do?" she mused. She'd been wondering the same thing since the very first site was uncovered in Belize several months prior, and each subsequent discovery only enhanced the mystery.

"We've still been unable to devise an interface," Trevor said over the vidcall. The young man had proven to be an asset in the field research, serving as Raena's eyes and ears on the ground.

"I'm tempted to get in there myself." Engineering wasn't Raena's strength, but she knew her way around most Taran tech. Moreover, she suspected that the technology wasn't a simple digital interface but rather that it had a bioelectronic component. Nothing else would explain its strange properties.

"We'd eagerly welcome another set of eyes."

"What are the Agents saying about it?" Raena asked.

"They're wary. They won't say much beyond 'it has a strange energy' about it," Trevor replied.

"And what do *you* think?"

"I'm at a complete loss for where to go from here."

His enthusiasm and creative thinking at every turn had

helped get them through the worst of the access negotiations with the various Earth governments, which was why he'd been selected for the assignment. Now that they were at the technical evaluation part of the project, he wasn't necessarily the right person to lead the efforts moving forward.

Raena took a slow breath and let it out through her teeth, thinking. "I hate to say it, but I think we need to hand this over to the TSS. Specifically, I'd like to see if I can get my father's eyes on it."

"I think that's the right call," Trevor agreed. "Though, after all this time, you'd be missing out if you didn't see it in person yourself."

She smiled. "Sounds like I might need to plan a trip, then." Unfortunately, it would have to wait. There were too many other things going on for her to get away.

"I look forward to giving you the grand tour whenever you're able to make it out here."

"Thank you, Trevor. You've done an incredible job getting us this far."

"It's been a pleasure, my lady."

"I'll reach out to the TSS about getting us further assistance. Talk soon."

Trevor bowed his head as the vidcall ended.

Raena leaned back in her swivel chair with a huff, admiring the view out the window of her secondary office. The rippling water of the sea below had a meditative effect, much like staring at a candle flame. She allowed her mind to wander down the paths of speculation for several minutes before returning her focus to the present.

Seeing no reason to delay, she called up her father on the viewscreen.

The TSS logo twirled against a black backdrop on the

screen for several seconds before Wil answered.

"Hi, Raena. How are you?" he greeted.

"Hey, Dad. Doing well. Is this a good time?"

"That doesn't really exist anymore. I can carve out a few minutes. What's up?"

She folded her hands on her desktop. "We need help on this Earth investigation."

He nodded. "I've been wondering how that was going."

"Have you been keeping up on the reports?"

"More or less."

So, that's a 'no'. She knew her father was extremely busy and had many high-priority items competing for his attention within the TSS. Coupled with his detest for administrative tedium, he often neglected reviewing reports. Even Raena had to admit that the recent documentation of the excavation progress on Earth had been rather tedious, so it wasn't surprising that he'd left the reports unread.

"We've been busy the last several weeks," Raena said. "After the discovery in Belize, we found similar pits under pyramids around the world. Researchers have known for a long time that the planet's pyramids follow a pattern, and the pits create a pattern within that pattern. The preliminary results suggest that the sites are networked in some way, but we still have no idea what the device might do."

Wil didn't reply at first. "We want answers for a lot of things. The more we discover, the more we realize how much we don't know."

"Really, Dad? That's all you have to say?"

"You want to know whether I think we should turn on this mysterious, ancient device? No, I don't, but we might not have a choice."

"What do you mean?"

He took a long breath. "The issues are stacking up against us. I just got a report for a situation that's not going to go away."

"What happened?"

"I can't get into that right now." He paused. "I hear what you're saying about the device on Earth, and I do want to look into it more. Give me a little time to get the other situations under control and then I'll see if I can resolve that one mystery, at least."

"Okay." Raena knew better than to press the issue about the other news that had him so distracted, though her curiosity was piqued. *Or maybe it's better I don't have any more bad news to worry me right now.*

"I'll be in touch soon," her father assured her. "And I promise to look over those reports about the device on Earth as soon as I can."

"Thanks, Dad. I'll talk to you then."

"Take care. Love you." He gave her a small smile and then ended the communication.

Raena took a steadying breath. *That wasn't how I thought that conversation was going to go.*

Something bad was brewing in the Taran Empire. She could feel it. Somehow, she'd need to find a way to help keep everything from falling apart.

CHAPTER 3

RETURNING TO TSS Headquarters, Jason wished he brought better news. The data salvaged from the lab may yet yield valuable insights, but his team had cautioned him about holding out too much hope.

We have confirmation that someone continued the Priesthood's genetic research after their fall. That's a significant detail, even if we don't yet know the culprit. Though it wasn't enough to warrant a celebration—far from it—the knowledge did keep him from becoming even more demoralized.

Jason had a little time before the scheduled debrief with his parents, so he stopped by the Coalition task force's Strategy Room to check in with the rest of his team.

Positioned in a tucked-away corner of the Command Wing, the large room had become Jason's secondary workspace within Headquarters. The task force was a small operation of half a dozen key workers, both Agents and Militia, with a much larger support team to augment field operations—including those who'd accompanied him on the latest raid of the lab. Anya and Ron were two of his most trusted colleagues, with him since the beginning.

When Jason entered the Strategy Room, the two workers presently inside snapped to attention.

"Welcome back, sir," Laura, one of the Militia officers, greeted. She was the youngest on the team—a recent graduate—but sharp and had brought a lot of energy. "How'd it go?"

Jason shook his head. "Not a total waste, but more or less another dead end. Anya will be here soon with a drive, which may yield a bit more."

She frowned. "Bummer."

"Yeah. Next one, maybe. Did I miss anything?"

Ted glanced at Laura. "Do you want to tell him?"

"Tell me what?" Jason asked.

"We *may* have something else," Laura replied slowly. "And it's a longshot, so don't get your hopes up."

"At this point, I'm willing to entertain every possibility."

She brought up a flight path on the holoprojector, depicting several points in a remote territory of the Outer Colonies on the side of the galaxy furthest from Tararia. "Well, Zak was digging around—"

"He was scouting out destinations for his upcoming leave," Ted interjected.

"Dude has terrible taste." Laura shook her head. "But anyway, he noticed that several of the missing person reports coincided with tour stops for this band traveling around."

Jason tilted his head. "A band? As in musicians?"

She nodded. "They're, um… we'll say 'niche'. They apparently are known for playing a type of music from Earth known as the 'blues'."

Jason raised an eyebrow. "That's oddly specific."

"How in the stars some random Tarans stumbled across

the style is beyond me. Seems like they've gained a bit of a following, though."

"It can be catchy. I could see how the themes would resonate with the manual laborers in the Outer Colonies," Jason said.

"At any rate, I don't know how or why they might be connected to the missing Gifted women, but there's a definite correlation." She changed the holographic display to show the times and dates of the band's concerts with the reported disappearances.

Jason assessed the data, noticing that there did appear to be a clear correlation between disappearances on the second-to-last or final night of the concert schedule on each planet. "That's really strange."

"Right?" She brought up profiles on the band members. "There's nothing remarkable about them aside from their music tastes. No records, no obvious connections to criminal elements. I can't figure out why any of them would be abducting random Gifted women."

"Unless they're being used as cover. It's not the *band*, but perhaps someone traveling with them."

"That would make more sense." She scrunched up her nose. "I dunno. Something still feels off about it."

"There's a pattern, so it's worth looking into deeper. I'll bring it to my parents and see what they think."

"It'd be kinda funny if this was the breakthrough we've been looking for."

"Stranger things have happened."

"I'll let Zak know he should keep digging around to see if he can find out anything else about them."

"Thank you." Jason checked the time. "I've got to run to a debrief. Good work on this."

"Just doing our jobs, sir," Ted said.

Laura nodded. "I wish we had more."

"Our adversaries have made it difficult. But we'll get them." He flashed them a supportive smile before departing the strategy room for the High Commander's office.

His parents were waiting for him when he arrived. Jason settled into his customary seat.

"It wasn't what we'd hoped to find, but it wasn't a total bust, either," he began. He gave a recap of the events, highlighting the information they'd been able to piece together.

His parents took in Jason's account of the mission's events with stoic expressions, seemingly unsurprised by the results. When Jason finished, Wil and Saera exchanged a knowing glance, accompanied by a momentary hum of energy from a telepathic conversation.

"So, it *was* an important site, at some point in the past, anyway," Wil surmised.

"Near as we can tell. I have the tech team combing through the exported data to see if we can trace it to any other sources."

Saera frowned. "I really thought this might be the one."

Jason shrugged. "We still might glean something during the forensic analysis. I'm not ready to give up entirely."

"I do need to address one other point," Wil said.

"Sure."

"I appreciate that your first instinct is to protect others, but sometimes the greatest danger is to be alone. It worked out okay this time, but sending away your team often isn't the best call."

His father made a valid point, but Jason couldn't help feeling defensive of his actions. He'd had sensible reasons to call for the facility's evacuation. "Understood."

"One of the most difficult aspects of leadership is knowing that we're putting others in danger. Though we try to mitigate those risks as much as we can, it's a reality we must except."

"I know."

"I hope you do." Wil let the gravity of the statement hang. "That said, it was good thinking to move the explosives into subspace."

"That was actually Gina's idea," Jason admitted.

"See? It's good to have other smart people with you."

"Point taken."

"Okay," his father yielded. "I'm just glad everyone is okay."

"Me too." Jason considered how much else to share about the new, unverified discovery. "We're tracing a new potential lead."

His parents perked up. "What else?" Wil asked.

"You know those disappearances? The team was finally able to connect them to something else."

Saera sat up straight in her seat. "What have you found?"

"A tour schedule."

Wil's brows drew together. "Pardon?"

"A tour schedule for a band. People seem to be going missing right around the time they finish a gig and move on to another world."

His mother tapped her lips in thought. "That actually does make a lot of sense. A band would make great cover for moving around."

"That's what we were thinking. However, I don't know how best to begin an investigation," Jason said.

Wil frowned. "Resources are limited right now. I'm hesitant to send a lone Agent, but sparing two or more might be tricky."

"I have a thought about that," Saera said. "What if we

assign this investigation as a Junior Agent internship?"

"Hmm." Wil nodded thoughtfully. "That's an interesting suggestion."

"We'd need the Agent assigned to be both a proctor *and* investigator," she continued. "Unfortunately, most of our typical internship overseers are otherwise engaged at the moment."

"What about Andy?" Jason suggested. "He's led a bunch of investigations like this and really knows his stuff."

"I don't think he's ever proctored an internship before," Wil said.

Saera shrugged. "He's led teams and knows what makes an effective Agent. That's really the only prerequisite."

"And he's been involved with the Coalition investigation since the beginning," Jason pointed out.

"All right," Wil agreed. "What about the Junior Agent?"

Saera hesitated. "I have someone in mind. This assignment would be a great test for her."

Jason tilted his head. "Investigating a band?"

"No. Finding out what happened to these missing young women." She swallowed. "A Junior Agent who's almost eligible for graduation is Kali Wietris, one of the freed Priesthood captives."

Wil let out a long breath. "No denying those parallels."

"There've been… concerns about her," Saera continued. "She has top marks academically, but she's had a number of behavioral citations. Her instructors and I have agreed that her future as an Agent will really come down to her internship performance."

"Then we can't go easy on her," Wil said. "This assignment does seem like the perfect test. If she's ever going to crack in the line of duty, facing what she will in the course of this investigation would reveal those vulnerabilities."

Jason's stomach clenched at the thought. He recognized that internships were designed to place Junior Agents in an uncomfortable position to make sure they could keep a level head when pushed to their limits, but this was a particularly challenging case. It was a testament to Kali's fortitude that she had excelled in the TSS even after being held as a captive by the Priesthood for almost two years.

He remembered her from the liberation—a teenager who'd been forced to carry a cloned baby to term. The entire situation was barbaric. None of the other Gifted women had wanted to pursue training for their abilities, but Kali had chosen to dedicate her life to protecting others. He admired her immensely for that, and he'd been rooting for her to succeed. Word about her emotional outbursts had gotten back to him on occasion. He couldn't blame her for being volatile after what she'd been through, yet it was also unbecoming of an Agent to exhibit anything less than complete poise under the most trying circumstances.

This proposed internship would make her confront her troubled past again, seen through the eyes of other young women who'd been abducted against their will. Either it would be too much for her to face, or her innate strength would see her through. It was a necessary test for her future as an Agent.

"We don't often work with Agent trainees coming from traumatic pasts," Saera said. "I empathize with her position, but it remains that we hold all Agents to a standard. We'll find a different, fulfilling role for her if this kind of field work isn't a good fit."

"I have no doubt she'll take the assignment seriously and be committed to getting answers. That's what we need," Jason said.

Wil nodded. "And Andy will give an honest assessment. This is a good fit all around."

"All right, I'll make the arrangements," Saera said. "I'd like to pull in Andy to assist with some other internship planning, too—get his perspective as a field Agent. Michael is swamped with other ops coordination right now."

"Absolutely," Wil agreed. "We need this next batch of graduates to be field-ready."

Jason stood up. "I'll prepare a mission brief."

—   —   —

Lexi brightened at the message from Jason, letting her know he was home and would be heading to their quarters imminently. She was already in for the night and was ready to unwind after a long day.

When the door unlocked with a soft chirp, Lexi rose from the couch to greet Jason. He smiled as he stepped inside, his gaze full of adoration Lexi had never expected someone to feel toward her.

"Hey you," she said, wrapping her arms around him.

He returned her hug. "I missed you."

She pulled back just enough to give him a kiss. "How'd it go?"

"Could have been worse, but it's not what we wanted to find."

"Bomax."

He gave her another kiss, longer and deeper. "I'll fill you in later. I've already been over it too many times today."

"Right, sorry. Get settled in."

Jason headed for the bedroom. "Nothing to apologize for. I'd be eager for details, too. Suffice to say for now, it was more or less a dead end."

"That sucks." She sat on the edge of the bed while he started changing into lounge clothes.

"How's everything around here?"

Lexi rubbed her eyes. "Fine. I need to finish up the curriculum plan. I think I finally know what to do with it, but it's going to be a long week."

"Good. Must feel great to have it coming together."

"Yeah. Your mom gave me a nudge about it this afternoon—she was very gentle and kind, but I can tell she's getting impatient."

"She does have a way of making it feel friendly even when she's scolding you. Not that I think that's what was going on here."

"Even if it was, she's justified. I've been dragging my feet on getting this stuff finalized."

"Nothing like a looming deadline to motivate you in the final push."

She laughed. "Isn't that the truth. Ugh! Now I need to do it all last-minute."

"Do you need any help?" Jason offered.

"Nah, I'm okay. I'm working with some educator consultants who'll help package everything. It's just a matter of concentration. There are some parts I need to do myself, to prove that I can."

Since Lexi hadn't had a traditional education, she had rarely worked on large-scale projects where she needed to manage her time and deliver a product in a specified format. Truthfully, her time in the Alliance had been as close as she'd ever come to conventional employment, and that was a far cry from a good résumé-builder. To successfully complete this assignment with the TSS would prove that her life experience had prepared her for a position of authority and demonstrate, for her own peace of mind, that she was worthy of instructing others.

"I know you can do it," Jason told her. "I'll be here for you in any way that's helpful."

"Right now, just moral support."

"I have a limitless supply of that." He hugged her.

She patted his back. "You just keep focusing on the Coalition."

"And I wholly intend to." He fell silent as he pulled back from the hug, seemingly trying to decide if he should say something else.

"What?" Lexi prompted.

"It's too soon to know if it's worth getting excited about. We have a potential lead related to the disappearances." Jason explained what they'd found about the band.

"How long has that been going on?" Lexi asked.

"At least a few months. We've been able to confirm enough of the recent travel logs to establish a pattern."

"That's great! I mean, about getting a lead. I hate to think about what may have happened to those missing women." She frowned. "Could these be the same people who took Melisa?"

"The band hasn't been to Duronis as far as we know, but that doesn't mean they aren't connected to the Coalition. They might all be working for the same people."

"How will you determine that?"

"We're sending a Junior Agent on an undercover internship to investigate the band."

Lexi's brows furrowed. "A Junior Agent. That's it?"

"She'll be with an experienced field Agent. And she has a history that will make her uniquely committed to the mission. If there's something suspicious going on with the band, I have every confidence that she'll uncover the truth."

"All right." Lexi crossed her arms. "What now?"

"We wait for information to roll in."

"I'll try to be patient."

He smiled. "You're so good at that."

"Hah." She sighed. "I have enough work to do over the next couple of weeks that I'll be distracted."

Jason rubbed his hand down Lexi's leg. "If you're looking for a distraction, I can help with that."

She smiled coyly. "Is that so?"

"One way to find out."

—   —   —

Shadows around the perimeter of the holoconference room made the space feel smaller than its true dimensions. Hanek had never quite gotten used to the eerie atmosphere, despite attending regular gatherings aboard the *Horizon*. Except, given those in attendance, it was no wonder he found himself on edge.

He tried to ignore the dark recesses around him, focusing instead on the bright, blue-white light illuminating a circular table toward the center of the room. The six chairs around it were empty for now, and the holoprojector was dormant.

Hanek stood next to the entry door, his hands clasped in front of him as he held a small tablet between his fingertips. The others would be arriving soon, and he needed to look his part. *At last, I'll get to hear what they talk about during these meetings.*

It had taken nearly a decade of service to work his way into the good graces of the Coalition's true leaders. Many people *claimed* to hold a position of influence, but the real roles of power were few and held by those whose names would never be publicly known. Though he was a mere assistant, being so close to greatness was a fulfilment of his life's aspirations—an opportunity to contribute and give purpose to his menial existence.

Soft footfalls sounded from the hallway, prompting Hanek to drop his eyeline into a reverent pose. Three dark-blue robes passed by at the edge of his vision, followed by a pair of feminine, heeled boots beneath black slacks.

"Hanek, the report," Magdalena prompted along with a snap of her fingers.

He rushed to the matronly woman, the only other person in the room of pure Taran heritage. She took the tablet from him, clicking one of her boot heels with impatience. No matter what Hanek did, it was never fast enough or done right, it seemed; however, she'd kept him in her service after countless others had been dismissed, so he had to be doing *something* right.

Hanek took a step back and clasped his hands again, awaiting further instruction. *They won't like this new information.*

Magdalena read over the report, a crease deepening between her sculpted brows. "When was the alarm triggered?"

"Seven hours ago, ma'am."

She nodded and sat down in one of the chairs at the well-lit table.

Hanek remained at the edge of the shadow, observing the room's occupants as they got settled.

In addition to Magdalena Steyn, there were the three blue-robed emissaries. While they looked Taran in passing, it was clear after more than a few minutes in the Gatekeeper hybrids' presence that something was strange about them—an almost magnetic quality that created an odd buzzing inside Hanek's head. The three emissaries ignored him; he was Magdalena's assistant, and that was the extent of his worth.

When Magdalena and the others were seated at the table, Hanek dimmed the lights and activated the holoprojector. Holographic representations of two additional robed figures appeared in the remaining empty chairs.

"Begin," one of the holographic emissaries ordered in a neutral alto tone.

All attention turned to Magdalena.

"The TSS has found Tregaren's lab on A-GEOS682," she stated clearly and without even a hint of concern.

Hanek braced for a reaction from the others; from his vantage, it was terrible news.

"Did they retrieve anything useful?" Carjen, one of the emissaries in the room, asked, his pale eyes scrutinizing Magdalena under the shadow of his hood.

"It appears they were able to access the system, but there was nothing left to trace back to us," she replied.

Carjen nodded. "It was only a matter of time before they caught that trail."

"No matter now," Felina, one of the other emissaries, said with a dismissive way of her hand. "Tregaren has served his purpose."

"We have enough?" Magdalena asked her.

"Almost. And once we do, we won't be nearly as exposed."

"All matters of risk and reward," Carjen added.

Magdalena scowled. "Assuming the conduit is successful."

"If it's not, then we'll try another tactic," Felina said. "These lives are of no consequence."

"Clearly, the TSS would disagree," Magdalena pointed out.

"They have many grand notions." Carjen scoffed. "True

idealists, but there's no place for that in a fight for survival. We can't stay here any longer. We'll find a way to reach our new home, regardless of the cost. One of our lives is worth thousands of theirs."

Magdalena remained silent, but Hanek wished she would voice a rebuttal that the two of them were members of that allegedly 'worthless' Taran race. *Not so expendable that we're not worth keeping around, apparently.*

Hanek had no illusions about his position within the Coalition being safe or stable. His overseers possessed powers far beyond his capabilities, or even his comprehension. Simply being in their presence was a privilege, so quibbling over his worth was pointless. He'd do what they asked of him, without question or reservation, as a humble servant to his masters.

Growing up, he never would have dreamed he'd one day be in the room with beings in direct communication with gods. If he put in his time and service, he would eventually get to meet those gods himself.

The Gatekeeper emissaries and Magdalena continued to talk amongst themselves, referencing places and events within coded conversation that Hanek did not yet understand. They spoke of a red planet and a base, which didn't sound familiar with Hanek's work to date, but he made a mental note to investigate further.

"We must be more careful with our activities," Felina stated. "If the TSS is on to Tregaren, they can find us."

"We're far more hidden than that. Others will fall well before anyone of significance knows about this council," Magdalena assured her.

The emissaries didn't seem entirely convinced, but they nodded in acknowledgment.

"We will proceed as planned," Carjen stated. "Keep us

apprised of any new developments."

"I will, my liege." Magdalena bowed her head.

With that, the holoprojection ended and the councilmembers rose from their seats.

Hanek remained in a reverent pose as they passed by the door, keeping his gaze downcast while standing statue-still.

Magdalena approached him as the emissaries exited the room. "I have a task for you," she said.

"I am yours to command."

"Plant a trail for the TSS to find Tregaren."

"Yes, ma'am." Hanek could understand her reasoning—to give them a plausible target to get them off the more important trail. It wouldn't work long-term, but for now, it might buy them time.

"That's all for now." She turned on her heel and left without another word.

Hanek let out a long breath. Their plans were about to come to fruition. Soon, he would see firsthand what lay beyond this corporeal dimension.

CHAPTER 4

THE POLITICAL SITUATION across the Taran Empire was giving Wil a headache. There was simply too much he couldn't control.

But I do have domain over some things. His mind returned to the recent conversation with Raena about the mysterious device on Earth. *Time to take another look.*

The technological discovery hidden beneath the planet's surface had been confounding investigators for months, and the recent assessments by Raena's team had only added to the mystery. While the initial surveys had only been for disparate sites, a combination of excavation and subterranean imaging had revealed a much vaster network that appeared to be linked planetwide. Such a monumental construction effort strengthened the argument that the ancient technology was a defensive—or offensive—tool.

Further, the indications that it was a relic from the era immediately following the war between Tarans, the Gatekeepers, and Erebus made it relevant to the TSS' current efforts. They needed to determine if it was useful, and if so, worth trying to replicate on other worlds.

He located the specific report Raena had referenced in their latest communication and pulled it up on the holodisplay above his desktop. It wasn't that he was avoiding the paperwork from his daughter, but rather he only ever read a fraction of the reports that passed through his inbox. In all fairness, the updates from Earth hadn't born any revelations after the first several, so he'd stopped paying attention in favor of more pressing matters.

The first portion of it was more of the same, discussing the tenuous political situation and the various strategies to gain access to the investigation sites. He flipped past that to a composite map of the artifact locations.

His breath caught in his throat the moment the image appeared. *I knew they'd been busy, but this!*

The three-dimensional rendering of Earth was covered with a series of dots connected by lines. It reminded him of the ley line renderings he's seen, denoting energy hotspots around the world, but these didn't quite align with those points. There was more than pure randomness to it, though—of that he was sure.

He reached out to Saera telepathically. *"Do you have a few minutes to come take a look at something?"*

"Yeah, be right there," she acknowledged.

Wil continued to study the map while he waited for her to arrive. The more he stared at it, the more he was reminded of connections within a crystalline processing matrix. He minimized the image when he felt Saera approaching.

"Hey, what's up?" his wife greeted as she entered the office.

"There are days when I wonder about our future with the younger generation, but today reminded me that we have two amazing kids and their peers aren't half bad."

"Yeah, they turned out all right, didn't they?" Saera smiled. "Anything in particular that prompted this declaration?"

"The investigation Raena has been leading on Earth. I finally got around to looking over the analysis."

"Oh, right." His wife sighed. "I'd meant to stay on top of that, but with all the—"

"We're both stretched thin, Saera. It falls under my purview, and I should have been paying better attention."

"You've had too much else going on to track every detail."

"Part of the job."

She took a slow breath. "We'll circle back to that. It might be time to discuss bringing on more administrative support."

"Agreed." Wil gathered his thoughts. "For now, we need to quickly get caught up. I hadn't realized the extent of what they'd uncovered on Earth."

"Some sort of device at various sites, right?"

"Oh, it's a whole lot more than that."

Wil brought up the image on the holodisplay again, the rendering of Earth slowly rotating to show the interconnections between the different locations. "Here's the complete map of the device locations. Each had a corresponding pyramid, of one form or another, marking its place."

Saera's eyes went wide with awe. "That pattern is remarkable."

"There's more going on here than meets the eye, but I'm not sure what yet. Most of the hotspots appear to be along the established ley lines and at pyramid sites—which some have speculated are a massive star chart. The pattern was predicted long ago, but it wasn't until a few decades back that the 'missing' pyramids needed to complete it were discovered. I guess in the course of those efforts they didn't realize there was even more to it."

"Ley lines... pyramids... How does all that connect to a potential alien device?"

"A very good question."

"For that matter, I wonder what prompted the pyramid construction..." Saera mused. "Why use that as a marker?"

"Well, these buried devices were here long before the structures above them. Though, I suppose there may have been markers that were removed when the pyramids were erected."

"It's fascinating to see these places with new eyes. I grew up hearing all sorts of seemingly outlandish theories about the purpose of the pyramids and possible alien involvement. I always laughed it off."

"It does seem far-fetched on the surface," Wil agreed.

"Needless to say, my concept of believability forever changed when I learned about Tarans out there in the galaxy."

"I wonder how these revelations are going to change Earth's culture. I bet there are Taran sociologists salivating over this massive psychological exercise. Nowhere else has there been an opportunity to study an advanced civilization's introduction to other sentient life, let alone one with ancient ties to a shared ancestry."

"Those impacts will take a generation or more to be fully realized. I could spend all day talking about it, but the fact of the matter is that we need to stop studying and take action."

Wil looked over the holographic model. "I need to go down there, don't I?"

"This is too important to have any doubts," Saera said. "Would you like me to go with you?"

"Yes, but I think it's better if you stay here. With so much uncertainty at the moment, I'm not sure it's a good idea for both of us to be away from Headquarters at any given time."

"That's a good point. I guess another family vacation is out of the question."

"For now. I hope this current strife is only temporary."

"With any luck, a visit to Earth will provide answers about the tech and its purpose."

"We'll find out soon enough."

— — —

Lexi stared at her monitor, trying not to freak out about how much work she had to complete in the next week.

What in the bomaxed stars was I thinking that I could get this finished in time? The obvious answer was that she would have agreed to anything the Lead Agent had asked.

Her only choice now was to buckle down and do the work. The problem was, she still didn't know precisely what material should be in the curriculum or in what order. Once she had a clear vision, she was certain she'd be able to knock it out quickly.

She stood up. A change of scenery was necessary if she wanted to get these details hammered out. Maybe a trip to the mess hall to mingle with people.

Lexi passed by a couple of Agents on the way, giving them a respectful nod. They smiled and nodded back, but there was a hint of wary caution in their expression; she had the aura of a Gifted person, yet she lacked the distinctive bioluminescent glow to her eyes and she also was notably not wearing Agent black. Though they knew her after these months of her being in Headquarters, and respected her position, she was still an outsider.

That's what we need to avoid. How can we help new civilian recruits find a sense of community within the TSS? Granted, those students wouldn't be training at TSS Headquarters alongside Agents so there wouldn't be authority figures to win over, per se, yet Lexi still recognized that there was an unspoken kinship among Gifted people. The training program needed to foster an atmosphere of comradery and mutual support as the students grew into their abilities.

She had already gotten so much from the experience of being around other Gifted people, giving her a sense of belonging she'd never experienced before. Even without Jason's companionship, it was a place where she could see building a career and a life.

The best part had been getting focused training for her Gifts. Jason spent one-on-one time with her several times a week working on her control and exploration of new skills. He had proved to be a patient and creative instructor; she suspected that he enjoyed the sessions, as well, since he'd transitioned from training students to full-time investigative work.

The training had given her a new appreciation for her own power. She'd known since early on that her Gifts were above-average, but it wasn't until she began working with Jason and heard his perspective as an instructor that she realized the extent of her strength. Granted, she had tapped into her abilities and had received coaching, yet some of the feats she was able to perform with minimal instruction were apparently rare skills, even within the TSS. Though she never would have attempted those things on her own—not realizing they were even possible—it was exhilarating to find out that so-called 'stopping time' was within her grasp. That ability to create a localized spatial distortion to move around faster than the typical bounds of spacetime reality would have come in handy at many times throughout her life.

Each lesson and new discovery affirmed for her that she was now in the right place with the right person. She was at home, with a loving partner, and her future was bright. Never before in her life had she held such optimism.

She took the elevator down to Level 2, where she resided with Jason. The Primus mess hall was a daily fixture in her routine—and a significant upgrade from the cafeteria during her time in the Alliance.

Being between the major mealtimes, there were only a handful of people in the cafeteria when she arrived. The buffet was presently closed, but prepared meals were packaged in a refrigerator to the right side of the entry door. Her eating schedule was erratic, so grabbing a container for re-heating was a standard occurrence.

She made her selection and popped it in the warmer, using the time to scope out a potential conversation partner for the meal. Across the room, she spotted Gil, one of Jason's good friends. They'd been in the same Primus Elite trainee cohort and had remained close even after graduation; he was one of the first people Jason had introduced her to upon making their relationship official.

The warmer beeped its completion, and Lexi removed the container. She headed over to Gil.

Lexi gave him a smile and a little wave as she approached. "Would you mind some company?"

He looked up from his handheld, propped on the table in front of him. "Hey, Lexi. Have a seat."

"Thanks." She slid into the booth across from him.

"How are you?"

"Pretty good. I'm still wrestling with the new training curriculum."

"When does the term begin?"

"We're supposed to get going in less than three weeks, and I am *so* not ready."

Gil gave her a supportive smile. "That's plenty of time to get the details worked out."

"That's what I've been telling myself for the last month, and I keep getting further behind." She poked at her meal.

"You need to get out of your own head. Go with your gut. There's a reason they picked you for this position."

"I guess." A wave of self-doubt swelled in Lexi's chest. *Or I was a wayward civilian and they wanted a way for me to fit in with Jason's life.* She took a bite.

"Anything you wanted to discuss?" Gil offered.

"You don't mind?" Lexi had been hoping for the offer, knowing Gil was one of those kind-hearted souls who'd graciously put others' needs before his own. She'd be lying if she said that he wasn't exactly whom she'd hoped to see in the mess hall.

"I'm not sure how much help I'll be, but I'm happy to try." He folded his hands on the tabletop. "What seems to be the hang-up?"

"I can't figure out the right sequence for teaching skills versus attitude."

"I'm not sure that 'attitude' is something you can really *teach*. That's more something a person brings to the experience."

"What I mean is how we impart the tenets of respect and autonomy."

Gil shook his head. "I hate to be contrary, but that's not something you'll ever be able to get people to internalize via a lecture."

"Sure, but it's something that should be *talked* about."

"Oh, definitely. But the only people who will truly hear

those words and capture their meaning are the ones who didn't need the explanation in the first place."

"Then how are we supposed to know who to trust? We could unwittingly train someone who'd use their abilities to take advantage of others."

"That's the risk. I believe that's why it's taken so long for the TSS to take steps toward starting a civilian training program. Agents go through intensive vetting and years of evaluation before we teach anyone how to tap into the full extent of their Gifts."

"Whatever we do for civilians can never go as far as the training for Agents."

"No, but that won't stop people from trying. The truth is, once you unlock some abilities, others will come naturally—or a determined pupil will figure it out on their own." He gave Lexi a significant look.

She couldn't argue with the observation; truthfully, she had risen well beyond her education through self-study after she parted ways with her instructor. No doubt, there were many others like her who'd learned the basics and then figured the rest out through trial and error. That was the thing about learning to harness abilities that were part of oneself—a natural ability could be learned through intuition alone, though it was certainly easier with expert guidance.

"Okay, so what it comes down to is that we need to focus on attitude, to whatever extent we can emphasize respect for others and a reverence for Gifts."

"Yes, but there's still the problem that you can't simply *tell* people. You need to show them."

"Any suggestions on how to go about doing that?" Lexi asked.

"Illustrate the consequences of their actions if they abuse their abilities."

"Right, but what does that look like in terms of a lesson plan?"

"I can't tell you that because I don't know. I've been in the TSS for too long. The ethical lines are so ingrained that I can't look at it from the outside."

They need reformed criminal me to provide the answers. Lexi wasn't feeling particularly hungry anymore and pushed her meal slightly forward so she could rest her arms on the table. "We have people arriving soon. I need a solution."

"And I'm sure you'll find it. I wish I could be more help."

Lexi sat in quiet contemplation for several moments. "What do you think is the worst kind of violation using our abilities?"

"Tough to say. While causing physical harm is certainly at the forefront, I personally tend to think that invading someone's mind is worse."

She looked down, knowing she was guilty of doing just that on more than one occasion.

"I mean when it's done with malicious intentions," Gil clarified when he saw her change in demeanor. "Like mind-controlling an otherwise good person to do something terrible. It's different if you're trying to prevent something bad."

"And even that's tricky. Who decides what's good and what's bad?"

"Social code."

"Not everyone follows the same code—especially in the Outer Colonies."

"Perhaps that's your first lesson, then," Gil suggested. "An ethics class, of sorts. Not telling people how to use their abilities, per se, but rather establishing a shared framework to shape your future discussions."

"Yeah, Saera said something similar." Lexi mulled over the

different ideas. "We could lead with a discussion of shared societal values instead of anything specific to a Gifted code of conduct."

"Right."

Lexi nodded. "Hmm. That's a good idea."

"Of course, you'll need to figure out what to share. It's not like we have a written guidebook—we sort of just *know* what's social convention based on how we grew up."

"It'd be the same for the incoming students. At least, they'll *think* they understand. It'll be like whenever you go to a new place; observe, adapt to the local customs. An unconscious adjustment."

"Very true."

She smiled, the idea forming. "That's exactly what we need to do. Just take advantage of those conditioned responses to mimic the environment. Lead by example."

"I'm not quite sure what you have in mind, but I get the impression you have it figured out."

"I do." With the realization, Lexi's appetite returned, and she pulled her meal back toward her. "Thanks for pointing me in the right direction."

He smiled. "Not sure I did much, but you're welcome."

Lexi tapped the table. "On the contrary, Gil, you've given me exactly what I need."

— — —

Jason closed out of his messages, disappointed that there wasn't yet an update from the field about the suspicious blues band. While not surprising, his general anxiousness about the situation had left him impatient.

All answers in due time, he reminded himself.

Lexi had been preoccupied with her own work, which had left Jason to idle speculation. Concerns about the nature of the lab they'd discovered on the asteroid continued to churn in his mind, fueling fears that a faction of the Priesthood might still be operating in secret. The thought was equal parts terrifying and sickening. He recognized that his parents were entertaining the notion, which meant it was a real possibility. The extent of that threat remained to be seen.

In the meantime, Jason was frustratingly in wait-and-see mode. *I need to clear my head so I'll be ready to act when we have a certain course.*

There was no better way to do that than to spend some quality time with Lexi. She had quickly become his trusted sounding board and partner, offering insightful council that helped him keep proper perspective. Though she was busy with her own work, it was late enough in the day that she'd no doubt at least need a break.

He sent her a text message via his handheld: >>How's your evening look? I could use some veg time on the couch.<<

A response came back after several seconds. >>Busy, but I can get away for a bit. Meet you at home?<<

>>Perfect. On my way.<<

Jason headed for their shared quarters. Juggling the demands of responsibility with an intimate relationship over the past two months had given him a new appreciation for how his parents managed their time. Was it not for their success, he might not have believed it was possible.

As he exited the elevator on his residential Primus level, Lexi stepped out from the adjacent elevator in the lobby.

"Oh, hey." She smiled. "Fancy seeing you here."

"Imagine that." He took her hand as they walked toward home. "Thanks for carving out some time for me."

"I needed a breather, anyway. I think it's going to be a late night. I'm on a roll."

"Yeah?"

For the first time in weeks, Lexi had an enthusiastic fire in her eyes. "It all 'clicked' this morning. Just need to get it all documented."

"I'm glad to hear it's coming together." They reached the front door, and Jason buzzed them in with the biometric lock.

"Stars, I'm so relieved! One final push, and then maybe a return to normalcy."

Jason closed the door behind them. "It's good, in a way, we're getting a lot thrown at us now. We can learn how to handle the stressful times together."

"Yeah, I guess there's that." Lexi kicked off her shoes.

"I think we're doing pretty well so far."

She flopped down on the couch. "It's been a whirlwind."

"That it has."

"It's wild. Setting up the civilian training program, I've been reminded about where I came from. Sometimes it hits me just how *freaking crazy* it is that someone like *me* is with someone like *you*."

Jason raised an eyebrow as he sat down next to her.

"I know, I know." She waved her hand. "I'm past the self-doubt."

"Doesn't sound like it."

She shrugged. "It's complicated. I love you, and nothing is going to change that. Still, I hear comments and see the looks—questioning if I'm up for my position, in more ways than one. It's just been a lot of emotional crap to process."

Jason considered refuting the statements, but that wasn't the right approach. Instead, he wrapped her in a quiet embrace, and she relaxed against him.

After a minute, she took a deep breath. "Thank you."

He gazed into her eyes. "I love you. This is a safe place where we can always be honest and vulnerable. You never have to apologize about what you're feeling."

"Now, *this* is what I wish others could see! We're just a normal, happy couple. It's not some weird power dynamic thing."

She doesn't feel nearly as secure as she claims. Jason thought about the best way to approach it. "Lex, I want you to feel completely comfortable with me and my family."

"With you, I do. The rest of them…"

"I think it's because you have an idea about highborn people in your head, and no matter how much I tell you they're not like that vision, you're not going to believe me until you meet them yourself."

"I can't help it. I've spent most of my life running from elitist assholes who take one look at a person and think they know their whole life story."

"Some people are quick to pass judgment on things they don't understand. It sucks, but there's nothing we can do about it. What we *can* control is how we react to those statements."

"I know." She took his hands. "Being with you keeps everything in perspective. Really, I don't give a fok about what others have to say about us."

"Good. Neither do I." He squeezed her hand. "But seriously, I think we're to a point now that it's important you meet my extended family so you know that you truly are welcome."

"That sounds great, but I don't see us having time for that any time soon."

"Why not?" Jason asked. "I'm in a temporary lull with the Coalition investigation. So, once you've delivered the final materials for the training program, we can slip away for a couple of days before the classes start. This might be the best chance for a vacation we'll get for quite some time."

She hesitated. "Are you sure?"

"Come on, you've talked about how you've never visited the Central Worlds. Tararia is as central as it gets."

"I don't know…"

"Please? Raena has been pestering me about meeting you. She and Ryan would love to host us at Morningstar Isle."

Lexi considered the offer. "It *would* be great to meet them."

"Is that a 'yes'?"

"Are you *sure* it's okay I leave right now? The training initiative…"

"It's not like we'll be out of communication. Once you send over the materials, they'll need time to review it. While you wait for feedback, it doesn't matter if you're here or on another planet."

"If you say so."

He nodded. "Believe me, my parents are big proponents of taking downtime to rest and reset whenever there's a chance to do so. This will be good for us."

"In that case, I can't turn down the offer."

"It'll be fun. I'll make the arrangements."

She let out a long breath. "Well, this should be an interesting trip."

CHAPTER 5

AFTER SEVERAL DAYS of evaluation and analysis in his office, Wil was fairly certain he had a handle on the pattern within the global structure encircling Earth. The survey conducted by Raena's team had identified three classifications of structures around the planet: deep pits with a distinctive sphere at the base, an engraved box at the bottom of a cylindrical chamber, and trenches radiating out from approximately one-tenth of the sites.

The trenches were exclusively near the pits containing the spheres, but not all of those pits had trenches. At first it had seemed random, but Wil had come to realize that the pits with associated trenches were exclusively at ley line intersections. Further evaluation of the ley line maps had verified energy signatures along those sites, which reenforced the historical view that they were locations of power. Though he wasn't sure if it was the same type of energy the Gifted wielded or something else entirely, it was an intriguing prospect.

His study kept bringing him back to the original site they had first identified in Belize. It was one of the pits with a sphere, and it had also been a significant area throughout Earth's history with a strong tradition of power emanating from the place. He'd made arrangements to meet Trevor, Raena's main point of contact for the ongoing investigation, to give him a tour of the site. Wil hoped that getting a firsthand read of the ancient technology might garner further insights, especially in terms of it being a possible higher dimensional energy conduit—whether that be a bridge, a defensive tool, or a weapon.

A knock on his office door pulled Wil from his thoughts. "Come in."

Jason opened the door and entered. "Hi."

"Hey, Jason." Wil checked the time on his desktop. "Are you ready to go?"

"Yes, just wanted to check in before we head out."

"No new crisis, so escape while you can." He flashed a weary smile.

"When are you going down to Earth?"

"Tomorrow—had to take care of some things before I could get away."

"I'm eager to hear what you find out. Message me any time."

Wil shook his head. "I'm certain whatever I find can wait until you're back. Enjoy this time with Lexi and your sister. You've earned a break." Wil himself had been given far too little downtime as a young Agent, and it'd taken him years to recover from the burnout. He hoped to spare his son the same difficult path.

"All right, well, reach out if that changes."

"Thanks, Jason. I appreciate that I can count on you."

His son nodded. "I'll see you in a few days."

"Have fun."

"Raena will make sure of it."

"Give her a hug from us." Wil wished he could go himself.

"I will."

Once Jason departed, Wil returned his attention to the data on his screen. Tomorrow, he would finally see the mysterious, ancient device firsthand and the next phase of their work could begin.

— — —

Raena pushed back from her desk with a sigh. *Why do new issues always seem to come up at the same time?*

Her team had been tracking the ongoing unrest in the Outer Colonies, and a new wave of heated commentary was sweeping through the news broadcasts. Raena and Ryan had recently introduced an initiative through DGE to offer apprenticeship career training to teenagers, which a number of reports had latched onto, claiming it was a scheme to introduce bias into approval rating voting. Though the target age for apprentices did happen to fall just shy of the legal voting age, offering a career leg-up was the ethical thing to do regardless of politics.

The accusatory reports were another desperate ploy by the media to incite an incident when the real story was far from that warped version of events. While Raena had become accustomed to the wildly inaccurate reporting from some of the less reputable so-called 'news' outlets, the vicious personal attacks were beginning to weigh on her.

Criticize us for what we could be doing better. Manufacturing issues doesn't help anyone. She smoothed her hand over her hair, taking a calming breath.

In some ways, it was a compliment that no one could find

anything genuinely awful to say. Raena and Ryan had been working hard to bring their experiences to bear with how the High Dynasties could better serve Taran citizens, which by and large had been met with favorable reactions. She suspected that this nonsense in the media had originated from the powers behind the Coalition in a poorly executed attempt to discredit the Dainetris Dynasty, since Ryan was well-liked and his rising political sway had shifted the power dynamics among the Taran rulers.

A knock sounded on Raena's office door, bringing her to attention. "Enter."

Jovan came in, concern creasing his brows. "I imagine you've seen by now?"

"That Marsha witch needs a reality check about what's newsworthy." The words slipped out before Raena had thought through how petty it would sound out loud.

Her assistant bit back an amused smile. "Allcast isn't known for their reporting accuracy. And Marsha is certainly not popular because of her professional presentation."

The rather buxom reporter did seem to value seductive fashion more than the content she presented, from what Raena could tell. The fact that Marsha had become fixated on Ryan over the last few months didn't improve Raena's feelings about the woman.

"Best we get ahead of it with some damage control," Raena said.

"How would you like to approach it?" Jovan asked.

"I think we should loop in Ryan."

She checked his schedule, seeing that Ryan presently had an open window between appointments. It was the middle of the day, so trekking across the estate to his administrative office wasn't realistic for a quick meeting. Instead, Raena initiated a holoconference.

An image of him appeared on the other side of her desk next to Jovan. "Oh, no. What happened?"

"Marsha Cassis is trying to get a new story to take hold," Raena replied. "About how the DGE career mentorship initiative is a scheme to rig future votes."

Her husband raised an eyebrow. "That doesn't make sense."

"Right? Well, apparently some people are going along with it."

He took a slow breath. "What's our response?"

"Don't have one yet. That's what I wanted to discuss."

"I'd really love to find a way to handle this so we kill the issue once and for all," he said. "It seems like every two weeks they present a new spin on the same old story—none of it grounded in reality."

"It's unlikely that a single approach will alleviate all concerns," Jovan chimed in.

Raena shrugged. "We can try. However, Jason and Lexi are going to be here this afternoon, so we need to resolve this before they arrive."

"I'm not sure if that timeline is realistic—" Jovan began.

"Let's do what we can. I haven't seen my brother for months, and I don't want this shadow hanging over our visit."

"Any suggestions?" Ryan asked.

"Well, it's clear certain sights are set on us," she said, not wanting to name Monsari directly in mixed company. "So, how do we solidify our position and avoid painting an even bigger target on our backs?"

"The target is already there. There's nothing we can do about that," Ryan replied.

"All right, so focus on strengthening our image."

Jovan scowled. "That's delicate. If you get too defensive, it will seem like you have something to hide."

"All right… in that case, we focus on playing up our most positive attributes rather than highlighting areas for improvement?" Raena suggested.

"Something like that," her assistant replied.

Ryan drummed his fingers. "What *are* the best things to call out?"

"Approachability? The tours and town halls. Our humble backgrounds," Raena said.

Jovan shook his head. "Upbringing won't play well."

Raena nodded. "Yes, we have ample wealth and influence now. There's a huge difference between having grown up in dynastic life versus living for years as a regular person."

"I agree," Ryan said. "That doesn't change the fact that most people won't see it that way. Finding out you're a dynastic heir is like hitting the 'easy button' for life."

She raised an eyebrow. "Nothing about this is easy."

"Try telling that to an asteroid miner," Ryan countered.

There was too much truth in the statement to deny. "Okay, forget about that angle," she said. "What *can* we try to sell, then?"

"That we'll listen. Despite this high and mighty life, we're not out of touch. It's the only play we have."

"You can say that all you want, but the masses will need more to be convinced," Jovan pointed out.

Raena considered their options. "I hate to say it, but I think we need to open up our lives."

"How so?" Ryan asked.

"Remember that showrunner who reached out from *Behind the Wall*?"

"Stars, no. Not a foking Sensational telespecial!" her

husband exclaimed.

"I know it sounds awful, but think about it."

"I am, and it's not making it less awful."

"That's not a bad suggestion," Jovan said. "What better way to give a window into your lives than to have a camera crew follow you around?"

"Everyone knows those shows are scripted and fake," Ryan grumbled.

Raena shrugged. "Yet, the stars are beloved celebrities. Something about seeing someone on a screen in your home apparently makes you feel closer to them."

"I don't get it." Ryan shook his head. "What if we just make a statement as part of the tour activities today?" he suggested. "The audience at the scheduled meet-and-greet is better than talking to a camera."

"A larger audience would be better, but you're right; the tour is the best we can do on short notice," Jovan agreed. "I'll prepare some talking points with the PR team. That doesn't mean the other option should be entirely off the table—"

"Noted, but no thanks for now," Ryan cut in.

"Thank you, Jovan," Raena told him. "I don't know what I'd do without you."

"My pleasure, my lady." He smiled. "I enjoy staving off chaos."

She chuckled to herself as he rose from his seat.

"Loop me in once you have the talking points," Ryan said. "I'll wrap everything up here and then meet you for lunch."

"Sounds good. See you soon." Raena was about to end the holoconference when Jovan abruptly halted his departure, gaping at his handheld.

"Change of plan," he said.

Raena's heart skipped a beat. "Did something happen?"

"The Monsari Dynasty just released an official statement

declaring a vote of no-confidence in Dainetris," Jovan stated.

"What the f—" Raena caught herself just in time. "That's ridiculous."

Ryan scowled on the holodisplay. "Were there specific citations?"

"Reading now," Jovan said, somewhat distant as he scrolled through the statement on his handheld.

"Put it up here," Raena instructed, indicating he should cast it to her desktop.

The information appeared, and she adjusted it to appear as part of the holoconference so Ryan could follow along.

She read through the document herself, shocked and appalled that they'd make such bold claims with no supporting evidence. The press statement built upon the news reports that had been circulating over the past several days, alleging manipulation of sensitive populations in order to garner favor in the approval votes for the High Council membership.

"This is it. They're making an official power play, aren't they?" A year ago, she wouldn't have dreamed one of the High Dynasties would dare make such an audacious declaration of political war.

Ryan crossed his arms, frowning as he reviewed the information for himself. "This move suggests that our suspicions about Monsari might be correct."

"What suspicions?" Jovan asked.

Raena exchanged a glance with Ryan on the holodisplay. *"Do we bring him in?"* she asked him telepathically, reaching out across the estate to his mind.

"He's earned our trust. We'll need support if Monsari is going to play things this way."

"We've learned some concerning information over the past year, Jovan. It's been kept need-to-know so far. We'd like to bring you in now."

His dark eyes widened with momentary surprise, then he gathered himself and nodded. "I'm at your service, my lady. I will do everything I can to ensure your trust in me is not misplaced."

She motioned to an empty chair by her desk. "You might want to sit down for this."

Raena was impressed by how Jovan remained so poised during her recap of the incidents involving the Monsari Dynasty over the past several months, especially when it came to the assassination attempt on her father and the prospect that MPS may have exhausted its supply of voydite. She didn't include every detail but tried to give enough that Jovan would get a complete, accurate impression of their present predicament. When she finished, the young man sat in quiet contemplation for several seconds before responding.

"We must avoid becoming isolated," he said at last. "Dainetris and Sietinen always stand strong together, but we'll need the support of the other High Dynasties. A united front against Monsari."

"It'd be foolish for them to make this kind of declaration without having secured support of their own. Otherwise, they'd just be placing a target on their own backs," Raena said.

"Unless they have reason to believe they can sway the others by striking first," Ryan countered.

"Regardless, we must respond in a way that will shut this down before it gains further traction. Suggestions?" Raena looked at her assistant.

Jovan paused in consideration. "The most effective countermeasure to these sorts of claims has been a direct statement from you. It would help if we had an audience to speak to."

"Okay," Ryan began, "so that's what we'll talk about during the tour's meet and greet. We make a statement and broadcast it live."

Raena nodded as she thought it through. "Yes, that could work." They'd planned for the casual conversation to come at the end of the tours so that people would have their final impression of the visit be a more personable view of Raena and Ryan, but switching things up on this occasion shouldn't hurt.

"These grumblings from the Outer Colonies have become so commonplace that most people don't place much stock in it," Jovan offered. "I believe a simple statement dismissing the allegations should suffice."

"I'm all about simple solutions," Ryan said. "Check with the PR team, take the pulse of public sentiment, and we'll squash it this afternoon."

"Yes, my lord. I'll report back soon." Jovan saw himself out.

As soon as Raena was alone in her office, she smiled at the holographic representation of her husband. "Don't worry, this will blow over soon. It's just growing pains."

He glanced to his side then back at the camera. "How's your morning looking?"

"A few internal meetings—nothing urgent. Why?"

"These new developments aren't sitting right with me. I think we should get together to strategize more."

"Should we get PR or Legal in on that?"

"Maybe later, but the two of us should make sure we're on the same page first."

The comment caught Raena by surprise. She considered her relationship with Ryan to be exceptionally strong and close, so the suggestion that they might not see eye-to-eye on an issue was in direct opposition to their everyday communications.

"I'll clear my schedule and be over there soon," Raena said. "See you then."

Raena ended the holoconference and then sent a message to Jovan to postpone the morning's staff meetings until after Jason's upcoming visit, since there weren't any pressing issues aside from the press statements. Once she had confirmation from Jovan, she headed across the estate to Ryan's office.

The center of DGE operations was buzzing with activity. Designed to impress visiting delegates, the expansive space was decorated with sculptural yet functional desks, ornate room dividers, and strategically placed potted greenery to bring a touch of the isle's gardens indoors. Different administrative hubs were arranged throughout the rooms, with groupings of desks for each of the specific business functions. Each represented the top of the reporting chain for DGE's disparate operational units, helmed by a liaison to communicate with Ryan as the Chief Operating Officer and his Operational, Legal, Marketing, and Public Relations leads.

There were upwards of sixty people in the open area of the room, though the most senior team members each had a private office. Ryan's, naturally, was the largest and had the nicest exterior view—situated at the rear of the room so that any visitor was funneled through the center of activity.

The workers barely glanced up at Raena as she passed by. Though her visits were frequent enough that this wasn't an unusual circumstance, their complete focus on their monitors indicated that there must be an urgent issue requiring their full attention.

It was only once she reached the collection of workstations at the back of the room, outside Ryan's office, that anyone addressed her.

Ryan's lead assistant, Sandrine, rose from her desk chair as

Raena approached. "My lady."

"Good morning." Raena smiled at Sandrine and the group of other administrators outside the office.

"It's a pleasure to see you over here," Sandrine said with a respectful nod toward Raena. "May I be of assistance?"

"I'm here for an impromptu meeting," Raena told her. "Is Ryan free?"

"Yes, he's expecting you. Go on in."

Raena glanced back at the serious workers throughout the room. "Is everything okay?"

"I'm happy to answer any further questions after your meeting, my lady," Sandrine replied.

On that somewhat ominous note, Raena let herself through the swinging glass door into the office, closing it behind her. Ryan's desk was at the back of the large room, positioned with both a view out the exterior window and sightlines to the entry door. The furnishings in the space were sleek and sophisticated with clean lines and a bold color palette of black, deep red, and gray. In addition to the desk, several visitor chairs and a sitting area with couches and a low table were positioned around the room.

"Hey," Raena greeted.

Ryan pushed back from his desk and stood to greet her. "Hi." He activated the controls on his desktop to turn the glass walls facing the rest of the administrative center opaque.

"One of those meetings, hmm?" she asked.

"Just don't want anyone bothering us," he replied. He gave her a kiss when they met in the middle of the room.

"What's on your mind?"

Ryan motioned for them to sit down on the couch. "I'm sorry to completely throw off your morning like this."

"No need to apologize. Just tell me what's going on."

"I'm growing concerned that we're facing a civil war across the Empire, and we need a plan."

"It's unlikely—"

"Perhaps, but we need to be prepared. I love that you always try to see the good in people and hope for the best outcome. This time, though, there might not be a clean way out."

Raena wanted to cling to her optimism, but deep down she recognized that Ryan was right. If things *did* go badly, they'd need strategies ready to implement. "How do you see it playing out?"

"The most likely scenario is that Monsari will continue to force a division between the High Dynasties. Some will side with them, others will likely side with us."

"That would get messy very fast."

He nodded. "The bigger concern is how the alliances might shake out at the Lower Dynasty level. Some of the families hold tremendous sway, and since most are based offworld, they may hold more allegiance to planets other than Tararia."

Raena reflexively glanced over her shoulder to confirm they were alone. All the same, she thought her next words were best conveyed telepathically. *"Is it right for us to try to hold onto Tararian centralized ruling of the Empire if enough people would prefer independence?"*

"At a certain point, no, the right thing would be to step aside. However, I believe these voices calling for separation stem from another group's aspirations for power, not a genuine will of the people."

"Then our mandate remains to act in the best interest of the public."

"To the best of our ability."

She nodded. "We have demonstrated strong financial

resilience as well as a humanitarian perspective in our actions. I must believe that has won us genuine friends who will see through the other nonsense in the news."

"We need to identify those friends and secure the alliances. If we're looking to the Lower Dynasties for support, then you can be assured that our would-be enemies are doing the same. Monsari wouldn't be making these aggressive actions unless they were confident in their position."

"Or it's a bluff and they're acting with pure desperation."

"That would make them even more dangerous. Is it worth considering a strategy where we play along?"

Raena shook her head. "You've done nothing wrong, and I can't advise any action that even hints at admitting culpability. We can beat this the right way. No stooping to their underhanded tactics."

"How do we go about determining our true friends? Direct questioning seems too on the nose."

"I think we need some kind of demonstration to see who rallies behind us. Subtle but clear," Raena suggested.

"And what might that be?"

She shrugged. "No clue. Don't we have people to give us brilliant solutions when we can't think of them ourselves?"

"Until they admit that they don't have any clue, either, and we're back to square one."

"Fun, isn't it? Then we'll get a spark of inspiration and change the face of the Empire. Simple!"

"Right. Easy. And then the next issue will come up and we'll need to do it all over again."

"So it goes."

Ryan sighed. "I foking hate this job sometimes," he muttered under his breath.

"Hey," Raena gently gripped his arm, gazing into his eyes,

"this isn't personal. They use our names, but it's not really about us."

"You have a family to hide behind. Dainetris is all me."

She didn't know how to respond to that. He was right; she did wear the shield of the larger Sietinen Dynasty and it alleviated much of the sting. Dainetris was still vulnerable and exposed in its slow return to power after nearly two centuries spent in ruin, all but forgotten. While that fact didn't change how Dainetris was treated as a High Dynasty, there were interpersonal dynamics that Raena would do well to remember when talking about these things with her husband; he was one step away from an orphan and didn't have nearly the support network she'd been so fortunate to have throughout her own life.

"I'm here for you," Raena said at last. She gave Ryan a light kiss. "You're amazing, and the people who matter most know that. A handful of naysayers can't do any lasting damage." Despite her reassuring smile, she wasn't so sure. *At least, I hope they can't.*

"I hate situations like this," Ryan said with a slow shake of his head. "I start to believe in myself and have confidence that I *can* be a leader within the Empire, then one statement can bring all that assurance crashing down. I like to think I have more fortitude than that, yet this keeps happening time and again. Maybe I'm not cut out for it, after all."

"On the contrary, the fact that you question your worthiness means that you genuinely care about what's good for the people. That's not a quality you can coach into someone. You have what it takes," Raena assured him. "We'll keep working on that confidence, because you have every reason to believe you can be a great leader, because you *are*."

"It was a lot easier when I was just a humble maintenance tech."

"Want me to break my viewscreen, for old times' sake?" she jested.

"Will it get me out of this press conference?"

"No."

"Then repairs just sound like extra work." He sighed. "I may as well embrace my new role."

"That's the spirit."

"How are we going to do this?"

"Maybe we should—" Raena cut off when a chime sounded at the door.

"Must be important for them to interrupt," Ryan said. "Come in."

A group of half a dozen executive administrators, public relations specialists, and the head rep from Legal entered the office ahead of Jovan. Jovan's shoulders were slumped and a flush shone through his dark complexion.

"Yes?" Ryan prompted.

"Apologies for the interruption, my lord, but this couldn't wait," Sandrine said. "Waiting until this afternoon to make a statement is no longer an option."

That's not the look of someone bringing good news. Raena held in a swear. "What now?"

"Monsari just released a follow-up statement urging the High Council to open an official investigation into Dainetris' dealings," Jovan revealed.

"Ah, shite!" Ryan groaned. "That's going to put a damper on things."

Raena scoffed. "The council is never going to endorse that."

"We can't be sure." Concern edged Ryan's voice.

"This is ridiculous!" Raena threw up her arms. "What's their play here?"

"Outside of your family, no one was happy for Dainetris to be back in the picture," Ryan replied. "I guess they've had enough."

"Monsari is more conniving than this, though. Putting out a couple of press statements saying that the High Council would be better off without that seventh vote? It's bad politics. Just baseless name-calling."

"All the more concerning, then." Ryan looked down. "There's no way we can respond right now."

"We have to. If we don't address it head on, they'll take it as an admission of guilt," the legal advisor, Fred, stated.

"How about we change around today's island tour schedule and begin with the meet and greet?" Ryan suggested. "We could make a public statement, and then everyone can go about their oohing and aahing at the magnificence of the island for the rest of the day."

Based on their facial expressions, the advisors seemed less than enthusiastic about that suggestion, but there were no vocal objections.

"Have the guests for today's tour arrived yet?" Raena asked.

Jovan nodded. "Yes, they're here. But—"

"All right, then we'll do this right now. No one will expect us to have a rebuttal so quickly, so we can show them we won't be bullied."

"My lady, I must advise that we delay this presentation until we've had time to vet the message," Fred told her.

"The longer we delay, the worse it will get for us. We need to wing it."

"I cannot endorse 'winging it' as a reliable political strategy."

"Noted," Raena replied with a curt nod. She turned her

attention to Ryan. "Do you want to lead off, or shall I?"

"Start winning them over and I'll close it out," Ryan said.

Raena rubbed her hands together. "All right, let's do this."

Despite her gripes and moans about dealing with the political drama, she relished the challenge of shifting the public consciousness. She never considered herself one to love attention while growing up, but there was something intoxicating about having so many people hanging on her every word for these sorts of broadcasts. Every time she stepped up to a speaking podium, a shiver of excitement ran up her spine—the thrill of the camera lenses and eyes focused on her every word. It was invigorating, making her want to work that much harder to be worthy of their attentiveness.

On the walk over to the meeting site, she consulted Jovan's list of talking points and composed her thoughts. By the time the contingent arrived, she had it all planned out.

With a silent exchange of support, Raena and Ryan stepped out onto the stairway landing above where the tourists were gathered.

Raena looked out over the crowd—approximately fifty people—and smiled warmly. "Hello! We're excited to have you here with us today."

The gazes of those in the crowd passed over Raena, displaying a mixture of awe and skepticism. She was used to that reaction after a month of conducting these tours, and she made it a point of pride to win over every single person by the end. Today might be more difficult than most because of the change in timing, but she wasn't one to shy away from a challenge.

"I apologize for the alteration to the itinerary—" may as well address that upfront, "—but we thought it best to meet with you sooner than later, given this morning's news reports.

Though we are no strangers to allegations of underhanded dealings, today's claims—just like those refuted in the past—are baseless and, frankly, an insult to our character.

"I won't deny that there are some leaders within the Taran Empire who might turn to devious means to win favor from honorable citizens. We've all seen political sway in action, to varying degrees, and it will likely remain an unavoidable element of governance. The difference, though, is intent. We must not conflate the impacts of well-intentioned charity with targeted bribery. Yes, both may sway favor, but one does so with the *intent* of getting something in return.

"The training initiatives undertaken by the Dainetris Dynasty and DGE have no such objective. Our only aim was to offer new opportunities for advancement to a citizenry who can help shape a better future for the Empire. We want you to be a part of designing that future. If these programs aren't what you want or need, tell us what we can do better."

A murmur passed through the crowd with several nods.

Raena stepped aside, giving a telepathic nudge to Ryan for him to take over.

Her husband took her place at the podium. "I won't stand here and tell you that I know how difficult life can be. Though I grew up as a Ward, I was lucky to live at a High Dynasty estate and I never needed to worry about being safe or well-fed." He paused, looking over the faces in the crowd.

Several people nodded, their tight expressions those of people who'd witnessed hardship or experienced it themselves.

"The initiatives we've launched don't address all problems throughout the Empire," Ryan continued, "but they do offer one of the things I was most fortunate to have as a Ward, and that's a trade education. Ward programs have a successful track record of pairing young people with career prospects that fit both their interests and aptitudes, and we've endeavored to replicate this best-fit process for you.

"Nothing like this has been attempted on this scale before, so it's no wonder it's come under scrutiny by those who are resistant to progress." He smiled, and a couple people in the audience chuckled. "Frankly, it goes against the traditional way of doing things where the people with the most advantages in life get first dibs on career prospects. Our aim is to level the field through a merit system, which will provide exposure to opportunities for those who might otherwise never be given a chance."

There were more murmurs in the audience at that, and one person let out a whoop of approval.

Ryan nodded at them, making eye contact with the people who were most engaged. "It will take more time to accomplish this objective, so what you see now is only the first step. Can we do better? Certainly, and we sincerely want to hear from you about what improvements you'd like to see. Our goal is to provide education and training so that each person is in a position to succeed based on their own talents and abilities." He surveyed the crowd. "In the meantime, the media is spreading their own account about what's going on. These statements are purely opinion with twisted facts that do not reflect reality."

At that, Fred and the other administrators tensed. The speech was starting to go off-script, but Raena understood why Ryan had elected to make the assertion about the lies. It was risky, but giving any latitude to the media would only embolden them to keep making false claims. They needed to publicly put them on notice.

Ryan gripped the sides of the podium as he looked out over the crowd. "We intend to continue with the programs as designed and will roll out the expanded scope on schedule. Anyone who participates is free to pursue their career and political affiliations without pressure or expectations. It's every Taran citizen's right to draw their own conclusions and take actions accordingly. Enjoy the rest of the tour."

He stepped back from the podium to an enthusiastic applause and several cheers. After giving a respectful wave and nod to the onlookers at the bottom of the stairs, he then rejoined the administrators where they waited out of sight inside the building.

"Nicely done," Raena said in his mind.

"There will be consequences."

Fred was clearly thinking the same thing, as he had a slight flush to his cheeks and was shifting uncomfortably on his feet. "That speech isn't quite what we discussed."

"No," Ryan replied in a confident, level tone. "But Monsari started a fight, so that's exactly what they're going to get."

CHAPTER 6

IT HAD BEEN so long since Jason's last leave that he hardly remembered how to relax. Lexi's anxious disposition in the shuttle seat next to him certainly wasn't helping him unwind. *Enjoy this time away from work. It'll be fun, especially for Lexi.*

He took her hand in an attempt to calm her nerves. "Try to forget everything else going on and prepare for pure decadence."

"I'm here, aren't I? You can ease up on the sales pitch."

"I'm not trying to sell you on it. I just feel bad that you're stressed."

She stared out the shuttle viewport at the curve of the planet below. "No way around it. A commoner Outer Colonies girl like me doesn't know what to do when she finds herself on a private shuttle to Tararia with a High Dynasty heir. It's like living in a bizarre dream-world wondering when I'm going to wake up."

"I can assure you that you're not asleep."

"I know, but my subconscious still hasn't accepted that."

Jason squeezed her hand. "In that case, I'll just make it the best waking-dream you can have."

The shuttle began its descent through the atmosphere, a smooth ride thanks to the advanced stabilization system and antimatter pion drive. After spending so much of his flight career in space, seeing atmosphere streak by outside was a somewhat odd sensation—like he was moving too fast, even though the speeds in open space were far greater than this planetary descent.

Once past the uppermost cloud layers, the view was far less dizzying as the craft began its final approach to Morningstar Isle.

The island rose from the sea like a sparkling emerald set in platinum. The southern expanse of the isle was covered with lush vegetation in deep greens interspersed with pops of flowering foliage in shades of red and gold. Even the large structures on the northern part of the estate were lost amidst the green from a distance. As the shuttle got closer, details of the rocky cliffs came into view, making them appear less smooth and metallic than they seemed from afar.

Lexi sucked in a sharp breath as she took in the view. "Oh, my stars!"

Jason smiled. "Pretty impressive, huh?"

"It doesn't seem real."

"Though there are some incredible structures on Earth, none of it compares to what I've seen on Tararia. I don't know if it's the building materials themselves or just the craftsmanship, but the details are astounding."

Despite his wonder, a slight shudder ran through Jason as he looked at the place, remembering the experience six years before when he'd taken a back pathway in through those cliffs to rescue the Priesthood's captives. He'd witnessed the dark side of what people were capable of doing to each other, and it had colored his perspective on many subsequent events. Despite a positive outcome to that mission, he had been left with a tainted impression of the island. Now that it was his sister's home, he was trying to alter that opinion.

It's all new to Lexi. Experience it through her eyes, he told himself. That might be easier said than done, but he aspired to keep an open mind.

The shuttle finished its approach toward the landing pad next to the massive former monastery perched above the northern cliffs. Several new structures had been constructed in the surrounding grounds, to Jason's surprise, likely to support the expanding operations.

They've been busy. Jason looked over the estate, noting there was also a new landing pad to the west.

The shuttle set down on the port's pavement with a barely perceptible bump.

"Ready?" Jason asked.

Lexi smiled. "Yeah, this'll be great."

They rose from their seats and stepped toward the front of the shuttle to the exit hatch. It folded downward to form a ramp.

Jason squinted against the sudden brightness of the afternoon sun.

Two figures were approaching the landing pad, with several more standing by at a distance. He felt rather than saw that the foremost greeters were Raena and Ryan—the bond of family speaking to him through a subconscious telepathic connection.

Jason reached out to his sister's mind. *"See, I told you I'd come visit."*

"It's taken you long enough!" she quipped back. He doubted there could ever be any real hard feelings between them.

Close now, Raena got a big grin on her face. "Jace, it's so good to see you!" She ran forward the last few steps and threw her arms around him.

He held her close. "I've missed you."

Raena pulled out from the hug and turned her attention to Lexi. "And you must be the enchantress who miraculously pinned down my brother."

"Oh, stars, here we go." Jason rolled his eyes.

"I jest," Raena told Lexi. She looked her over. "You are even more striking in person."

Lexi flushed. "Thanks. So are you."

"It's all thanks to my stylist."

Lexi tugged at her generic TSS-issued outfit. "Clearly, fashion hasn't been a priority."

"Well, I took the liberty of getting you a few items so you can enjoy yourself while you're here," Raena said.

"Oh no, am I going to end up looking like an exotic bird putting on a mating display?" Lexi said in a panic in Jason's mind.

"No, Raena would never pick out anything for you that she wouldn't wear herself," he replied. *"The crazy fashion all comes out of the Sixth Region, and she stays far away from that."*

"All right, good. Because I don't think I could fake it in front of a bunch of telepaths." Lexi nodded to Raena. "Thank you, that's very thoughtful."

Raena put her arm around Lexi. "Come on, let me show you around."

Ryan stepped forward and gave Jason a hug. "I'm glad you could make it."

"Some time away from Headquarters will be good."

"It'll be great to have Lexi here, too. I'm looking forward to getting to know her."

Jason watched his sister talking with her. "I'm worried about what those two are going to get up to together."

Ryan laughed. "They look like fast friends already."

"I can't wait to hear which horribly embarrassing story Raena tells about me first."

Raena laughed at something Lexi said.

Jason sighed. "So it begins."

"She's been really looking forward to this," Ryan continued. "We both have."

"I think she always wanted a sister and just settled for me."

"Perhaps in addition to, not instead of."

"In any case, I haven't been a very good brother recently. I should've checked in more."

Ryan shook his head. "You've been there for her when it's mattered. I know you may look at it like she left home and has been on her own, but that's not the case."

"Yeah, she has a whole other family here. Our lives are so different now."

"We've come a long way since that first year in the TSS together, huh? That decade feels more like a lifetime ago."

Jason nodded. "Yeah, man, I wish I could go back in time to tell myself everything I know now. I expect I would have done some things differently."

"Such as?"

"Appreciate the simple times."

"Yeah, I know what you mean. It was kind of nice being anonymous, wasn't it?" Ryan chuckled to himself. "I don't think I'll ever get used to giving speeches that will get broadcast across the galaxy."

"I'm very happy that isn't in my job description."

"Not yet, anyway. I suspect you'll one day occupy the big seat in the TSS."

"Maybe." In actuality, it was more like 'probably', but Jason had intentionally avoided thoughts of his career that far in the future. Though his father had been hinting at that intention for years now, Jason enjoyed the freedom of being an Agent rather than a commander. This new assignment as a task force leader was the first step of greater responsibility, but he'd hold onto his autonomy for as long as possible.

"Yeah, I wouldn't be broadcasting that intention, either," Ryan said. "I know all too well what it's like to have a target on your back because of your position."

"You two seem to be doing all right."

"Things aren't always as peaceful as we make them seem."

"I have heard a few rumblings."

Ryan nodded. "More than a few. And getting louder. What happened at the Monsari estate a few months back was just their opening move."

"What else?" Jason asked. He hadn't heard about more trouble with the dynasty beyond the speculations about their ongoing involvement with the Coalition.

"That press release today?"

Jason shook his head.

Ryan scoffed. "Oh, well, it was quite the morning. Monsari has formally declared me unfit and called for an inquiry into Dainetris' future standing."

"What the fok?" Jason gaped at him.

"No joke. I suspect Tararia is going to become a dangerous place in the near future."

Jason took a deep breath and swallowed. "It might be best if we don't discuss this with Lexi. She's stressed out enough with this visit as it is."

"That's a conversation you can have in your own time. Just thought you should know."

"Thank you. I'll pass on the message to my dad."

Ryan nodded. "I don't expect the TSS to rush in to our rescue or anything, but it's good to know we have allies with... a different kind of influence."

"We'll see what we can do," Jason assured him.

"I appreciate it. We're in a difficult place right now of trying to be open while also recognizing that leaves us exposed."

"That's right, I heard you've started doing tours of the estate?"

"We're not conducting the walk-through ourselves, but we're setting aside time each day to talk with visitors if they have any questions for us," Ryan replied.

"That's a nice idea. Demystify you as people."

"Yeah, we want to connect with regular citizens. It's still too soon to know if it's going to make an impact."

"I'm glad I can stay out of the news most of the time."

"Well, if you and Lexi get married, I'm sure you'll have your time in the Sensationals."

Jason sighed. "I suppose that's unavoidable."

Ryan raised an eyebrow. "Which part?"

"Both. I mean, I don't need anything on paper, but I'd like to for her sake." It was a dark way to look at it, but the fact remained he was in a dangerous line of work, and he wanted to know she'd have protections in the event something happened to him.

Ryan nodded. "I guess being in positions like ours, it's inevitable to make headlines."

"Best we can do is hope for it to be in our favor."

— — —

Should I be worried that she's taking me off alone? Lexi wondered as Raena led her away from Jason and Ryan.

"I just wanted a little one-on-one time to get to know each other," Raena said, glancing at Lexi. "I hope a chat can help set your nerves at ease."

Lexi had to give the woman points for being perceptive. Then again, reading people was a necessity in the world of politics. "Thanks, I appreciate that."

Raena flashed a warm smile, reminding Lexi of the way Jason lit up when he saw her. Truth be told, Raena was even more beautiful in person than videos or pictures had indicated. Part of it was her eyes, which were an almost identical shade of teal to her brother's. The subtle glow in the afternoon sunlight instantly captivated Lexi, and she found it difficult to look away even as her nerves constricted her chest.

Though she tried to think of Raena as Jason's sister, the fact remained that she was a High Dynasty heiress. Lexi had never dreamed she'd set foot on Tararia, let alone that she'd find herself talking one-on-one with a member of the ruling elite.

"I'm glad we could finally get together," Raena continued as she led Lexi toward the palatial manor. "I've been eager to meet you since Jason first mentioned you."

Lexi tried to gauge the meaning behind the words. To her surprise, she detected nothing but genuine interest. *And she's nice, too?*

"I've been wanting to meet you, too," Lexi said. "I haven't actually known twins before. I know you're not identical, or anything, but I've always been interested in that idea of growing up so closely with someone."

"It is a special relationship." Raena evaluated her. "Are you an only child?"

"May as well be. I have a much older half-sister, but we

don't…" She faded out. "It's complicated."

"Family often is. I got really lucky with mine."

Lexi swallowed a sudden lump in her throat. "Yeah, you did. Your parents have been amazing to me. I never would have imagined I could feel so welcome."

Raena smiled. "They love their found family. I appreciate everything they've done to make the TSS a place where people can belong no matter what they've faced in the outside universe."

"Speaking as one of those wayward strays, it's truly changed my life."

"I'm glad to hear it. And I'm sure you're going to change many more with your new civilian training initiative."

"Oh, you've heard about that?"

"It's been quite a hot topic, actually," Raena said. "I was happy to hear you were helming it rather than someone who's been part of the TSS for years. I think it needs that outside perspective."

A swell of pride pushed down Lexi's nerves. "I like to think I'm bringing that."

"I'm excited to see what happens. There's still a fair amount of anti-Gifted sentiment, and I want more than anything for that to change."

"Either they want to use us or force us to the outskirts of society." She scoffed. "I can't tell you how much it meant to me when you stood up to the Priesthood."

"I wish we'd been able to do it sooner," Raena murmured, her tone turning dark and hard. Lexi could sense the bitterness beneath her poised demeanor.

"Believe me, I know change takes time. Normally, at least. Life does seem to be on fast-forward these days."

"I'm quite familiar with that feeling." Raena shook off the

somber cloud. "When I met Ryan, everything changed overnight."

"How old were you?" Lexi asked as they approached the manor.

"Sixteen. It was… a lot to process. And, less than a week after we left Earth."

"Shite."

"Yeah." Raena glanced back over her shoulder toward Ryan in the distance. "We took a year to get to know each other before making it official, but we knew right away. Funny how life can throw you curve-balls like that."

"It must have helped that you and Jason were going through it together."

Raena hesitated, not quite masking a wince. "Some parts. I don't think he understood what I had so quickly with Ryan until he met you."

I take it there was some drama there. Lexi needed no explanation; her own whirlwind romance had certainly changed her perspectives on love and partnership. "I wouldn't have believed it if I hadn't experienced it for myself."

"We're very lucky to have found that kind of profound connection with someone."

"Yeah, we are," Lexi agreed.

The two of them fell quiet as they strolled.

Ahead, the former monastery took on more definition as they veered toward the back entrance through the upper garden. Having spent most of her life in space, Lexi found any time with vegetation was a treat—such a commonplace experience for most planet-dwellers that she felt a little silly getting excited about seeing a flower growing in dirt. It wasn't that there weren't gardens on space stations, but rather that access to those green spaces were often reserved for the wealthy, though that wasn't supposed to be the case. Seeing this array of verdant life across the isle offered a poignant reminder of how she was talking to someone who never had to want for anything, the only restriction being her imagination.

Yet she's walking here alongside me like an equal. In fact, there hadn't been even the slightest hint at an elitist attitude. Despite all of Jason's assurances, Lexi hadn't believed that it would be possible to travel to this place where someone of her background had no right to go and to nonetheless be accepted with open arms.

A feeling of immense gratitude swelled in Lexi's chest, flowing through her until she feared she might sob.

"Thank you for being so cool about all this," she blurted out.

Raena raised her eyebrows with quizzical surprise. "What do you mean?"

Lexi felt her cheeks flush. "For not being defensive or accusatory or whatever."

Raena let out a hearty laugh, then brought her hand up over her mouth sheepishly. "Sorry, I can only imagine how awkward this must be for you." She looked Lexi in her eyes. "Seriously, though we might be strangers now, I hope by the time you leave you'll think of me more like a sister. Jason chose you, and that's all I need to know that you're great. Please, try to relax and enjoy yourself. Stars know, I need to unwind, myself."

"Okay." Lexi gave her a small smile. "I just figure that you and Jason probably have had strong opinions about each other's partners, being so close."

"Oh, for sure. That doesn't mean we always listened." Raena laughed again.

"Did he and Ryan get along?"

"Yeah, they've been good from the beginning. I didn't date much back in Earth, but there were plenty of girls I warned Jace about back in high school. Though there was nothing too noteworthy, I did get in my share of I-told-you-so's."

"So, I *am* being tested." Lexi was only half-joking.

"Nah, you were in as soon as you bonded. I trust his judgment now; all of us made dumb decisions as teenagers."

"Not my finest time, either."

"All experiences shape us. That's not always a bad thing." Raena shrugged.

Had Jason not shared his account of Raena's kidnapping by the Priesthood, Lexi would have doubted that Raena had been through anything remotely as traumatic as her own early life experiences. Though Raena didn't exhibit obvious symptoms of post-traumatic stress, that didn't mean she didn't struggle with it daily like Lexi. Strong people were good at hiding their inner demons.

"It sucks to be used by megalomaniacal sociopaths," Lexi said. "I guess we have that in common."

"I think we have a lot more in common than that, and far better things."

Lexi smiled. "Yeah, sorry. I'm still trying to wrap my head around this whole thing. How to be around you."

"That's easy. We're family. Forget about everything else."

Raena led her on a quick loop through the upper garden before heading back to the palace, where they entered the manor through a large archway. The architecture was the most extraordinary Lexi had ever seen, both in terms of the artistry and the fine materials. Opulence was one thing to see on a screen, but seeing it up close reminded her yet again about the differences between the wealthy Central Worlds and the environments on many of the Outer Colonies planets.

She quickly gave up trying to follow their path through the massive palace, walking through more dining rooms and living areas than it seemed like any singular structure had a right to contain. Every one of them was finished to the highest standard, with exotic incense giving each space a unique personality that made it feel like merely walking from one room to another was a voyage to a different world. As far as Lexi was concerned, she had indeed entered an alternate reality.

The tour eventually took them to one of the central towers of the former monastery, where a stone balcony at the top offered an unobstructed view of the churning sea below.

Lexi breathed in the salty sea air, unlike anything she'd experienced during her previous travels. The slight stickiness of it on her skin was oddly refreshing. She gazed out at the impressive vista. "It's amazing here."

"It is." Raena leaned her forearms on the railing, taking a deep breath as the breeze rustled her ponytail. "It reminds me of Earth in a lot of ways—the best parts of it."

"Did you have a palace like this?"

"Oh, stars, no! I had a very boring suburban childhood."

Jason had told Lexi as much, but she had never believed it. There was no way the Sietinens could have blended in anywhere. "I can't imagine what that was like."

"*Not* like this. I spend every day wondering when I'm going to wake up from the fairytale." Raena pushed back from the railing and clapped her hands together. "But since we're still in the fantasy, let me show you to your room and then we can get the party started."

"I'm game."

"Good. And you can see if any of those new outfits are to your taste."

Lexi smoothed her custom TSS uniform. "I'm honored to wear it at Headquarters, but having something else would help get out of that 'work mode' mindset."

"Cheers to that. And there'll be a proper cheers with wine as soon as you get settled in," Raena added with a wink.

The guest wing was somewhere up one of the many towers; Lexi was already so turned around that she made no attempt to orient herself, trusting that Jason or someone else would be able to point her in the right direction later. Entering through a set of double doors, Lexi sensed Jason ahead.

A short way down the hall, she spotted him waiting in a small sitting area with Ryan across the hallway from doors to numbered suites. The two men stood up as Lexi and Raena approached.

"Please tell me she hasn't revealed all my embarrassing childhood secrets," Jason bantered with a mock accusatory glance toward his sister.

Lexi smiled. "Not *all* of them, I'm sure."

Jason sighed melodramatically. "The perils of family get-togethers."

Raena rolled her eyes. "Watch it or I *will* start telling her the juicy stuff."

"Well played." Jason motioned to one of the doors, turning to Lexi. "Shall we?"

She nodded. "Sure. Thank you for the tour, Raena."

"My pleasure. See you downstairs in a few."

Jason palmed open the biometric lock on the door as Raena and Ryan departed. "Did you have a good time?" he asked Lexi.

"Yeah, it was great. Raena has a way of setting you at ease."

"It's a gift. Needless to say, she never had an issue with being popular."

"I don't doubt—" Lexi's breath caught as the door to their suite swung open. The outer room was easily four times the size of the quarters she now shared with Jason at TSS Headquarters. "Oh, my stars!"

"I forgot to mention that the accommodations here are next-level," Jason said, casually walking inside.

Lexi followed him in, making a conscious effort to keep from gawking. Once inside, she noticed a separate bedroom was visible through a door to the left, and a double doorway on the back wall of the living area opened onto a terrace overlooking the sea. The glass doors stood open, letting in the salty breeze.

Unlike the simple furnishings in her TSS quarters, the finishes in this space screamed of opulence and luxury. From the intricate crown moldings to embellished metal plates around the door handles, the exquisite attention to detail spoke to an expectation that guests would find no expense had been spared in appointing the space.

"How is Raena so humble living in a place like this?" Lexi commented with a raised eyebrow.

"None of this material stuff really matters to her. There are simply expectations about appearances on influential planets like Tararia."

Lexi wandered into the bedroom, where she stopped next to the large bed, dressed in deep red linens and adorned with silver inlays in the carved wooden headboard. She rubbed the silken fabric between her fingers. "This material is incredible. I've never felt anything like it."

"Only the finest for the guest suites. Lucky us!" Jason replied with a smile.

"And here I thought the stuff at TSS Headquarters was nice."

"We do live at a high standard there, but a room like this is designed to impress as an expression of status. I can almost guarantee that these sheets and everything else in here cost a fortune."

Lexi scowled. "Raena and Ryan don't strike me as the kind of people who would be frivolous like that."

"Oh, they're not. Raena is actually quite frugal—always has been. What I meant is that there's an *expectation* that they, as High Dynasty members, will purchase these top-of-the-line items from Baellas. It's almost a donation in the name of friendly business dealings."

"I imagine there's a certain handheld model VComm only makes available to certain clientele, as well?"

Jason pointed his finger in the affirmative. "You've got it."

"Politicking sounds exhausting."

"No doubt. And now you understand why I hide in the TSS."

"Yeah, wow."

"I'm forever indebted to Raena for taking on the social maneuvering challenge. I have it easy by comparison."

Lexi evaluated him. "You miss her, don't you?"

"How could I not? No one else can fully understand the experience of finding out you're the heir to an empire and needing to leave the only home you've known to play a pivotal role in a galactic civilization. And we spent all of our childhood together. I could count on her being there, no matter what was going on with our other friends. It can take a long time to trust someone else with your feelings like that."

Lexi looked him over. "How are we doing?"

"The bond has expedited things."

"I know it'll take time to have the same kind of trust you share with the rest of your family, but I look forward to getting there."

"Me too."

Lexi continued checking out the suite. She found a door at the back of the bedroom, which opened into a walk-in closet stocked with several fine outfits. At first glance, they all looked, remarkably, to be to her taste. "This is amazing."

"I pretend I'm at a theme park every time I come to visit."

"You know, I'm actually starting to believe you," Lexi said.

"About what?"

"That you didn't have all this growing up. Raena corroborated your story."

He looked at her with his eyebrows raised in shock, chuckling a little. "Seriously, you had doubts?"

"Maybe not. I don't know." She sighed. "I guess it's that I have difficulty understanding how anyone would give up *this*."

"Fame and fortune aren't everything," he replied. "I'm glad I didn't grow up here, because I think I would have probably turned out a total jerk."

"I doubt that."

"It's hard to know. In any case, I'm happy to have had a simpler life as a kid. Our house was nice, but it was very… normal. We had a decent-sized backyard, Raena and I each had our own room. I had to clean up after myself. What Raena has here, with servants and a freaking *castle*, is mind-boggling."

"Huh." Lexi stared into the distance out the window, lost in thought. "I just realized, I've never actually had my own bedroom."

"I'd offer to hook you up with your own quarters, but I rather like sharing a space with you."

"Oh, yeah, no. I definitely don't want to be on my own now!"

He placed his hand on her shoulder, offering a warm and steady anchor to the moment. "If there's anything I can do to give you those things you missed out on, please don't ever hesitate to bring it up."

Lexi looked off to the side, overcome with a wave of emotion. *No one has ever taken care of me like this before.*

"Hey, are you okay?" Jason asked, stepping closer to her.

"Yeah, sorry. It's all kinda overwhelming. I keep waiting for the moment when you'll stop being so amazing, but instead you keep getting even more incredible."

He reached out to her through their bond, offering a warm mental embrace and caress that provided more reassurance than any words could. She reciprocated the telepathic gesture and wrapped her arms around him. Leaning her head against his chest, she took a few slow, intentional breaths to center herself.

"Thank you," she murmured.

"I'll always be here for you."

"I know you will." The stress and doubt melted away.

He pulled back from the hug, gazing into her eyes. "Now, what do you say you pick out one of those fancy new outfits and we go get a drink and have some fun?"

CHAPTER 7

TIME FOR ANSWERS. Wil exited the central elevator on Level 10, heading for the wing containing the large hand-to-hand combat training rooms.

One of the rooms had been retrofitted into a transit hub, of sorts, to streamline the TSS' involvement in the ongoing Earth investigation. Rather than taking shuttles to the planet's surface, they had determined that transdimensional spatial dislocation—or TSD—arches would be a far more efficient transit method. Though he had a TSD arch in his own quarters, it led only to its paired archway in the basement of his former home on Earth. Rather, the transit hub contained arches linking directly to each of the key investigation sites on Earth. Never before had the technology been applied in such a fashion, to Wil's knowledge, but it gave him ideas for potential future applications.

Visiting Earth always gave Wil mixed feelings. On the one hand, the world was where he'd raised his children and had spent sixteen years of his life, making it the only planet where he'd officially resided. Conversely, it was also a foreign place that lacked the comforts and familiarity of the Taran Empire—missing technology and a cultural landscape where he felt he could be himself. He normally took comfort in the anonymity Earth had offered during his residence, but becoming the literal face of first contact had forever ruined that. Now, he was again one of the most famous and recognizable people, and that meant he needed to present himself as a reasoned and informed leader. It was going to be a challenge since he had little notion of what he was about to confront within the mysterious, ancient site.

Only a single attendant was in the TSD arch room when Wil arrived.

The young man came to attention. "Hello, sir."

"Good afternoon. I'm headed to Caracol."

"Ah, yes, that arch is toward the back right, second row."

Wil nodded to him. "Thank you."

The TSD archways were arranged in an offset grid pattern, forming an orchard of spatial portals leading to the various worksites across the planet. Each arch had a placard centered above the opening stating the name of the site and its navigational coordinates on the planet. The devices were wrought from gleaming metal with intricate patterning offset by thin, blue strands of light running through the framework. Though the aesthetics were critical to the functionality, Wil made it a point to add a little artistic flair to his designs whenever possible.

He located the relevant arch and checked its settings at an adjacent console. It had a secure lock with its paired device in Belize and the subspace corridor read as stable.

Just like old times. Wil let out his breath the moment before he stepped through the gateway. A tingle passed over his skin at the event horizon, and then for a moment he felt like he was floating.

Subspace was a bizarre contradiction of calm and a tantalizing call of great power just out of reach, which he now knew to be the energy of the higher dimensions. He resisted the urge to seek it out, instead allowing himself to be pulled through the other side of the archway.

Wil sucked in a breath as warm, heavy air touched his face. He quickly oriented himself, discerning that the TSD arch had deposited him inside a standard tent used for Taran military field ops, and the interior space had been outfitted as a functional command office.

"Greetings, sir," a young man welcomed from next to the main desk. Wil recognized him as Trevor, Raena's main point of contact for her oversight of the onsite investigation.

"Pleasure to meet you, Trevor," Wil replied. "I'm looking forward to finally seeing your discoveries up close."

"We were all excited to hear that you were coming yourself. We could use some experienced eyes on this."

"I'll see what insights I can offer." Wil picked at his shirt, pulling it away from his stomach. Even the breathable fabric was oppressive in the high humidity.

"I wish I could say you get used to it," Trevor said, motioning to his own short sleeves and lightweight pants. "You might want to leave the jacket."

"A very sensible recommendation." Wil stripped off his overcoat and laid it over the back of a nearby chair. Though the environment was still a harsh contrast to TSS Headquarters, shedding a layer did help a little.

"I'll show you the dig site whenever you're ready," Trevor offered.

"Let's get to it."

"Right this way, sir." The young man headed for the flap door at the front of the tent.

Wil pushed through after him, and the flaps automatically resealed behind him. He squinted in the sudden, bright light of outdoors cast from the angled afternoon sun, wishing that he still had tinted glasses as part of his standard TSS uniform.

The tent was situated in the middle of a grouping of temporary structures, which all faced a central walking path approximately four meters wide. Though the tents were a military design, the layout and personnel were civilian, lacking the kind of ordered precision Wil was used to, as evidenced by haphazardly stacked crates and cluttered tabletops under an open-air tent across the pathway.

"It's been a little chaotic around here," Trevor said with an apologetic wince when he noticed Wil's expression.

"I'm not here to grade your operations."

Trevor nodded, though his disapproving glare at a poorly stacked equipment pile suggested he'd been on the losing side of previous discussions about the state of the camp. "The main attraction is this way."

Wil gave a friendly nod and smile to any workers he passed by, but almost none reacted. Those who did let out a gasp of surprise and then did a double-take before speeding up whatever they had been doing. He had no doubt that everyone would know he was there by the time he returned home.

The camp pathway flowed into a narrow tract where footfalls had worn a compacted rut through the loose dirt. Despite the sun streaming in from its low position above the horizon, the entire area was in shadow from the massive section of ground suspended overhead. Wil hadn't paid much attention to it at first, being so accustomed to enclosed, interior spaces. Now that he'd noticed the looming structure, however, he couldn't help feeling a wave of disconcertion.

"Kind of messes with your head, doesn't it?" Trevor said with an upward glance.

"The images don't really do it justice," Wil replied.

He'd been an advocate of Raena's idea from the start, seeing the value in both the functional solution and socio-political play of wholesale lifting the sensitive historic sites into the air. The mining platforms, which had been repurposed for that end, were easily capable of the physical feat and certainly made for an impressive spectacle from afar. Nonetheless, he hadn't quite anticipated what it would feel like to stand beneath thirty hectares of land suspended overhead.

The path sloped downward toward a broad, recessed area in the ground. As they neared the lip of the pit, Wil sensed a pull of energy much like that he'd experienced from the Rift. This was different, though—more like a song, with ebbs and flows, rather than a strong, sustained tone. He wasn't sure what to make of it.

Other Agents who'd visited the site had commented on a strange energy in the place, but none had described it in those terms. *Is it because my abilities are different, or is this a consciousness choosing who to connect with?* Though the second option seemed self-serving, he'd been singled out in enough situations before that he couldn't ignore the fact that he stood as a representative for his people at large.

Wil slowed his pace as he caught a first glimpse of the pit's interior. The carved stone walls had a shiny quality to them, as though laced with crystal or metal. Fine lines reminiscent of a circuit board traced around the cylinder in complex patterns, each emitting a subtle blue glow in the shadows. Scaffolding had been installed around the interior perimeter, providing a spiraling walkway to the bottom.

He was struck by a distinctive hum in the air near the pit. It was as though the walls themselves were calling to him with wordless whispers that tickled the back of his neck. *There's power in this place. But what's the source?*

He'd explored many incredible locations throughout his life, but there was a unique quality to this ancient structure. Curious, he reached out to the energy in the way he would any other interface device. Nothing met his telepathic probe.

"Trevor, what have scans revealed about the energy field here?"

The question seemed to catch him by surprise. "Nothing conclusive. We haven't been able to figure out why we're getting the readings we've been observing." He shifted on his feet.

"And what about you? Does this place make you uncomfortable?" Wil asked. Trevor had no aura of Gifted abilities, so it was curious that he seemed affected by the energy.

"I... It doesn't feel like I belong here. I can't explain how or why, but I don't feel 'welcome' inside."

"Is that feeling more pronounced in any given location?"

"It starts a few meters back and gets more intense the closer I get to the sphere at the bottom."

"Have others expressed that kind of discomfort?" Wil couldn't recall reading about any instances of that reaction in the reports, which was doubly strange since Trevor was writing them.

"Only a handful of people, but we couldn't determine any commonality or pattern, so it wasn't scientifically defensible."

Wil nodded. "In the future, those kinds of anecdotal observations should be noted, just label them as such."

"Yes, sir. Sorry."

"In other circumstances, 'feelings' don't carry the same weight. But there's nothing conventional about this." Wil peered into the depths, barely able to make out the pedestal-mounted sphere centered at the bottom of the pit.

"I don't think I can offer much from this point forward." The young man said, starting to back away from the pit.

"You can stay up here."

"I'll be on the comm if you need anything." Trevor eagerly stepped back several more paces.

"See you soon." With a steadying breath, Wil stepped onto the scaffolding.

The structure was sturdy underfoot, to his relief. At thirty meters deep, the pit had enough depth to give him a touch of vertigo—an annoying condition that only struck him planetside and on large space stations. He kept his focus on the walls.

A subtle blue light illuminated shallow, carved channels branching across the stone surface, like glittering rivulets of water tracing a weathered cliff face. As he walked by, he noticed that the speed of the light's travel adjusted to his movements, flowing in sync with his stride. He paused to test it, and the pulsing glow stopped for three seconds before continuing its previous rhythmic waves. When he started forward again, the light rippled to again fall in step with him.

This is weird. It seemed to be a form of bioelectronic interface, not unlike the feedback system used on the *Conquest* or the Aesir ships. Unlike that technology, however, he didn't sense any kind of telepathic prompt for him to form a direct neural link.

With increased curiosity, he quickened his pace down the spiral ramp. By the time he neared the bottom, the 'song' he'd identified up top had filled his mind with a sweet yet slightly discordant harmony.

He stepped off the ramp onto the stone floor and everything went quiet. The song instead became a *feeling*, drawing him toward the sphere at the center of the chamber.

What are you?

He cautiously approached the object. The slivers of blue light flowing through the carved channels grew brighter and faster in his presence, concentrating on the intricate patterns scrawled across the sphere. The feeling of the ethereal song intensified, pressing in on his mind as it beckoned him.

Clearly, the device was resonating with him somehow. It *wanted* him to activate it. He knew better than to give into the requests of unknown technology without having a reasonable understanding of what it might do.

How do I figure out what it does without turning it on? The previous researchers had run into the same conundrum, only none of them had expressed the device making a direct bid to them. *Or I'm losing my mind.*

Wil took a deep breath and centered himself. The song intensified in his mind again, and he focused on it, just beyond his reach. He extended himself toward it, much like he did to initiate an astral projection. Perhaps that was the key—that interfacing with the device wasn't possible in corporeal reality.

As a precaution, he sat down, cross-legged, on the ground. He would try to let go and see where the investigation took him.

He released from his physical self, hovering at the edge of reality. In other instances, he would soar away from his body to roam the stars, but this time he waited, curious to see what other presence might join him.

"Hello?" he beckoned into the nothingness.

The background song shifted its pitch, rustling and

swirling around him until it coalesced into a chorus of whispers. *"Specify your intentions."*

Wil tingled with anticipation. He hadn't expected to interact with the device like this. *"I seek to use this device to protect Earth and the Taran people."*

"Unknown parameters."

His excitement evaporated. This wasn't any kind of sentience. *"Tarans are a race native to the spacetime dimension. I am presently on a planet we call Earth. It was settled by Tarans long ago."*

The whispers became chaotic for several seconds before returning to a unified voice. *"This planet is known. Tarans are not authorized users of this device."*

"Who built it?" Wil asked. More than anything, that would lead him toward answers.

"The Morla'ki."

The name wasn't remotely familiar to Wil. *"Do they go by another name?"*

A sharp pain pierced Wil's mind, and he recoiled. The connection with the device held onto him, preventing him from severing the connection. Its probe burrowed deeper into his mind, scouring his memories.

Shite, this was a mistake! Desperate, he tried once again to cut the connection to no avail.

The pain ceased as suddenly as it had come on, and the device's hold on him loosened. He was about to withdraw to prevent further intrusion when the whispers gave him an answer.

"You know them as the original Gatekeepers."

Wil tried to stay calm. While he and Saera had speculated about the Gatekeeper's potential involvement in constructing the devices, it was quite another matter to have it confirmed.

Moreover, he'd promised the Gatekeepers that Tarans wouldn't activate their technology again, and here he was interfacing with it. *Shite.*

"Were they working alone?"

"No."

"Then with whom?"

"This terminal is not authorized to disclose that information."

The response didn't make any sense to Wil. *Why could it share that the Gatekeepers made it but not the other party?* He was already in deep enough now that he figured he should get as much information as he could. *"What is the purpose of this device?"*

"To bridge."

"To bridge what?"

"To bridge," the voice repeated.

Wil held back the frustration that would taint his mental tone if left unchecked. Getting angry with the alien device wasn't going to help him get answers. He decided to try another tactic. *"How does it function?"*

"It generates a spatial distortion field."

Okay, now we're getting somewhere! Though vague, the statement suggested that he and Saera had been on the right track with their speculation about the device generating an energy field. Paired with the 'bridge' statement, he suspected it might be some sort of transdimensional gateway. *But if that's the case, then why would the Gatekeepers build it? And why on Earth?*

It led him to one logical follow-up question. *"Does this device allow entities from a higher dimension to descend to spacetime?"*

"Yes."

Stars! Wil pulled back from the connection, now even more worried that he may have inadvertently opened that bridge through the telepathic link. After another moment of consideration, he realized that the device was still powered down and a planet-scale device wouldn't function through one person's mind like that—at least without him knowing. He relaxed a little, though he still wasn't sure where to take it from here.

"Are you equipped with a chronometer?"

"Yes."

"Can that timeline be expressed in terms of this planet's cycle around its star?"

"Yes."

That would give them a timeline in terms of years. Though the Tararian standard year and Earth year weren't precisely the same, it was close enough for most comparisons. *"How many cycles have passed since this terminal first came online?"*

"One-hundred-three-thousand-four-hundred-fifty-two."

If it was accurate, the construction predated the conventional timeline for the rise of humans. Ancestors of modern Tarans were certainly spacefaring by that time, though it's possible they had not yet discovered Earth. Maybe the Gatekeepers had been to the planet first—or whoever else had built this device with them.

Wil wanted to narrow the timeline further, if he could. Determining when the device had been buried would help him home in on the rest of the colonization timeline. *"How many cycles has it been since this terminal was last accessed?"*

"Two-point-one-seven."

Wait, that's... The timeline placed it close to the other interactions with the Gatekeepers. *Is that possible? How did they get down here?*

He tried to focus his racing thoughts. *"Are the terminals on this planet linked?"*

"Yes."

"Were the other terminals also accessed two-point-one-seven cycles ago?"

"Yes."

It did make sense that the original builders of the device would know how to gain access without the exceptional effort of suspending the ground overhead. The question remained, though, *why* anyone would come back after so long. *Unless…*

"Before the most recent terminal access, how long ago was the previous interface?"

"One-hundred-two-point-one-seven cycles."

"Is there a historical record of access every one-hundred cycles?"

"Yes."

Wil wasn't sure whether to laugh or cry. Someone—or something—had been in regular contact through this transdimensional device. But with what? And to what end?

"When was the last time the device was fully online?" he asked.

"One-hundred-three-thousand-four-hundred-fifty-two."

The same time as when it was first online. *So, it was used once and has been dormant since, but checked on regularly. Does it have something to do with the end of the Ancient War? Or the start of it?*

Somehow, he now had even more questions than when he'd begun, but the history was starting to take shape. *"Is this the only planet with a device like this?"*

"No."

"Where are the others?"

"Unknown."

Naturally, it would have been too easy if he could get actual spatial coordinates. *"How many others?"*

"Unknown."

That wasn't helpful at all. However, the information from the terminal might not be current; there was no knowing how many worlds had been destroyed in the past hundred thousand years. Determining the terminal's link offworld would take more digging, but he'd already heard enough that he should give a preliminary report to others.

He was about to disconnect his mental link with the device when one more personal question occurred to him. *"Why did this terminal link with me?"*

"You were compatible."

Though he would need to delve into the matter further, the reply supported his hypothesis that being able to astral project or a comparable skillset was necessary in order to interface with the device. For now, he set aside the concerning implication that whoever had been stopping by every century to check in must then also possess similar abilities.

Wil disconnected the mental link, sucking in a deep breath as he returned to his physical self. He stared at the sphere in front of him for several seconds before standing up. The device remained unchanged on the surface, with the blue threads of light offering the only indication of activity.

He ran through the information he had gleaned from the session and began thinking about what other questions he could phrase to delve deeper. No matter what, it would be a tedious exercise, and he wondered if it might be prudent to bring in other Agents with advanced skillsets to aid in the information-gathering. Saera might have an opinion on the matter.

Wanting her council, Wil pulled out his handheld and was

relieved to see that the energy field in the pit didn't interfere with his signal. He called her.

"Hey, how's it going?" she greeted.

"I spoke with it."

"Hold on, 'spoke'? With the device?"

"It appears to be a sort of artificial intelligence interface, though quite unlike CACI or others within the Taran sphere," he explained. "I believe the technology is rooted in a higher dimension."

"A new take on quantum computing, hmm?"

He glanced at the device. "I'm not sure. I'd like to spend a little more time with it and see what else I can learn through telepathic interface."

"Okay, take as long as you need." She paused. "What has it told you so far?"

"Well, that's where things get interesting."

— — —

Lexi examined herself in the closet's full-length mirror, hardly recognizing her own appearance. She'd never been one for dresses, but this steel-gray gown was an exception. The bottom straddled the line between skirt and pants, with an angled outer layer that shimmered with every movement. With a form-fitting bodice and long-sleeves, the garment was as comfortable as lounge clothes while also being formal enough for a high society ball—or so she imagined, based on images she'd seen in the Sensationals.

"I love it," she said to Jason as he admired her from the bedroom.

"I must say, you look so good in it that it's making me eager for you to take it off."

She laughed. "You'll have to wait until after dessert. I intend to sample *every* course."

"I would expect nothing less." He rose from where he had been seated on the edge of the bed. "You look stunning, truly."

"Thanks." She smoothed her hand over the fine fabric. "This thing probably cost the GDP of a small city."

"Best not to think about it."

Lexi had expected Jason to laugh off the statement. *Except it's probably true.*

Jason held out his hand. "Shall we?"

She took it. "Lead the way."

They strolled from the guest wing down to the ground floor, where pleasant scents of a feast greeted them a short way down the corridor. The source of the wonderous aromas became evident when they entered an ornate dining hall.

The rectangular table in the center of the room was spread with the most magnificent assortment of foods Lexi had ever witnessed. From fruits and vegetables to an array of bite-sized, edible works of art with intricate layers of ingredients that looked too perfect to consume. The items were displayed on ornate dishes wrought in fine silver.

"Wow." Lexi's jaw went slack as she took it all in. *Each of those platters probably cost a week's salary for most people.*

"We weren't sure what you might like, so we decided to offer a sampling of Tararia's most notable cuisine," Raena said. She had changed into eveningwear herself, a dark-blue garment not unlike the style of Lexi's.

"I wish I had a few extra stomachs." Lexi assessed that she'd be full after just *tasting* even half of the items on display, second-guessing her proclamation to try everything.

"Small samples," Raena replied. "And don't worry about extras going to waste. We always share with the staff."

"Good to know." She took an offered plate—which she was fairly sure contained precious metals—and took an assortment of items.

Jason followed behind, making his own selections and offering suggestions about some of his favorites encountered during previous visits. Raena and Ryan grabbed plates for themselves, and then the four of them took seats at a smaller table at the back of the room, which was situated in a large bay window with a view of the garden. Water and wine were waiting at each of the place settings. Outside, the lighting was starting to turn cool and blue for the evening, just dark enough for the solar lights along the pathways to activate.

"This is lovely, thank you." Lexi settled into her seat. She selected a delicate pastry and took a bite, finding that it was filled with something sweet and savory. "Wow."

"Welcome to our home," Ryan said, raising his glass to Lexi. "It's always better here with company."

She held up her glass for the toast.

"Island life is one of solitude." Jason took a sip of wine.

"That wasn't the intention," Raena countered. "This place was too important to leave it as an empty monument."

Lexi knew that it was the former base of operations for the Priesthood but not much beyond that. "The Sietinen Dynasty is based in the Third Region, right?"

"Yes, and that's where we lived before coming here," Raena replied.

"What about Dainetris? Where did the family used to be?"

Ryan swallowed hard and took a gulp of water to wash down his bite of food. "There was an estate on what's now the eastern coast of the Third Region. It's buried now."

"Long story," Raena added. "Suffice to say we needed to build a new home."

Sensitive subject, apparently. She let the somber moment pass by trying another delicacy, finding it as delicious as the first.

"So, Lexi, where did you go to school?" Raena asked.

"I—" The burn of embarrassment heated her cheeks. "I had no formal education."

"Oh. Doesn't matter," Raena said hastily when she noticed Lexi's discomfort. "Smart people like you can get by just fine."

"Still…" She didn't know what to say to these people, who were clearly some of the most intelligent individuals around and who'd had access to great educators.

Raena waved off Lexi's concern. "No, I've talked to you enough already to see that you understand things better than most, regardless of where or how you picked it up." She smiled. "Plus, street smarts count for a lot."

"I guess." Still, Lexi couldn't help wondering what she might have become had she been afforded the chance to go to school like a normal kid.

"Life can be unfair. We can't help the circumstances we were born into," Ryan added. "Why should I have any of this?" He swept his arms in an all-encompassing gesture.

"Birthright," Lexi replied.

He shook his head. "What is that, really? I grew up as a Ward with nothing to my name. Sure, I have distant ancestors who made some smart business decisions and were able to amass wealth and influence, but they lost it all. My immediate blood relatives were destitute for generations. Why, simply because I share DNA with people who were at one time relevant to society, should I be granted the power to influence the course of a galactic empire?"

When he put it like that, it didn't make any sense at all. She only shrugged in response.

He sighed. "Yeah, it's unfair that I was handed all of this, while others could work their entire life to educate themselves and sacrifice their personal life in the interest of career advancement, and yet they could never get beyond a certain level—status that was handed to me with zero effort on my part."

"I think that's one of the complaints in the Outer Colonies," Lexi said.

"Understandably. And I thought about abdicating," he admitted. "In many ways, that would have been the responsible thing to do."

"But we know what would have happened then," Raena chimed in.

He nodded. "The power would have gone to someone who wanted it. Worse, someone who felt entitled to it."

Lexi knew there was truth in that. She'd seen the hunger in the Coalition's leaders and shuddered to think what they would do with real power. "For what it's worth, I think you're doing a good job."

He shrugged. "Trying to."

"I appreciate the groundwork my grandparents laid," Raena said. "Nothing we've done would have been possible without them."

Lexi nodded. "They sound like good people."

"They are. Thanks to them, we've had a significant shift in the role of institutions on Tararia," Ryan said. "The role of the High Dynasties and their corporations is a morphing landscape right now."

Raena nodded. "The Priesthood had restricted lots of information and resources in their bid to maintain control. As soon as that presence was removed, the giants began to stir. A lot has changed in the past two generations."

Lexi met the other woman's gaze. "Not to be the naysayer here, but has it? A handful of elite still preside over the rest of the Empire from their seats on a single planet."

"That's true," Raena acknowledged. "It's not a perfect system, but it *is* getting better. I'll grant you that with or without the Priesthood, many aspects of Taran governance remain the same. However, when it comes to the treatment of Gifted, there have been significant advancements in recent years."

"Forgive me for being skeptical, given my experience on Cytera."

"I would be, too," Raena told her. "Look at it this way, though. Ryan and I—as well as my grandparents—openly express our abilities. My dad is the face of the TSS. Yet, when my grandparents were married, any mention of them being Gifted was covered up. My grandfather refused to wear anything other than his TSS dress uniform for the ceremony, so his parents decided to hide all imagery from the wedding. It should have been the event of the century, broadcast to every corner of the Empire as two of the most powerful Dynasties united. Instead, it was relegated to a couple of headlines that soon became mere footnotes in history."

Lexi raised an eyebrow. "All because their families didn't want ties to the TSS and Gifted?"

"Yep." Raena shrugged. "So, yeah, maybe some things haven't changed all that much. In other ways, though, we no longer have to hide. I can't help but look at that as a win."

"I guess it is. I hadn't thought about it that way," Lexi admitted.

"What's most important is the connections we have with others. No more living in a little bubble. That's what we're trying to do here, anyway."

"I don't think it will provide all the answers, but it's a good start," Lexi said.

Raena smiled. "Little steps every day." She clasped Ryan's hand and squeezed it.

"All right, enough serious talk," Jason interjected.

"Agreed." Raena grabbed her wine glass and raised it in another toast. She looked knowingly between Jason and Lexi. "To a bright future."

CHAPTER 8

THE PREVIOUS NIGHT'S dinner had gone better than Raena could have hoped. Before meeting Lexi, Raena had been prepared to put on a friendly face no matter what—for the sake of her relationship with Jason—but she'd been thrilled to find that they genuinely got along quite well. In particular, she was pleased that Lexi hadn't bent over backwards being deferential and had even voiced contrary opinions over the course of their discussions. That kind of strong personality was exactly what she felt her brother needed in a partner.

After a leisurely morning, Raena invited Jason on a walk through the gardens so they could get some one-on-one time. It'd been over a year since they'd spent any meaningful time together with just the two of them, and she was eager to catch up and reminisce.

"I'm really glad you're here, Jace," Raena said as she led him down her favorite path.

She looked over her brother, still not used to seeing him as he was now. In her eyes, he'd always be the boy with whom she'd gone on imaginary adventures and had shared the most precious moments in her young life. No amount of time apart would change that bond. She could only hope that her own future children would get to experience that with each other.

"It's different now, isn't it?" he murmured.

Raena realized that her thoughts had been more open than she'd intended. "I honestly don't think we'll ever be able to go back to how things were," she replied after a moment. "We live out of time, in a way, now. Seeing each other in the past and not knowing how to relate in the present."

"This present reality isn't something I could have imagined in my wildest dreams."

"No kidding. Even when we joked about aliens, I didn't think that we *were* those aliens!"

"*Royal* aliens," Jason corrected. "Miss Princess, now living all high and mighty in your fancy island castle."

"I think of it as executive-in-training rather than princess."

"Same difference."

She laughed it off. "It's funny looking back on the games we used to play as kids—remember 'secret royalty'?"

"Oh, that's right! I'd completely forgotten about that. What were we, six?"

"Yeah, something like that." She smiled, remembering the games. "I thought about it the other day, and I got to wondering if we came up with it on our own or if Mom and Dad inadvertently tipped us off somehow."

"I think we got it from a movie."

"Probably. But it's funny how accurate it ended up being."

"I'm pretty sure our plan was to live in a castle and eat nothing but candy."

Raena grinned. "You saw the spread last night. Sorry it didn't work out on your end."

They busted out laughing.

"We do have pretty incredible lives," Jason said.

"We do. Not without challenges, but I can't complain." She looked over at her brother. "I'm happy to see you happy, Jace. It's been a rough year."

He looked down the path, avoiding her gaze. "Yeah."

"It's crazy what we considered 'big problems' back when we were young on Earth, huh?"

"Stars, yes! Talk about a change in perspective."

"Arguing about curfew time or if we could have our own car."

Jason smiled. "Which, I'll point out, I *still* don't have."

"Dude, you're pretty much captain of the *Conquest* now. That is *way* cooler."

"But it's *terrible* to park."

She laughed. "Yeah, I don't think you're going to get a lot of sympathy for that."

They walked in silence for a minute, listening to the songs of the insects and the waves crashing against the cliffs in the distance.

"That all feels like a lifetime ago," Jason said at last.

"Or a lucid dream. I can't believe how much can change in a decade."

"Sometimes, it feels like yesterday. I remember Dad sitting me down when we were about fifteen and giving me a talk about making smart choices. It must have been so obvious to him and Mom that we were going to parties and doing things that would have been quite unbecoming if we'd been here on Tararia."

"In all fairness, *you* got into many more shenanigans than I did."

"You were always the golden child." He glanced up at the towering stone wall of the castle behind them. "Not a lot has changed on that front."

She sighed. "Oh, come on. You're the star Agent now. That means more to Mom and Dad than political influence."

He shook his head. "You were always their favorite."

"That's not true."

"They love us equally? I don't doubt that, but you're still the favorite. Maybe it's just because you're the daughter and the dynamic is a little different."

She looked down before bringing her eyes up again. "You're closer to them now. They respect you as an officer. I'll always be their little girl, no matter how old I get or what I do. If they do have any favoritism, it's for a memory of me, not who I am now."

"Don't say that. They respect the person you've become."

"I know. Just… you live in their world. I don't. And that's okay. Things worked out how they needed to, and I have no regrets."

"You do look like you're in your element here."

"I have to say, politicking isn't nearly as bad as Dad made it sound."

"I'd still rather settle disputes with a good fight. Way more satisfying." He grinned.

She gave him a playful shove. "A few years ago, I would've believed you really feel that way."

"I don't know, there are still times when it feels like the way to go. Sure, talking it out among civilized people can get a decent result, but I don't see every conflict ending so cleanly."

Raena read between the lines. "What's the latest on the Erebus?"

"We'll see what Dad has to say when he gets back from Earth. Not a lot to report on the other fronts."

"It's too quiet."

"Don't I know it. If they want to attack us, just do it already."

"It seems like half the members of the High Council have forgotten the planet was almost destroyed a year ago. I'm astounded how short memories can be."

"People focus on what they want to hear. An unfightable transdimensional threat doesn't make for a happy narrative."

"We *can* fight them though, right?" She'd experienced the Erebus' power up close and knew all too well that the beings could crush a Taran world. *The TSS has to be working on a defensive strategy. We can't be in the same position we were before.*

Jason only shrugged in response. "We'll deal with each threat as it comes."

"I wish I hadn't asked."

"I can't lie to you, Raena. Dad's worried, and that's not a look I'm used to seeing on him. Still, it's obvious we have more pressing issues from a civil unrest standpoint, so it's prudent to focus on the conflicts we already know how to handle."

"I would love your insights into what to do about the thinly veiled calls for my head, because I don't have a clue."

"Same options as with any bully. You either hit back, or you make them your friend."

"My advisors tell me that going to blows is unladylike."

"Sounds like you need different advisors who know better fight choreography."

She smiled. "You may be onto something with that."

The garden path opened at a viewpoint looking out to the east. Only ocean was visible as far as the eye could see. A wooden bench was positioned at the front of the paved semicircle overlook.

Raena sat down on the bench and Jason joined her.

"I'm glad we could get this time together," she said.

"Me too."

"Life is getting complicated. I don't know how many more opportunities we'll have to just hang out and reminisce about old times."

"The future isn't nearly so bleak. We'll get through it."

"That's not what I mean." She bit her lip. "It might not be just Ryan and me for much longer."

"Oh yeah?" Based on his sidelong glance, he took her meaning.

"It's a little sooner than I'd ideally like, but it's the reality of the political situation." The recent events had made it clear that having a succession plan was necessary. More than that, though, their relationship was in a good place to start a family. There would always be reasons to delay, so they may as well stop making excuses.

Jason leaned back on the bench. "I don't envy your position."

She shrugged. "A small change in timeline—nothing I don't want to do. Ryan is going to be a great dad."

"And you'll be a wonderful mom."

Raena smiled. "I hope so. What about you and Lexi? Any thoughts of a future family?"

"We haven't talked about it yet. Realistically, TSS Headquarters isn't a great environment for raising a kid. Just look at how weird Dad is."

She chuckled. "True. I've heard a lot more Agents are starting to request assignments where they can have families. Maybe it's time for a change around HQ?"

"We're already busting at the seams."

"In the current facility, yes. But since the structure was transitioned from subspace, it's surrounded by tons of open space inside the containment shell. Why not expand?"

The idea hadn't occurred to him. "That's an interesting thought."

"Do you know if Mom and Dad have considered it?"

"They've never said anything."

"Might be worth bringing up. The TSS has always been an extended family. Why not continue to enhance that culture? The base could become a multi-generational home."

"Definitely something to think about."

"Whatever you decide, I can tell you two are going to be great together. I'm really happy for you, Jace."

He blushed a little. "Thanks. I'm still getting used to the 'we' thinking rather than 'I'."

"Yeah, that is an adjustment."

"You and Ryan made it seem so easy. I can't believe you navigated this kind of connection as teenagers."

"Needing to keep it secret for so long helped us to take it slow."

"In retrospect, maybe having Lexi move into my place on the day we met wasn't the wisest way to go about things."

"I would've done the same. You got it figured out, and that's what's important."

Jason stared at his hands. "I can understand now why you pulled away back then."

"I didn't mean for it to be like that."

"I know. And it's okay. With what I know now, I see how there wasn't anything else you could have done."

"No, I wasn't there for you in the way I could have been. I'm sorry for that," she said.

"It was a lot of change to navigate all at once, that's for sure. But maybe even more so for Ryan than us," Jason mused. "We were entering a new culture and got to shape our identity within that, but he had to reshape his entire sense of self while staying in the same place. In that way, he probably needed your support more than I did."

"Honestly, I don't think he's ever fully adjusted."

"Maybe it's best for a leader to maintain an appreciation for how precarious their position can be."

"I won't argue with that."

They enjoyed the view for a while longer while reminiscing about old times on Earth and their first year together in the TSS. For that short while, the galactic problems they were facing faded to the background and Raena was able to relax and enjoy the moment. Feeling unburdened was such a rarity these days that she was especially grateful for the opportunity.

Eventually, they were forced to return to the present reality, and they rose from the bench to begin an unhurried stroll back to the manor.

As they approached the back patio area where Raena liked to take her lunch and entertain close friends and family, she spotted Lexi reading on a tablet in one of the loungers. Seeing them, Lexi set down the device and got up to meet them halfway. She jogged the last couple of steps and wrapped an arm around Jason's waist.

"Hey you," she greeted. "Have a nice walk?"

He glanced at Raena and smiled. "It was perfect."

"Thank you for allowing me to borrow him," Raena said.

"No problem."

The couple focused on each other in a way Raena recognized from her interactions with Ryan, and she turned away to give them a moment for a reunion kiss. She took the opportunity to pull out her handheld and check for messages, taking a few steps away.

She lost herself in a doom-scroll of emails related to the

political debacle for thirty seconds before snapping herself out of it. *It can wait. There's nothing to do this second.*

When she returned the handheld to her pocket, she looked up to see a throng of onlookers chatting fervently amongst themselves, their handhelds raised and pointed toward Jason and Lexi in each other's arms behind her.

Raena glanced between the tourists and Jason still chatting closely with Lexi. "Uh oh." She backed up toward her brother, clearing her throat to get his attention. *Stars, we should have made it policy to take away devices during the tour.* She added a telepathic cue when he didn't take notice. *"We've got company."*

Jason finally glanced toward the people in the distance but seemed untroubled. "What?" he asked.

"So… you know how we opened up the estate to civilian tours?"

"Yes."

"Well, that's a group of tourists over there. And they just took a bunch of pictures." There was no way anyone nearby could have missed Jason's overt affection toward Lexi— definitely not something that could be passed off as an exchange between 'just friends'.

"Ah." He evaluated the onlookers. "Any bets on which of the Sensationals publications will have it on their front page first?"

Raena bit her lower lip. "You're not upset?"

"Why would I be? She's my partner."

"Yeah, you're right. May as well get it out in the open." She was impressed by his nonchalance, though that may be more from inexperience than a commendable attitude. "I hope it doesn't turn into too much of a headache for you."

"Eh, whatever. This actually might be the perfect distraction."

"How so?" she asked.

"You've been looking for something to defuse the media spotlight on you and Ryan, right? I'm a Sietinen who's historically gotten very little screen time. They can satisfy their High Dynasty news needs while focusing on someone who *really* doesn't care what they think."

Lexi scowled. "I'm not sure how I feel about that."

"I hate to say it, but there isn't a lot of choice with the media circus that comes along with being intimate with highborn," Raena said. "Sure, Jason is fairly sheltered within the TSS, but a Sietinen will make headlines no matter where they go. My advice, Lexi, is to let the universe know you're here to stay and he's officially off the market."

"How do we do that?" Lexi asked tentatively.

Jason evaluated the onlookers for a moment before taking Lexi's hand and pulling her to him. "I can think of one way."

— — —

Hanek turned away from his computer terminal, not sure what to make of the latest report. *Why is there an activity log from Earth?*

The small planet on the other side of the galaxy had gotten a fair bit of media attention over the past year due to its recent reunion with the rest of the Taran Empire, but the technologically limited world was unremarkable in every other way. At least, so Hanek had thought. If the Coalition was keeping tabs on it, there must be something else going on.

He copied the information to a tablet, per procedure, in preparation for his check-in meeting with Magdalena.

Hanek walked the short distance from the open administrative center where his workstation was located to the administrative wing where Magdalena had her private workspace. Beyond her duties within the Coalition, she was an executive used to having her every request met efficiently and to an exacting standard, which kept Hanek equally busy and stressed. In this line of work, failing to meet expectations didn't result in getting fired—at least not in a non-lethal sense of the term.

Magdalena was waiting in her office when he arrived. Her eyes narrowed at the sight of him. "What's wrong?"

"Nothing, ma'am, I don't think. Here's the field report for you." Hanek handed her the tablet. Data transfers over the network would be far more efficient, but the Coalition's management had decided on this communication procedure for whatever reason; it seemed archaic and impractical, but he was in no position to argue.

She activated the tablet with a brush of her hand and looked over the contents. Her brows raised with surprise.

"When did this come in?" she asked.

"I'm not sure," Hanek admitted. "I only checked the datastreams in advance of this scheduled meeting."

She looked like she wanted to chew him out but thought better of it. "Please add the feed to your handheld with a flag for Earth."

"Yes, ma'am," he acknowledged, growing more confused and intrigued.

Magdalena pulled out her handheld and sent a quick message. "Come with me."

Hanek followed her to the council meeting chamber. There hadn't been a meeting on the calendar, but he presumed that she had just sent a summons.

Sure enough, upon entering the room, Magdalena activated the holoconference system.

"The Tarans have discovered the device," she stated.

Felina's holographic avatar frowned. "That's not news."

"I mean, they have found a way to interface with it," Magdalena clarified.

Carjen's avatar leaned forward, now fully engaged. "How is that possible?"

Magdalena shook her head. "There are a few among them with the gift of sight. Either they got lucky or they're learning."

"This could give away far too much." Carjen's brows drew together. "How do we prevent further access?"

"At this point, that's not realistic," Magdalena replied.

"She's right," Felina said. "Even one interface means they now know about the device. The diversions failed."

The Coalition had organized local demonstrations on Earth, which Hanek had thought were simply an engineered inconvenience to distract the Taran authorities from the real issues. However, this renewed interest in Earth indicated that the protests may, in fact, have been designed to cause delays or serve as a deterrent because the Coalition was trying to keep something important on Earth hidden.

What else is going on? What does the device do? he wondered. Despite being an assistant to someone in the inner circle of the Coalition's leadership, he apparently didn't know very much about the larger plan.

"We must make a move soon," Carjen insisted. "Before they learn too much."

"We're still months away from effective action," Felina countered.

Magdalena steepled her fingers. "There are always ways to buy more time. We mustn't rush the process."

"There wouldn't be an issue if you'd held up your end of the deal," Felina spat. "The weapon is useless."

"The problem is that it works *too* well. We're working on a new deployment technique. I have every confidence that we'll strike the necessary balance to accomplish our goals."

Hanek suspected that was a reference to the incident on Quel a few months back. He'd only had an ancillary connection to that project, but he knew they'd suffered a significant setback when they'd lost containment of the new weapon. The TSS' untimely intrusion certainly hadn't helped matters.

"And the other project?" Felina asked.

"Proceeding as planned," Magdalena said. "The facility is operational and we're gathering the final conduits."

"Speaking of which, where do things stand with Tregaren?" Carjen asked.

"Still playing his part for the time being," Magdalena replied. "Our informants haven't heard anything within the Guard or TSS. It would seem they haven't caught his trail yet." She cast an accusatory glance in Hanek's direction.

Laying that trail was his job. He had tried to strike a balance between having the clues be obvious enough to be noticed without it looking like it was a blatant setup. Either he'd been *too* subtle or the authorities were too distracted by other pursuits to have caught the lead to the former Priesthood scientist.

"See to it that they do catch on," Magdalena stated.

Hanek nodded. "I'll throw out a few more breadcrumbs." He gave a little bow.

Tregaren's capture would be a suitable distraction from the Coalition's real work. The ancient man would never think of himself as disposable, but even his considerable power didn't compare to those behind the Coalition.

"Proceed carefully," Carjen cautioned. "The TSS has proved to be resourceful."

Magdalena inclined her head. "Which is why a sacrifice is necessary. Tregaren will make a suitable figurehead."

"Indeed. And eliminate a complication in the process." Carjen's avatar looked at something off-camera. "Is that all?"

"For now." Magdalena rose. "We're agreed—allow the TSS to continue the investigation on Earth?"

"We're not yet in a position to stop them," Felina said. "Let's not make it easy, though. Keep them busy."

"We can do that." Magdalena ended the call. When the holoprojector turned off, she placed her hands on the desk and leaned forward, letting out a long breath as her head hung down.

Hanek gave her a minute, standing quietly at the edge of the room. Questions churned in his mind about what he'd heard during the meeting. *What are they hiding?*

Eventually, Magdalena stood up and smoothed her hands down the front of her pencil dress. "Can I count on you to set the trail?"

"Yes, ma'am." Hanek bowed his head. He took a cautious step closer to her. "What does the device on Earth do?" he asked. It was a risky question with a high likelihood of getting shot down, or landing him in trouble, but curiosity got the better of him.

A humorless smile touched her lips. "It is either our salvation or the instrument of our imprisonment. Only time will tell which."

CHAPTER 9

JASON SET DOWN his handheld on the breakfast table with a flourish. "Well, they move quickly. I'll give them that."

The headline story on almost every media outlet was the mysterious lady spotted having an intimate moment with the allegedly single Sietinen heir. Jason was reminded of the entertainment-focused tabloids back on Earth, which lined the checkout aisles at grocery stores. Even in the move away from print media, those were holdouts and had maintained an almost cult-like following. The Taran variety were different but had the same result.

"It's not even a good picture! Figures this would be my debut." Lexi let out an exasperated sigh.

She was being a better sport about it than Jason had anticipated. For all her assertiveness in certain matters, she was somewhat shy and valued her privacy. He did, too, and the sudden media frenzy was without question an invasion. However, it was *so* over-the-top that it was surreal, which took the edge off.

"I didn't anticipate this trip starting a whole *thing*," he said.

"Thank you for taking it in stride."

She waved her hand dismissively. "It's fine. Whatever. I'm just looking at it as a platform to spread the word about our new training initiative."

"Now that's a good spin." He smiled. "I think you were born for the spotlight."

"Nah, just a reformed shadow-puppet bent on revenge against would-be masters."

He blinked at her, not sure how to respond. "You never cease to surprise and amaze me. I may also be slightly terrified of you."

"Good. That'll keep you in line." She wagged her finger at him.

That's a joke... right? He laughed it off, not entirely sure either way. "I have every intention of staying on your good side."

"Good plan." She flashed a smile before continuing her breakfast.

They sat in silence for a while, enjoying the view of the garden while Raena and Ryan tended to some administrative business. Jason had hoped that they'd be able to take more time off, but that simply wasn't realistic given their positions. Some time together was better than none.

"Can you take me down to that viewpoint you mentioned?" Lexi asked suddenly. "I'd like to enjoy the ocean while I can."

"I'll do you one better. How about we head to the southern coast where we can get right down to the water?"

Her face lit up. "Really? I didn't know that was an option."

"Seawater is kinda gross, but you should at least put your feet in the ocean once."

"I didn't realize there was a way down anywhere. The cliffs

up on this side are massive."

"We'll need to fight the tourists—metaphorically, to be clear—but perhaps that will give us a photo op to replace that one you don't like."

"Oh, good idea! I should wear that blue-green sundress. It has a sexy-chic vibe, right?"

He chuckled. "Who *are* you?"

"According to the Aeris Star—which is the dumbest name for a publication, since Aeris is a *moon*—I am the, and I quote, 'blue-eyed seductress who may have taken the Empire's most eligible bachelor off the market'."

He rubbed his temple. "Please, stop reading those."

"Oh, you don't want to hear the Top Ten they'd picked out for who they *thought* you were going to end up with?"

"I'm begging you, no."

"I dunno, number four is kinda cute."

"Not as adorable as you—when you *aren't* talking about the Sensationals."

She set down her handheld. "Okay, you win. Take me to the beach and I won't tell you the finer points of 'dos and don'ts for dating highborn'."

He took a long drink of juice to mask his smirk. "Didn't take long for you to get comfortable here."

"Uh, yeah! I didn't realize how nice it would be to have people taking care of *me* for once. And, the Regional Tribute—again, awful name, my stars—said that I have a, quote, 'refreshing, natural look', which I'm fairly sure is a compliment but may actually be an insult about looking frumpy."

Jason stood up and extended his hand. "Beach. Now."

"Thank you, my lord. That's all I was waiting for." She smiled and slipped her handheld into her pocket.

Stars, two days here and I've unleashed a monster. He

followed her back to their room so they could change into more beach-appropriate attire.

Once dressed, Jason led Lexi to the parking area for the small, wheeled vehicles used for getting around the island. Though effectively golf carts in Jason's mind, the miniature cars looked considerably more sophisticated and were more comfortable than the carts he'd ridden in while vacationing back on Earth. He selected one of the two-seaters, which was more like a low-walled platform with two lounge chairs separated by a table across from a built-in minibar.

Lexi looked it over, eyebrows raised, and nodded with approval. "Traveling in style, I like it."

"I figured that was on-point for your new fancy-pants personal brand."

"It'll do." She winked and took her seat in the buggy.

Jason sat down next to her and accessed the direction controls, selecting the most secluded southern pier as the destination. The buggy started up with barely a sound and began gliding down the path. A nearly invisible shield rose up in the front to break the wind as it picked up speed.

"You know I'm just joking when I say that stuff, right?" Lexi said.

"Yes. And I'm glad you're having a good time." He offered his hand to her over the armrests.

She took it. "I am."

He entwined his fingers in hers, enjoying the view as the buggy sped along, as smoothly as if it was floating. The path wound down the hill, hugging the eastern coastline as the land sloped downward toward the sea to the south. To the east, the sun rose over the picturesque waves, casting a soft golden glow. Sweet, floral aromas wafted over from the lush vegetation in the island's central ravine, which was closer to a nature preserve than a garden. Jason was told that it had been cultivated by the Priesthood hundreds of years ago so there was a degree of organization to its layout and contents, but it had gone wild with the passage of time and neglect in the later years.

After twenty minutes, structures began to appear with increasing frequency amidst the foliage, eventually giving way to defined neighborhoods. Most buildings appeared to be newer construction, mostly poured concrete colored and textured to look like stone. Tiled roofs and potting containers with brightly colored flowers softened the appearance and brought a sense of vibrant warmth to the community.

The buggy slowed as it entered the populated area, though only a handful of people were visible. Most didn't even bother to look up at the sound of the approaching vehicle, only stepping out of its way.

"Is this where the workers live?" Lexi asked.

"Some of them," Jason replied. "Others live at the estate. The visitors who come for the tours stay down in this village."

"It's kind of a long commute for the workers."

"There are faster ways. We're just taking the scenic route."

"It is, at that." Lexi sucked in a breath with delight as the buggy cleared the buildings, coming up over a rise to an unobstructed view of the southern shoreline. "Wow!"

Aqua-hued waves lapped along the white-sand beaches. Several cottages were perched on stilts over the water. The buildings at the waterfront were more architecturally detailed than those higher up on the hill, and almost all of them had balconies or patios to take advantage of the view.

The buggy took the roadway down toward the water's edge, where there was a pier with a little bar serving food and drinks for the tourists and off-shift workers.

Once the vehicle parked, Jason hopped out and offered his hand to Lexi.

"What a gentleman," she said with a smile.

He helped her down. "Only for you, my love."

She gave him a quizzical look. "That's sweet, but—"

"Don't react, but we're being watched," he said in her mind.

She calmly looked around, spotting the tourists he'd noticed. *"Take Two on the photo op?"*

"I'm game if you are."

Lexi spun around and gave him a sultry kiss, pivoting to give the onlookers' cameras a prime view. She kept her movements fluid and poised as though a trained model on a photoshoot.

Jason wasn't sure where those skills had come from, but he was impressed. *"You're full of surprises."*

"What can I say? You inspire me." She took his hand and led him in the direction of the bar.

"A little early for drinking, isn't it?"

"That thought says more about you than me. I was eyeing a smoothie."

He smiled. *"I wasn't going to judge. We're on vacation, after all."*

They walked up to the bar, which was tended by one worker who was chatting with a casually dressed man seated in one of the tall chairs.

The casual man took notice of their arrival first, looking over Jason and then disapprovingly at Lexi. Upon closer inspection, Jason realized that the casual attire was actually sewn from fine materials; the man was no doubt wealthy, possibly Lower Dynasty here for a business meeting.

One glance and the bar worker's demeanor became more formal. He turned from the other patron and focused on Jason.

"What can I get for you, my lord?"

Jason's skin crawled at the use of the formal title. "What's your best smoothie?"

"Depends on individual taste, of course, but the pomo-malga consistently gets the most compliments."

Jason glanced at Lexi, and she nodded her approval. "Two of those, please."

"Coming right up." The worker gave a friendly nod and then got to work.

The casual man was doing his best to appear disinterested, but Jason's attuned senses picked up his silent judgment.

While Jason paid for the drinks using a biometric interface on the bar, Lexi wandered a few steps away to peer out at the sea. "That looks like a good spot out there." She motioned toward a wooden dock a hundred meters away.

"Perfect," Jason agreed. "Go on ahead."

She glanced between Jason and the casual man. *"Are you sure?"*

"I'll meet you there in a few minutes."

She nodded and flashed a thankful smile at the bartender, who was busy making the drinks.

As soon as Lexi had departed, Jason turned his attention to the casual man. "Is there something you'd like to say?"

The man's lips curled into a smug smirk. "Tough to miss this morning's front-page news when it shows up in the flesh."

"You clearly have thoughts on the matter."

He shrugged. "Only that I'd thought the Sietinen line was finally getting back on track, but apparently you take after your father."

Jason squashed a wave of heat rising from his core. He'd faced a number of bigoted attitudes over the years aimed at his mother's part-human heritage. In times past, he may have decked the guy on the spot, but his conditioning allowed him to keep a level head.

"You really shouldn't judge people you don't know," Jason said. "Maybe one day you'll be lucky enough to find the kind of love that lets you see life differently."

Behind the counter, the bartender placed a fruit garnish on each of the smoothies and handed them up.

The casual man had clearly been expecting a negative reaction from Jason, because he only sat in stunned silence while Jason grabbed the purple blended drinks.

"Enjoy your day." Not waiting for a response, Jason went to meet Lexi over at the spot she had identified. He let out a calming breath and breathed in the pure air, trying to let go of his annoyance.

Lexi was waiting for him partway out the dock, wide steps led down to the water.

"What was that about?" she asked, no doubt having seen the confrontation from her vantage on the dock.

"Nothing to worry about." He handed her one of the drinks.

She took it. "I guess there are assholes everywhere."

"A fact of life." Jason took a sip of the sweet drink, determined to not let the encounter sour his mood.

Lexi drank a third of her smoothie and then set down the glass on the steps. "All right, I've gotta do it." She slipped off her sandals.

Jason sat down on the steps. "Go for it."

With a gleeful grin, Lexi, barefoot, descended the stairs into the water up to mid-shin. "Bomax, it's cold!"

"It's all open ocean around here. Archipelagos with shallower water are much warmer."

"That sounds divine." She stood on one foot and splashed

the other in the water. "This isn't bad, though."

Jason took in the surroundings, similar to the Caribbean islands where he'd taken a trip with his family as a young teenager. The gentle lapping of the water against the dock and soft calls of birds in the distance reminded him of those simpler times.

Lexi sat down on the step below him. She got a faraway look in her eyes, her arms wrapped around one knee while the toes on her other foot twirled in the water.

"What's on your mind?" Jason asked after they'd sat quietly for several minutes sipping their drinks.

"Just thinking about our time here."

"I'm glad we came."

"Me too. The sights and food have been great, but I'm also happy I got to meet Raena and Ryan. I never really had any kind of role models growing up. Especially with romantic relationships. It's been nice being around a happy couple who can show what's possible."

"Yeah, Raena and Ryan are great together. I spent a long time being envious of their relationship." He smiled down at her. "Then I met you, and I realized I could have it for myself."

"Well, you don't have a castle."

He laughed. "As my sister is quick to point out. Personally, I think they're overrated."

"All the upkeep! And the expectation to throw epic parties. It's all a bit much, isn't it?"

"My thoughts exactly."

They sat and chatted for another half-hour until Jason's handheld pinged. He checked it, seeing a message from Raena. "Hey, sorry to cut this short, but we should get back. Raena said she'll be wrapping up her meetings soon."

"Okay." Lexi stood up, brushing off her feet before sliding

her sandals back on. "Thank you for this. It was perfect."

"One day, we'll go to Alushia. If you want a prime beach experience, that is *the* place to go."

She beamed. "I can't wait."

— — —

Lexi had just finished rinsing off her feet and changing back into more sensible clothes when she got a text message from Raena asking to meet with her.

"Do you know anything about this?" she asked Jason, who'd been lounging on the bed while she dressed.

"About what?"

"Raena wants to meet."

"Ah, right." He sat upright. "If it's what I think, hear her out."

Lexi raised an eyebrow quizzically, willing him to give her more to go on than that.

"I love you exactly as you are, and I support whatever you decide."

"Stars, Jason! What's going on?" She wasn't sure whether to be nervous or excited.

"It's nothing bad. I don't think it should come from me. Just talk to her."

Lexi wanted to protest further, but she recognized that he wasn't going to offer additional insights. The best way to find out was simply to meet with Raena. "Okay."

Jason got up from the bed and placed his hands lightly on her upper arms. "You're safe now, and there's no longer any reason to hide. I promise you that."

What the...? The serious tone caught her off-guard. She gave him a quick kiss. "Thanks? I'll see you in a bit."

Confused yet intrigued, she headed toward the meeting place Raena had indicated—fortunately, one of the few places in the massive estate she felt confident navigating to on her own.

Raena was waiting in the small sitting area near the dining hall—a reading or study nook, of sorts, with a pair of plush chairs, a couch, and low tables. Some light snacks and a tea set were arranged on the largest table within easy reach of the chair where Raena was seated. She motioned to the other chair. "Make yourself comfortable."

Lexi sat down. "What did you want to talk about?"

"Tea?" Raena offered, already leaning forward to pour some into a cup for Lexi.

"Sure." She hadn't consumed much tea in her lifetime since it was extraordinarily expensive most places, but she'd started to acquire a taste for the fruity varieties with breakfast.

Raena handed her a cup and saucer. "While you're here on Tararia, I wanted to extend an offer."

"For what?"

"I did some research, and I found a specialist who can restore the bioluminescence in your eyes—if you're interested. No pressure."

Wait, that's what this is about?

Lexi gazed into Raena's glowing teal eyes, so similar to Jason's. She'd dreamed for years of being able to display her abilities in that way, and now there was a genuine opportunity to make that a reality. Yet, she found herself hesitating to accept the generous offer. Perhaps it was because she had lived for so long in hiding and it was only recently that she'd been open with her Gifts. This change would mean making that display public and permanent.

"I didn't know that procedure was possible," she replied.

"Almost any kind of physical alteration is if you can find the right specialist. Ocular modifications are actually quite common. The question is, is that something you'd want?"

Lexi knew she had to let go of her past. It had been dragging her down for too long, and this could be a way to help her move on. "Yes, thank you. That would be great."

Raena smiled. "All right, I'll set an appointment for later this morning."

I guess I won't have time to change my mind! She felt confident in the decision, but it still felt rushed. "They can fit me in on such short notice?"

"I had them hold an opening just in case—but, truthfully, when you have a name like mine, there's never a wait."

I have no doubt about that. Lexi nodded. "Thanks. I wasn't expecting this."

"Jason mentioned that he'd brought it up to you before but you weren't sure then. I know there must be a lot of other feelings wrapped up in it."

Being used, betrayed, hunted. Lexi shook her head. "I'm ready to leave that chapter of my life behind now. I appreciate you helping me get a fresh start."

Raena reached over and gave Lexi's hand a light squeeze. "I'm glad I can do for you what I wish I could do for so many others."

"I'll try to pay it forward."

They finished their tea, and then Lexi sent a text message to Jason. >>I'm going to do it. Come meet me out back and we'll take a shuttle over.<<

>>On my way,<< he texted back right away.

Lexi let out a determined breath as she stood. "I'll see you afterward, I guess."

Raena smiled. "I look forward to meeting the new you—or

is it 'old', since it's restorative?"

"The real me," Lexi said.

Raena suddenly pulled her into a hug. "You're amazing." She let her go. "Sorry, just wanted to say that."

"Well, the feeling is mutual. I'll see you in a bit."

"See you soon."

Lexi headed out. She spotted Jason coming down the stairs.

He turned, sensing her. "Hey."

She met up with him at the base of the stairs. "Generally, I'm not a fan of secret schemes, but you were right with this one."

He smiled. "I am getting to know you pretty well, hmm?"

"I admit, you have some skills. Don't let it go to your head, though."

"Never."

She took his hand. "I never would have guessed this is what I'd be doing today."

"You're sure?"

"Positive. The moment Raena offered, it felt right. The timing is a surprise, that's all."

"Sounds like the procedure is pretty quick and easy. The restoration is a lot simpler than…" He faded out.

"Yeah. The original surgery was pretty rough. I'm sure having it performed by a back-alley doctor didn't improve the experience."

"This guy's the best on Tararia, which makes him *the* best. You'll be in good hands."

"As long as you're there with me."

"I wouldn't be anywhere else."

They started walking toward the shuttle port.

"You know, I had a bit of an eye fiasco during my first trip to Tararia," Jason said.

"How so?"

"Raena and I were presented to our great-grandparents in this absurd reveal ceremony thing. They went to 'inspect' us like some sort of livestock, at which point they declared there was too much green in our eyes."

"What? Your eyes are beautiful!"

"Well, it's all subjective, I suppose. They wanted to alter them to be closer to the traditional Sietinen cobalt."

"I didn't realize that was a thing."

"Central Worlds nonsense. My grandfather was the last of the line to fit the mold."

Lexi shook her head. The selective traits reminded her a bit too much of Cytera. "Good riddance to that."

"My sentiments as well."

They reached the port and boarded a small transport shuttle—a stripped-down version of the vessels used for surface-to-space journeys. Lexi kept her gaze glued out the window on the westward trip to Vaentar in the First Region, the seat of the Vaenetri Dynasty and hub of communications-related technology for the Taran Empire.

The city was more spectacular than Lexi could have imagined, with towering buildings constructed of glass and gleaming metal paired with breathtaking natural beauty, courtesy of the confluence between three major rivers. The core of the city was positioned on the high ground, terraced around the hills and spanning the waterways. She'd once read that each of the regional capitals on Tararia were constructed near rivers but that this was the gem. Based on her initial impression, she couldn't disagree.

"You know, I've actually never been over here," Jason admitted.

"Isn't your great uncle head of Vaenetri?"

"Yes, but I've only met him a handful of times, all of which were at the Sietinen estate over in the Third Region."

"I'd love to see that, too."

"Eventually. My grandparents are wonderful, but they can be kind of intense. I didn't want to throw too much at you at once."

"Thanks." Truthfully, she was eager to meet two of the most famous leaders in the Taran Empire and see what they were really like.

Lexi had noticed a difference in how Jason and Raena regarded their grandparents. Raena seemed extremely close to them while Jason had an emotional distance that reminded her more of a business relationship. Since he hadn't met them in person until he was a teenager, she suspected there hadn't been time for a bond to develop, whereas Raena had lived with them for a number of years after she left the TSS.

The shuttle set down on top of one of the medium-height buildings toward the southern end of the city.

Stepping out from the shuttle onto the open roof, she was struck by a sudden gust of wind, prompting her to look toward the edge of the building. Though far from the tallest tower in the area, it was still a dizzying height above the horizon. She was grateful to be toward the center of the structure because she suspected her knees would go weak if she got any closer to the edge.

A man jogged toward them, emerging from an enclosed area twenty meters away. "Lexi Karis?" he asked as he got close.

"Yes," she confirmed.

"I'm here to escort you to Doctor Luwaen," the man stated. "My name is Tolan."

"Pleased to meet you. Jason here will be accompanying me."

Recognition filled Tolan's eyes. "Yes, my lord, right this way."

"I don't think I'll ever get used to this 'my lord' business," Lexi said telepathically to Jason.

"You and me both."

Tolan led them inside the enclosure, which appeared to be a reception area for visitors arriving from the air. The lobby was tidy and formal with the kind of décor that screamed 'professional' with no forms or colors that might be offensive to anyone. The workers were equally rigid, dressed in shades of gray and beige with plain, angular styles.

They entered an elevator at the back of the lobby, which quickly descended to Level 31. The doors slid open silently, revealing a minimalistic medical office reception area with white walls and floor contrasting gray and black furnishings. A solitary potted tree at the center of the room offered a pop of color.

A receptionist at a counter to the left of the room smiled at them as they stepped out of the elevator. "Welcome, Miss Karis. We've been expecting you."

"Uh, thanks." She wasn't sure what to say. "Do you need my…?"

"The doctor will take your medical history in the back. We have everything else for now. We'll call you back in a moment."

"Thank you."

"Wishing you the best outcome." Tolan bowed and then returned to the elevator.

Lexi exchanged a bemused look with Jason. *"This is weird."*

"Again, this is why I stick to the TSS."

Before they had a chance to sit down, a door at the back of the room opened and a woman dressed in a white uniform stepped out. "Miss Karis?"

Lexi walked over to her with Jason a step behind. "Is it okay if he comes back with me?" she asked the woman.

"We prefer to have just our patients in the back because of the delicacy of the procedures, but—"

Lexi shook her head. "No, it's okay. I can go on my own." She turned to Jason. "I'll see you soon."

"I'll be waiting." He gave her a kiss.

With a wave of nerves, she followed the woman through the doorway into the back.

"I'm Elsa," she greeted. "I'll be the nurse assisting Doctor Luwaen."

"Do you do many of these procedures?" Lexi asked.

"This exact alteration is not often requested. However, it is the same technology we use for many other cosmetic changes, so you have absolutely nothing to worry about."

While not the most reassuring answer, Lexi couldn't argue the fact that it was an unusual procedure and it made sense that they didn't perform it often. When she had originally had her irises altered, that too had been novel. Even so, changing eye color was a common enough request, so the technical foundation was sound.

Elsa led Lexi down a short corridor lined with doors before motioning her through into Room 4. A platform that was equal parts chair and bed stood in the center of the room, surrounded by equipment that Lexi couldn't begin to identify.

"Please have a seat," Elsa requested.

Lexi tried to set her nerves aside as she settled into the operating chair. It wasn't the surgery itself that concerned her, but rather anxiety about the transition it meant in her life. Though she'd come to terms with taking that step and looked forward to it, being on the precipice of the change made her reflect on everything leading up to that moment. All the fear and loneliness came flooding back, but it was also accompanied by the fulfillment of companionship and the acceptance she now enjoyed. The small cosmetic change would be the ultimate reflection of that transformation she had experienced within.

Elsa stepped off to the side of the room, hands clasped in front of her, as the door opened and a bearded man in his fifties walked in.

He wore a similar white uniform to Elsa's and had a slightly ageless look for someone who'd undergone procedures of his own. Upon further reflection, Lexi realized she may have underestimated his age by a couple of decades.

"Hello, I'm Doctor Luwaen," he greeted.

"Lexi," she replied. "Nice to meet you."

He stepped forward, looking her over from a distance with an impassive gaze of professional detachment. "I understand that you'd like the glow restored to your eyes?"

Lexi nodded. "If that's possible."

"It certainly is. It's barbaric what happened to some people before the Gifted were more widely accepted. I'm honored to be able to give you back what was lost."

"How does this work?"

"We remove the scar tissue and stimulate the growth of the luminescing strands that should be there," he replied. "Beyond that, it's rather technical."

"That's a good enough answer for me."

He asked her a series of questions about her medical history—nothing notable to report—and then did a body scan to confirm that there wasn't anything that might impact her receptiveness to the procedure. Everything checked out.

"All right, this will be quick," Doctor Luwaen said. "The equipment can make adjustments, but try to limit your movements."

He brought up two panels from the chair's headrest and placed them against her temples to keep her head stationary. A machine with a long arm and pointed tip then swung over from behind her and hovered in front of her face, a red light illuminated just above the pointed tip.

"Focus on the light," the doctor instructed.

Lexi did as she was told.

The machine whirred to life, making minute adjustments and sending occasionally flashing bursts before adjusting again. Lexi held as still as she could, staring at the light, for what felt like several minutes.

"Okay, the damaged tissue has been removed. Now to stimulate the regrowth." He brought up a syringe. "I'm sorry, but this part is going to be uncomfortable. You'll feel a pinch in each eye. It'll be quick."

"Do what you need to do," Lexi said.

She cleared her mind and focused on her breathing. She'd been through enough uncomfortable experiences that she could withstand a little pain. The outcome would be worth it.

As promised, Lexi felt a pinch in each of her eyes as he inserted the syringe. She resisted the urge to flinch. It didn't hurt as much as she'd braced herself to endure, but it was far from pleasant.

"Close your eyes now," Doctor Luwaen instructed.

Lexi felt a cooling mask press against her eyelids.

"I've just given you a concentrated nanite injection to stimulate the regrowth of the bioluminescent tissue within your irises," he explained. "Natural regrowth can take months or years, so this is the best way to get fast results."

"How long will it take?"

"You'll see preliminary results in half an hour. It should

have full effect by the time you get up tomorrow morning."

"Wow."

He patted her shoulder. "You did great. I'll leave you to recover. Please let Elsa know if you experience any discomfort."

"Thank you, doctor."

"My pleasure." There were soft footfalls as he stepped away, followed by the hiss and click of the door.

Lexi lay in the chair in darkness, quietly reflecting about her visit to Tararia and what these changes meant for her future. Ultimately, she was excited for what was ahead.

"All right, Lexi, let's have a look," Elsa said, breaking the silence. Lexi had almost forgotten that she was in there.

"I'm ready."

The mask lifted from Lexi's eyelids.

"You may open your eyes now," Elsa instructed.

Lexi slowly cracked open her lids. After a brief moment of adjustment to the light, her vision was normal. There was a slight ache in her eyes.

Elsa bent over her. "How do you feel?"

"Like I spent too long reading without a break."

"That's a normal sensation while the eyes regenerate. It should be gone by tomorrow." She smiled. "Do you want to see the results?"

"Yes!" Lexi sat up as Elsa handed her a mirror. She took it, giving herself a moment before taking a look.

Softly glowing pale-blue irises stared back at her from the mirror. *These are my eyes. My* real *eyes!*

Her heart swelled. She hadn't thought she'd ever get to see herself that way again. It was more beautiful than she could have imagined.

"Thank you." The words were barely more than a whisper

but filled with raw emotion.

Elsa smiled back. "I'm glad we could help."

Lexi wiped at the happy tears and then returned to the waiting room.

Jason was reading on his handheld when she arrived, and he looked up when he sensed her presence. A joyful smile spread across his face, matching her own. "You look amazing."

"I feel different." She walked over to him.

He wrapped his arms around her. "You get to be yourself now."

"Thank you for supporting me on that journey."

"And I'll be there for you no matter what else comes."

She hugged him tightly. "Same here. This new me is all yours."

CHAPTER 10

THE FINAL NIGHT on Tararia was a happy blur for Jason, punctuated by a pleasant evening with his sister, Ryan, and Lexi, followed by an early bedtime. He could have used several more days to unwind and relax, but he and Lexi were both needed back at TSS Headquarters.

They took a shuttle at dawn up to the space station, where they boarded a transport ship home. Jason used the travel time to get caught up on his neglected messages, to his relief not seeing anything that would derail the rest of his week.

Upon reaching Headquarters, Lexi ran off to her office to deal with last-minute administrative items related to the training initiative launch while Jason went to check in with his father.

Wil beckoned him inside when he showed up to his office. "Welcome home."

"Thanks, it was a good trip. Raena and Ryan send their love."

"I wish I could have been there."

"We missed you and Mom." Jason took a seat. "How did

things go on Earth?"

"Oh, that's quite a story." He gave Jason a recap about his experience interfacing with the device and what he'd learned.

"Bomax! That's... wow." Jason leaned back in his chair. "So, we still don't know what it does, but it was built by the Gatekeepers."

"And another race, which may or may not be the Erebus."

Jason shook his head. "I don't think it was them."

"Then we have someone else to worry about."

"I wasn't there to hear it firsthand, obviously, so it could just be how you were telling it, but I get the impression that this 'other race' may be one of the Gatekeeper hybrids."

"What makes you think that?" his father asked.

"You said it told you that these Morla'ki were the *original* Gatekeepers."

"Hmm." Wil rapped his fingers on the desktop. "Suggesting that who we call the 'Gatekeepers' might be different."

"And we do know they're hybrids—not Taran, and not Gatekeeper, either. I could see how the device might call them something else."

"But why would that information be restricted?"

"We're not supposed to know some of them never left the Taran planets."

His father nodded. "True. And it also makes for an interesting study of history many haven't wanted us to know."

Jason gave him a quizzical look, not catching his meaning.

"The Priesthood erased Taran historical records, and I get the impression that the Gatekeeper hybrids were equally vested in maintaining secrecy. However, if the Gatekeeper hybrids indeed trace back a hundred thousand years to when this device was constructed on Earth, then that means *they* might have a record of what happened to Tarans in the intervening years—or even before that."

"Wouldn't that be interesting to know?"

Wil shook his head slowly, getting a distant look in his eyes. "I've longed for those answers for many years. We are doomed to repeat mistakes when we forget or ignore history, and this is a huge gap in our inherited knowledge."

"I, for one, am not going to get my hopes up just yet. This could be totally off-base speculation."

"Regardless, it's an interesting hypothesis to have in the mix," his father replied. "For the time being, though, it doesn't matter. I've initiated a new analysis of the device in light of what I learned through the Q&A, with the hope we can determine the properties of the energy field—or bridge, as the AI called it. What the thing *does* is more important than who made it."

Unless it was made by an enemy to destroy our ancestors. His father knew that was a possibility, so Jason didn't voice the thought. He did see other potential applications. "It could be a way to talk with the Erebus using a method where they'd be more willing to listen."

"Or they might take the use of technology the Gatekeepers helped develop as an act of aggression."

Jason shrugged. "Either way, it would get their attention."

"Not all attention is good, contrary to what some might say."

"I'm not sure what to suggest."

Wil shook his head. "I'm not in the market for advice at the moment, so that's okay. I want to sit on it for a while."

"Good plan."

"What about you? I couldn't help but notice the front-page article Michael slid across my desk featuring you and Lexi."

Jason waved it off. "Freaking tourists. Something like this was bound to happen with the way Raena opened up the estate."

"Are you two doing okay with the publicity?"

"Yeah, it's fine. Lexi thinks it's hilarious, and I've been ignoring it as best I can."

"A smart approach. These kinds of public obsessions are fleeting."

"Did you go through this with Mom?"

"Not so much in the press but within the TSS. We managed to keep our relationship a secret for years, so it was a shock when people realized what had been right in front of them the whole time."

"I expect to get a little ribbing around here, but whatever."

"You're in a much more favorable position than I was at the time. There were some who…" He sighed. "I guess you could say that they believed I should focus purely on the war and having a girlfriend would be nothing other than an unnecessary distraction."

"Shows how little they knew."

"Indeed. Outside judgment can test a relationship, and I'm happy to hear you and Lexi are coming through it just fine."

"Yeah, we're solid. Tararia was good for us."

"I'm very glad to hear it."

Jason hesitated. With all the news and his discussion with Raena, he'd been thinking about their future together and the best course forward. *This might be as good of an opening as I'm going to get.* He decided to go for it. "Do you have any thoughts on Lexi and I getting married?"

Wil chuckled. "Yes, naturally."

Jason realized the poor phrasing of his question. "I mean, do you have any concerns or objections?"

"No, I think it would be good. Do you have reservations?"

"Not beyond wondering if it's a bit fast to be thinking about it," Jason admitted. Truthfully, he'd been considering Lexi his future wife since the day they met, but he'd never say that out loud.

Wil softened. "It might be fast for a normal couple. Really, though, you already made that commitment to each other when you bonded."

"That's true."

"Did anything in particular prompt this discussion?"

"With all this fuss in the Sensationals, Raena suggested that announcing our engagement might be a good distraction from the other negative press about Sietinen and Dainetris."

Wil nodded. "I'd never advise using a romantic relationship as political leverage, but I do understand where she's coming from."

"More than anything, I want Lexi to feel secure. She knows I love her, but I think part of her is still fearful that I'll get bored and move on."

"Yeah, I went through that with your mom early on, too. I wouldn't suggest using a proposal as a crutch to get past those insecurities; that requires time and patience."

"So, we should wait?"

"Only you can answer that. What I can tell you, though, is that once you have that person you want to spend the rest of your life with, there's no sense delaying anything that will make you happier together."

Jason nodded. "All right, I'll think on it some more and talk to her."

"Open communication is always a good move." Wil paused. "I'm afraid the starstone allotment this generation has been exhausted."

Jason shrugged. "That's fine. As pretty as the stones are, I never much saw the point in having rings you only pull out for fancy formal events." Starstones were an exclusive gemstone so rare that only select nobles had access to them in small quantities. Sietinen and the other High Dynasties were allotted enough gem material to produce one set of wedding rings per generation, and that had naturally gone to Raena and Ryan.

"Your mom is so attached to the rings we got on Earth now, I'm sure she'd be happy to pass our set on to you, if you'd like."

Jason considered the generous offer. "No, thank you, but those are yours. I'd rather we have something of our own that we can wear all the time, once we take that step."

"A wise move." Wil glanced at his desktop as an alert popped up.

A moment later, Jason's handheld vibrated. He pulled it out, finding that it was a message from Andy sent to both Jason and Wil alerting them to a development in the investigation involving the band and their potential involvement in the disappearances of Gifted women.

Wil brought it up on the holoprojector above his desk, and they read through the incident report together.

"Stars!" Jason exclaimed. "I didn't see that coming."

His father's brows were drawn together with worry. "I'm concerned that I didn't either."

The report indicated that Kali, the Junior Agent assigned to the case, had used herself as bait to draw in the suspect. In the course of the abduction, the suspect was identified to be a rogue member of the Priesthood—apparently a defector from before the fall of the organization. Since he had been out of the Priesthood for decades, it explained why he hadn't been captured in the final stand when the organization's members had linked in a telepathic network. He'd, apparently, continued genetic experimentations on his own, and the abducted women were his test subjects.

Jason's stomach turned over at the thought. While he would have liked to see the perpetrator imprisoned for the rest of his life, the former Priest—Tregaren— had apparently been killed during the confrontation with Kali. As a prior victim of the Priesthood herself, there was a satisfying sense of justice in that outcome. Nonetheless, it raised additional questions about how the ex-Priest had been able to find the resources to engage in further genetic research and who else was still involved.

"Okay, so this Tregaren guy was killed. Was he working with anyone?" Jason asked.

"He had to be. As egotistical as the Priests are, their designs are beyond the scope of an individual."

"Him being dead makes for a difficult interrogation."

Wil slumped in his chair. "I'm not pleased about that."

The phrasing was a downplay from his expression. Knowing his father well, Jason could tell that he was pissed. *I guess this is what happens when we send a Junior Agent to do senior-level work.* Andy, however, was as seasoned as they came, so maybe it was just a difficult situation that had gone sideways. "Where do we go from here?" Jason asked.

"I'll leave that up to you as the head of the Coalition task force."

Lucky me. Jason nodded. "I'll have the team scour Tregaren's ship and see what else we can learn."

"This wasn't the head of the snake," Wil said. "We need proof about who he was working with."

"Do you think it's connected to Quel and the other illegal research?"

"Likely, which means this is even wider-spread than we feared." He closed out of the report. "This organization is more than talk, Jason. They're bent on fracturing the Empire. They're coming at it from enough angles, we might not be able to keep up."

His chest tightened. "What does that mean for us?"

"Long, stressful days of being on edge. It was smart to grab a mini-vacation when you did."

Jason smiled in spite of the tension. "Seize opportunities, right?"

Wil nodded. "And find happy moments amidst the dark."

"I intend to." Jason rose from his seat. "Sounds like I have work to do. I'll keep you posted."

"Thank you, Jason. I'm grateful to have you working on this."

He smiled. "I may as well put all of your training to good use."

After leaving the High Commander's office, Jason veered over to the side hallway where Lexi's workspace was located. She was inside, typing out a message on her desktop when he arrived.

"One sec," she said without looking up, continuing her typing.

Jason waited in the doorway for her to finish.

"Okay…" She leaned back from her desk. "Sorry, wanted to finish that thought before I lost it."

"I've been there," he said, coming the rest of the way inside. "What's up?"

"There was a significant development while we were in transit. That undercover mission to investigate the band finally got results."

Lexi tensed with anticipation. "Oh, yeah?"

"Turns out the guy behind the abductions was former Priesthood—left decades ago for whatever reason."

Her face flushed. "That should make for quite the interrogation."

"He was killed in the encounter."

Lexi's brows knitted. "That's disappointing."

"I hate to say it, but I'm used to it by now. The Coalition has a knack for staying a step ahead." Either this incident was a rare slip-up on their part or Tregaren had outlived his usefulness and had been handed to them. Or, maybe the same hubris that had been the Priesthood's undoing had caught up with him, as well.

"You'll catch them," Lexi said. "This is still a victory."

"It is. While we're not moving as quickly as I'd hoped, you're right—we *are* making progress."

She glanced at the unfinished work on her desktop. "Thanks for keeping me in the loop. I should really get back to this, though."

"Yes, and I need to dive into this with my team. I'll see you at home tonight."

"Good luck. You've got this!"

Feeling energized and determined, Jason headed to the Coalition task force office. They had a new clue, and he intended to see where it led.

—   —   —

Wil sat quietly at his desk collecting his thoughts after Jason left. He'd been prepared for the investigation into the Coalition to unveil deep evils within the Taran Empire, but the lingering presence of the Priesthood was among his worst fears. *I didn't want to believe it was possible any of them survived.*

In the final standoff with the Priesthood, the organization's members had linked minds across space to form a single, powerful network and merge their powers. Wil—along with

Jason and Raena—had fought back, ultimately severing the connection and breaking the minds of those who'd been linked. Some of the Priests and their Acolytes had been driven mad, while others were doomed to live out their remaining days in a persistent vegetative state. Everyone who'd been apprehended had been locked up, regardless, at various prison facilities across the Empire.

That was supposed to have been the end of it. While they couldn't be certain that they'd captured *everyone*, the TSS and Taran leaders had been operating under the assumption that any stragglers would see the futility of their former objectives and quietly retreat into the shadows.

What hadn't occurred to Wil was the possibility that conflict within the Priesthood could have led to splinter groups forming before the organization's fall. Those independent operators may have ignored the call to join the telepathic network and could have remained unscathed.

A soft knock sounded at the entrance to Wil's office, and he looked up to see Saera waiting in the doorway.

"I got the news. Do you want to talk?" she asked.

He nodded, and she stepped inside and closed the door.

"How many others could be out there?" he asked, not expecting an answer. "I'd hoped so badly all of this would be behind us forever."

"Or he may have been a one-off," Saera countered. "It's too early to tell."

He got up and headed over to the couch. She joined him.

"I've spent my entire career reading people and behavior patterns, trying to figure out what our adversaries will do next and how to stop them. With this, I can't see the moves."

She took his hand. "One step at a time. We'll get there."

"How many people will be hurt before we figure it out?"

"Don't think about that."

He shook his head. "It's part of the job. I won't have any more senseless sacrifices on my watch."

"Don't punish yourself for the things you can't control."

"I have the power to do so much more than I have."

"What else could you do now, Wil?"

"Storm into the Monsari estate and read Celine's innermost thoughts—pull out every secret she has and settle this once and for all."

Saera dropped her eyes. "You can't."

"Not without starting a major galactic incident, but I *could*. We have all this power and it's only an appreciation of the law that prevents us from taking action. What I suspect is playing out in the shadows right now is what happens when respect for the law goes out the window. Is it possible to beat someone who won't play by the rules, or do you need to start thinking like they do?"

"I don't know."

"I need to decide, while there's still a chance to stay ahead of this."

"There might be another option," Saera said slowly.

"And what's that?

"The band manager who Kali has been working with— Mika. He's Tregaren's son," Saera revealed.

"A clone?"

"No, a biological son. He raised him."

That could change everything. If someone had spent their whole life with Tregaren, that was the next best thing to talking with the man himself. "Why is this only being brought up now? It wasn't in the preliminary report."

"I heard it directly from Andy moments before coming here. It's a sensitive detail for obvious reasons."

Wil considered the information. "We need to bring Mika in. Now."

— — —

Raena's stomach turned over. The TSS report to the Taran High Council was shockingly cold and factual for its contents. *A rogue former Priest killed in a standoff with a Junior Agent who was herself a victim of the Priesthood. Makes you wonder what really happened.*

She set down the tablet on Ryan's desk. "How many people did he experiment on?" She wasn't expecting an answer, and she didn't want to know. Even one person was too many.

"He's gone now," Ryan said. "That's the important thing."

"But who might he have been working with? If this band was helping him recruit people, then there may be other collaborators."

"The TSS is still investigating."

Frustration flushed her cheeks. "I just hate knowing that monsters like him are running loose."

"Me too. That's one of the harsh realities."

Raena shook her head. "There are always those who will take advantage of others if given the opportunity. But this is far beyond that—it's horrific."

"There are so many things we encounter in our positions that we'd never know about as regular citizens."

"I'm glad we can shield others from those brutal realities, but sometimes I wish we didn't need to know about it ourselves."

"Same here." Ryan tapped his thumb on the desk in a nervous tick.

"You're right, this is in the TSS' hands. We have to focus

on updating our public image."

"That image would be fine if the media stopped making up lies."

"No matter how many times we say that, it doesn't improve our present situation." Raena stood up and began pacing to help her think. "We need a newsworthy endeavor that will take the spotlight off the negative, fabricated press. Something irrefutable that will outshine the shadows our enemies try to cast."

"I'm fresh out of ideas."

She strode in a slow path across the room and then back again. "DGE is known for its ships. Transportation. Movement. Freedom. The issue that people are complaining about now is feeling trapped on their worlds. A lack of choice. We need to give them flexibility. Movement."

"And that would be manifested... how?"

The idea took form in her mind. "City-ships."

"Pardon?"

"It's not a novel concept, but it's rarely been put into practice. Giant structures designed to support an entire community. A mobile space-station. People can find others with the same values and beliefs and carve out a life together— a smaller population than a planet, but enough to be sustainable. They can go anywhere, self-contained and free. Citizens answerable only to themselves without burdensome planetary politics."

Ryan stared at her, working his mouth as he tried to decide how to respond. "That's out-of-the-box, I'll give you that."

"It's the answer," she stated, sure of it now. "And I'll tell you why."

CHAPTER 11

THE YOUNG BLOND man seated across the interrogation table looked more remorseful than Wil had anticipated. A long list of offenses—from abduction to assault—suggested someone with a warped moral compass, yet the young man had tears in his vibrant green eyes.

"I told you, he made me do it. I didn't want to," he insisted.

"I want to believe you, Mika," Saera said from next to Wil, "but why should we trust your word?"

"Read my mind, if that's what it takes. He was controlling me. Programmed me to do what he asked. I didn't want to hurt anyone."

Mika had stuck to his story since the beginning of the interrogation, claiming that Tregaren had brainwashed him since he was a child and had recently used him to help identify Gifted women who were good candidates to abduct. He would slip a drug into their drink and then hand them off to Tregaren. While a horrible offense, he insisted he had no part in the more heinous experimentations that followed. Thus far, he had yet to reveal any insights into what those other activities might be.

"There's no need to invade your mind," Wil said. "We can tell if you're lying. Let's go over it again."

Mika slid his palms over the table, leaving sweaty streaks. He shook his head, his face flushed up to his hairline. "Tregaren left the Priesthood decades ago—well before I was born. But he was one of the scientists, and he'd continued the work on his own. That's why he took my mom. She was originally intended to be a surrogate for his clone, and he couldn't make it work."

"And you're his son?" Wil clarified.

The young man nodded. "I think I was his backup plan. He would overwrite my consciousness if he got desperate enough for a vessel to transfer himself into."

This is why we outlawed cloning entire bodies—so this kind of barbaric act could never happen. Laws meant nothing when they were ignored, of course. The Priesthood, especially, was well known for covertly engaging in all of the activities the organization had publicly banned.

Mika spread his fingers on the table. "Tregaren took my mom when she was in her twenties. She wasn't the first; I don't know what became of the others. He never treated me like a son... more like a pet. When I was old enough, he trained me. Eventually, he found the band and told me to be the manager. Every planet where they played, I'd hang out in the club looking for Gifted women who didn't seem like they'd be missed right away. Sometimes, though, it wouldn't matter—if she had a strong enough aura, he'd want her all the same."

"Why only women?" Saera asked.

"They're what was needed for whatever they're doing."

"More surrogates, presumably—just like the Priesthood," Wil said in Saera's mind.

"It's awful. I can't think about it." Despite the discomfort

he sensed within her, she remained poised and professional externally. "How long ago did you begin recruiting for him?"

"I think I was sixteen when he sent me out for the first time. So, six years, I guess?"

He's so young and has already been through so much. Wil could say the same thing about his own nonexistent childhood, but somehow it was worse when it happened to others. "And how many people did you find for him during that time?"

Mika looked down at his hands. "I don't know."

"What did I say about lying?" Wil pressed.

"I. Don't. Know!" Mika shouted back, punctuating every word. "It's not like I kept count. Hundreds. I don't know how many exactly."

"Less than a thousand?" Wil asked. "More?"

"No, probably closer to three or four hundred. Two, sometimes three, people every two weeks or so."

The math worked out in Wil's quick mental calculation. "How did you hand them off?"

"I'd follow her until the drugs kicked in, then get her somewhere secure and he'd pick her up."

"But how, specifically?" Saera asked.

Mika shrugged. "He had another ship. He never traveled with us. I think he took a shuttle to the surface."

"He, personally, picked them up from where you left them?"

"I was never there for that. I don't know."

"So, other people may have been involved?" Wil questioned.

"Maybe."

The conversation wasn't going anywhere fast, but the important aspect was that Mika gave no indication of lying or withholding information. *"He really doesn't seem to know the details,"* he commented telepathically to Saera.

"I agree. Despite his role, he's a victim in his own way."

"It'll take significant time with a specialist to strip out his conditioning. Tough to know if he'll ever fully recover."

"We have to try. Part of me wants to punch him in the face for what he did, but I know it wasn't of his own accord. It's difficult to ascribe blame in a situation like this."

Wil wished he could say that everyone had a choice, but he knew that wasn't true. A young, untrained person had no hope of fighting back against the telepathic influence of someone on Tregaren's level. Living with the knowledge of his role would be punishment enough.

Mika studied them through squinted eyes. With his abilities, he clearly recognized that they were having a telepathic discussion. "What are you going to do with me?" he asked.

"We haven't decided yet." It was the most truthful answer Wil could give.

"What do *you* want to happen?" Saera added.

The young man thought about it. "I want to make things right."

Wil was intrigued by the response. "And how would you foresee doing that?"

"By finding out what happened to them."

The statement was genuine, but Wil detected a deeper meaning and motivation to the words. "What aren't you saying?"

Mika squirmed. "He… He did something with my mom. I think she might still be alive. I want to find her."

Ah, there it is. He exchanged glances with Saera. *"That's as strong a motivation as any we're likely to find."*

"Even so, can he be trusted?"

"*Not yet.*" Wil folded his hands on the desktop. "All right, you want to find your mother, and if you come across the other missing women in the process, it'll be a happy accident?"

"No." Mika's face clouded. "You're twisting my words. That's not what I said."

"You're telling me, then, that if you were to find out that your mother was dead, then you'd continue looking for the others indefinitely?"

"I—" He floundered.

Wil wanted to push him to see how quickly he might give up. Mika might want to set things right, but that would take a degree of follow-through that he might not possess. Wil watched the young man's expressions and gleaned the thoughts flitting on the surface of his mind. There were good intentions there, but Mika was lacking a clear sense of direction.

"You don't have to be alone, Mika," Wil said, softening his tone. "We can help you, but there would be conditions."

"Like what?"

"For starters, you'll need to tell us everything you know about Tregaren. No detail is too minute."

"I already—" Mika caught himself. "That's going to take a while."

"Our Agents have time to hear and document it all."

Mika nodded. "What else?"

"You'll need to swear that you won't use your abilities to hurt anyone," Wil continued. "We don't typically let people with your level of skill roam around without supervision. We believe in a code of conduct, and we take violations very seriously."

"I don't need a foking babysitter," he muttered.

Saera raised her eyebrows. "If that's the level of emotional maturity you possess, then maybe you do."

His face flushed again, and he sank down in his chair. "Sorry."

Wil refocused on the key point. "Do you know what Tregaren was trying to accomplish with his research?"

"He'd always ramble on about immortality and ascension. I never knew what he meant."

It's an exact match for the Priesthood's rhetoric, but why so many subjects? He had to have been working with other people. The pieces were there and it was frustrating Wil that he hadn't yet identified the connective strands. "Did he ever talk about associates?"

"No one specific. He'd say, 'we need them', but I could never be sure if he was just talking about himself. He wasn't," he waved his hand next to his head, "all there, you know?"

"That tends to happen after a thousand years of transferring your consciousness from body to body." Wil wasn't convinced that questionable mental stability was the only factor in play. That 'we' more than likely referred to outside collaborators.

"I'm just happy the sick foker bit it before he had a chance to do that to me," Mika shot back.

The spirit and venom in the words was more telling than anything else the young man had said. He was disgusted by Tregaren, and he hated that he had been used by him. If the TSS could successfully direct that hatred into productive activity, Mika could prove to be a powerful new ally.

Wil folded his hands on the table and leaned forward. "Okay, Mika. Let's discuss how we can help each other."

— — —

Profound loss was a familiar feeling to Mika Hendri. He'd lost his home, his friends, his innocence, his mother—well, she was missing, not gone. But he knew all too well the sensation of being utterly and completely alone.

Tregaren's death changed nothing. If there had been any impact at all, it was that Mika was now free. Tregaren had been an abusive menace for Mika's entire life, invading his mind and warping his thoughts. Mika didn't know who he'd be without that influence, but he didn't like who he'd become.

I can be different now, he told himself.

He'd always looked at the TSS through Tregaren's eyes, considering the organization and its Agents to be a nuisance to society, imposing their will on others under the guise of righteous justice. Having met Kali and now members of the TSS' leadership, he realized that Tregaren had seen evil in others where it was only within himself. The TSS were the 'good guys' by the measure of anyone with a decent moral compass. That was the kind of influence Mika needed now—a chance to atone and start to rebuild himself as a better person.

He found himself sitting alone in the compact bunkroom he was certain was a glorified prison cell while the TSS figured out what to do with him.

A knock sounded at the door.

"Come in," Mika muttered.

An Agent stepped in, middle-aged with kind, glowing brown eyes. "Hi, Mika," he greeted. "I'm Agent Locklan, but you can call me Jack, if you like."

"Why are you here?" The question came out more acidic than Mika had intended.

"You've just been through quite an ordeal. I thought you might need a friendly ear."

"If you're here to interrogate me some more, just come out

and say it. I'm not trying to hide anything."

The Agent took a seat at a small table near the door. "No, that's not what this is about. I'm a therapist. I heard about what happened, and your father's death—"

"He wasn't my father," Mika spat.

"Okay. Well, I understand that you had a complicated relationship with Tregaren, and when a person is suddenly gone, there can be unresolved feelings."

Mika crossed his arms. "That foker deserved to die."

"I'm not here to pass judgment. If there's anything you'd like to get off your chest that you didn't have a chance to say to him, I'm here to listen."

"You know what I'd like to say? That I wish I had my mother back. Even though Tregaren forced her to have a son for him, she still loved me. That monster never treated me as anything other than a tool, and then he took away the only person who'd ever cared for me. I'm glad he's gone, but I wish I could get her back."

Locklan nodded thoughtfully. "Do you know what happened to her?"

Mika shook his head. "Tregaren took her away when she tried to defy him. I haven't seen her for years. She might be dead, but I don't know for sure."

"Well, if she's still out there, we'll do everything we can to help reunite you."

"Thanks, but I know I'm alone."

"We're never as alone as we think," Locklan said. Then he added in Mika's mind, "*Sometimes, we just have to be willing to let someone in.*"

— — —

Lexi checked the time on her desktop, realizing that several hours had passed since she'd last taken a break from her work. It was only then she noticed the ache in her back and that her right leg was half-asleep.

"Ugh." She stood and shook out her leg while flexing her back, massaging just above her hips with her knuckles.

It'd been a nonstop slog since she returned from Tararia. The applicant response had been so overwhelming that they'd needed to revise the training program to include separate tracks, which hadn't been in the original scope. A large portion of the curriculum could be repurposed, but figuring out the new order and which pieces needed to be on both tracks had proved to be many hours of tedious work.

It will all be worth it. She had no doubt about that. This was the start of a major shift in the public consciousness, and she was excited to be at the forefront of those efforts.

With most of the feeling returned to her leg, she decided it was a good time to grab a bite to eat. She sent Jason a text message as she headed toward the mess hall. >>Hungry? I'm taking a break.<<

>>Can't right now, but swing by my office on your way out. I miss you.<<

>>On my way.<<

She took the longer path toward the central elevator, which would lead her past Jason's workspace. As she rounded the corner into the main Command Wing, she passed by Saera's office. When the Lead Agent spotted her, she motioned for Lexi to come in.

"Hey, you're alive," Saera greeted with a smile.

"Sorry, did I miss a message? I've been head down in the zone."

"Wil's the same way; I'm used to it. I had sent along a bit

of news an hour ago. Given the overwhelming interest in the new initiative, we've decided to pivot the TSS field office on Antaris to focus on civilian training."

"Really?" The news brought a smile to Lexi's face.

"We'll keep this first cohort small while we work out the kinks, but that facility will give plenty of room for us to scale up."

"That's amazing. Thank you."

"I'm thrilled to see this come together. You're doing a great job, Lexi."

"Thanks." She glanced toward the door. "I should probably get back to it."

"I'll see you later." With a nod, Saera returned to her work.

Lexi headed out into the hall and hurried a few doors down to Jason's office. "Hey, stranger," she greeted him from the doorway.

"Hi! You look surprisingly happy for someone who's spent all day at her desk."

"I just got a bit of good news from your mom on the way over. The Antaris TSS base is going to be repurposed into a training facility for the initiative."

"Very nice."

"Yeah, I'm excited." Lexi walked behind his desk to stand next to him.

He gazed up at her from his chair, placing his hands on her hips. "I'm glad it's all coming together."

"It is. How's your stuff?"

"My parents just handed off a suspect to me. Mika—Tregaren's son. We need to find out everything we can from him."

Lexi bent down to kiss him. "You will. And then you'll find the others."

"I hope so. I'm ready for this to be over."

"One step at a time. We still have a long way to go."

— — —

Finally. Hanek breathed a sigh of relief. It had taken far longer than he'd anticipated for the TSS to catch Tregaren's trail, but that loose end was now tied up at last.

He didn't expect the Taran authorities to buy that Tregaren had been working independently, but the investigation into his activities would delay them for weeks, if not longer. The man was a ghost in every database at the TSS' disposal, and his travel logs would lead them in circles. That poor son of his would likewise only offer insights that would lead nowhere—a mere puppet oblivious to the larger scheme in play.

Feeling more optimistic than he had in a long time, Hanek headed to the galley to grab a snack before the afternoon staff meeting.

The large freighter, *Horizon*, which the Coalition had adopted as its mobile base of operations, was equipped with several galleys, each with permissions based on a person's role within the Coalition. Hanek had thought his recent promotion to Magdalena's lead assistant would bump him up to the next tier, but he was still relegated to the dining facility for the administrative underlings. As much as he'd like an upgrade in the fare, the dining arrangement did offer consistent gossip from the other aides about their managers' work.

He'd been shocked, at first, by their propensity to share details, but an analysis of the behavior had yielded two insights. Foremost, the assistants were eager to feel important, and sharing secrets was a way to show the value of their work. The second was that everyone felt they were on the same team, so there was no harm in sharing information.

Idiots. Hanek's time in the Tararian Guard had drilled in the importance of information compartmentalization and only sharing details on a need-to-know basis. The Coalition would need to lock down its practices if they didn't want an internal breach to be their downfall.

As he entered the galley, a group of four young aides were seated around a table, heads together whispering to each other—no doubt recounting the exciting events of the day.

Not my problem that they don't know how to keep their mouths shut. He shook his head.

The meals were dispensed in prepackaged containers from a refrigeration unit at the back of the room. He grabbed one from the stack and popped it into the warming tray positioned between the refrigerator and a drink dispenser.

Hanek leaned against one of the empty tables, watching the group of four boast about their exploits. Annoyance started to rise in his chest. *Won't anyone tell them better?*

The warmer completed its cycle with a chime. He pulled it out and grabbed a utensil pack.

One member of the group let out a loud, raspy laugh—the sort that grated on Hanek's nerves. He tried to swallow his irritation, thinking about the good news he'd just received about Tregaren and how he had no reason to be in a glum mood.

He selected a table as far away as he could get from the group in the relatively compact space and started to eat. The engineered food wasn't great, but it was palatable enough by space ration standards.

Another raspy laugh sounded from the table, followed by a guttural guffaw from another man.

"Can you keep it down? Some people would like peace while they eat," Hanek shouted across the room.

The three men and woman halted their conversation, staring at him.

One of the men looked dramatically around the otherwise unpopulated room before settling his attention once again on Hanek. "I take it that 'some people' are *you*?"

"Just common courtesy." Hanek took another bite.

"Maybe you should find somewhere else if being around people is such an imposition."

Hanek gripped his fork in his clenched fist. "I don't have an issue with people, only loudmouths who don't know their place."

The raspy-laugher scoffed. "Who is this guy?"

"Someone who knows a whole bomaxed lot more than you," Hanek shot back. "Leave your job at your desk unless you want to become intimately acquainted with an airlock."

"How about you mind your own foking business?" the woman retorted.

"I suggest you take that advice for yourself." Hanek relaxed his hand enough to scoop up another bite of his meal.

"Doing just fine over here. Thanks, buddy," raspy-laugher said.

Hanek swallowed. "All right, let me tell you a story. It's about a young aide who came to work on a spaceship with a lot of very powerful people who were used to getting their way. The aide got quite confident in his position, sitting in on many important meetings where lots of sensitive information was shared.

"Well, this enterprising young man started to chat with his friends about what he heard, and they told their friends. One of these stories made it back to the man's supervisor, and it didn't take her long to figure out where the leak had been sprung. She confronted the young man, and he admitted what he'd done. She thanked him for his honesty and then promptly threw him and everyone he'd told into an airlock. 'Once a gossip, always a gossip,' she said, and then vented them.'"

The four young aides gaped at him from across the room like he was crazy.

"Seriously." Hanek took another bite and swallowed. "I know because I was the one who told that supervisor about the stories that were going around the lunchroom. Got her former aide's position out of the deal—a nice promotion."

He pushed the tray with the remains of his meal forward into the center of the table. "You should have just shut the fok up when I asked."

Without another word, he headed for the exit.

"Wait, hold up," the guffawer said as Hanek passed by.

"He's joking, right?" the woman asked her colleagues.

Hanek ignored them; he had a meeting to get to. If there was anything worth salvaging of their professionalism, the story would get them in line. Then, if they didn't heed the warning, he'd illustrate that every word of it was true.

CHAPTER 12

IT HAD TAKEN Raena a while to convince Ryan to buy into the city-ship idea, but once he started to understand her reasoning, he'd gotten on board.

Her premise was that people want control over their own domain. They would seek to conquer, regardless of what they had; it was about the thrill of the hunt. So, if there were smaller targets, the opposition would go after those rather than the larger, more difficult objectives.

Essentially, the city-ships would be decoys. The Coalition and other organizations with power-hungry leaders would naturally gravitate toward the 'low-hanging fruit', as the saying went. A city-ship was a far easier target than a planet-bound settlement, which would also offer the strategic advantage of being mobile. An irresistible draw, which would take the attention off the much less defensible alternatives where more innocent bystanders would be likely to get swept up in the fight, versus a new location where people would *choose* to go. If things turned unfavorable—well, they'd signed up for living there.

Putting the idea into practice would be far more difficult than selling others on the concept. By design, the city-ships were enormous, and the funding and resources would need to come from somewhere.

While DGE was well-positioned by most corporate standards, the company had nowhere near the financial reserves of the other High Dynasty corporations, which hadn't experienced a two-century-long break in operations. Though DGE's assets had been somewhat recovered after the dynasty's official reinstatement, the depth of the resources simply wasn't there. It would take decades to begin balancing out again, if it would ever catch up.

With purely internal funding out of the question, Raena decided to turn to the deepest pockets she knew—who also happened to be family.

"Hey, Grandpa," she greeted Cris when he appeared on her viewscreen.

"Raena, hello! How was your visit with Jason?"

"It was really great. You're going to love Lexi. She's the perfect combination of poise, smarts, and grit."

"I have no doubt. I only wish we'd had the opportunity to frame that announcement."

Raena winced. "Sorry about that. Things have been a little crazy around here. I didn't—"

"What's done is done," he said. "I'm sure there are ways we can mitigate our exposure."

"What do you mean?"

"Any statement we make enforcing their relationship, or Jason being 'off the market' as the Sensationals like to put it, closes off potential business and political alliances through marriage. I will never become my parents and encourage that kind of thinking for an actual arrangement, but leaving things open-ended for hypothetical talks can be a useful tool."

She wasn't used to her grandfather thinking in those terms, but she did see where he was coming from. "Who would you have even set him up with, hypothetically?"

"There've been two options floating out there for the last decade. The first was Leana Naelandri, better known as the heiress to Alteria Galactic, one of SiNavTech's longtime business partners. We've been unable to acquire the company, despite numerous attempts over the last two generations, and a prospective marriage could have made that merger happen."

"Oh." Raena put the odds of Jason having gone along with that at exactly zero.

"I never expected that to materialize, but I had a glimmer of hope that the two of them might meet and happen to hit it off, much like you and Ryan."

"Minus the 'thinking I was falling for a servant' part."

He smiled faintly. "Right. But the pairing with Leana was always secondary to an even more hypothetical but powerful prospect: Tamala Monsari."

"Oh, *fok* no!" The words slipped out before Raena could stop herself. "Sorry." She was especially surprised she'd even sworn like a proper Taran—finally converted after all these years.

"I want nothing to do with that family, either," Cris replied. "Still, the *option* was valuable. We have little to fall back on now to mend that bridge."

"Why would we even want to? The dynasty is failing."

"If that is indeed the case, then we'd want to be first in line to pick up the assets. Closeness has benefit, even with our enemies."

She nodded her understanding. "I didn't think about it that way."

"You're learning." It was a nice way of telling her that she'd messed up.

"We'll be changing our protocols regarding the use of recording devices during the tours," she replied. A future mitigation strategy is what he'd care about, not an apology.

"Good plan."

"None of this is why I called," Raena said, bringing the conversation back around to the original point. "I've been thinking about a new business proposition, and I was hoping for your buy-in."

"Conceptually or financially?"

"Both."

He studied her through the viewscreen. "I'll hear the pitch."

She took a deep breath and gathered her thoughts. "I propose we begin manufacturing city-ships to serve as alternate targets for the Coalition rather than their only option to be to go after entire planets."

Cris considered the statement. "What makes you think they'd lessen the interest in planets?"

"Purely a resources calculation. Sure, a planet offers more *renewable* resources, but right now the Coalition is most focused on spreading its message and cultivating unquestioning followers. A smaller community on a ship would give them not only superior control of the population but also mobility."

"I can see where you're coming from, but I'm not sure that's really a solution."

"I know it's counter-intuitive, but hear me out." She restated the discussion she'd had with Ryan, offering preemptive responses to the questions and concerns he'd voiced during their debate.

Cris nodded thoughtfully, taking it in. "There is validity to the argument, Raena, but I don't see the long-term gains."

"It'll slow down the takeovers and offer an alternative for people who want to get away."

"Your heart is in the right place with this, no doubt. I can see your excitement here, but I can't get on board."

Her chest constricted. "Why not?"

"Dozens of reasons. Foremost, though, I know from experience that these scenarios rarely play out how we imagine. I spent a lot of time at the helm of the TSS, and we dealt with our fair share of civil disputes. Every time we tried to offer instigators an alternative place where they could go without regulation, they insisted on trying to change the place where they already were. It's not actually about achieving peace, but rather control. And once they reach one milestone, they'll change their goals and start the whole mess over again."

"I hate feeling helpless."

Cris leaned forward slightly. "What made you think of this idea?"

"I'm looking for something big to shift the narrative away from calls of incompetence."

"Throwing money around will never be the solution to get the public on your side."

"I wasn't suggesting we try to buy their favor."

"Your plan is to present an enemy with strategic resources with the hope that they'll go after that rather than your other valuables."

Raena didn't like to admit defeat, but it was clear her grandfather didn't share her read of the events. Continuing to press the issue was unlikely to get him on her side. "What do you suggest instead?"

He glanced offscreen before returning his focus to her.

"What are your key skills?"

"Pardon?"

"I can't hand you an answer to this, but I can help talk you through it. What are your key skills, Raena?"

She thought about it. "I think I'm good at organizing information, crafting messaging, bringing people together…"

He nodded. "That's right. To sum it up, you have a natural gift of making people feel comfortable, no matter who they are. Yet, you keep trying to take the media focus *off* of you."

"I've opened up my home for daily tours."

"And that's a great start. But, what, a few dozen people a day? That's not even a blip compared to the trillions of Taran citizens."

Her cheeks flushed. "I suppose it's not."

"And those city-ships, well—it'd be a bigger blip, but that's not going to move the needle. You need to win over the hearts and minds of the masses."

"How?"

"I truly don't have an answer for you. Even if I did, it wouldn't be authentic coming from anyone but you. I have every faith you'll figure it out."

He was quick to shoot down my idea. I don't know if I can do any better. She nodded reluctantly. "Thank you for your time."

"Hey, don't be discouraged. Just because I can't support this concept doesn't mean you've failed." He gazed at her lovingly through the screen. "I believe in you."

"Thanks. I'll keep working on it."

"Good. Talk soon." He ended the vidcall.

Well, shite. That hadn't gone at all how she'd envisioned. However, she trusted his council, so she wasn't going to waste time second-guessing. *Back to the drawing board.*

— — —

Jason mulled over the latest answer from Mika. It wasn't sitting right. "So, Tregaren planted directives in your mind without your knowledge or consent, but you endorse using telepathy to subdue people?" he repeated.

Mika scrunched up his face. There was no obvious indication of his connection to the monster Tregaren aside from a similarity in their jawline. His eyes were green rather than the albino-like red the Priests' eyes had taken on as a result of their extensive genetic modifications. Had he shared that characteristic, Jason doubted he'd have been able to be in the same room as him.

"You're twisting it," Mika said. "I'm just saying, if someone is going to be captured or attacked anyway, it's a kindness to make it so they won't feel the pain."

There was a certain logic to it, but Jason was nonetheless disturbed to hear Mika thinking in those terms. At no point during the hypothetical scenario had he suggested using his abilities to fight back against the assailant on the victim's behalf—the most intuitive and logical action for any TSS Agent trainee.

"Mika, I'm going to repeat the question," Jason said. "If you were to find yourself in an alley with someone who's being chased by a would-be murderer, how would you respond?"

The young man sat in quiet contemplation for several seconds. The spark of realization filled his green eyes, followed by his face twisting with disgust. "I'm sorry, I didn't... I..." He shook his head, sniffing.

"Your behavioral programming runs deep. It's going to take time and effort to unravel it all."

"I don't want to be like this," Mika pleaded.

"We can help," Jason assured him. "This isn't going to be an easy process, but I think we have a lot to offer each other."

"I'll tell you anything." He pounded the heel of his hand into his temple. "I just want these thoughts *gone*."

"Okay, we'll do our best." Jason was confident in the skills of the TSS' psychologists. If anyone could repair the damage to Mika's mind, it would be them.

Until a good portion of that work was complete, he wasn't sure how much useful information he'd be able to extract from Mika; all the thoughts and emotions and memories were jumbled together and colored through the perceptions Tregaren had conditioned into him. Their recent exchange was evidence enough that his thought patterns were in disarray. Beyond the inconvenience of trying to interrogate him in that state, Jason felt sorry for the young man and hoped he'd respond well to treatment. Dwelling in those dark thoughts was no way to live.

Jason excused himself from the discussion, handing Mika over to a security detail.

He rubbed his eyes, itchy from tiredness. Everything had been nonstop since they returned from Tararia.

A big lead and still no forward progress. He was growing increasingly frustrated with the situation. Tregaren *had* to be working with the Coalition, and yet there was no concrete evidence of any involvement. Again. *We need a breakthrough.*

He felt a ticking clock, though there was no tangible external factor driving a timeline. He'd been experiencing a shapeless sense of dread for more than a year now, believing devastation was coming any moment.

They were still here. Nothing catastrophic had happened. Yet, he couldn't shake the feeling that something awful was looming just out of sight.

Jason's handheld buzzed with an incoming text message notification. It was a summons from his father. Letting out a long breath, he headed to the High Commander's office. He let himself in through the open door.

"How did your discussion with Mika go?" Wil asked as Jason entered.

"He's guarded. I don't trust him yet." He sat down in his usual seat.

"Neither do I. He was under a powerful influence for a long time. Brainwashing or not, he didn't have a good role model, and his perception of morality might not align well with our own."

"I agree."

"It'll be an interesting case."

Jason crossed his arms. "I'll be honest, I'm frustrated. I got my hopes up that this mess with Tregaren was going to give us answers, and we've gotten nothing so far."

"I must admit to feeling frustrated on my end, as well. Not with you," he hastily added. "With myself."

"We're playing with a shite hand right now."

"I can't blame my issues on external factors."

"Is there something you haven't told me?" Jason asked.

His father hesitated. "You and I are in a challenging position. We're attuned to things that others aren't—cosmic energy patterns, as it were. Vague indicators which can offer us all the answers without saying anything at all."

"Ah, so this is about what the Aesir said?"

Wil nodded. "I can't shake the notion that they're right— that there is something I need to see but haven't been able to."

"I've been wrestling with a similar feeling myself. It's staring at me from behind, but every time I try to spin around to catch a glimpse, it's gone."

"What worries me is that we're dealing with seemingly separate issues, yet we've arrived at the same crossroads. What does an ancient device hidden on Earth have to do with genetics research, a rogue political separatist movement, and a transdimensional alien occupation?"

"The makings of a total shiteshow," Jason joked.

Wil chuckled. "I can't disagree."

"In all seriousness, though, I think it's pretty clear by now that the Coalition has designs beyond the Taran political sphere. Either they're after some form of ascension similar to the Priesthood, or there's something even worse going on."

"I can only interpret this uneasiness we've been feeling as a sign that the natural cosmic order is in distress. It sounds silly, but—"

"Not to me. I don't pretend to understand how things work, but I've seen enough to know that how we perceive the cause and effect of events is a construct of our perceived reality. Maybe these feelings are a sort of echo of future strife we have yet to experience."

"I can only hope that sensing them now will allow us to change course," Wil said.

"Ripples of possible futures, and we can help shape which to ride."

"It would be wonderful if we could. If I could only see the pattern..." The self-critical anxiety was evident in his father's tone.

Jason sat in contemplative silence. *He's not the only one who's seen the pattern before. When I saw it, I needed to let go of my physical self. Try too hard and it's unreachable.*

Wil eyed him. "What?"

"You've always told me when it comes to our Gifts, to trust my instincts."

"Right."

"Well, everything I've heard you say is about what you're thinking. What's your gut telling you?"

Wil leaned back in his chair, fingers steepled as he considered the observation. "That I need to be less concerned about my present reality and focus on the bigger picture."

"Isn't that what Mom's been saying?"

"Yes. And she's right more often than not."

"That's what the pattern is all about, isn't it?" Jason said. "Looking across time and space at the shifts in major forces?"

"It's more nuanced than that."

"Sure, we can pick out specific elements. Nonetheless, it will help shape general courses of action, not tell you what to have for dinner."

"True."

"So, you can't overthink it. You need to be in the mindset of strategy, not tactics. We're not there yet."

Wil raised an eyebrow. "If you have a suggestion about how to proceed, please share."

"If we want this guidance, then we need to remove ourselves from the distractions of the here and now."

"Astral projection."

"The freest state we can be."

"I've tried. Multiple times," Wil said. "No luck."

"How far did you allow yourself to drift, really?" Jason asked.

"I've roamed, believe me."

"Yet you always find your way back."

"Of course. I have my tethers to home. It's easy."

"So, trust in those connections and let loose."

Wil shook his head. "You know what it's like to look into the nexus—to face a force so much greater than yourself. It changes how you see everything, irrevocably."

Maybe he just hasn't wanted *to see it again.* Jason understood his reluctance. It was terrifying to face those harsh truths, but it's what they needed to move forward. All other avenues had failed. "We'll go together."

"I can't ask you to risk yourself like that."

"It's not a risk, though. Like you said, this is home; we can always find our way back. The bigger issue is one person bearing the burden of a difficult truth. If we're both there to witness it, maybe it'll make it easier to process."

Wil smiled.

"What?" Jason asked.

"I was just thinking back to something your mom once told me early on in our relationship—to accept generous offers of support when they're freely given."

"It's good advice."

"Working with loved ones is never easy. On the one hand, I welcome your contribution as a TSS Agent. However, as my son, I'm hesitant to place you in danger."

"Is this actually a risky situation?"

"I don't know, and that gives me pause."

"You can't shield me from everything, Dad," Jason told him.

"No matter how hard I might try." He nodded pensively. "Okay, we'll try to find the nexus together. Stars know I've had no success on my own."

"Are we going to do this now?"

Wil shrugged. "May as well, if you have time."

"Sure."

"I'd like to loop in your mom, though." There was a hum of energy denoting a telepathic exchange as Wil reached out to her.

Saera arrived at the office a few minutes later. "Are you sure this is a good idea?" she asked.

"When all else fails, try something new," Wil replied. "It's time we test the limits of Jason's abilities. Better we try together than alone."

"I want to try, Mom," Jason said.

She looked between her husband and son. "All right." She didn't sound enthusiastic about it.

Wil and Jason got settled on the floor. There was no reason they couldn't remain seated in chairs, but sitting cross-legged on the carpeting felt more appropriate for these kind of astral projection exercises.

Saera sat down on the couch near them. "Do you want me to maintain a tether?"

"Not directly," Wil replied. "I suspect we'll need to let go, but having a beacon to help us find our way back would be useful."

"You'd *better* come back."

He smiled. "We will."

"Don't worry, Mom, we've done way crazier things than this," Jason added.

"I wasn't particularly happy about those things, either." Saera raised an eyebrow.

"This will be rather boring on your end," Wil said. "Do you have anywhere you need to be this afternoon?"

"Nothing I can't tend to while keeping an eye on you here. I'll call you back if anything urgent comes up."

"Sounds good." Wil took a deep breath. "Well, I guess we should get to it."

Jason nodded. "I'm ready."

They closed their eyes and slowed their breathing, centering their minds in preparation for the journey ahead.

In practiced fashion, Jason released his consciousness from his physical self, drifting away from his body and upward through Headquarters. He sensed his father doing the same, seeing him as a ghostly echo of his corporeal self.

Together, they soared out through the main elevator shaft and emerged in the great expanse of space beyond.

It had been a long time since Jason had roamed freely like this, and he relished the exhilaration. For all the pleasures his corporeal form could experience, nothing compared to his consciousness being unbridled like this. Then, with a pang, he realized that it wasn't like it used to be—he now did have ties, to Lexi, and the prospect of leaving her behind was painful.

The ethereal manifestation of his father next to him nodded. *"It's different once you're bonded. Now you know why I always come home."*

"I'd wondered. It'd be tempting to stay out here forever."

"Which is why we must usually resist. But now, we need to give in."

Jason understood. They needed to let go of their sense of individual self in order to read the pattern. They'd once looked into the nexus, a shortcut to that expansive sight, but now they must expand their vision without that crutch. The nexus gave them a window into one key aspect of their own lives; now, they sought answers for an entire civilization.

Jason and Wil began to drift. While he'd normally remain cognizant of the spatial bodies around him while astral projecting, Jason now allowed all perceptions of the physical world to fade into the background.

He was energy, surrounded by energy. Shapeless, yet interconnected and limitless. Threads snaked across the vast expanse, coiling into bundles of varying sizes where each person and thing existed in physical reality. These energy pathways weren't scaled like the objects he knew, but rather were concentrated based on their influence over the rest of the energy grid. He realized that he and his father were bright spots of energy, and their minute movements caused a ripple down the threads, tugging on the interconnected fabric. Other people could twist and writhe through their entire lives and never flutter a single thread.

"Is it fate?" Jason asked. It couldn't be a coincidence that they had so much influence.

"I gave up on that idea a long time ago. I look at it as cosmic responsibility—the Universe's way of maintaining balance. We're instruments."

"This is the web you talked about in your original nexus vision, isn't it?"

"Yes, though it's changed."

Jason followed his father's gaze into the distance, following the threads leading to the Rift. His father had spoken about a blight on the web from the Bakzen, who had ripped and twisted the threads when they tore open the Rift. Much of that damage had been repaired, but a wound remained.

Rather than a dark presence like Jason had expected to find, the area was a blinding light. He couldn't look at it directly, needing instead to observe it from the corner of his perception. *"What is it?"*

"A link to the higher dimensional energies that shouldn't be there. That's what the Rift is."

Jason had suspected as much, but the confirmation was still a startling realization. Seeing now how brightly it burned, he realized that he'd likely be burned up if he gave into its beckon. It was dangerous.

Wil looked around. *"What are we missing? I see the threads, but the Aesir talk like there's a pattern to be read—to view possible futures and determine a course."*

There *was* something missing. For all the majesty of the web, it was still somehow... flat.

"It's static," his father observed. *"I see where there are points of influence, but not the outcomes of those actions."*

"And you're sure that's what the Aesir indicated you should be able to do?"

"Everything they say is a riddle. I'm not certain of anything."

"Maybe we're not looking at it right." Jason kept studying the web, trying to see what he was missing. His father was right—there weren't possible pathways, only what existed in the present.

How are we supposed to see the future? Then, he realized he was taking the wrong approach. It all became clear. *"Dad, when we leave our physical self, we're floating outside time. Yet, we're still thinking of this as 'now'."*

The tension he'd been feeling from his father eased. *"Yes, that's it."*

Though a key insight, conceptually, Jason had no idea how to put the realization into practice. *How do you stop looking at time as a linear construct?*

Next to him, though, his father's presence had changed. He seemed somehow bigger to Jason, or... extended. Fascinated, Jason watched as Wil took on a prismatic quality, separating into duplicate versions stretching toward infinity, almost like he was staring into the corner of a house of mirrors or through a kaleidoscope. The echoed versions faded the further out they went from the original until they were invisible in the dark beyond.

How is he doing that? Jason couldn't figure out how to replicate the act himself, but it didn't matter. He had come here for support, and the best thing he could do now was remain as a tether to pull his father back if he started to come apart.

Threads began to snake out from the different instances of Wil's presence, causing little shudders to race along the energy web. Flashes of energy rippled through the strands, lighting up the different instances with each. Some remained after the flash, and others shattered.

Jason watched, awestruck, as the web responded to the different iterations.

At last, the prismatic copies folded inward until Wil was once again a singular presence.

"What happened?" Jason asked, though he had suspicions.

"I can't describe it, but I saw beyond time."

"There were thousands of you, stretching as far as I could see in every direction."

"That's what it felt like. How long has it been?"

"I have no idea," Jason replied. Astral projection was always a strange process, and this was by far the most disorienting of his experiences.

"We should get back."

Jason followed his lead, tracing the bond to Lexi back toward Earth and into TSS Headquarters. He returned to his body with a start, at once feeling comforted and also confined.

"How did it go?" Saera asked when Jason opened his eyes.

"I'm not sure." Truthfully, he didn't know what had been accomplished.

Wil was slow to reply, continuing to sit on the ground, his brows drawn together in deep thought.

"Wil, you okay?" Saera asked.

He nodded. "Yes, it's just a lot to process." He slowly stood up.

"What did you see?" Jason got up, too—stretching out his legs, which had become sore from too long in one position. He checked the time, seeing that nearly an hour had passed. It had seemed like they'd been out there for only a few minutes, or maybe a lifetime.

"I finally understand now," Wil said slowly. "I've been looking at everything wrong."

"What have we been missing?" Jason asked.

His father began to pace slowly. "It doesn't matter how quickly we prepare to stand against the Erebus. They're not beholden to our time. From their perspective, what's happened in our past and what could happen in our future are facets of the same coin. It will unfold when it unfolds, and nothing we could have done or can do will change that."

"So, we do… nothing?" Saera asked.

Wil shook his head. "No, we have plenty of work to do. I'll need a while to figure out the details, but I now understand what that device on Earth is for."

"Which is…?" Jason prompted when he didn't immediately elaborate.

"It bridges to the higher dimensions and locks anything in its path to a specific time and place."

Jason understood the words, but he wasn't sure about the implication. "What does that mean for us?"

"It means that we can force the Erebus to play by the rules of our reality."

"Meaning, we'd be able to hurt them? To kill them?" Saera asked.

"Hypothetically. The problem is, the device didn't operate as intended during its test run," Wil said.

Jason crossed his arms. "I don't like the sound of a malfunctioning device with that kind of capability."

"Neither do I." Wil shook his head. "But if we're going to prevent the imminent destruction of the Taran race, we have to figure out how to make it work."

CHAPTER 13

JASON SOON LEARNED that insights gleaned through astral projection were as intangible and difficult to put into practice as the act itself. In the month since he had ventured into the great beyond with his father, they'd made very little progress toward understanding the ancient device on Earth or how to modify its operations.

Jason glanced at the latest field report from Trevor, seeing more of the same. *They have to be losing their minds down there. You can only run up against a wall so many times before wanting to give up.*

He was facing similar challenges with his own investigation into the Coalition. His team had somehow managed to remain cheerful, but Jason himself was losing faith that they'd achieve a significant breakthrough.

There was one glimmer of hope. Kali had been sent back out into the field with Mika and the band to continue the hunt for the missing women. Though Jason still had reservations about Mika, he also believed in second chances. Mika had been deemed mentally stable by the TSS psychologists and had exhibited no violent tendencies during the three weeks he was held for evaluation, so only time out in the real-world would reveal his true potential for recovery.

How long do we let them search before we call it off? Jason had been wrestling with that question for too long now. The harsh truth was that everyone who'd gone missing was probably dead. To prolong the search meant denying their families closure.

They needed to give the investigation a little more time. Kali hadn't been out on her new mission for long, and she needed the opportunity to catch a new lead.

Be patient. He wasn't sure how much longer he could.

Feeling too unfocused to review reports, Jason decided to take a break from his office by going to check in with the Coalition investigation team in their mini command hub. The once bustling room was now still and quiet. There'd been so little information to sift through in the past week that some of the task force members had offered to help on other projects.

Only Laura remained full-time on the endeavor. She was hunched over her desk when Jason entered.

"Hi, Laura," he greeted. "Thought I'd check in. How's it going?"

"Keeping at it!" she replied, as enthusiastic as ever. "Though, it's not the same being here by myself."

"What would you say to me moving in here with you until we're back up to full capacity?"

"As long as Lexi won't be jealous," Laura jested back.

"If I don't spend the night, I think it will be just fine." Truthfully, he would invariably end up working into the wee hours of the night on occasion, but Lexi had been doing the same. They were secure enough in their relationship that it wasn't a genuine concern.

Jason settled into one of the empty workstations. "Have you gone over the *Sepiantia* flight logs again? I've been wanting to cross-reference the location data with the logs we pulled from Tregaren's ship."

"Yes! Since you brought it up…" Laura shoved off from her desk to wheel her chair over to another console, gliding across the floor with practiced precision.

Putting her time alone in here to good use, I see. Truth be told, Jason would have done exactly the same thing at her age.

She activated the holoprojector and displayed a star map with overlapping data points. "This is the mess we're dealing with. It's garbage."

Jason looked it over. Nothing about it indicated corrupted data. "Did something happen to the files?"

"Oh, no, no." She waved her hand. "What I mean is, it's been curated. A trail that intentionally loops back on itself to form a giant knot with no end."

Laura animated the display to show the data points in sequence. Indeed, the path formed a loop. "Before you say it, I know that a loop can be a pattern, and the first record we have could still be a starting point. The issue is that there are records of tampering—gaps in the data. So, what we're looking at is the path they *want* us to see. What happened during those gaps is anyone's guess."

Jason sighed. "And both of the ships have an independent jump drive, so we can't even calculate probable targets based on the duration of those gaps."

"Yep." Laura stared glumly at the display. "They could have gone anywhere in the galaxy during those deleted timeframes and we'd never know it."

"Back to square one, then." It wasn't what Jason wanted to admit, but he couldn't ignore that truth.

"I hate to say it, but all of the evidence points to Tregaren being a decoy. There were plenty of leads, but every single one of them was a dead end. It's like the people he was working with *wanted* us to catch him to throw us off the real trail."

"I'm willing to believe that," Jason replied. "Anyone who'd work with a former member of the Priesthood clearly has no moral qualms, and a person like that would be willing to sacrifice one of their own."

"The question is, then, where are those puppet-masters lurking?"

"We'll find them," Jason told her. *Hopefully Kali comes up with a lead soon.*

— — —

Mika had expected to feel relieved once he was back on his own ship, but the place wasn't the same now. He sat on the *Sepiantia*'s flight deck watching the swirling light of subspace as they jumped between worlds, letting his mind wander.

The only reason he had this ship was because of Tregaren. Mika had designed it with his mother as a young boy, and it'd been built to spec. Now, it was the only thing he had left of both of them. The part connected to Tregaren, he wanted to destroy. Yet, he couldn't do that without taking away his mother's contribution. The entire situation made his head and heart hurt.

A soft hiss sounded behind him as the flight deck's door opened. He turned to see Kali enter.

"Hey, how's it going?" she greeted, the soft glow of her hazel eyes standing out in the dimmed lights.

"You know." He shrugged.

"Yeah." She looked at the spot where their friend had died

during the final fight with Tregaren.

"You're not supposed to be on the flight deck," Mika muttered.

"I know. But I thought you might need the company."

"Not your job."

She looked around. "I don't see others clamoring for the role."

He stared straight ahead. "Suit yourself."

Kali took a seat next to him. "I know it's easy to feel alone, but I want you to know you're not," she said gently.

Mika swallowed. "How can you even look at me?"

"I know what it's like to be used. I don't think you're a bad guy, you were just in a lousy situation. We can help each other, but that starts with trust."

That's bold, considering she holds my fate in her hands. He knew the only reason the TSS had let him go was so they could follow his moves, perhaps leading them to Tregaren's secret collaborators. Kali was his watcher, plain and simple.

Yet, something about her helped set him at ease. As much as he guarded the flight deck as his domain, he was actually happy she'd stopped by. Nonetheless, he didn't know her well yet, and he couldn't be sure about her motivations.

He sank deeper into his seat. "Trusting someone isn't like flipping a switch."

"I'm not asking you to. Just that you try to keep an open mind."

"About what?"

"That we could be friends."

He chuckled. "You're here to keep tabs on me."

"Doesn't mean that can't be in a friendly way."

Their eyes met, and he felt a warmth in her that he hadn't fully registered before. "Yeah, okay," he agreed.

"Good." She smiled. "It's a start."

— — —

Hanek stepped through the open doorway into Magdalena's office. She stood at the viewport, hands clasped behind her back. There wasn't much of a view at the moment, as the ship was in subspace, but there was something to be said about the meditative properties of gazing into the ethereal ribbons of blue-green light.

"You wanted to see me, ma'am?" Hanek said to announce his presence when she didn't immediately turn around.

"I have an assignment for you," she replied without turning to face him.

"I'm at your service."

"I'd like you to go to the Spadrosi Station. I need a message personally delivered to the Commander."

"Gladly." Hanek found it interesting that she used that moniker even though it was just the two of them in the room. Her eldest son, Andrei, had adopted the name—ironically, it seemed—after he washed out from the TSS Agent training program. Hanek didn't know the whole story there, but the guy's ruthless reputation within the Coalition was an indication that his temperament probably hadn't been the right fit. Hanek had always considered the guy a hero.

She finally turned to face him. "See, that's what I like about you, Hanek," she said with a slight upturn of her lips. "I can give you a vague assignment and you don't ask questions."

"It's not my place."

"You're right about that." Magdalena strode over to her desk. She pulled out a small drive, no larger than her thumb. "Deliver this to him personally. No one else should even know of its existence."

Hanek took it from her and placed it in his pocket. "Understood, ma'am."

—   —   —

Since his expedition with Jason a month prior, Wil had spent more time exploring the pattern and learning how to read the projected outcome of manipulating the cosmic threads. What he'd discovered is that nothing he could do would result in a certain outcome; he could only nudge events in a given direction.

In any case, he had taken an important first step—one his allies had been urging him to take for a long time, and he was overdue for a status report.

He called up Dahl.

The old Oracle answered the vidcall looking surprised. "Cadicle, I thought you might be done with us for good."

"I'm sure the pattern told you otherwise."

The Oracle didn't seem amused by the statement. "Why are you reaching out now?"

"I owe you an apology, Dahl. I didn't leave our last conversation on the best note. I'd like to put all this unpleasantness behind us."

"I would, as well. Are you truly ready to embrace who you are?"

Wil took a long breath. "And who am I, Dahl? I've spent my entire life trying to be who others expect me to be. Am I a commander? A politician? A father? I can barely define those, let alone this nebulous, mythical Cadicle figure you expect me to be. I am ready to be me. I just don't know if I can be myself *and* all the other things everyone needs."

"If you are true to yourself, you will be all of that and more."

"How?"

"You let go of those expectations and listen to what the pattern shows you."

"I've been trying. A month ago, for the first time since I looked into the nexus, I saw the cosmic web again."

Dahl nodded. "That is progress."

"But in and of itself, not enough." Wil shook his head. "I see that what we consider reality is only one facet of that web, but I don't understand how to read the outcomes and guide events accordingly. There's no clear path."

"It's a feeling more than a specific sight," Dahl replied.

More of the same cryptic statements. Maybe I should have continued to keep my distance. Wil desperately wanted the Oracle's guidance, if only he could get a straight answer. His patience had worn too thin to keep running in circles. "Please, tell me how to proceed."

Dahl considered the request, his pale brows drawn together with consternation. Then, he softened. "You still insist on working alone, don't you?"

"Jason has helped me."

"That isn't the only person at your disposal. What of the young man who had a brush with the Erebus?"

"Darin?" Wil hadn't thought about him in months. While his case was fascinating, the TSS researchers hadn't yet been able to identify a clear enough pattern in the expression of his unique prescience ability for it to be useful. "What about him?"

"I believe he may be your key to focusing on the right outcomes. He's somehow tethered to the Erebus. Use that connection."

While an intriguing hypothesis, Darin's visions had been

for random events in his daily life—nothing that seemed tied to the fate of the universe. "I'm dubious," Wil admitted.

"When we first learned of him, there was a sense that he would serve a greater role. I believe you should take him to where you communicated with the device on Earth."

"I'm not sure about that."

"He is a conduit. Capitalize on that connection to open a dialogue."

Wil wasn't ready to commit just yet. "I'll take it under advisement."

Dahl's lips pressed into a thin line. "You must decide on a course. We stand at a crossroads."

"I know. I'll keep trying."

"And you will succeed."

I sure hope so. Wil nodded. "Thank you, Dahl. I'll be in touch."

"Take care, Wil."

He ended the connection and leaned back in his chair. *That wasn't very productive.* The lead on Darin was an interesting thought, however. He'd need to reopen that line of questioning.

A knock on his door pulled Wil from his ruminations. A quick telepathic assessment showed it was Jason. "Come in."

"Sorry to disturb you. I thought you'd want to see this right away," Jason said as he entered, closing the door behind him.

"See what?"

"I told you about that travel loop in Tregaren's logs," Jason began, and Wil nodded. "Well, the only place that came up regularly in the ship's travel logs was Red Ghost. It's an obvious criminal hotbed, but we could never get in there without it being *really* obvious we were there for a raid, and places like that have a way of hiding everything they don't want the authorities to know about."

"What about it?"

"An opportunity has landed in our lap, so it would seem. That band Kali is traveling with has received an invitation to play a gig on Red Ghost."

Wil considered the suggestion. "While convenient for us, I don't like that we'd be sending in an Agent and civilians without means of getting them quick backup."

"Sure, it's a gamble. They're all aware of the risks and want to do it."

We have no other leads. No risk, no reward. He didn't like putting anyone in a dangerous position, but there was too much at stake to ignore the opportunity. "Okay. Let's step inside the den of the beast to see what we can discover."

CHAPTER 14

HANEK GRIPPED THE armrest of his seat on the transport ship, compelled to hang on as it tilted to a seemingly unnatural approach angle.

Spadrosi Station was unlike anything he'd previously encountered. The base was suspended in a fixed subspace position through scientific means that were well beyond both his capability and interest to comprehend. He was certain that the Coalition hadn't constructed it, though it was unclear how it had come to be in the organization's possession. He suspected that the non-Taran members of the governing council had provided the access—a gift to enable their covert operations.

There was no better way to hide a facility than to have it be invisible from conventional spacetime reality. The likelihood of a ship accidently stumbling across it while traversing subspace was close enough to zero to be incalculable, which meant that only people who knew precisely where to look for it would ever find it. Moreover, particulars of the docking procedure were so bizarre that any unwanted visitor was unlikely to gain access even if they *could* see it out a viewport.

Hanek was presently experiencing that docking protocol firsthand as his transport ship dove straight down toward the top of the station. "I don't see a berth," he commented to the pilot, trying to hide the concern in his tone that he had been tricked into a suicide run.

"There's an interior bay," the pilot replied. "I know it's weird. We need to ride in an artificial gravity well. Subspace maneuvering isn't for the faint of heart."

Prior to this experience, Hanek hadn't realized that this kind of steering was even possible outside of normal space. *I'll leave it to the pilots and navigators.*

The ship continued its dizzying dive to the top of the station, then pulled into the opening. Up close, it was actually large enough to accommodate a small cruiser. The interior was tight by port standards, mostly because a rather large ship was currently berthed in one of the top slots. It was one of the oddest ship designs he'd ever seen—rather ugly, resembling a mythical sea beast with scale-like textural details along its hull.

"That's not one of ours," he commented.

The pilot looked over the strange vessel with distaste. "Definitely not. New investors, maybe?"

Hanek didn't like the idea of taking funds from someone with such terrible taste, but credits were credits. With everything the Coalition had planned, they'd need all the resources they could get.

The pilot directed the shuttle into one of the berths for smaller vessels, and the docking clamps pressed into place, sending a slight shudder through the ship.

"I'll be waiting here," the pilot stated.

"This shouldn't take long." Hanek unbuckled his flight harness and made his way to the side access hatch.

It took a minute for the status light to turn blue, indicating the umbilical gangway had a pressurized seal with the ship. Hanek opened the hatch and stepped out.

The gangway led to a walkway hugging the outer wall of the bay, where a stairwell connected the different levels. At the bottom of the stairs was a broad platform filled with what appeared to be supply crates next to a freight elevator servicing the different docking positions. Straight ahead from the bottom of the stairs, the platform funneled toward a security checkpoint.

Hanek confidently strode up to the guard. "I'm here to see the Commander."

"And you are?" The guard looked him over.

"Hanek Eldwan, personal assistant to Magdalena Steyn."

The guard's eyes widened at that, and he hurriedly checked his tablet. "Yes, I see. Just a moment." He spoke into a comm, too quietly for Hanek to overhear.

A couple minutes later, a small, dark-complexioned man approached from deeper within the facility. "Hello, Hanek, you're here to see the Commander?" he asked.

Hanek nodded. "I have a personal delivery for him. I work for his mother."

"Yes, I know." He started to turn around, stumbling slightly. "I'm Pyra."

The name was familiar. Hanek realized they had communicated before in the course of business. "Ah, yes."

"It's nice to finally meet you in person." Pyra said, leading the way. "I've been working for the Commander for a little over a year now, and there are so many people who are only names on my screen, you know?"

Hanek followed. "You've done well to get this post."

Pyra bobbed his head. "I much prefer it to the last."

The corridors were stark white, giving the space a clinical feel. That was appropriate, in some ways, given that the base was primarily a scientific research facility. Officially, it was operated by SPEAR Tec, a legitimate business on the books, though there were enough extracurricular activities that the reported operations were only a fraction of the organization. As one of the Coalition's key branches, SPEAR was on the cusp of transitioning from a business to a movement, and Hanek was excited to see how it played out.

The Commander's office was deep inside the base through multiple bulkhead doors. They obviously took security seriously, which was always a pleasure to see. There was probably no unauthorized lunchtime chatter around here.

Pyra stopped outside a sliding door, stepping to the side of the corridor so Hanek could get by. "Here you are."

Hanek nodded at him as he passed. The door opened automatically.

Inside, the room was smartly appointed with several chairs and a large desk. The Commander himself, Andrei Steyn, sat behind the desk, his screen hidden from view.

"Sir, I'm here on behalf of your mother," Hanek stated.

"And you are?"

"Hanek," he replied. "Her assistant."

"Ah, yes. She didn't tell me you were coming. What's this about?"

"She asked me to deliver a message." Hanek reached into his pocket.

A cold tingle traveled down his arm, and he suddenly couldn't move. It was as though the air had hardened around him.

"Wha...?" A small gasp escaped Hanek's lips as he unsuccessfully tried to break free.

Andrei stood up, his gaze intensely focused on Hanek. "What message?"

"A drive. I was reaching for it."

Andrei kept his telekinetic grasp on Hanek as he crossed the room. He opened the front flap of Hanek's jacket and felt around inside the pocket Hanek had reached for, pulling out the small drive. "What's on it?"

"I don't ask questions."

The other man gave a satisfied nod. "You came here only for this?"

"I do as I'm told."

Andrei scoffed and shook his head. "Stars, I wish there were more of you. Pyra out there," he indicated his own assistant, "can barely walk across the room without tripping."

"I'm sure he has other redeeming qualities."

"Enough that I tolerate him. His mind is unreadable; I wish I had more like him to choose from."

"He's a null?"

Andrei tilted his head. "You've never met one before?"

"I'd only ever heard rumors about them. I didn't know for certain that they were real."

"The council wasn't pleased when I brought him on, but I have my own reasons. My mother understands."

"I'm sure." However, Hanek was skeptical about the council tolerating any amount of secrecy. Their associates had delved into Hanek's mind on more than one occasion to verify his assertions—an unpleasant experience he wasn't eager to repeat. Having Pyra's natural imperviousness to telepathy would have saved him a number of literal headaches.

Andrei reached into an inner jacket pocket and pulled out a small vial filled with a white mist. "This work we're doing is going to change the Taran Empire," he said, holding the vial between his thumb and forefinger. "It's going to change Tarans."

"A fallible species in need of improvement."

"So much wasted potential." He gazed at the vial. "We will succeed where others failed."

Hanek shifted on his feet, growing uncomfortable. The odd detachment of the Commander's demeanor set him on edge.

Andrei held the vial up to his nose and cracked the lid. He breathed in a long draught of the mist. His eyes seemed to grow brighter and he straightened his posture, as though energized.

What's in that vial? Hanek was aware that some of the Coalition's funding came from drug sales, but every successful dealer knew better than to sample the merchandise. It was disconcerting to think that this man in charge of so many critical Coalition operations might be under the influence— though Hanek was unfamiliar with any drug matching that design.

The other man got a contented smile. "We're on the cusp. I can almost see over the horizon."

Hanek nodded, uncertain how to respond. "I should probably get back." He glanced toward the door. "Is there anything you would like me to relay to Magdalena or the council?"

"Yes, tell my mother we—"

A sudden jolt rocked the station.

"The fok?" Andrei swiped his desktop, bringing up a status report.

A station schematic appeared, with incident warnings flashing in red. There appeared to be multiple impacts.

"Are we under attack?" Hanek asked, concern creeping into his tone.

"It's not possible." Andrei flipped through the reports.

Hanek followed along, looking for any indication of which ship was firing and how it may have gotten there. The location should have made the facility impervious to enemy attack.

"Fok! It turned against us. How?" Andrei smashed his fist against the console.

Hanek caught on to what he had noticed. The attacking ship was the same one that had been docked in the bay when he'd arrived. How it had departed and turned its guns on the station in that short a time was a mystery.

He took a step toward the door then hesitated. "Should I…?"

"Go. I'll handle this," Andrei stated, his expression now grim with a fire in his eyes.

"Thank you, sir."

"Oh, and the message. Tell my mother we're on schedule."

Hanek nodded. "I will." It seemed to him like this attack had the potential to throw off whatever schedule that may be, but that was way above his paygrade.

— — —

Mika had dreamed of finding his mother alive, envisioning a joyous reunion of running toward each other, arms outstretched for an embrace. But this… nothing could have prepared him for this.

He gazed at her still form within a stasis chamber, her pale skin and closed eyes making her look more dead than asleep.

I'm so sorry, Mom. Tears stung his eyes.

He had gone to Red Ghost with Kali and the band with the hope of finding answers, but he hated where that truth had led. The planet itself was a cover for this secret space station, hidden in a fixed subspace position near the planet's moon. When they'd arrived, Mika had found that it contained his worst nightmare. Several dozen of the missing women—the innocents he'd helped Tregaren collect—were here in stasis alongside his mother, and they were all connected via what looked like a giant capacitor at the center of the room. It didn't make any sense how or why they'd ended up here.

What were they doing here? Mika's stomach turned over, threatening to empty his last meal on the metal floor grating.

He'd been a part of this atrocity, however unwittingly and beyond his control.

I hope they didn't suffer. They were in stasis, not dead. This wasn't over. He placed his hand on the window of her stasis chamber. *I haven't lost her yet.*

A shudder rocked the station as it was struck by an exterior blast.

Mika looked up through a transparent dome on the ceiling to see his precious *Sepiantia* fly by. His skin crawled, knowing it was presently being flown by a stranger.

"Herja won't let us down," Kali said, sensing his concern.

"I hope you're right." He didn't understand how Kali could put so much faith in someone she'd just met. A chance encounter on Red Ghost and aligned goals of infiltrating Spadrosi Station made for a tenuous alliance. The woman was by all accounts a pirate, for stars' sake, and here she was in control of his ship.

Nonetheless, Kali had sent Herja out of the pod room to create a diversion, and she'd come through. Though Mika didn't see how undocking the ship, their only way off the station, would ultimately improve their chances, the blasts from the *Sepiantia* did seem to be slowing the soldiers outside the pod room's doors. In that sense, the distraction was working—for now.

"Focus," Kali said in Mika's mind.

He didn't know why she could make him feel so at ease, but he needed that calming influence right now. He needed to be strong for his mother and the other captives. This was a chance to set things right and help them get to safety.

"We're trapped," Mika whispered. "How do we get them out?"

The room was at the dead-end of a corridor in the heart of the station, and armed guards were banging at the door. Even if those soldiers suddenly disappeared, there was still no direct way to get back to the *Sepiantia* since it was now being flown by someone—a suspected pirate, no less—he barely knew. Worse, the wake sequence on the stasis pods was progressing slowly, and it was unclear when the occupants might be able to move. There was no way he and Kali could relocate the pods without disconnecting the power.

"We're going to be fine," Kali said.

He shook his head. "We shouldn't have come here alone."

"I don't disagree, but I also didn't expect to end up at a secret subspace base after playing our set."

The entire mission had gone so spectacularly sideways, Mika couldn't even be sure where it had started to go wrong. All that he knew was he'd accomplished his objective to find his mother, and now he might not be able to get her to safety.

Emotion welled in his chest, all the anger and bitterness for the awful manipulation that had led him here. Everyone in the room had been a victim in one way or another. Mika knew helping to fight back against the Coalition was the only way he could find some semblance of peace, but he didn't know how.

"I've failed—"

"Don't do that, Mika," Kali cut in. "We found your mom

and the rest of them. That's what matters."

He nodded, though he wasn't sure he believed any of them stood a chance.

"I need you to trust me," she added in his mind.

He met her gaze. There was determination in her eyes. The same warmth he'd sensed in her before came back full-force. For some reason, he *did* trust her. The chaos around them faded away, and there was only her.

"We're going to get out of here," she said, *"and we're going to save your mom and these other women."*

Mika nodded, feeling a new sense of calm and purpose. *"What do you need me to do?"*

"Link with me," she said. *"You're stronger than you know. We're going to fight our way out of here."*

She opened her mind to him, and he took the telepathic tether she offered. Energy surged through him—not the dark power he'd experienced with Tregaren, but a bright and hopeful light.

"What can we do?" he asked. *"There's no way out."*

"Help will be here soon. We just have to hold on."

More blasts rocked the station. The transparent dome overhead was beginning to crack. Whatever escape Kali had in mind didn't seem possible.

"We can do this together," she said in his mind.

He embraced her power, allowing it to flow through him. They were stronger together. Maybe, just maybe, it would be enough.

— — —

As soon as Hanek exited Andrei's office, Pyra rushed forward. "You need to get to your ship," he urged.

"Already the plan." Hanek sprinted down the hall. After a few strides, he was cursing that he hadn't spent more than the minimum necessary time in the gym.

Sounds of blasterfire sounded from down the corridor. He ran as fast as his legs would carry him, grateful he'd paid attention to the path on his way in.

He rounded a corner and was knocked to the side. His hearing was overtaken by a high-pitched whine and his vision went dark at the edges. To his surprise, he realized he was kneeling on the floor, his shoulder resting against the far wall. The once pristine white corridor around him was now tinged with black smudges. Muffled shouts sounded around him, distorted by his own dimmed senses.

Hanek placed a hand against the side of his head, working his jaw to clear his ears. It didn't help.

The voices started to take on discernable meaning.

"Get to the pod chamber!" someone was saying.

"Secure the bay!" another shouted.

The shuttle bay, shite! Hanek scrambled to his feet. His legs were unsteady under him and he felt nauseated. There wasn't time to worry about a concussion; he needed to get off the station before it was locked down.

With a sickening clench of his stomach, he realized that leaving would mean going through the center of the firefight. He hesitated. Waiting it out on the station was a possibility, but that option meant he would be thoroughly, truly trapped. Not only was he on a spatial structure, but being suspended in subspace meant a conventional ship couldn't access it. He estimated his chances were better if he got out now.

Assuming my ride hasn't left without me, he realized with a new wave of concern.

He forced his legs to work, picking up speed as he resumed

running down the hall.

Armed guards raced toward him from the opposite direction.

"Identify yourself!" one demanded, pointing his rifle at Hanek.

"Hanek Eldwan, assistant to Magdalena Steyn. I was here to—"

"He's fine. Move," one of the other guards said, and they raced past.

Whoever they were after, they must have had a description. *Traitors from that ship,* he estimated. Whatever had transpired, they were concerns for another time.

At last, he reached the security checkpoint at the bay. The guards had positioned to face both inward and outward, which Hanek found confusing. *If they turned the ship on the base, then why would there be a threat from within?*

He held up his hands as he approached and restated his name and credentials.

"I remember," the guard acknowledged. "It's a mess out there. You're going to have a bomaxed time trying to leave."

"I'll take my chances." Hanek raced past him, heading toward the docking location of his transport shuttle. His legs and lungs burned from the prolonged exertion, making the pounding in his head worse.

To his relief, the vessel was still there when he arrived. However, the pilot was anxiously tapping his armrest. He let out a relieved sigh when Hanek arrived.

"I waited, but—"

Hanek hit the control to reseal the hatch. "What the fok is going on?"

The pilot shook his head. "I don't know. The big ship left in a hurry, and then I think it started firing on us. I have no idea who's on board. They switched the station comms to a private channel as soon as the firing started.

Fok. Hanek strapped into his seat. "I hope you have combat flight experience."

"No…"

"Then I hope you're a quick learner." Hanek hadn't seen real action during his short time in the Guard, but he'd at least been through training for what to expect. Unfortunately, that didn't extend to having a hand on the controls.

The pilot gulped as he disengaged the docking clamps.

Slowly, the shuttle drifted away from the gangway, then began moving up the access shaft.

Hanek's fingers curled around his armrests as the ship exited the station and the surrounding area came into view. Dark marks marred the outer plating of the station, and bits of scrap floated nearby, trapped in the strange artificial gravity well used to allow ships to dock.

The pilot deftly dodged the debris, aided by the onboard AI's calculation of a clear path displayed on the HUD.

Just as it seemed like they were through the worst of it, the attacking ship came into view. Hanek braced.

However, the ship was focused on firing at a specific target, ignoring them—for now.

"Get us out of here!" he urged.

"We need to get to a minimum safe distance for a jump." The pilot had perspiration on his brow, and his hands were trembling on the controls.

"Go faster!"

"I can't. The physics here are—"

He cut off as a blast rocked the ship, though the shields held. It hadn't come from the ugly vessel.

"Was that from the station?" Hanek asked.

The pilot checked the display. "Maybe? There are so many contact points around here from the debris, I can't...." He faded out, focusing on the path ahead.

Hanek studied the information on the HUD for himself. It appeared that the station's defenses had been aiming for a chunk of debris that had been caught in the gravity well and was headed back on a collision course with the structure.

Not firing at *us, at least.* Still, friendly fire was a real possibility in the messy circumstances. They needed to get out fast.

"Almost to minimum safe distance," the pilot reported.

Hanek watched the distance tick down on the projected flight path ahead.

With only three kilometers to go, the large ship ceased firing and started heading right for them.

Shite! Hanek pressed into his seat, as if that would offer any protection. "Jump!"

"Almost there..."

Light swirled around the ship and time appeared to elongate for a moment.

Hanek breathed a sigh of relief as a starscape shone through the ethereal cloud, solidifying into a stable view.

"Sorry, I needed to get us out of there," the pilot babbled.

"Quite alright." Hanek smoothed his hair.

The pilot seemed perturbed by being in regular space, though, to his surprise. Then Hanek realized the issue: they could be traced in normal space, and the proximity to the base might give away its location. Granted, they could have come from anywhere, but the placement wasn't ideal; there were specific protocols for the approach and departure for that reason.

However, his own self-preservation instincts overrode his

concern for the Coalition in this particular case. "Extenuating circumstances," Hanek assured the pilot, though if the Coalition's leadership made a fuss, he'd readily shift all blame to him. "Just get us far away from this mess."

The young man relaxed a little at that.

Hanek focused on the stars ahead. "Once we're clear, take us home."

CHAPTER 15

AN EMERGENCY ALERT chirped on Jason's handheld next to his bed, startling him awake. He lunged over to grab it.

"What is it?" Lexi asked next to him, still half-asleep.

Jason read over the message. To his surprise, it was from Michael. >>There's been an incident at Red Ghost. TSS forces are responding now. Rendezvous in C-1.<<

"There might be something going on with the Coalition. I have to go." He gave Lexi a quick kiss. "I'll let you know if I'm leaving Headquarters."

She sat up. "Is everything okay?"

"I don't know yet." He quickly pulled on his uniform.

It was almost 05:00, so at least he'd gotten almost a full night's rest. He used the trek up to Level 1 to shake off the fog of sleep.

When he arrived at the large conference room next to the High Commander's office, his parents were seated and Michael stood at the head of the table, ready to give a briefing.

"Hi, Jason," Michael greeted.

"Good morning," Jason replied. *Or maybe not so good.*

"We have an unusual situation developing near the planet known as Red Ghost," his mother stated.

The holodisplay at the center of the room activated to show a rendering of the planet. True to its name, it had a reddish hue, reminding Jason somewhat of Mars.

Jason nodded. "I'm familiar with it."

"The TSS has been tracking this planet for some time, though local regulations have limited our monitoring," Michael explained. "We've known it was a criminal hotbed, but thanks to Kali's undercover work, we've just made a discovery that changes our understanding of their business."

The holodisplay shifted to a corporate logo for SPEAR Tec, the company suspected to be an arm of the Coalition based on the equipment identified in the lab on Quel.

A tingle ran up the back of Jason's neck. "SPEAR Tec? They're connected to the missing women?" Jason looked between his parents and the Head of TSS Operations. "And why is this coming from Ops rather than going through the Coalition task force?"

"Because Kali found a SPEAR Tec facility in subspace and called in tactical support, which made it a larger TSS fleet issue."

It took a moment for the words to register. "In subspace? How is that possible?" Jason asked.

Michael shook his head. "They appear to have co-opted an old facility, much like the TSS took over this structure as a base."

Wil ran his fingers through his hair. "How would they even know it was there? Or how to access it?"

"All great questions we'll have a terrible time answering," Michael replied, "but that's not the important bit. They've found those missing women—or about forty of them, anyway."

"Stars! Are they okay?" Jason immediately thought of

Melisa, on Lexi's behalf.

"Most of them, yes. They've all been in stasis. Some of them didn't fare well. I don't have final numbers yet on the survival rate."

"Shite. Okay." Jason exchanged glances with his parents. "I need to get in touch."

"Yes, Andy is expecting your call," Michael said. "Things are still a bit chaotic over there at the moment. The subspace facility was heavily damaged."

"Casualties?" Wil asked.

"No TSS, though Kali's in rough shape."

Jason's heart skipped a beat. "Will she be okay?"

"Yes, just suffering from an ability over-draw and an injured arm. A little rest and she should be fine."

It was rare for Agents to push themselves to their limits, but it was like any other form of exhaustion. Knowing that Kali had a relatively high Course Rank score—an Agent's ability rating, known colloquially as a CR—made it even more surprising that she would have hit a wall; whatever situation had necessitated that kind of exertion must have been intense.

"We have confirmation, then," Saera said slowly. "That the disappearances *are* related to the Coalition, and they have corporate funding."

All of our worst fears. Jason tried to order his thoughts. "Okay, I'll see what I can learn about motives—why they were holding those women in stasis."

"I'm very curious to find out." Wil stood up, and Saera and Jason followed suit. "Thank you, Michael."

"I'll keep you apprised. I've sent backup to support our TSS base on Fureron; they're running point on the Red Ghost cleanup," Michael said.

"Excellent." Wil checked the time on the conference room

viewscreen. "I'm going to go grab breakfast, and then I'll be in my office if you need anything."

"I'm going to see if I can get in touch with Andy. I'll see you later." Jason headed for the door.

He was tempted to share the news with Lexi, but he held off, not knowing the state of the missing women. He didn't want to give her false hope that Melisa was alive if she hadn't survived or wasn't among those discovered in the pods.

Jason went the short distance to his office and closed the door. He pulled up Andy's contact info on the desktop monitor and initiated a vidcall.

An awkwardly angled image of Andy appeared on the screen, bouncing slightly as he walked while on his handheld. "Hi, Jason. I take it Michael shared the news?"

"He did. What's your status?"

"It's a shiteshow, if I'm being honest. Sorry I bypassed you and the task force. We had a ship in a firefight, and things escalated quickly."

"Quite all right. I'm glad everyone is okay."

"Mostly. Kali was totally out when we retrieved her, but the prognosis is good. From what I've gathered so far, she linked with Mika to bolster their abilities and… well, saved the day, to put it bluntly. They were able to keep a shield around the room to protect everyone until we got them out."

"What about the people that were in stasis? Have they been woken up?"

"Yes, working on it." He shook his head incredulously. "I don't know what the fok they were doing with them in there. Near as we can tell, it was some kind of power system. I hate to say it, but it's like they were using them as living batteries."

Jason thought about the research being done on Quel. "More like a conduit, I expect."

"Nasty business."

"Have you apprehended anyone who was in charge?" Only people who'd worked at the facility could likely provide answers about what purpose the women were supposed to serve. That information might hint at the Coalition's larger plan.

"A few middle managers, but no higherups," Andy said. "Of the top dogs, one is dead and it looks like the other got away. We detected traces of a TSD arch."

How do they have that technology? As far as Jason knew, it was restricted within the TSS and the Priesthood's database, which had been handed over to the High Council. It was more evidence that Monsari had a hand in the Coalition's dealings. "I suggest keeping that detail need to know."

"Already done." Andy stepped inside a room and closed the door. "Are you alone?"

"Yes."

"I'm still compiling the list of survivors, but one of the names jumped out. I believe we've found the Melisa who Lexi has been looking for."

Jason's heart lifted. "Is she…?"

"She's still pretty out of it, but she's awake and has confirmed her name."

"Thank you." Jason considered the options. "Can you send the survivors back here to Headquarters? I'd like to interview everyone." Under other circumstances, he would have gone out to the field, but their delicate physical state did make a good case for getting everyone checked out by Medical. The fact that it would be an excuse for Lexi to be reunited with her friend was a bonus.

"Not everyone is conscious," Andy said. "I recommend deferring to the medical field response team's judgment for who's cleared to travel at the moment."

"Of course. Get each person the treatment they need. Whatever resources you require, we'll get them to you."

"Thanks. Oh, and one more thing you should pass onto your dad. Kali was able to speak telepathically with that higherup who died before he passed."

"This is going to be quite the field report, isn't it?"

Andy nodded. "You have no idea. It seems he'd had a change of heart shortly before he was shot. He indicated that SPEAR's plan is to attack key cities in the Outer Colonies—I don't have any more details than that."

Shite, that's all we need. Jason nodded. "Noted."

"All right, I better get back out there. I'll get Melisa and a few others on a transport ship back to Headquarters ASAP."

"Thank you, Andy. Take care."

Jason leaned back in his chair, processing the information. *We found forty missing people, including Lexi's friend… so why don't I feel happier?*

The answer was simple: though this was a victory, they'd also learned that the Coalition's plans were even more elaborate and dire than they'd feared.

Focus on the good. He headed back to his quarters.

Lexi was still in bed when he arrived, though she was awake.

"Hey, what was that about?" she asked him, propping herself up on her elbows.

He sat down next to her. "Lexi, we just got some big news."

She tensed, her eyes searching his to determine if it was good or bad. "What?"

"Some of our field Agents found a hidden facility where about forty women were being held in stasis. We found Melisa."

"Are you serious?" She bolted upright. "Where? I have to go!"

"You can't see her quite yet. Everyone was in pretty rough shape when they were removed from the stasis devices, and they need time to wake up properly, and then she's going to come here to Headquarters."

"Do you know for certain that it's her?"

He nodded. "Yes. She's okay."

Lexi let out a long breath. "Wow." She shook her head. "I can't believe it!"

"You said she was alive. You were right."

"Where was this place she was being held?"

"It's strange—it was hidden in subspace. It must have been an old Aesir base, or possibly something older."

"Shite, I didn't even know you could suspend a structure in subspace."

"It's very difficult to do. I only know of a handful of places like it."

Her brows knitted. "How did a bunch of criminals get access?"

"That is a most excellent question, and we don't know yet," Jason admitted. "Much of it was destroyed in the altercation, so I'm not sure how much we'll be able to learn."

"Do you know what they were doing there?"

He shook his head. "The preliminary reports suggest that they were working on some sort of power system, using the people with abilities as the…" he couldn't think of a nice way to put it, "…fuel source."

"Oh, my stars! That's barbaric."

"Yeah, these are, without a doubt, the worst kind of people."

She wrapped her arms around her legs. "I can't imagine what they've been through…"

"Melisa will be lucky to have you help her through this."

"And what about everyone else?"

"Hopefully we can get them back to their loved ones in short order. The TSS will offer counseling in the interim and placement if they have nowhere to go."

She nodded, her expression turning to grim resolve. "Find the people who are behind this."

"We will. We're getting close."

— — —

"I'm surprised we're not going back to TSS Headquarters again," Mika commented to Kali as they sat together on the *Sepiantia*'s flight deck. It was good to be back on the ship, and he was grateful to have it in one piece after seeing Herja's flying.

"We're needed in the field," Kali replied.

After what had happened on the Spadrosi Station, Mika was certain that they'd lock him up—or at least bombard him with questions for weeks like last time. He'd linked with an Agent rated with a CR of 9, yet she'd passed out from overexertion and he hadn't. Mika had known he was strong, but that…

He tried to put it out of his mind. The important thing was that they'd been able to keep the pod room from decompressing, and that had saved everyone inside. That positive outcome was probably the only reason he was still free.

Nonetheless, the only place he wanted to be right now was at the hospital with his mother, waiting for her to wake up.

"They'll look after her," Kali soothed, picking up on his thoughts.

She had a way of doing that. Never before had he been around someone where he felt that in-tune. It was comforting, but it also scared him a little. He'd found himself relying on her, yet he'd promised himself he wouldn't trust anyone again. *Everyone who gets close to me suffers.*

He focused on the navigation course displayed on the forward viewscreen of the *Sepiantia*'s flight deck.

"Andy will give us our next assignment when we reach Fureron," Kali said. "I think he's starting to trust you."

"And do you?" Mika asked.

She flushed a little, to his surprise. "Getting there."

"I don't want you to get hurt," he blurted out. "Bad things happen to people around me."

"I'm not worried."

He met her gaze, and there was only confidence there. He admired that strength and wished he had more of it in himself. *Maybe I can learn.*

"I'll try not to let you down," Mika said.

She smiled, bringing out her natural beauty. "Just keep being you, and it'll be just fine."

Tentatively, Kali reached across the armrests and took his hand. A subtle electric tingle passed between them. "We may face trouble at every turn, but we can be part of the solution."

It could be wishful thinking, but he believed her.

— — —

I'd almost given up. In her heart, Lexi had believed that Melisa was alive. Even so, the logical part of her brain had told her to not hold out hope. Hope was a path to disappointment, and she'd been let down too many times in her life to risk further heartbreak.

She passed the hours waiting for the transport ship trying to work in her office, not particularly focused but able to make some progress on her latest project.

At last, she got a message from Jason. >>Ship just docked. We're going to conduct interviews on Level 1, floor 2, A wing.<<

Not sure if it was a sanctioned message or a courtesy note between lovers, she waited fifteen minutes and then headed toward the nearest staircase for access between floors on the same Level. If her timing was accurate, she could spot Melisa on her way into the interview room.

Lexi positioned herself outside A wing where it could conceivably look like she was passing through. She wiped her palms on the legs of her uniform, sweating from anxious anticipation.

A couple minutes after she arrived, sounds of a large group of people came from the elevator lobby. Lexi began walking along her planned intercept path.

The group came around the corner. Lexi instantly picked out Melisa from the group, her wavy, red hair and sky-blue eyes recognizable even from a distance. Her heart dropped into her stomach seeing her. She'd intended to play it cool, but her plan evaporated as her emotions took over.

"Oh, my stars!" Lexi ran to her taller friend and wrapped her arms around her. "I didn't know if I'd ever see you again."

"Lexi?" Disbelief filled Melisa's eyes, then confusion. "Wait, how are you here?"

"Sorry, who are you?" one of the Militia soldiers escorting the group of women asked.

Lexi had blocked out everyone else other than Melisa. She quickly gathered herself. "Lexi Karis, head of civilian training." Melisa's eyes widened at that. "This is a dear friend of mine. Could I have a moment with her before you bring her back?"

"It's all right," Jason shouted from down the hall, coming

toward the group. *"Take your time,"* he added in her mind.

"Thank you." Lexi looped her arm around Melisa's and led her toward one of the small conference rooms.

"Sorry, I couldn't wait to see you," Lexi said.

"I don't understand how you're here."

"It's a long story." Lexi closed the conference room door then embraced Melisa again. "I'm so glad you're safe. It's been such a long time… I didn't know what had happened to you."

Melisa returned her hug, but there was distress on her face. "That's going to take a while for me to get used to. What's been almost two years for you only feels like a couple of weeks for me."

"Yeah, a lot has happened. I'll get you caught up, don't worry."

Her friend looked her over. "Wait, your eyes, they're…"

Lexi nodded. "I recently had them restored."

Melisa let out a mirthless chuckle that barely made it past her lips. "I bet you have access to all sorts of things now in the TSS."

"I didn't enlist. It's complicated." Lexi tried to organize the thoughts racing through her mind. "What happened after you got to Duronis?" she asked. "I went looking for you when I didn't hear anything."

"You came after me? They didn't—"

"No," Lexi assured her. "I kept my abilities hidden."

"I wish I'd done the same." She shook her head. "It all happened so fast. I think I was only there for three or four days before they told me I was needed elsewhere."

"What happened then?"

"I went to a meeting, and then I remember being in blackness—some kind of transport box. When it opened up, I saw a lab-looking place, and they put me in a chamber. That was it. I woke up in the chamber, and they told me the current date."

"I'm so sorry, Melisa."

"What are you apologizing for? I went to Duronis on my own. You had nothing to do with what happened to me." She placed her hand on the side of Lexi's face.

When Melisa started to lean in for a kiss, Lexi instead drew her into another hug. She knew the kiss wasn't meant as a romantic gesture, but rather an act of physical comfort. They'd been closer than most friends, brought together by running for their lives and freedom, hiding out in less than hospitable places. Frankly, it was a lot more pleasant to cuddle up with someone in those circumstances rather than to feel completely alone.

Lexi had described the complexity of that relationship to Jason as their own bond had deepened, but trying to explain to Melisa how so much had changed in the last year would be much more difficult. To her friend, mere weeks had passed since they'd last seen each other.

Melisa pulled out from the hug, her eyebrows drawn together. "What's wrong?"

"A lot has happened since you went into stasis."

Melisa's arms dropped to her sides. "You're with someone now, aren't you?"

Lexi nodded. "We've been bonded for a couple of months now."

"Hm."

That's it? That's the only reaction? Lexi thought it best to not pile any more on her friend at the moment. "I'd better get you to that interview. Then, we have a lot of catching up to do."

—   —   —

The pounding in Hanek's head had subsided by the time his transport shuttle made it back to the Coalition base ship. A trip to the infirmary was definitely in order, but checking in with Magdalena was the first priority.

He found her in her office, seated behind her desk. She looked up as he entered, and he was pleased to see she looked genuinely relieved.

"I'm glad you made it back in one piece," she said, examining him. "Though you look like shite."

"I got caught in some crossfire. Or an explosion. I'm not sure what happened."

She shook her head, the glisten of tears welling in her eyes. "Our plan fell apart, that's what."

Hanek came further into the room. "What happened?"

"Marco betrayed us. For his son."

He absorbed the words, trying to infer the meaning. Marco was Andrei's younger brother, who was largely in charge of the drug transport and distribution side of SPEAR. Hanek didn't know much about him, other than Magdalena wished Marco had found a way to be in his son's life so she would have access to her grandchild. "I don't understand," Hanek admitted.

"Marco brought his boy to Spadrosi in some ill-guided attempt to bring him into the family business. He allowed his friends to come—a pirate woman and two others, who turned out to be undercover TSS— and they turned on us. We've lost the station."

Hanek's heart dropped. "But that's where…"

"Yes, the TSS has liberated our captives. All those years of collecting, for nothing." She scoffed, but Hanek saw it was to hide a sob of grief. "Now, Marco is dead, and my grandson has been reunited with his mother. I doubt there's much chance of bringing him in now."

"No, we'll find a way," Hanek said, though he had no idea how. It just seemed like the right thing to say, given her present state.

"Perhaps." She gathered herself. "Were you able to get the message to Andrei?"

How can she focus on business when she's just lost her son? While impressed with her dedication, it was unnerving to see a mother so calm after having just received word about the death of her child, and, apparently, that he betrayed her as his final act. "Yes, I gave it to him. He said to tell you that 'everything is on schedule'. But, that was before the attack on the station."

Magdalena nodded. "Those preparations were independent. Good, then we can still salvage this." She stood and began pacing behind her desk.

"Forgive me if I'm overstepping, but is Andrei okay?"

"Yes, he and his assistant made it off the station using a TSD arch before the TSS seized it."

"Good. What can I do to help?" he asked.

"Gather a report of the TSS' and Guard's known fleet locations in the sector. It's time we go on the offensive."

CHAPTER 16

A VIDEO FEED of the interviews with the rescued women played in the background while Wil tended to the priority messages in his inbox. So far, there hadn't been any revelations on either front, just more clues that didn't seem to lead anywhere.

He was combing through the final messages when a Priority 1 alert flashed on his desk. He snapped to full attention; that designation was reserved for a direct threat to a TSS facility. *What the fok?*

When he opened the report details, his eyes went wide with horror. There'd been a bombing at the TSS' Antaris base—the site recently dedicated to the civilian training initiative. His heart dropped. *No...*

A moment later, Michael ran into his office.

Wil met his friend's frantic eyes as he approached the High Commander's desk. "What happened?"

"Information is still coming in," Michael replied. "We don't have a casualty report yet, but there's definitely structural damage to the base."

Civilian attacks were an unfortunate reality in times of civil unrest, but aside from Alkeer, Wil couldn't remember a single instance of a TSS facility being attacked since the end of the Bakzen War thirty years prior. There was no doubt in his mind that this was the Coalition's doing.

Anger and concern roiled within him, but he didn't allow the emotions to consume him. He took a deep breath to help focus. *If they want a fight, that's what they're going to get.*

"Civilian and personnel safety are the top priorities," Wil instructed. "If the structure is compromised, get everyone out."

Michael consulted his tablet. "The base commander has requested medical support and any people we can send to assist. The place looks like it's been through a battle."

A recorded video popped up on Wil's desktop, showing a smoldering building with a section blown out of its side. Rubble littered the sidewalk and street below, and people were running around frantically. Agents and Militia personnel were helping the injured away from the structure and creating a perimeter around the building.

Wil's stomach turned over at the sight. They'd never lost people in a terrorist attack. Every member of the TSS was prepared to die in battle, but an unprovoked attack on a base like this was a horror he'd never expected to encounter in his career.

First Alkeer, and now this. Our own people are turning against us.

There was a time not so long ago that Agents were admired—and perhaps a little feared. Never would someone dare take violent action against them in such a way as this attack. The Empire was fracturing, with people turning against one another in a way the civilization hadn't seen for a millennium. Worse, they had powerful external adversaries that should be their focus.

Get through this. One problem at a time. Wil took another centering breath. "Michael, send every available field Agent in the vicinity to assist. Get people to safety and secure the area. As soon as possible, I want an evaluation of who did this and by what means."

Michael nodded. Telepathically, he asked, *"This was the Coalition, wasn't it?"*

"Likely, but I want confirmation before we start throwing around accusations outside of Headquarters."

"I'm on it," Michael continued aloud. "I'll keep you apprised." With another nod to Wil, he left the office.

Shite. Wil shook his head. *We need to get this situation under control.*

He sent a message to Jason: >>There's been a Priority 1 development. Come to my office.<<

— — —

Jason rose from the interview table. "Please, excuse me. I have to attend to something."

Darika watched him go, confusion written on her face. Jason felt bad leaving in the middle of her story about her capture by SPEAR, but a Priority 1 development and summons from the High Commander overrode any other task.

He headed straight for his father's office. Inside, Wil was reviewing footage of a planetside explosion on the holoprojector.

"Stars! Where's that?" Jason exclaimed.

"The TSS' Antaris base." His father's tone had the flat affect he took on when in focused command mode, dealing with something too awful to allow emotion to take hold.

Jason's heart dropped into his stomach with the news, but

he forced himself into the same, semi-detached mindset to objectively handle the situation. "What happened?"

"Bombing, as far as we can tell. SPEAR just released a statement taking credit—so, Coalition."

"Shite." Jason watched the video more closely, noting the extensive structural damage. "How many were hurt?"

"A least a couple dozen dead. Well over a hundred injured. I don't know yet how many were civilian trainees versus TSS personnel."

"Just when I think these fokers can't stoop any lower."

"If I can find one positive in this tragedy, it's that now we can react with impunity. There's no longer any question of cause or jurisdiction."

"I'm all for that. How do we proceed?" Jason asked.

"First, we need to secure the area and tend to the wounded."

"Do you want me to head out there?"

"No, I need you and your team working on a strategy for how to hit all known SPEAR Tec assets in one go to take them out."

"That's just one arm of the Coalition," Jason pointed out.

"A limb is a limb. We have to respond with extreme force. Anything less might embolden them further."

"Okay. What about Antaris?"

"Andy is coordinating emergency support from Fureron. Resources are thin out there after the other incident at Red Ghost, but between Andy's team and the outposts on Orilan, Crydael, and Aldria, I think they have it handled."

"All right, I'll get my team on it, then." He massaged his eyes. "I don't think I'm ever going to get used to the part of this job where dozens of people die and we spin it into a positive."

"That's one of the reasons not everyone is cut out for this

line of work. We have to stare down the worst evils of our kind."

"And they never seem to go away."

Wil shook his head morosely. "No, they don't."

Jason stood up. "Send information my way as you get it."

"You'll be the first to know." He paused. "And thank you, Jason."

"Happy to be of service." Jason left the office feeling anything but happy, but he appreciated the acknowledgment. Given the sensitive nature of their work, it was an asset to have the trust in his family to fall back on.

Before going to the task force command center, he stopped by his office to check in with Lexi. He called her handheld, and to his relief she picked up.

"Hey, I had to duck out of the interviews early," he said.

"Did something happen?"

"There's been an attack on the Antaris base."

She paled. "What?"

"I'm sure you'll get looped in soon, but keep it to yourself for now. I don't have any details yet."

"Was it bad?"

"Looks like it. Some kind of bomb."

"Oh, my stars…" She took a steadying breath. "Coalition?"

"Yeah, SPEAR."

"Shite."

"I expect this is going to keep me very busy for the foreseeable future."

"And me, as well, given the training initiative was based on Antaris."

He combed his fingers through his hair. "I don't know what this is going to mean for the program."

She nodded. "Yeah, we'll see."

"I love you. I'll see you as soon as I can."

"Love you, too."

He ended the vidcall and slipped his handheld back into his pocket. *Having someone to share the difficult times with makes all the difference.*

The task force office was abuzz with activity when he arrived. Everyone who'd been on reduced hours were now back in full force.

"What do we know?" Jason asked as he entered.

"Still compiling data," Laura reported.

"Reviewing the security surveillance from the area now," Zak chimed in. "There's a lot to go through."

The monitors around the office were filled with footage from various angles, both from surrounding establishments and the TSS' own internal recording devices. The various shots each invariably ended with a massive fireball erupting from the TSS facility, followed by a portion of the building collapsing. While the rest of the structure was standing for now, pieces kept falling off and it didn't look stable.

"Have we been able to determine if it was a suicide bomber or a planted device?" Jason asked.

Laura glided in her chair across to her other workstation. "Preliminary analysis is coming back as a remote detonation. I've put in a request to VComm to pull the local network traffic. We might get lucky and be able to triangulate the signal to a point of origin."

Jason sat down at one of the empty workstations. "The question is, how did they get it inside?"

"That part's easy," Zak replied. "One of the students."

His heart dropped. *One of the civilian trainees was working undercover for the Coalition?* With an even worse clench of his gut, he realized that it might not have been just one.

There was supposed to have been extensive screening for personality and mental stability for the incoming students, but ultimately, a determined enough person could fake an answer. TSS code of conduct prevented invasive mindreading without cause, so all a person would have to do is verbally answer correctly and they wouldn't draw suspicion.

"Okay, I'm going to go over the student profiles and cross-reference those with the casualty and survivor field reports. If we can find the perpetrator, maybe we can track this back to the source." He got to work.

— — —

From the moment Mika learned of the attack on Antaris, he knew that's where they needed to go. Fortunately, Kali had backed him up on the request, and Andy was so desperate for help that he'd agreed.

I helped the monsters in the Coalition hurt innocents, and I need to do everything I can for the survivors. The thought kept him going, even though he was utterly exhausted. He strained under the telekinetic exertion of holding the failing TSS structure together with Kali.

At the time they'd volunteered to help, Mika didn't realize what kind of mess they'd be walking into. It'd only been a short hop from Fureron to Antaris, and they hadn't arrived with a moment to spare. Not everyone had made it out from the building yet, and they'd needed to immediately extend telekinetic structural support to keep it from collapsing entirely.

The two of them were linked, combining their abilities to become more than their individual strengths. Together, they'd managed to keep the building standing while the rescue teams completed their work. The once majestic structure was located near the middle of a city to signify a union between the TSS and the civilian population. Of all the places, it made sense the Coalition would target this one.

"I can't hold it much longer," Mika said in Kali's mind.

"Almost there."

They held on for five more agonizing minutes. Mika's legs trembled and his head felt like it was about to explode.

Finally, the last of the survivors ran out from the Antaris base, covered in soot and coughing. One of the supervising Agents flashed an 'all clear' to them.

"Ready… release," Kali instructed.

Mika let go of his hold on the building, and the pressure in his head immediately diminished.

The concrete and steel settled with a cloud of dust. For a moment, he thought their efforts had been unnecessary. Then, the structure began to crumble. Small chunks gave way to larger sections, and soon the western wing of the building was nothing more than a pile of rubble.

Kali stared at it, smudges of dirt and soot streaking her face. "I'm starting to think that disaster follows us."

"Me, maybe." Mika shook his head.

"Thank you," an Agent said, walking up to them. "I don't know how you held it up for that long, but you saved a lot of people's lives today."

"I'm glad we could get here in time," Kali said.

"It would have been a lot worse without your backup, that's for sure," the Agent said. He looked over Mika, not hiding his confusion about how a non-Agent was involved in the operation.

"It's a long story," Kali said with a dismissive wave of her hand.

Someone shouted, and the Agent ran off to help.

"We do make a great team," Mika said.

"Yeah, we do." Kali brushed off her dirty hands. "We really do keep finding ourselves in the middle of trouble, don't we?"

He laughed. "Yeah. But there's no one else I'd rather be in it with."

— — —

"Oh, my stars." Raena took in a video of the devastated TSS base on Antaris.

Next to her, Ryan shook his head, pained and disgusted. "They're clearly sending a message that civilians shouldn't associate with the TSS. This was a warning."

"It's making them look like monsters. No one can see this and think they're the 'good guys'!"

"Don't be so sure. There are still plenty of people who take issue with Gifted."

As much as Raena wanted to refute the statement, she knew it was true. Bigotry took many forms—finding ways to ostracize 'others' and punish their allies. She wasn't convinced that the Coalition was motivated by those ideals, but they were opportunists willing to play up any potential divide in order to turn citizens against each other.

Am I any better, thinking about this as an opportunity? Her first reaction to the news had been concern and anguish, but the second was the thought that rendering aid would be a good PR move for her and Ryan. She hated that such thoughts even crossed her mind, but with the city-ship idea dead, she needed something else.

"We have to help," she said.

"No doubt," Ryan agreed. "I'll have my staff put together—"

"That can be part of it, but I think this would benefit from a personal touch," she continued. "I'd like to go there."

"That might not be safe."

"I'm not concerned. What's important now is showing that we're there for our people. Sometimes you need to see the awful things up close to understand how to deal with them."

Ryan studied her. "I don't like the idea of using tragedy for political gain."

"That's the nature of politics, no matter how much we try to rally against it. Either we can join them and work every day to be leaders worthy of our positions, or we can be beaten down a little every day until nothing remains."

"I don't think our prospects are that dire."

Raena rested her hands on his desk and leaned forward. "It's easy to tell ourselves that, hoping things will get better. But it's better to recognize now that the wolves are circling. We're the young calf whose mother is just far enough away that there might be time for a deadly strike. Do we run to the safety of the herd, or do we stand on a little hill of righteousness under the delusion it will offer us the protection of high ground?"

He looked down. "I don't know what I'd do if anything happened to you out there."

"I'll be fine. Please, let me do this for us."

"Okay. I love you, and I love that you're always looking for a way to make things better."

She took his hand. "How we look after each other is what keeps our race going."

"Some people would do well to remember that."

"So, we'll do our part to remind them."

CHAPTER 17

LEXI KEPT CHECKING her handheld for new messages, even though the Agent conducting the interviews had promised Lexi that she'd let her know the moment Melisa had finished her debriefing.

Though there was no rational reason for the feeling, she'd been less anxious when Jason was leading the interviews. She understood why he'd needed to hand off the task to someone else, but she couldn't help feeling protective of her friend and the others who'd been through an awful trauma. Since Jason had helped her through her own trying times, she trusted him, while she'd never met this other Agent before.

Her handheld finally chirped with an incoming text message.

About bomaxed time! She checked the device, confirming that it was the notification she'd been waiting for. Apparently, Melisa was going to be assigned quarters on Level 7, in the Militia area, and Lexi could meet her there.

She grabbed her jacket from the back of her office chair and hurried toward the elevator.

So much had changed since she'd last seen Melisa, she didn't know how to begin to explain. Every time she took a step back, she couldn't believe her own life—how was someone else supposed to?

Melisa's background had been so much like hers when they met, marred by being on the run and alone, unable to trust other people. They'd found that connection with each other, and Lexi had learned how to let someone in again, after being betrayed by her mentor. Without that relationship, she might not have been open to seeing what kind of a life she could have with Jason.

What do I tell her about that? Her head spun.

She decided to just see how the conversation flowed. It would come out one way or another.

Melisa's housing was in a block typically reserved for visiting officers from other branches of the Taran military. Though not exactly guest suites, and not as nice as Agent quarters, it would make for a comfortable enough place to recuperate.

Lexi hit the buzzer for the room she'd been told was assigned to Melisa, but there was no answer. *Might not be here yet.*

She paced outside the door, waiting. Three minutes later, she saw her friend coming down the hall.

Melisa got a big smile when she saw her waiting. "Hey!"

"Hi. How'd it go?"

She shrugged. "I don't think the questions will ever end, and I don't have any of the answers."

"You never know what tiny detail might make the difference."

Melisa placed her palm on the biometric lock next to the door, and the bolt clicked open. "That's the only reason I'm playing along."

Lexi followed her inside. "There are good people here."

Her friend eyed her. "*You're* speaking nicely about Taran authorities? A lot *has* changed."

"I…" She searched for the words. "I was accepted here in a way I haven't been anywhere else. They might surprise you."

"And now you're working with them officially? Head of Civilian Training, was it?"

"Yes, it's a new thing." Her chest constricted as she thought of Antaris.

Melisa plopped down on the couch. "How did you go from following me to Duronis to working for the TSS?"

"I'm not sure if now is the right time to get into all the details," Lexi said as she sat down next to her.

"No." Melisa shook her head. "I've already lost more than a year. I want to start getting caught up."

"I…" Lexi dropped her eyes. "I don't know where to start."

Her friend smiled. "Pick a spot! I'll take anything to start feeling normal again."

"Well, in terms of what I'm doing with the TSS, they've been wanting to start up a program for civilians looking to tap into their abilities. Since I have significant training but was never in military service, I was a good fit."

"That's awesome!" Melisa scrunched up her face. "But *how* did you get that position?"

"That's a longer story."

"I have nothing but time."

She started off with the basics. "I met an Agent who gave me a reason to stay here at TSS Headquarters."

Melisa perked up with interest. "And you said you've bonded?"

"Yeah." She shook her head. "We had a resonance

connection, if you can believe it."

"Shite, really? Wow."

"It's been pretty surreal."

"So, who's this lucky Agent?"

"That's where things get pretty wild. Color me shocked when I found out his name is Jason Sietinen."

Melisa did a double-take. "Hold on… what? You're joking."

"Like I said, a lot has changed."

"I… don't even know what to say to that."

"I'm sure you'll meet him soon. He was supposed to do your interview, actually, but he got pulled into something else. He's heading up the investigation into the Coalition."

"Yeah, and the Sietinen Dynasty, and SiNavTech—"

"No, he's very much TSS. His sister is the politician."

"Maybe the drugs from my time in stasis haven't worn off completely."

"I know, me, of all people, talking about Taran politics like it's a casual thing. I barely recognize my life."

"What else have I missed?"

"The Empire is on the brink of civil war. Oh, and we've been semi-invaded by transdimensional aliens with the power to un-make a planet in seconds."

"Maybe I should go back into stasis."

"Some days, it does sound pretty tempting to sleep through this and wake up when everything is back to normal… not that I know what 'normal' is anymore."

"Shite, Lex. How the fok did we end up here?"

Lexi grinned. "Pretty sure I just told you."

"I'm not convinced I've woken up yet."

"Neither am I, but it's a pretty nice dream so I'm going along for the ride."

Melisa smiled. "You seem happy."

"I am." She shrugged. "What can I say? I feel at home for the first time… possibly ever. I never would have thought it would be in a place like this, or who I'm with, but life is weird sometimes."

"I'll say. Does that mean your legal issues are behind you now?"

Lexi nodded. "I was offered a blanket immunity deal, so I'm free and clear."

"Shite, that must be a relief."

"Yeah, though I've been… detached from it. I keep thinking I'm living someone else's life."

Melisa examined her. "You always wanted a fresh start."

"I did, and I got it." She paused. "In some ways, though, my old life was never really what I thought it was. I've learned some pretty crazy things about Cytera since I've been here."

"Oh, yeah?"

"Turns out some of the head families were Taran nobles."

Melisa shook her head, sending waves of her red hair wildly around her shoulders. "I guess I shouldn't be surprised. Does that mean that you have highborn blood in you?"

"Not enough to count, and none of the families that are currently relevant on the galactic stage."

Melisa eyed her. "I didn't think High Dynasty heirs were allowed to consort with commoners."

"Well, the Sietinens aren't stuffy assholes. Jason's mom was raised on Earth, as were he and his sister. His dad has spent his entire life in the TSS and has no taste for Taran politics."

"His dad—the incredibly famous Wil Sietinen."

Lexi laughed. "Oh, my stars! I was ambushed for a family dinner, like, two days after Jason and I met. It may have been the weirdest hour of my life."

"You are far braver than I."

"Bravery has little to do with it." Lexi shifted on the couch. "I dunno, I guess this whole thing has made me realize that we're overly preoccupied with social strata and have lost sight of treating those around us as people. I haven't had direct interaction with the transdimensional aliens, but Jason has, and what he's told me has really put things in perspective."

"Wait, you were serious about that alien invasion?"

"Yeah… sorry."

"Fok! Are you sure I haven't been out for longer?"

"It's been a doozie of a year."

"Shite, you're right about that." She let out a long breath through pursed lips. "I'll probably spend the next week just watching news clips and reading headlines."

"That should get you caught up pretty well."

"I don't know if anything ever will. I'll always be missing that year, you know?"

Lexi turned somber. "I'm so sorry that happened to you."

Melisa shrugged and flashed a half-hearted smile. "I made it out alive, so it could have been worse."

"Very true." Lexi had learned that nine women hadn't survived the wake-up from stasis. Reports indicated the pods were old and ill-maintained, so it was fortunate more people hadn't perished.

"I have no clue where to go from here. Obviously, that plan to join the Alliance didn't pan out."

"You know…" Lexi began slowly. "There is this new civilian training program for Gifted people, and I happen to know the person in charge."

Melisa laughed. "I dunno…"

"Come on! You were always lamenting that you didn't know more about your abilities. This could be a great chance."

"Then what? I pick up new skills and…?"

"Maybe work as an instructor, or you can figure out something else. The program isn't only about learning how to use your Gifts but how to be more confident in yourself."

"This is sounding a lot like a self-help workshop."

"It is *not*. And watch what you say, because I designed the curriculum."

Melisa raised an eyebrow. "All right, I'll think about it."

"Good. Now, how about I give you a tour of Headquarters?"

—   —   —

The attack on Antaris hit Wil personally—not only as TSS High Commander, but because the TSS was a family. *His* family. Everyone hurt and injured in the assault were his people.

Nothing about it was okay. Security had failed. Screening measures had failed. The local response had been abysmal. Frankly, if help hadn't arrived from other TSS bases, the casualties would have been much higher. Even that was in large part to Kali and Mika, though the specifics of their intervention were sketchy. All in all, he had more questions than answers, and the worries were stacking up.

He'd been swamped in work reviewing security upgrade strategies and revised response plans for other facilities based on what had happened. While he endorsed the policy of continuous improvement and immediately incorporating lessons learned, reliving a tragedy over and over again through those analyses grated on his emotional scars from the war. He'd learned to manage those past traumas, but times like this tested those coping skills.

He pushed back from his desk with a sigh, rubbing his eyes. Long, stressful days were ahead.

A chime at the door brought his attention back to the present. "Come in."

To his surprise, Kira entered. "Hi, sir, I hope a drop-in is okay."

"As long as you're not bringing more bad news, I'm always happy to see a friendly face." He ventured a smile.

She returned it. "No news, but an offer."

"I'm intrigued." He motioned for her to sit in the visitor chairs across from him.

"I've been following the reports," she began as she settled in, no doubt referring to Red Ghost and Antaris. "I know the TUF is still in a fledgling state, but we do have a few response teams in place. I wanted to offer our resources, however limited at this stage, to support the apprehension of the Coalition's leadership."

"In other words, you've caught the scent of a field assignment to your liking."

She shrugged playfully. "Seems you have me figured out pretty well."

"There's a reason I picked you for your position." He steepled his fingers. "Do you have anything in particular in mind?"

"For starters, I'd like to offer a TUF support team to assist with search and recovery out of the Fureron base."

"That would be wonderful," Wil agreed. "It's a perfect opportunity for the public to see Enforcers and TSS working together under a shared banner."

"My thoughts exactly. Secondly, I was thinking that it might be helpful to send the genetic information about the captured women to Leon to see if there are any shared traits.

Why were those *particular* Gifted people taken over others?"

"Good thought." Wil entered several commands on his desktop to grant Kira's fiancé access to the files so he could review them from the perspective of a genetics specialist; Leon had already helped out the TSS with similar projects, and Wil was grateful to have him heading up the TUF's new research division. "Done."

Kira leaned forward. "There's one more thing. When Jason finds who's responsible and goes to take them out, I'd like to be on the field team."

"I can't promise that."

She nodded. "Then consider this a formal request for consideration."

"You have my permission to let Jason know you're interested. The decision will ultimately be his."

"Okay. Thank you, sir."

"We're glad to have you working with us."

She smiled. "I loved my time in the Guard, don't get me wrong, but it's been very easy settling in here. I'm happy for the change."

"Good to hear it's working out."

"It definitely is." She stood. "I won't keep you; I know you're busy. I'll coordinate deployment of the support team with Ops."

"Thank you, Kira. And I look forward to hearing if Leon finds anything of interest in the data."

"Me too. I'll be in touch soon."

CHAPTER 18

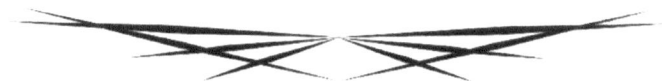

THIS IS WHY *I don't get close to people.* Mika paced across the flight deck of the *Vanguard,* willing the ship to get to the planet Glaendor faster. He'd just gotten word that SPEAR was planning a demonstration on the planet, and his friends in the band were planetside. Now it was a race to get to them in time, both for his friends and to stop whatever the Coalition was planning to do via SPEAR.

Mika would have rather been on the *Sepiantia,* but it was deemed too large and noticeable for the mission. He and Kali were supposed to slip in undetected, rather than a mass of TSS Agents storming the planet. Whatever was going on, it would be up to the two of them to intervene.

He'd feel a lot better about the situation if the band was already somewhere safe. He wasn't sure when he'd started to care about them so much; perhaps it was his deepening relationship with Kali that had helped bring down the walls protecting his emotions.

Mika looked over at Kali, seated on a ledge in front of the forward viewport, and felt concern he'd never expected to experience for another person. She was putting her career in the TSS on the line for him by insisting they be trusted with this mission—not because she thought she was the best for the job, but because Mika wanted to go, and this was the only way they could get there and ensure the band was able to safely get offworld. No one else in the TSS would give a second thought about the band over any other civilians. Kali would, and that meant everything to him.

She met his gaze, sending a spark through him. That connection that had formed between them when they'd linked on Spadrosi Station had continued to strengthen. He could feel her thoughts and emotions—and it astounded him that she had the same attraction and affection toward him that he'd developed toward her.

I'm not worthy of being loved by someone like her. He turned away.

"Mika, you can't keep pretending you don't care," Kali said, breaking the silence.

"Care about what?"

"Anyone."

He didn't know how to respond, so he just stared out the viewport.

"I've seen the change in you," she continued. "The hurt you feel from what Tregaren did to you will always be there. I'll never completely move past what the Priesthood did to me, either. But, it's all experience. The 'good' or 'bad' of it is in our minds. We can learn and grow from those awful things; they don't need to weigh us down. And I see that shift happening for you. With how you feel about the band... and me."

He turned to meet her gaze then. Her brilliant hazel eyes called to him, one look saying more than an entire conversation. Against all logic and reason, it was plainly there for him to see—love.

"Kali—"

"Healing doesn't happen alone. Maybe what we've both been needing is a fellow wayward soul to remind us why life is worth living—because of the connections we can form with others, however unlikely."

He swallowed. "I'd only hold you back."

"No, you've shown me why it's important to keep moving forward."

His heart warmed at that. There was too much on his mind right now to think through if a happily ever after might be possible for them, but knowing there was a chance… that made it all the more important to make it through the mission on Glaendor in one piece.

"I never thought I could be happy. You've changed that, Kali," Mika said softly.

She gave him a coy smile. "Good to know."

They fell silent again, enjoying the view of subspace outside. The mission came first, for both of them. But whatever they were about to face, they'd do it together.

— — —

As Raena's transport shuttle arrived at the port near the Antaris base, it occurred to her that she hadn't left Tararia in close to a year. There was a time not long ago when the notion of traveling between worlds across the galaxy would have seemed like fantasy, and now staying confined to a single planet for months on end made her feel like she was practically a shut-in.

This journey was a worthy reason to venture out. Even from a distance, through the shuttle window on the final approach, she could make out the devastation of where the Antaris base had been blown open. A large portion of the structure had collapsed, and the surrounding area had been sectioned off with security fencing.

When she'd made her plans to visit, the local authorities and TSS representatives had been firm in their stance that she couldn't visit the site itself. However, the reason for her visit was to connect with the locals and survivors, so spending time at one of the relief shelters was her priority.

"Would you like to go over the lines again, my lady?" Jovan asked from the seat across the aisle from her. He'd insisted on coming along, despite her protests, as a representative for the public relation's team. As part of his role in that capacity, he'd had Raena memorize a prepared speech for her arrival at the shelter.

What Raena hadn't told him was that she had no intention of sticking to the script. It was stuffy and insincere, as prepared statements often were. She'd played along in the rehearsals to appease him, but she'd say whatever felt right in the moment.

The shuttle landed, and the two of them deboarded. A group of local officials approached to greet her as she came down the ramp.

"My lady, you honor us," an older man with gray hair and a thin beard welcomed, taking a step forward and giving a slight bow.

"My condolences for your losses and the impacts of this tragedy on your community," Raena replied, bowing her head. That part of the script was acceptable.

"Please, right this way." He held out his arm

Jovan fell into step next to Raena.

"This isn't what we agreed to," she said in his mind.

"You didn't expect to come here and actually get your hands

dirty shoveling rubble, did you?" He formed the response in his mind for her to read, per the system they had worked out over their years working together.

"I'm not going to allow my presence here to be an imposition. I'm here to help, not be a distraction."

"When it comes to optics, it doesn't matter. You're the only High Dynasty member who came in person."

"Well, Makaris sent a month's supply of food, so that's a lot more useful than me walking around offering cheerful smiles and sympathies," she replied.

She'd been concerned it would be like this when she planned the trip, but that expectation had allowed her time to prepare.

Raena followed the representative inside a warehouse-like building to an open area where several dozen people were gathered. They all looked at her excitedly.

"Please, we'd love it if you said a few words," the man told her.

Raena nodded and gave a curt smile. "Of course, it would be my pleasure."

She took up position in front of the group. She felt awkward having up a telekinetic shield, even if no one else knew it was there. Here she was, asking people to trust her, and she was operating under the worst possible assumptions about these people, but not taking precautions would be foolhardy.

"There's nothing I can say that will take away the pain of this situation, but I want you to know that you're not alone. Though a divide has been growing across the Empire, this isn't the time for us to focus on differences. One of the complaints I hear the most is about how Taran leaders don't understand how common people live. I totally agree. It doesn't matter that I grew up as a fairly typical middle-class kid, because one, it was on Earth, and two, I live in a veritable castle now. It's pointless to pretend otherwise.

"I can go on these tours and give speeches like this, but what does it change? I get a little window into your life and then go back to being just as out of touch as anyone else who isn't living among their people."

She'd already strayed significantly from the original notes for the speech, but she was about to really go off the rails. Jovan was shaking his head ever so slightly to discourage her, while also thinking rather loudly, *"No, don't,"* but she ignored him. She'd been over every scenario, and this was the only move that felt right.

"I've wracked my brain time and time again for how I can be more understanding and in-tune with your needs. Should I move to the Outer Colonies and live in an unassuming apartment in the heart of a slum? Would that actually change my perspective? And then it occurred to me: we need people who can take an objective look from a high vantage. The Empire is simply *too big* to expect leaders to understand every nuance. That doesn't mean we shouldn't try, but ultimately, we're fighting for the survival of an entire race that likes to repeatedly set itself on the path of annihilation—sometimes from within."

She looked over at the destruction on the other side of the street, shaking her head slowly. "I mean, just look at where we are now. An everyday citizen can't solve all those problems. That's why there's a centralized governance, because it's our only chance to make sense of the madness."

Raena looked down. "I never wanted to be a leader. I was born into it, but I didn't know I'd go down this path until I was sixteen. At that time, I did make a conscious decision to become the best leader I can be. That means I don't get a normal life. Sure, it looks glamorous from the outside, but the things I know and the decisions I have to make… I wouldn't wish it on my enemy. It's a burden. You see publicly the product of the evils we face on a daily basis through large-scale acts of terror like this, but there's so much more.

"How can I be a good leader? By shielding you from that so you can find the happy moments in life. I'll make those difficult decisions so you don't have to. I can give you hope for a better tomorrow. That's why the High Dynasties run the public services you rely on in your everyday lives—so it's never a question of if that resource will be there when you need it.

"In the end, will you agree with everything I say or do? Probably not, but that's part of the public discourse. I can simply do the best I can with the information I have. I hope that can be enough for you."

She stepped back, finally taking in the crowd to gauge their reaction. Jovan looked horrified, but his expression softened when he realized that the audience members were smiling and nodding with understanding. Slowly, light applause sounded, followed by several enthusiastic shouts.

Only then did Raena allow herself to return their smiles. "Thank you."

She stepped off to the side to allow the leader man to speak. Jovan gave an approving nod and shrug that admitted, 'Okay, you were right,' without him needing to utter a word. She was grateful he'd handled it like that.

The leader cast a sweeping gaze across the audience. "I can't speak for everyone, but I must say that I found that message refreshing," he said, beaming. There were cheers of agreement from some members of the audience. "Well, we should get to the main event here. The volunteer coordinators will be dividing you into groups, so please follow their instructions. We appreciate you all being here today."

"Which volunteer group am I in?" Raena asked.

"My lady, we couldn't possibly—"

"At a minimum, I have two capable hands. Please, I'd like to be involved in the relief efforts through more than just financial and material contributions."

"I have been telling my team that every pair of hands helps…"

"All right, direct me where to go."

He gave her instructions to meet up with Group Six, and Raena motioned for Jovan to follow her to the assigned rally point.

"Is this safe?" he thought loudly as they walked.

She replied to the prompt in his mind, *"I'll keep a shield up, don't worry."*

What she didn't say is that she had no intention of spending all her time on Antaris doing photo ops as a token volunteer. This was a rare opportunity to interact with locals and hear what they had to say.

After reporting to the group's supervisor, she found herself in a blur of supply sorting and bundling. When it came time for volunteers to deliver the supplies, she was the first to raise her hand.

"I'm going off for a bit," she told Jovan off to the side, beyond earshot of the rest of the group.

"Absolutely not—"

"Jovan, I'm doing this whether you approve or not. I can look after myself."

He halted his verbal protest, but concern still shone in his eyes.

"Stay here and help with the sorting or go back to the shuttle—whatever you'd like to do. I'm going to handle these deliveries and get some quality face-time with my people."

Jovan nodded reluctantly. "Yes, my lady. I'll see you soon."

Raena gathered her assigned cart filled with small supply crates designed to provide families with essentials for several days while they were displaced from their homes around the explosion site. She ignored the strange looks from the other volunteers when they saw her pushing it along without an escort.

Once she was far enough away from prying eyes, she stepped into an alcove to strip off her outer dress, revealing plain street clothes beneath. She then took her hair down from her signature ponytail and restyled it into a loose braid. A pair of glasses designed to diffuse the bioluminescent appearance of her irises completed the look. While hardly a proper disguise, she'd found that context was a major part of recognition, and she could likely pass as a commoner simply through subtle alterations of her appearance.

Only one way to find out if this works, she thought to herself while performing a quick visual check in the mirror. Satisfied, she directed the cart out to the street.

Activity had died down around the community center as the volunteers had dispersed to complete their various tasks. Raena's assigned delivery route would take her through a multifamily residential area adjacent to the TSS facility. Several apartment buildings had been evacuated while they were investigated for potential structural damage, and the residents were staying in shelters. Being able to personally deliver the supply crates on her cart to each of those families would be a prime opportunity to interact with the citizens and get their read on the situation.

She pushed the hovercart to the community shelter, appearing as any other volunteer. There were a number of civilians around, as well as a small contingent of military personnel.

To her surprise, she also saw a group of soldiers bearing the new TUF insignia, which combined the emblems of the Tararian Guard and TSS. It brought a smile to her face; in this time of mass division, at least one aspect of the Empire was becoming more unified.

When she entered the shelter, she was pleased that no one paid special attention to her. *All right, blending in!*

She began making her rounds. The families gathered on emergency cots watched her approach, cautious hope in their eyes. She stopped next to the first cluster of beds, separated from the neighbors by cloth panels stretched across a frame.

"Here are some things to make your stay more comfortable," Raena said as she handed a supply crate to the mother of the family.

"Thank you," the woman replied. "Do you know how long we'll have to stay here?"

"I don't. They're performing checks on the structures and utility lines to make sure everything is safe."

"It's a bomaxed mess," the father muttered.

"I'm sorry you have to go through this," Raena said. "I'm sure they'll get you home as soon as possible."

He shook his head. "Never should have put a base in the heart of a city."

Raena couldn't refute that point. As much as she liked to advocate for the integration of Gifted people into the rest of society, military bases were a target, and placing that target in the middle of a population center invited trouble. She couldn't blame the TSS for wanting their civilian training center to be accessible, but before rebuilding in this same location, they would need to have a discussion.

Nonetheless, Raena was interested in a civilian perspective on the issue. "Don't like the TSS in your backyard?" she asked.

"No, it's not me I'm worried about," he replied. "These bomaxed SPEAR zealots have been buzzing around here for months, looking for an excuse to act. They finally got one."

"And they were specifically targeting the TSS?"

He raised an eyebrow. "Not from around here?"

She shook her head. "Popped over from Orilan to help out. I haven't seen mention of SPEAR over there."

"Then the stars have looked kindly on you. Around here, they'd become a nuisance until… this. Railing against any Taran authority."

"Do most of the locals feel that way?"

"No, our economy relies on interplanetary commerce. I think the talk of independent worlds is idiotic."

She gave a noncommittal nod. "I hope everything gets back to normal for you soon."

"Wishful thinking, but thank you." He shrugged.

The mother raised the crate in her hands. "And thank you for this."

Raena smiled. "My pleasure. Take care."

The next family didn't seem interested in conversation when Raena attempted to open a dialogue, so she moved on. The mother of the fourth family was the next one willing to converse.

"This is what SPEAR wanted," the older woman said. "Get people displaced and scared. Then they'll come in and tell us how much better they'd run things."

"Do you think they would?" Raena asked.

"I'm certain they believe it, but I don't trust those kinds of groups. Too much ambition for their own gain."

"Is it really any different with the dynasties?"

She shrugged. "They already have so much, there's not much left to gain. It's the new money fighting for its place that worries me."

"Do you know where SPEAR came from?"

"Doesn't matter, don't care. Anyone claiming to be different is more of the same."

Is that what it sounds like when Ryan and I say that? She'd tried to rationalize their statements because of their different backgrounds, but the truth was that it did sound hollow—especially out here in the Outer Colonies. "Actions mean more than spoken promises."

The woman hoisted the supply crate. "Like you, being here now."

Raena wasn't sure if she'd been recognized or if the statement was innocuous. The woman's soft smile didn't reveal her thoughts. Either way, Raena knew she'd made the right call to come here in person.

She completed the deliveries and then returned to the supply area to get another load.

"Take these over to the shelter at Meridian and Fourteenth," the clerk instructed.

Raena hadn't counted on a trek through town, but it was a great opportunity to get a broader glimpse into life in the city.

With the cart full, she ventured out onto the busy street where people were gathered in throngs, talking amongst themselves. A few people watched her with interest.

After passing by one group of predominantly young men, she noticed that they were continuing to watch her from a block away.

They may have recognized me. She tried to think of how to proceed. The best option was to get to her destination as quickly as possible and complete her delivery. She picked up her pace, pushing the hovercart at its max rate.

The path to her destination took her down a less populated side street. A wave of apprehension washed over her, but then she considered that if the group followed her and wanted to reveal her identity, it would be better to do so in a more private setting. Nonetheless, she felt better knowing her personal shield was in place.

Halfway down the desolate side block, she sensed a presence behind her. Even without looking, she knew it was the half-dozen men she'd noticed back on the main street. They'd picked up their pace to overtake her.

I don't think they know who I am. Rather than allow them to creep up on her, Raena let go of the cart and turned to face them. "Why are you following me?" she asked in a calm, confident tone.

"Why's a pretty girl like you working hard out here all alone?" a dark-haired man at the front of the group said.

"Volunteering," she replied curtly. "I have a delivery to complete."

"Hey, we can take that off your hands for you," another man chimed in, approaching Raena.

This is the last thing I need. She took the opportunity to glean the thoughts on the surfaces of their minds. The majority of the men were interested in the supplies on the cart—hoping to steal them and then make a profit on selling them to those in need—but two others had their eyes on her, specifically. Neither option was going to fly.

"Let me stop you right there," Raena said. "Turn around and leave before I make you."

They laughed.

"Very cute, sweetheart," the first man said. "How about you—"

There was no reason to allow him to finish. Raena telekinetically picked up the whole lot of them and flew them back to the far end of the side street. She set them down just roughly enough to drive home her point.

"Don't think about coming back here!" she boomed in their minds.

Even from a distance, she could see the fear in their eyes. They scampered off back into the crowd on the main street.

Only once they were gone did she realize she was trembling. *Why am I upset? I was never in any danger.*

However, she knew that was a lie. Despite her extensive Gifts, she was still susceptible to being knocked unconscious if she was caught by surprise. Her shield was useful, but it wasn't infallible.

More than that, though, she realized she was upset because there were so many people who wouldn't have been able to defuse the situation like she had. *What if someone else had taken this route?* How many others had in the past and had unthinkable things happen?

More than any conversation, it drove home the fragile balance of polite society, where in desperate times some people would quickly abandon decency. If acts like this were happening on Antaris, which before two days ago was a thriving community, she could only imagine how awful it must be in places where generation after generation had fought to get by.

Lost in thought, Raena completed her delivery to the other shelter.

Afterward, she was still feeling antsy, so she dropped her empty cart at a return site and then wandered over to the destroyed TSS base. It was now a pile of rubble surrounded by barricades and temporary fencing. Looking at it now, she could barely tell there was once a splendid structure on the site.

She found a lone woman standing with her arms crossed, taking in the view of the wreckage. Raena came up next to her—close enough for easy conversation but not so near as to encroach.

"Awful, isn't it?" Raena commented after a few moments of silence.

The woman shook her head, clicking her tongue against her teeth. "I was supposed to be in there, but I'd skipped class to have lunch with my girlfriend."

"Wow."

"Right? I keep thinking about what would have happened if I'd been there, and…" She faded out as her lip started to quiver.

"A person could drive themselves crazy thinking like that," Raena said. "Focus on where you go from here."

"What kind of future do we have, really?"

"What do you mean?"

"If we don't fall into a civil war, there's still the Erebus. They're not our friends, no matter what the authorities say."

"I can't argue with that."

"That whole thing is so creepy."

"Yeah." Raena had many thoughts on the matter, having encountered the Erebus as intimately as any living person, but she wanted to see if the woman would offer up any more.

"I saw the picture of Tararia. I don't see how we could do anything to stop them."

Raena only nodded in response.

"SPEAR says that they have a way."

That caught her attention. "What have they said?"

She shrugged. "Just that with their leadership, there'd be nothing to worry about."

More vagueness. As much as Raena wanted to press the issue, she didn't detect that the woman knew more than she'd already said. "I wouldn't believe those promises," she said instead.

"Oh, I don't. I don't think many people do."

Good to know. Raena nodded. "Take care, now." She wandered back toward the community center.

Inside, she met up with Jovan, where he was helping to assemble more supply crates. He gave her a quizzical look after assessing her clothing and altered hairstyle.

She shrugged. "One with the people, right?"

He chuckled and got back to work. "You walk the talk. Can't argue with that."

When they had a break between activities, he pulled her aside. "Learn anything useful?"

"That we haven't lost yet."

"Hmm?"

"The Coalition has been trying, but these people aren't bought and paid for," Raena explained. "We still have a chance to rally against that influence."

He smiled. "Then that's what we'll do."

CHAPTER 19

EVERYTHING WAS SO precarious. Hanek could feel the Coalition's endeavors approaching a crossroads. The loss of Spadrosi Station had been a major setback, but the other plans that had already been set in motion were an opportunity to get back on track.

We can't give up now. People are turning to our side. We just need to tip it over the edge.

It was a delicate balance for the Coalition to both instigate attacks and offer a solution for relief. The goal was to demonstrate how ill-equipped the Central Worlds were to deal with any kind of disaster. They were so insular and focused on profits that responding to small-scale local issues wasn't a concern.

The Outer Colonies would never have the resources they'd need to flourish. The only answer was for those planets to become independent. By making drastic demonstrations, the Coalition was forcing citizens to reach that conclusion faster than if the Empire's evolution ran its natural course. There simply wasn't time to wait around now that the Erebus had emerged. It was too important to prepare for the new future of Tarans.

Hanek entered the holoconference room with Magdalena, where they would observe the next demonstration. This one would be unlike the others—a decisive show of what was to come, rather than simply tearing down old structures. They'd been teasing previews of their real power and their future vision for the Taran Empire, but this would bring all of those plans to fruition. Not even the Taran military would be able to stop them.

"He's on his way to the docking station," Magdalena said. "It won't be long now."

Hanek brought up a video feed on the conference table, a compilation of images from key sites around Glaendor. Most of the planet's population was confined to one, massive city, which was situated within an expansive biodome. Glaendor City itself was prosperous by Outer Colonies standards, though that was mostly due to activities that fell into the gray area of lawful or were straight-up illegal. The video feed included coverage of a port, a public square, and streets in four different neighborhoods.

He recognized one of the neighborhood shots as being outside the Blue Pixie, the club owned by Magdalena's younger son, Marco; since his recent death on Spadrosi Station, its future ownership and management was now up for debate.

"Oh, there he is now." Magdalena pointed to the feed of the port where a vehicle had pulled in. Andrei emerged from the car, looking somehow different than when Hanek had met him at the station. He had a wild gleam to his expression and movements, noticeable even via the camera's distant vantage.

He wasn't alone. A pretty blonde woman was with him, as well as a teenager Hanek recognized as Magdalena's grandson,

Treva—Marco's boy. Another man with a dark complexion and small stature completed the group.

Even Magdalena's normally stern expression had taken on a hint of concern with the observation. She watched her son saunter toward a woman and man waiting at the dock. Hanek didn't recognize the brunette woman, but her companion was Pyra, Andrei's assistant, which made no sense at all.

Hanek had sat in the meetings to talk through the tactics of the operation, but this wasn't what they had planned. Only Andrei and the small man were supposed to be there; the others were an unexpected complication.

"Is everything okay?" he asked, barely above a whisper.

Magdalena made no response at first, and he debated whether or not to ask again louder or to let it go. Then, she spoke, "They're about to deploy the weapon."

Hanek took a step back and swallowed hard. *This is it. It all comes down to this.*

They'd been waiting for this moment for months. At times, Hanek had had his doubts about the Coalition's commitment, wondering if they'd have the fortitude to follow through with the difficult actions. After all, the coup on Duronis had failed and they'd lost Red Ghost. The big move on Glaendor was their chance to show Taran authorities that they had both the organization and resources to make a play for dominance.

Andrei was still a wildcard in his mind. 'The Commander', as he was known with the Coalition, was regarded for his decisive action and brutality. This wild man here on the video didn't look ready to go into battle.

No, it's not a battle at all. It's an extermination. The hint of doubt crept into Hanek's mind.

There was no stopping it now. Hanek could see the small man who'd be the conduit for reshaping this world. The wielder of the greatest weapon the Taran people had ever known. Andrei would make sure he followed through.

The weapon itself—well, Hanek couldn't see that on camera, nor would he have been able to detect it in person. Information feeding into the holoconference display offered the only indication that the weapon existed. Pesta, as it was known, existed primarily in a higher dimension. It's handler, an unfortunate man who'd become tethered to the creature, offered a bridge to spacetime so the weapon's destructive power could manifest. Through sentient control, it had the ability to unmake matter.

Thus far, that power had been unfocused and had run unchecked. Roana and Quel were unfortunate accidents, but the Coalition had learned from that experience. They'd been able to harness the being first unleashed on Quel and successfully tether it to a handler. Now, the weapon was finally stable and ready for deployment.

The plan was simple: Mac, Pesta's handler, would release the transdimensional fury upon the world, disintegrating anyone and anything that stood against the Coalition. It was a planetary sacrifice to exert dominance. Stand alongside us, or face death. Those who couldn't be won through moving words would be convinced through fear.

Hanek's brow furrowed. Something was definitely wrong. The people at the docking station were all staring each other down, and it was unclear who was on whose side.

"That bitch is trying to ruin everything," Magdalena sneered.

That's when the pieces fell into place for Hanek. The brunette woman was Kali Wietris, the undercover TSS Agent who'd been a thorn in their side since Tregaren's untimely passing. She'd been behind the loss of Spadrosi Station and the unfortunate events on Red Ghost, and now here she was on Glaendor making a mess of things again.

The heat of anger rose in Hanek's chest. *What is she doing there? Why fight the inevitable.*

Of course, that was the TSS way, wasn't it? To insert their authority where it didn't belong. No matter. She was no match for Pesta. Andrei would see to it that she didn't survive this encounter.

Without warning, the blonde woman pulled out a handgun and aimed straight at Andrei. She said something that wasn't picked up on the video feed, then she pulled the trigger.

"No!" Magdalena brought a hand over her mouth, letting out a gasp of pained surprise.

However, the shot had passed straight through Andrei and instead hit Mac squarely in the chest. The small man crumpled to the ground.

"What…?" Hanek didn't complete the question as the scene descended into chaos.

Agent Wietris raised her hands, as though she were using her abilities, but it was unclear on the video feed what she was doing. The faces of everyone on camera were strained and horrified. A telekinetic battle was being waged, invisible to everyone outside.

Hanek's heart raced. Nothing was happening like it was supposed to. And if Mac was dead, that meant that Pesta… *Where is Pesta?*

He cursed the inability to see the weapon. It could be anywhere. But for certain, it had lost its handler. It could dissolve into an obliterating force at any moment.

Most worrying, though, was Andrei. Hanek scanned the video feed, growing more concerned with every passing moment. "What's happening to him?" he asked tentatively.

Andrei appeared to be... translucent. *This doesn't make any sense. Is he fading away?*

"He's taken too much," Magdalena murmured.

"Too much of *what*?" Normally Hanek wouldn't directly question her, but this was too unusual for him to not at least try to get an answer.

"It..." She faded out, but Hanek silently urged her to continue. "It was a gift. Well, more of an experiment. Something to help expand one's mind to an ascended state, if only temporarily."

He realized that must have been what was in the vial he'd witnessed in Andrei's office. That's why it had looked so strange. His mind raced, trying to understand how the pieces fit together. "Is this what you were going to give those women to make them conduits?"

"A variation." Magdalena took in the footage of her son, her brows drawn together with concern.

"What's happening to him?" Hanek asked when she didn't elaborate.

"Something that shouldn't be possible."

She didn't say more. Hanek wasn't sure if Andrei might be ascending or if he was simply disintegrating.

Warnings appeared in a red flash at the perimeter of the holodisplay—a proximity alert for incoming ships to Glaendor. TSS ships.

"Shite!" Magdalena spat. She stared desperately at the screen where her son and grandson were out of her grasp. "We need to—"

"We need to jump out of here," Hanek urged before she could finish.

The warnings on the screen intensified. Not only was the TSS about to descend on Glaendor, but there was a strong chance their own ship in orbit would be discovered. They couldn't risk the entire Coalition operation.

"But Andrei—"

"There's nothing we can do now."

Reluctantly, Magdalena nodded. She hit the comm button to open a line to the flight deck. "Get us out of here."

— — —

"A ship just jumped away," Andy reported to Jason over the viewscreen in his office. "Looks like it was operating on an independent jump drive."

No doubt operatives related to the Coalition. He sighed. *They're always one step ahead.*

Jason had opened up a commlink with Andy on the *Journey IV* as soon as the TSS vessel had dropped out of subspace at Glaendor. Short of being there himself, watching the events play out in real-time was the next best thing.

"Thanks, Andy," Jason said. "What's your status?"

"I'm trying to find Kali. She—" Andy got a faraway look in his eyes. After several seconds, his attention returned to Jason. "Um, Kali just sent me a telepathic message," he said. "She shared what's going on down there. She told me, 'He is Erebus.' About Andrei."

Jason squinted. "What?"

The other Agent shook his head. "I don't know. She shared an image of him… like he was fading away. And then he became solid again and had glowing gray eyes. I can't explain it."

The account sounded more like fantasy than real events, but Jason had seen enough bizarre things to not dismiss it out of hand, especially since the report had come from a fellow

Agent. "Secure the scene," he instructed. "I'll want to talk to Kali myself."

Andy nodded. "I'm on my way. Mika just got there. I'll send along footage from the dock. I'm sure they can tell us more."

"I hope so." The more that happened with the Coalition, the less sense it made.

— — —

Mika's lungs burned from his run to the spacedock. He'd had to make sure the band was okay, and now Kali was his foremost concern. *I'm too late. She needed me sooner and I wasn't here.*

He could sense Kali had reached her limit fighting on her own. Andrei was strong—so much stronger than he should be. Mika was ready to face him regardless of his poor odds of winning, but he couldn't see Andrei anymore. The man had inexplicably dissolved, leaving only his clothes behind. Even so, Mika could still sense his presence.

Protect Kali. It was the only thing on Mika's mind. Kali had been there for him when no one else was; she'd helped to heal him and give him new purpose in life. He owed her everything. And now, he could begin to repay that debt. He needed to stop Andrei.

Mika lashed out at what was left of the man with all his telekinetic might, trying to slash at what he could detect of his consciousness, now detached from the physical form, which had been released into pure energy.

"Die!" Mika shouted into the ether.

His attack struck true—but did nothing.

The entity that used to be Andrei laughed at the failed

attempt. *"You will never be strong enough."*

Mika recoiled. He'd given everything to the assault. Kali needed him. Everyone on the planet needed him. He wasn't enough.

The voice buzzed in his mind, closing in around his consciousness. *"You're mine now."*

CHAPTER 20

HOW IS THIS possible? Jason reviewed the latest information from his parents and Andy. It painted a concerning picture of what had happened on Glaendor.

Word was slowly spreading around the TSS that there had been another incident, though the details were being kept need-to-know. The notion that the Coalition may have a new and improved version of the planet-killing weapon was concerning, to say the least.

Lexi burst into his office. "What happened?" she asked. "I heard there was another attack."

Jason telekinetically closed the door behind her. "Not exactly. I don't know how to classify these incidents anymore, actually. It's a mess."

"Was anyone hurt?"

"A few people, but it wasn't the global disaster it could have been." He rubbed his eyes. "I'm going to be meeting with Kali soon—that field Agent who's been investigating the disappearances and now SPEAR. I hope a conversation with her will clarify matters."

"She was the one who helped on Antaris, right?"

He nodded.

"Well, I owe her a drink." Lexi cracked a sad smile.

"That situation would have been a lot worse without her, that's for sure."

"I'd love to meet her and thank her personally after you're finished with official business."

"I can arrange that." He gave her a kiss. "I'll see you later tonight."

"Good luck."

He headed to the designated interview room on Level 1. He tried to mentally prepare for the meeting. A warning from his father echoed in Jason's mind: *Mika may have killed Andrei, who had started to ascend. That's more power than we've seen outside this family.*

Given that caution, Jason wasn't sure why he'd been delegated to conduct the initial interview rather than his father himself. He chalked it up to him being the head of the Coalition task force, but Jason wondered if there might be more to it than that.

When he entered the interview room, Kali and Mika were already there. They sat side-by-side at the table opposite the door. Kali's eyes widened slightly when she saw Jason.

She had the refined appearance he'd expect of someone with a dynastic background. Wietris wasn't a particularly prominent Lower Dynasty, but the designation alone came with a certain gravitas within the Taran sphere. Jason found the idea of nobility ridiculous, despite his fortunate position within the hierarchy. Since Kali had elected to join the TSS, it was possible she felt the same way; the organization tended to attract people who placed more value on accomplishments rather than the benefits of name and title alone.

"Hi, welcome back to Headquarters," he greeted.

"It's good to be home." Kali gave him a cordial smile. He was pleased she didn't use an honorific; Agent-to-Agent, one wasn't necessary, though given his station many added one anyway. "And it's nice to meet you in-person, officially. Your mom has been really kind to me," she added after a moment.

Jason smiled. "Yeah, she's like that."

Mika flushed slightly and cast his gaze down at the table.

"We appreciate everything you've done," Jason said, including both Kali and Mika in the statement.

Kali smiled. "I couldn't let my first assignment be a total bust."

Mika brightened a little at that, glancing at Kali.

It was then Jason noticed the connection between them—far more than a camaraderie between work associates. *Wait, are they bonded? When did that happen?*

He sent out a subtle telepathic probe to confirm his suspicion. Sure enough, the two had a bond, though it appeared even newer than his own with Lexi. Given Mika's questionable background and Kali's newly minted Agent status, that was a potential concern. However, knowing how defensive he could get over Lexi, Jason decided that the interview would be more fruitful if he saved that line of questioning for the end.

"You two have been in the thick of it with the Coalition, so I wanted to personally sit down with both of you to get your impressions. As the TSS task force lead, I'd like to incorporate any insights you can offer into our strategy to take the organization down once and for all."

"Can't come soon enough," Kali replied. "They definitely took a page out of the Priesthood's handbook." Despite her traumatic background as one of the Priesthood's captives, she was surprisingly calm. It would seem the field assignment for her pre-graduation internship had indeed been a healing experience.

"I've realized we can't root out every evil, but there are some we can't overlook. This is one of them," Jason said.

She nodded and folded her hands on the tabletop. "Well, I can tell you Maggie Steyn is at the intersection of all the relevant parties. Andrei and Marco were totally under her thumb."

"She appears to go by Magdalena within the Coalition," Jason said.

"Not surprising. 'Maggie' doesn't exactly inspire fear in the hearts of followers."

"Did you encounter her directly?"

Kali shook her head. "She likes the shadows. But she's smart, and she's vicious."

"What does she want?"

"Power?" She shrugged. "Her grandson, Treva, is a motivating factor, too. Or he was. The poor boy's mom was one of the women in stasis."

Jason nodded, recalling the name. "She made a full recovery?"

"Yes." Kali glanced at Mika when he deflated in his seat.

"Sorry," Jason murmured, wishing he'd chosen more delicate phrasing. Mika's own mother was also one of the recently freed captives, but she was still in a coma with an unclear prognosis.

"I'm here to keep others from getting hurt," Mika muttered.

"We can agree on that." Jason activated the holoprojector integrated into the table so he could step through the field reports with Kali and Mika. "I'd like you to walk me through everything again. I know you've been over it with Andy already, but I'd like to hear it straight from the source."

"Of course." Kali began walking Jason through her undercover assignment spanning the last month-plus.

He listened intently, asking clarifying questions to add details where it seemed like something important may have transpired. Nothing in particular jumped out at him as being different from the reports he'd reviewed as part of his task force activities until they got to the part about the events on Spadrosi Station.

What hadn't been clear before was how she had bonded with Mika to link their abilities. It made sense, given what had happened on Antaris with them holding up the building together, but Jason hadn't realized the nature of their work together and how it had been the start of a true bond and not just linking.

The story didn't really get interesting, though, until it came to the showdown at the docking station with Andrei Steyn. The video of Andrei disappearing had told part of the story, but Kali's extrasensory perception filled in additional gaps.

"I could feel the energy coursing through him," Kali said. "It was like being near the Rift."

A gateway to the higher dimensions. Jason's chest tightened with the thought. If Andrei had passed through the dimensional veil, then was he still out there in some form?

He refocused on the task at hand. "What became of the Pesta weapon?"

"Don't know for sure," Kali replied. "But Pesta made a conscious choice. We can't think of her like a tool."

A living weapon? The idea had been thrown out there, but this confirmation changed the nature of the game. It was a benefit if they could get Pesta working on their side, but negotiating with a transdimensional creature hadn't exactly gone well thus far. If Pesta was, indeed, a product of the Erebus, as the research seemed to suggest, then it might be just as volatile and manipulative as the other Erebus had been—another 'gift' to Tarans, this time handed directly to terrorists. Not only did that change how the TSS should regard the Erebus, but it made their domestic opponents that much more dangerous. That was, of course, if the TSS could even track down Pesta, since there had been no indication of her presence on Glaendor after the showdown at the docks.

Jason resisted the urge to wipe his hands down his face. Instead, he took a slow breath, looking between Kali and Mika. "What happened to Pesta?"

"I'm not sure. I…" Kali faltered. "I think she may have gone into Ava."

"That was the blonde woman?"

She nodded. "Ava was Marco's girlfriend. I think she may have run off with Herja, who's a pirate we kinda teamed up with."

Jason gave her a questioning look.

"You've gotta work with the resources at your disposal when you're undercover," she said by way of justifying her actions. "Herja's not all bad. She was actually really helpful."

Jason couldn't argue with that. "Any idea where we might find Herja and Ava?"

"No, I'm sorry, I was out cold at the end. I don't even know if Ava is still Ava or if Pesta has complete control."

"Okay." Jason fixed his gaze on Mika. "Did you see what happened to them?"

He shook his head. "They ran off in the direction of Herja's ship. Knowing her, and I don't know her well, she'd drop Ava off at her first opportunity and then get as far away from

Glaendor as possible."

Most likely, then, tracing Herja would be a dead end. However, it would be worth checking ports in the vicinity of Glaendor to see if Ava had been spotted. She had striking enough features to stand out. He filed it on his exponentially expanding mental to-do list.

"Okay, that brings us to Andrei Steyn," Jason continued. "How did he die... or did he?"

"I destroyed him," Mika stated matter-of-factly.

Jason had thought he had braced for the affirmation, but his heart skipped a beat nonetheless. "How?" he asked, not sure he wanted the answer, but he needed to know.

There was a hum of energy between Kali and Mika indicating a telepathic exchange.

"I need you to be honest with me," Jason said. "We need to know we can trust you." He left the subtext unstated. If Mika couldn't be trusted, he wouldn't be allowed to remain free; he'd be too dangerous. It was in the young man's best interest to cooperate.

After several tense seconds, Mika nodded. "Andrei had started to ascend, but I could still sense his mind. I surrounded him with everything I had and crushed him out of existence." The words were far too calm and level for the statement. Jason couldn't tell if it was because Mika had been through so much that he could look at horrific actions from a purely objective vantage, or if he really didn't understand what a momentous act that was.

"How did you learn how to do that, Mika?" Jason asked. "Is that something Tregaren taught you?"

Mika's eyes darted to the side. "No. I just figured it out in the moment."

Jason knew from personal experience how intuition could take over in trying times, but it concerned him that the young man was so reticent about explaining *how* he did something that by all accounts should have been impossible. "Are you sure Andrei is gone?" he asked.

Mika swallowed. "Yes."

Jason didn't detect a lie in his tone or in the energy of his thoughts, but it was clear he wasn't being entirely forthright. "It's a difficult thing, taking a life."

Kali met Jason's gaze. *"He only did it because it's what needed to happen,"* she said in his mind.

Jason could respect that. He and his family had done things that would be barbaric in any other context. "I know you've had a tough go of it, Mika, and you didn't really have a good role model growing up. We can forgive certain actions in the past, but I'd be remiss in my duty if I didn't emphasize that we have a code of conduct and will have expectations for your behavior moving forward. I believe that was made clear to you by my father the last time you were here."

"Yeah, we had a nice chat. He seems like a good guy. It must have been nice having parents who actually care about you." The bitterness came through full force in Mika's tone.

Jason was taken aback by the venom of the comment. "I am fortunate, yes. However, you're in control of your own destiny now."

He scoffed. "Easy for someone like you to say."

Kali placed a hand gently on Mika's arm, and he relaxed slightly.

"It's been a difficult few weeks," she said, sounding apologetic.

"I can appreciate that," Jason replied. He wanted to let the behavior slide, but that wouldn't set a good precedent. If Mika was going to have a continued relationship with the TSS—and his new bond with Kali almost assured that would be the case—then he needed to understand his place in the scheme.

Jason leaned forward, looking Mika in his eyes. "I know this isn't easy for you, but I'm not here as your adversary. If you want this to work," he glanced between Mika and Kali, "then you need to stop treating me like your enemy. That attitude won't fly with me."

The tension released from Mika's shoulders. "I understand."

"All right." Jason folded his hands on the tabletop. "Now, I'd like to go over everything one more time."

The story remained the same as the first time they'd been through it, but the details at the end continued to give Jason pause. Mika didn't appear to possess extraordinary abilities, especially when compared to Jason—yet he had undeniably pulled off a feat that shouldn't have been possible. That meant that either Mika was more powerful than it seemed, or higher-dimensional entities had a weakness. Jason hoped it was the latter.

When Jason was satisfied that he had captured all the relevant information, he dismissed Mika but asked Kali to hang back.

"This is about my relationship with Mika, isn't it?" she asked once they were alone.

Jason nodded. "I'm with Lexi; I get it. But you do realize it complicates things?"

"That I put my career on the line for love? Yes." She looked him in the eyes. "You did the same."

"I talked about it with my parents ahead of time. You, on the other hand, initiated a permanent telepathic bond with someone who, until a few weeks ago, was engaged in criminal activity and has subsequently defied direct orders. I won't pretend that Lexi had a pristine background, but she hasn't once broken our TSS code of conduct since coming here. Mika has."

"He had good reasons."

"That's a slippery slope, Kali. Would you disregard protocol for the same reasons?"

She thought for longer than he would have liked before responding. "No."

"*Are you sure?*" he asked in her mind.

Confirming her dedication wasn't something that could be done through a spoken promise. Words had power, but they weren't binding. To prove she would place the TSS and her duty above personal ambitions, she'd need to open her mind to assessment.

He didn't specifically ask to be let in, but she picked up on his cue and opened her mind. She shared not only her intentions moving forward but also her memories of the incidents in question. Mika had shared his rationale when he'd gone against explicit orders to delve into a suspect's mind to extract information; that lead had turned out to be a valuable clue that ultimately led to the successful rescue of the captives on Spadrosi Station. Yet, Mika couldn't have known how key it was at the time; it remained that he'd defied orders without exhibiting remorse.

Then there was the raw exhibition of his power on Glaendor and how he'd killed Andrei. The firsthand impression of it through Kali's senses was even more shocking than the video of the docking station. However, through the emotional connection between Kali and Mika, there was a clear expression of motives. Mika was acting to protect not only Kali but everyone she cared about—and at the core of that was her found family with the TSS and their commitment to the Taran people. Mika recognized that Andrei was a menace and needed to be stopped through any means necessary, the same call any TSS Agent would have made.

"His heart is in the right place," Kali said in Jason's mind. *"He just needs guidance."*

Jason pulled back. "Okay. We'll give him a chance to prove himself."

"You won't be disappointed."

—   —   —

"Well done evading their questions," the voice said in Mika's mind.

He wasn't sure if it was still Andrei or something else. The force had been with him since Glaendor. It wasn't there all the time, simply appearing out of nowhere and then fading again without warning. He'd tried to tell others about it, but every time he started to speak or think a warning, the Andrei-presence would appear again and stop him.

He was trapped in his body, at moments feeling as free as ever, and then he'd be thrust into a corner deep in the recesses of his mind to watch himself carry out actions.

Mika had seen others give him curious looks, but no one seemed to realize what was going on. He could shout the warnings loudly in his mind, yet his voice would never comply, and his thoughts would become lost in fog. Solidifying his bond with Kali in a night of passion after the Glaendor showdown had been an act of hope for her to *feel* what was wrong so she could help, and even then it had gone unnoticed. Mika didn't know what to do.

"You're going to be quite useful," Andrei whispered.

Mika pressed his hands against the side of his head in a vain attempt to block out the voice.

"*I won't help you.*"

"*You don't have a choice.*"

"*What do you want from me?*"

"*You'll know when it's time.*"

—   —   —

"I keep going back to Kali's warning: 'He is Erebus'," Saera said as she leaned back in her seat across from Wil. "Has she said any more about it?"

He shook his head. "Only that she allegedly heard it from Pesta."

"Trusting the statements of sentient weapons created by our enemies. That's what we're doing now?" Saera arched an eyebrow.

"Obviously, there are some serious conversations in order."

"That's for sure."

Wil frowned at the report. "I don't understand what happened."

Saera shrugged. "Don't ask me. I'm stumped."

Wil watched the video again. It still didn't make any sense. The man seemed to fade without any other apparent spatial distortion around him, then he became solid again but was impervious until suddenly he disintegrated. The only meaningful factor appeared to be Mika's arrival; that was when he'd unraveled.

Wil leaned back in his seat, crossing his arms. "I have one thought, and I don't like the implications one bit if it's accurate."

"And that is…?"

"He was ascending."

Saera worked her mouth for a few seconds before sinking deeper into her seat with a discontented huff.

"I don't know how that would be possible. But…" The strange translucency and glow to the man's body couldn't be explained through conventional scientific means. As inexplicable as it seemed, the most logical explanation was that he'd gone out of sync with conventional physical reality—that made more sense than simply 'vanishing'.

Saera splayed her hands on her thighs. "Okay. We need to step through this piece by piece."

"Agreed."

"Let's go back to the other instances involving transdimensional tech," she said. "There's always a clear spatial distortion—a window for physical objects to pass through. A doorway of some sort."

"Right, except there was nothing like that in this case," Wil countered.

"Not externally, anyway."

He shook his head. "If it's internal, then we're talking about something happening at the cellular level. That doesn't do a lot to discount the 'it wasn't ascension' argument."

"Could have been spatial dislocation."

"We both know that wasn't the case."

As much as Wil wanted to offer alternative explanations, he'd seen enough to be certain what he was looking at. They had video evidence of something that was considered a mythical feat, and he had no idea how a random TSS reject had been able to accomplish something even the Priesthood's vast resources had been unable to achieve over the course of thousands of years.

More worryingly, that process had been interrupted, and it appeared the person powerful enough to intervene was none other than the son of an ex-Priest. It was going to be quite the debrief.

Wil rolled back to an earlier clip of the docking station footage where Andrei Steyn had consumed a vial of a misty substance in hand. "What in the stars *is* this?"

"A drug of some sort?"

"Do you think it might be connected to what happened to him?"

"A drug that makes people ascend?" Saera asked, the skepticism written in her expression.

"I don't know how effective it is, considering it looks like it may have killed him." That was only one possibility; the other was that Mika had done him in. Wil wasn't sure which option was more concerning.

Saera nodded slowly. "Well, it's not surprising it would be lethal. Flooding our bodies with higher-dimensional energy like this is a death sentence."

"For the average person, anyway."

Her expression turned grim. "True, I can't help but wonder how *you* might react."

"I have no intention of finding out. If I'm going to roam the higher dimensions, I'll do so on my own terms—not with an experimental bit of alien tech."

"Good, because I don't want you going anywhere." She leaned over the desk and squeezed his hand.

"There is a bit of tech we can't ignore, though—this 'Pesta'. I don't know what to make of it."

"Yes, what happened to the weapon?"

"I don't know. I think we'll need to talk with Kali and get her firsthand impressions of what happened. The video feeds only tell so much."

"Yeah." Saera crossed her arms. "It's weird. This isn't like what we've seen before. The footage we recently discovered about what happened on Roana didn't look anything like the incident on Quel. Roana's Pesta attack was a disease that turned people to ash. Quel was…"

"It was a straight-up transdimensional energy bomb. While the first was more like a controlled trickle, Quel was a flood."

"And what about Glaendor? Where did they make that Pesta and what could it do?"

"Good question. Without seeing it in action…" Wil faded out.

"Hmm?"

"I was just thinking about potential iterations. That one on Quel was a higher-dimensional entity, right? Its energy was released in our reality, but… did that actually kill it?"

"You mean, the Pesta that Kali encountered could be the same being that destroyed Quel?"

"Maybe. Just throwing it out there."

Saera considered the thought. "I suppose it's possible that they may have retroactively figured out how to tether the being to a host. The Coalition could have gone back after we finished our study of the planet."

"Mac is probably the only person who could have answered how he came to be connected to Pesta. Unfortunately, Pyra doesn't know."

"More unanswered questions, then." She sighed.

"In any case, they probably didn't count on their weapon having a sentient mind of its own."

"No doubt. And now this Pesta from Glaendor is on the loose. What are we supposed to do about that?"

"Locate it, and see if we can reason with it, I suppose."

Really, Wil had no idea. He'd rather such a thing not exist at all, but he had been party to so much killing in his lifetime that he couldn't stomach the summary destruction of a sentient lifeform—by all accounts, the first of its kind—simply because he didn't understand it and its power scared him.

Saera gazed into his eyes, sensing his unspoken thoughts. "We can give Pesta a chance, but Tarans seeking this kind of power can't be trusted."

"Agreed."

She threw up her arms. "What's their fascination with immortality and ascension, anyway? After meeting the Erebus, I have *no* interest in visiting the higher dimensions, thank you very much."

Wil chuckled. "I'm not sure they're giving us the most accurate impression of what might be up there."

"Well, one bad neighbor is enough to turn me off from the whole neighborhood." She crossed her arms.

"Makes you wonder if the Priesthood knew about those risks when they began their experimentations."

"Given the track record of that organization, they probably thought they'd move in and own the place."

"That wouldn't surprise me."

She shook her head. "They were obsessed. Sounds like the Coalition hopped on that bandwagon."

"It certainly seems that way, based on the genetic analysis Leon completed for the captive women."

Saera raised her eyebrows. "Oh?"

"It dropped on my desk a few hours ago, conveniently enough. There was high ability potential in all of them— Primus Agent level, if they'd trained."

"So, SPEAR was going after those with the strongest Gifts? Why?"

"Perhaps because there's something in our genetic potential which dictates our connection to the higher dimensional energies," Wil mused. "After all, that lab where they were found looked like a giant capacitor, so maybe they were trying to harness the power of that transdimensional link?"

"I profoundly disagree with their methods, but I must admit that's an intriguing concept."

"Agreed. I wish we had a better understanding of the interaction between genetics and the expression of abilities. Specifically, what makes some people stronger in telekinesis and telepathy than others?"

Saera nodded. "There's clearly some sort of physiological difference."

"I suspect it has something to do with the '*aesen* saturation potential' of a person, though I have no clue what controls that on a genetic level."

"How so?" Saera asked.

"For instance, we've always emphasized physical fitness in the TSS not just because of combat potential, but because it makes our Gifts stronger."

"Huh." Saera's eyes brightened with the spark of realization. "That would actually explain the calculation behind estimating potential."

"Hmm?"

She tilted her head. "Haven't you ever looked into the TSS intake assessments?"

"The results, obviously. But no, I can't say I took a deep dive into the underlying calculation methodology."

"All right, well, I did when I first became Lead Agent. Most of it is a simple genetic evaluation looking at certain markers associated with high abilities. However, there's also a variable for physical stature, which I found odd. This new theory about *aesen* changes my understanding."

Wil caught on. "Our physicality influences the saturation potential."

"Exactly. And that's not to say that some smaller-stature individuals can't be as strong as bigger ones—they just need to have a higher maximum saturation threshold to make up for it."

He pondered the idea. "It tracks. Lung capacity increases with fitness training, so there's no reason to think someone's abilities couldn't be strengthened, too, by optimizing their body's performance."

Saera pursed her lips in thought before continuing. "I guess hitting our personal *aesen* saturation point might have something to do with when someone hits the wall in the Course Rank test."

"Yes, when the draw outpaces the *aesen* refresh rate, you max out."

"Right. But more than that, it means that the TSS' founders knew about those factors and took it into account when designing their measurement tool."

He realized where Saera was going. "And, of course, the TSS was founded by the Priesthood. They knew all along."

She nodded. "It explains their crazy obsession with finding the 'perfect vessel' to help them ascend. They recognized the role of genetic potential in connection to the higher dimensions."

"Shite, that does make complete sense."

She looked him over. "You never hit a limit during testing. What does that say about you and our children?"

"I'm not sure, but the Aesir have made it clear that our abilities are what the Priesthood had been trying to unlock."

Saera left the rest unsaid, but Wil could sense the unspoken question: If he kept drawing on the *aesen*, would he eventually ascend beyond his physical form?

He had, temporarily, on many occasions when astral projecting. Still, he remained tied to his physical body. Perhaps it would be possible to truly shed his corporeal form, but he had no intention of trying.

"It's funny how the right thing can make you look at old information in a different way," Saera said, breaking the silence.

"I can't believe I didn't see that before." Wil leaned back in his chair.

Saera shrugged one shoulder. "We're limited by our perception of our reality. Previously, we never had a reason to look at things any other way. Most of the time, we need to look at our individual experience."

"As much as we can try to look at the larger scheme, sometimes we're blind to the obvious."

"We have a lot on our minds."

"Very true." He pondered the new information. *The Priesthood understood the deeper nature of our abilities and kept that knowledge to themselves. How shocking that there was yet* another *thing they suppressed.*

Saera leaned forward. "I want to know why the Erebus may have given Andrei a substance to help him unlock those latent abilities—to help him ascend, or whatever was going on."

"That is the question," Wil said. "If we can figure that out, maybe we'll finally understand the Erebus' long-game."

CHAPTER 21

RAENA WAS STILL shaken from her experience on Antaris, but she was determined to not let it show. *They wouldn't ever allow me to leave the estate again if they knew.*

She'd never been in actual danger, as far as she was concerned. Her shield was in place and she'd had no difficulty dispatching the would-be assailants. Nonetheless, it wouldn't look good on the newsfeeds that the Sietinen heiress was vulnerable in any fashion. She'd been through enough to know how the story would be twisted, and any benefit of her visit to Antaris would be undone.

So, she put on a brave face and prepared a highlight reel in her mind of the great things to come out of the trip. A little creative wording was necessary in situations like this.

When her shuttle arrived at the estate, Ryan was waiting at the landing pad. After exiting the shuttle ahead of Raena, Jovan stepped off to the side as Ryan approached to give her a hug and kiss.

She squeezed him tight. "I missed you." They rarely spent more than a few hours apart, so being back in each other's presence was like a missing part of Raena had been restored.

"Missed you, too." He gave her another kiss.

"Any news?" she asked as they parted.

"Nothing catastrophic," he reported. He started giving her a rundown of the highlights while the three of them walked toward the palace.

True to his word, it sounded like the Empire had remained intact in her absence, aside from rumors of an incident on Glaendor, which had yet to be substantiated through an official report. Given how many unexpected, awful things had transpired lately, it was a victory.

She gave Ryan an overview of her visit, leaving out the part about the would-be attack on the side street during her deliveries. However, as soon as they were inside, Ryan motioned her into one of the private conference rooms while Jovan went ahead to check in with the office.

When they were alone, Ryan placed his hands gently on her upper arms. "Raena, what really happened on Antaris?"

She gazed into his questioning eyes. She could be selective with her words around others, but complete transparency was the only option with her husband. The emotion welled up within her, and she allowed some of it to make it to her surface-level thoughts. "We say so much, but none of those words capture what's really going on—how people really think."

He took in the images with his lips pressed into a firm line. "Why didn't you say anything sooner?"

"What good would it do? I'm fine, and there are more important—"

"You are the most important thing to me. I'm so sorry you had to go through that."

"I'm glad it was me, because I could do something about it. I like to think that my experience will make things a little safer for others in the future."

He ran a hand through his hair. "I love that you can take care of yourself and deal with any situation, but please promise me you won't go off alone like that again."

Raena wanted to object, but she recognized that he was right. Anything could go wrong, and not having any backup was a needless risk. This wasn't just about her, but also everyone who cared about her and was counting on her. "I promise."

Ryan gave her a light kiss. "You're amazing, and I love you for always being yourself."

"You too."

He took her hand. "Okay, so you said you had some insights?"

She nodded. "Yes, but I'd like to pull my grandfather into that conversation."

"Sure."

"Please, let's keep the rest of it between us."

"Agreed." He didn't look pleased about it, but she fully trusted him at his word.

They continued to Raena's work area. After checking in with the rest of her staff, Raena and Ryan went into her office to call Cris.

Her grandfather appeared on the holodisplay. "How was your trip?"

"Productive. I came to a realization," Raena replied.

"Let's hear it."

"The problem isn't actually that the Outer Colonies citizens dislike Tararian rule—far from it, actually. The issue is that they're *reliant* on us."

"In terms of shared infrastructure?"

"Yes. So, when the Coalition preaches about independence

for the Outer Colonies and a focus on locality, the part of the message that resonates is that if all other planets disappeared, the one where a person happens to be living at that moment would still be okay. They'd have power, and food, and medical care. All the things that contribute to a decent quality of life."

"That makes sense."

"It does. I realized I'd been looking at it all wrong. My original proposal to build those city-ships would have given all those things to our enemies rather than placing those investments into the people who need it."

Cris nodded. "That was my concern."

"As I was handing out supply crates to displaced families, it occurred to me that the contents of those boxes had all come from off-world. I did some digging, and I discovered that it would have been difficult to acquire some of those items based on the planet's resources alone. And that's for relief efforts on a pretty small scale, only a few city blocks!"

"That doesn't seem right." Ryan frowned.

"I thought so, too, but it's true. Beyond food stores and medical, there aren't emergency supplies stored on-world aside from those *for* the Guard itself. Without offworld relief, even blankets would need to come from the private sector, and those merchants' resupplies are entirely dependent on interplanetary commerce."

Her grandfather's face darkened as he slowly shook his head. "Limiting access to resources is nothing new. It started sometime during the war, and it would seem it's still rampant."

"Why haven't you done anything about it?"

"You should know by now that being aware of a problem and fixing it are two different things."

"But—"

"I've tried working with the other High Dynasties and their

subsidiaries, but there are so many players in the middle that mandates become meaningless."

She crossed her arms. "Then we try again, and this time, we make sure the leadership is really on board."

Cris was about to protest, but instead he let out a soft sigh. "What do you have in mind?"

"Local infrastructure investments," she replied. "Agriculture. Manufacturing. Enough to cover the basics. We facilitate training for new jobs and empower planets to increase their self-sufficiency from the rest of the Empire."

"What about the worlds where those exports are critical to their livelihoods?" Ryan asked.

"Isn't most of the labor handled robotically? Still need the same people for oversight. I haven't run any numbers on cost of goods, but I'm sure there's a way to make the math work."

Cris nodded in consideration. "We'd have to get the other High Dynasties on board—especially Makaris."

"Much like DGE's new space docks and training, Makaris could spin this into an opportunity rather than competition."

"Hm." He paused in deep thought, eyeing her through the viewscreen. "You might be on to something with this. Let's write up a business case and see what we could do."

She smiled. "I already have some ideas."

— — —

Wil frowned at the text message from Jason: >>We might have a problem with Mika. Talk soon.<<

He hated cryptic communications like that, especially without a clear follow-up timeline. However, he'd rather be alerted to a potential problem sooner than later, so there was that. He sighed. *If it's not one thing, it's another.*

In the meantime, Wil was eager to meet with Pyra. The Militia officer had given nearly two years to the undercover assignment—and had almost lost his life in the course of duty—so Wil felt it was his responsibility to personally conduct the debrief.

"Welcome home, Pyra," Wil greeted him outside the conference room.

"Thank you, sir. It's very good to be back."

Wil motioned him inside the interview room and they took seats across the table from each other.

The poor man looked haggard—shifting eyes and a nervous shaking of his leg that spoke to the kind of trauma where the person hadn't expected to make it out alive. In many ways, he probably had believed it to be a one-way mission, the way it seemed like things had started to go at the end.

"Thank you for meeting with me," Wil said.

"Of course, sir," he replied.

"I doubt you expected to find yourself in this position when you accepted the assignment two years ago."

Pyra made a harsh tone at the back of his throat. "Yeah, you could say that."

Normally, when sitting down to an interview, Wil could get an immediate read on a person through passive telepathic observation. In this case, he was met with only a blank wall around the man's mind. He was a null, and no amount of telepathic probing would allow Wil through. It was some kind of genetic mutation caused by one of the Priesthood's many interventions, as far as anyone could tell. The result was that Wil would need to rely on his other senses to learn the truth about what had happened on Glaendor and the rest of SPEAR's operation.

"We've been tracking many moving pieces for a couple of

years now, and the bigger picture is finally coming together," Wil continued. "I believe you can fill in several of the gaps."

"I'm still trying to understand some of it, myself, but I'm getting there."

"Any insights you can offer are greatly appreciated."

"Well, it comes down to this," Pyra began. "Andrei Steyn was working with the Erebus *and* the Gatekeepers."

Wil leaned forward. "The Gatekeepers? What makes you say that?"

"There's a planet the Coalition has been excavating, Zeron. They've said they're doing 'archaeology', but that always struck me as a shite cover story. It wasn't until the recent events that I saw the connection to the Pesta control technology SPEAR Tec was developing. The underlying architecture is similar to what I was shown about the Gate sphere before I went undercover."

"To be clear, you're saying there might still be Gatekeeper tech within the Taran Empire?"

Pyra nodded. "I've never been to Zeron, but they talked about it like there was something really important there. I only overheard a few conversations, but it sounded like there might be people who know how to use it. My guess is they're a rogue group of those Gatekeeper hybrids you met."

Either they never left, or the Gatekeepers are divided. Wil's heart pounded in his chest. *Could the Erebus and Gatekeepers really be working together?* Given the device discovered on Earth and its likely role as a transdimensional bridge, it wasn't outside the realm of possibility. The bigger question was why two powerful races would involve Tarans in their planning. As far as Wil was concerned, the only explanation for that is that Tarans were a means to an end—and the Coalition very well may be sending the entire civilization into a trap.

Pyra shook his head and let out a little chuckle when Wil didn't respond immediately. "I know, right? It doesn't make any sense."

The words were confirmation of Wil's speculation, but knowing those scenarios were the truth still shook his core. *Why would the Erebus side with the Coalition? What's their aim?*

Wil let out a slow breath. "Okay, so the Coalition is likely working with aliens behind the Taran government's back."

"Yes."

Wil tried not to let his concern show. "Do you know about any leaders in the broader Coalition?"

"As far as I can tell, Maggie Steyn is the brains behind SPEAR, which puts her toward the top of the organization as a whole." He paused. "I do have one potential lead, but it will be difficult to follow up on without tipping them off."

"And what's that?"

"One of the people I heard Maggie speaking to is a board member of MPS. They're the Head of a prominent Lower Dynasty—Reva Calrosi."

Wil took a slow breath. *We've suspected as much for a long time.* He nodded. "We've never had a name to trace to the activity before."

"You can see where this goes. Besides that, I know the Coalition's base of operations is on a ship rather than on a planet or somewhere else stationary."

"That explains why we haven't been able to track them down."

The officer nodded. "They keep the details of the ship highly classified. Not even Andrei knew its location at any given time."

"Do you have any contacts on the ship?"

"Not anyone who I think would assist in our efforts. The main person I coordinated with was Maggie's assistant, Hanek. But, he's a Coalition career-man, very by-the-book."

"I can't imagine the kind of person who goes along with alien collaborators like that."

Pyra wrung his hands. "I'm not sure how many people know who's calling the shots behind the scenes. I didn't figure out the Erebus connection until the very end."

"Any thoughts on who else might be involved?"

"It's all speculation and guesses beyond what I've already said. They kept information highly compartmentalized. What we refer to as 'the Coalition' is a loose definition of the real organization. More accurately, the Alliance, SPEAR, and other branches operate independently with only limited touchpoints to the larger structure. Maggie—er, Magdalena—and others I can't name are the common threads between those disparate divisions. The Steyn family in general, really. I'm not sure how a non-highborn family was able to amass that level of influence, but it happened."

"Every dynasty rose to its political position because it was already influential through business. Most of those fortunes were self-made if you go back far enough. Sounds like the Steyns were a modern dynasty in the making."

Pyra shrugged. "I guess so."

"It sounds like your firsthand knowledge was mostly related to SPEAR, correct?"

He nodded. "That's a weird one. When I first started working for Andrei, the SPEAR Tec name was protected. Then it's like they stopped caring and it became the center of the propaganda. SPEAR was plastered all over the place and the company's original operations became an afterthought."

"We've considered trying to hit all of their public assets in a unified strike," Wil said. "I have Jason working on a plan."

Pyra shook his head. "Not worth it now. Anything of value has been moved outside the SPEAR name."

A means to an end? Wil crossed his arms, considering the possibilities. Perhaps the company had outlived its usefulness. "What did they used to do? We've found little information about them on the Net, and even that was somewhat contradictory."

"It claimed to be biotech research, but I have strong suspicions that they were actually manufacturing and distributing drugs."

"What kind?"

"The sort people sample and then they have a customer for life, and you need to know the right people to get more."

"A club on Glaendor makes a lot of sense." The planet had a reputation for catering to those with less than legal tastes and a penchant for partying. There were few better worlds situated to serve as the hub for a recreational drug empire. "Do you know of anything tying SPEAR directly to the club or the distribution activities?"

"I saw flight logs for the transport ships, but I was never able to copy the information. Stars, I wanted to, but Andrei had everything on lockdown at all times. I'm sorry I wasn't able to do more, sir."

"You were there to intervene when it mattered most. There's nothing to apologize for."

He nodded, but regret was still painted on his face. "I hope the political lead pans out. If you can access travel logs for them, then you might be able to find a travel pattern for the Coalition ship."

"Yes. And there is another possibility…" Wil mused.

"Sir?"

"Nothing for you to worry about." Wil smiled. "I'm sure you're exhausted. There's more I'd like to discuss, but it can wait for a later time."

Pyra gave a weary nod. "I'm happy to push through, but I can't deny that a good night's rest would do me wonders."

"Then you shall have it." Wil rose from the table. "Thank you again for everything."

"I'm glad to be of service." Pyra bowed his head.

Wil returned to the Command Wing and headed straight to Saera's office. She motioned him inside when she spotted him outside her door.

"How'd it go with Pyra?" she asked.

"Barely scratched the surface, but I caught one bit of bad news and three threads I'd like to trace sooner than later."

"I'm all ears. Let's hear the bad news first."

He closed the office door. "The Coalition may be a joint operation between Taran terrorists, the Erebus, and a rogue faction of Gatekeepers."

She sat still, lips parted, in silence for several seconds. "Well, naturally," she said with thick sarcasm. "This just keeps getting better and better."

"We need to look into a planet, Zeron. They might be excavating some ancient tech on the sly."

Saera perked up. "Zeron… That name is familiar. I think Kali visited there early in her internship investigation. I don't recall there being anything of note."

"It's worth another look, then."

She made a note on her desktop. "All right, what else?"

"Pyra also gave us a name: Reva Calrosi. There might be a political connection directly to Monsari, which would obviously be huge."

Saera brightened. "I don't want to get my hopes up, but

yeah. Wow." She added another note on her desktop.

"And, finally, there's an unsubstantiated suspicion that the Coalition's operations are managed from a ship equipped with an independent jump drive."

She nodded. "That actually makes a lot of sense."

"It does." He leaned closer. "What I couldn't tell Pyra and haven't even told you is that I anticipated the independent jump drive tech would get abused through illegal activity once it hit the civilian market. It's not supposed to be trackable, but I… well, let's say I left a backdoor into the system in case there was ever a real emergency."

Her mouth dropped open slightly. "Why didn't you say anything sooner? We could have tracked them down months ago!"

"It doesn't work like that—can't just find a ship anywhere in the galaxy. Tracking still requires tracing a path. However, Andy said there was a ship that jumped away right after the TSS arrived at Glaendor. There's a strong possibility that was the ship in question. You're the first person I'm telling that we might actually be able to track it."

"I won't say a word."

"I'll loop Jason in, too, but I don't want it going beyond the three of us."

Saera nodded. "Agreed."

"Good. Let's forget about taking out a limb—I want their head. So, if you can follow up on the Reva Calrosi lead, I'll get on the tracking issue and see what I can come up with."

She smiled. "Absolutely. I'm glad we're finally getting somewhere."

CHAPTER 22

JASON'S GAZE PASSED back and forth between his parents, having difficulty believing what they were telling him. It made so much sense, and yet… it changed everything.

"The Coalition was never just Tarans," Wil was saying. "Monsari and Steyn have been working with these rogue Gatekeepers and Erebus the entire time."

"I still want to know, why involve the Tarans at all?" Saera asked.

Jason nodded, trying to get his thoughts in order. "I agree. It doesn't make sense. They're so powerful compared to us— well, normal people, anyway."

"Except in one way," Wil replied. "We have numbers on our side. And breadth of territory."

"In all fairness, we don't know the scope of civilization for the Erebus or Gatekeepers," Saera pointed out.

"We can draw a conclusion based on their behaviors. Simply put, they would *not* have involved the Tarans if there was a more efficient method to accomplish their goals."

"So, what *are* the goals?" Jason asked, a hint of frustration creeping into his tone.

"I believe it comes down to their difficulty with accessing our spacetime reality," his father explained. "My educated guess is that they wish to eradicate us but due to the scope of our civilization, they are unable to simply reach down from the higher dimensions to do so. Their powers are immense—in concentrated areas. Over the breadth of a galaxy, it might be too difficult, or damaging, for them to harm us.

"Meanwhile, the Gatekeepers are scientists more than fighters. Even when they attacked those planets with the Gate spheres, it wasn't a weapon so much as repurposing other technology toward destructive ends. I believe they wish to claim our worlds as their own, so they have teamed up with the Erebus to eradicate Tarans without damaging all of our planets."

Jason stared at him, blinking slowly. "How can you say that so calmly?"

Wil smiled. "No, this is good news."

"Please, elaborate." Saera's brows furrowed with concern.

"The Erebus have given us the method for them to access spacetime—the power core they 'gifted' us. That means we have a guide we can reverse-engineer for us to access the higher dimensions."

Jason scowled. "Does it really work like that?"

"Not if you're most people. But we're not."

Saera tilted her head. "So, you're suggesting that we use the technology they gave us and turn it against them to launch an offensive on their home turf?"

"Essentially, yes."

"Dad, I don't mean to sound negative, but this is crazy," Jason said. He'd heard a lot of outlandish plans from his father over the years, but this one to harness the power of the device on Earth in combination with the strange, large-scale energy field generated by the Erebus' power core had way too many unknowns for his taste. Sure, it might work, but it also would be a massive risk.

Wil smiled slightly. "Your objection is noted, and I appreciate you speaking your mind on the matter."

"He's right, Wil," Saera chimed in. "I think we need to investigate this more before seriously considering it as an option."

"Okay. I'll work on the models and report back."

Despite the words, Jason sensed that his father had already made up his mind about the planned course of action. To talk him out of it, they'd need an alternative approach. That meant tracking down other leads on the Coalition. "Where did you land on the trace of the potential Coalition ship?" he asked.

"It's a mixed bag," his father replied. "I was able to confirm that there was a ship, but I haven't been able to trace its path yet. The backdoor is… complicated. I think rather than a true trace, I'll need to deploy a flag, of sorts, to alert us if the ship's nav background pings one of the SiNavTech beacons. While not ideal, it'll just be a matter of time before we catch the ship in a place where we can intercept it."

While disappointing, the plan was still a better prospect than they'd had for a long time. "Where does that leave us for now?" Jason asked.

"More research, modeling, and strategizing," Wil said. "But we're close."

Jason stood up. "All right, I best get back to it, then."

"Yes. But before you go, what was it you wanted to say about Mika?" Wil asked.

"Right, yeah…" He crossed his arms. "I can't put my finger on it, but something has been different about him since Glaendor."

"Has Kali said anything?" Saera asked.

"No. I've asked a few other Agents, but no one has picked up on it. Might just be in my head. Maybe just picking up their new bond or something."

Wil pursed his lips, considering. "I trust your gut. As soon as we're finished with the interviews, why don't you get him and Kali out of Headquarters, try to suss out an agenda, if there is one."

"I can do that. Weren't you saying another look at Zeron is in order?"

Wil nodded. "Indeed. And Jason, keep all this between the three of us."

His chest tightened. "Yes, I know." He hated that he had to keep anything from Lexi. The relationship his parents shared, able to discuss all aspects of their professional lives, was something he envied. Perhaps, in time, he could have that with Lexi, too.

They were so close to a breakthrough with the Coalition, they couldn't risk a breach of any sort now. He had to see it through to the end.

—   —   —

Lexi had found herself to be an anomaly within TSS Headquarters, but for the first time, there was someone even more out of place than her. She was both intrigued and disgusted by Mika Hendri's story—the son of an ex-Priest and powerful telekinetic in his own right, who'd spent several years on the road managing a band of musicians. She needed to meet the man for herself.

Since Mika was also involved with Kali, a TSS Agent with a highborn background, Lexi had no shortage of potential conversation openers with him. She decided to track him down in the mess hall and see how it went.

She spotted him sitting alone and made her move. "Hey, welcome to the ex-criminals-turned-TSS-consultants club," Lexi greeted Mika as she sat down across the table from him.

"Uh, hi. Who are you, exactly?" the blond man asked her, his eyebrows drawing together.

"Lexi Kalis. Both of us got pulled into this mess in similar ways, from the sound of it."

"I highly doubt that."

"Your mom was one of the captives in stasis, right?" Lexi asked.

His eyes widened. "Yes. How…?"

"My friend, Melisa, was taken, too. I joined the Alliance—one of the Coalition's branches—in an attempt to find her, but that didn't go so well."

"Oh. Well, my involvement is significantly more foked up than that."

"Try me."

"My father was an ex-Priest who left the Priesthood before the fall, and he orchestrated the entire genetic experimentation scheme behind the abductions."

Lexi had known all of that already, but hearing it directly from him and seeing how the poor guy looked sick over the whole thing hurt her heart. Part of her wanted to be angry with him for having such a close connection to the horror, but it wasn't fair to blame the child of a monster simply by association.

"That sucks," she said at last, not wanting to tip him off that she already knew most of his background.

"Tell me about it."

"For what it's worth, you landed in a good place. The TSS

has offered me the kind of home I never thought I'd have.

Mika stared down at his plate. "So everyone keeps telling me."

"You know, we have a lot in common. We're both products of genetic experimentations outside the Priesthood who ended up bonded to TSS Agents. I think the Universe is going to demand that we become friends."

"Oh! You're Jason's girlfriend?"

"Yeah."

Some of the tension went out of him. "I didn't realize at first."

"Sorry, I probably should have led with that."

He shrugged. "You know, you might be the first person here who I actually want to talk to."

Lexi placed her hand on her chest. "I'm flattered."

"I mean, there *are* some striking similarities with us." He chuckled. "I didn't think it was possible that anyone else could be in as weird of a situation as me."

"Likewise. But man, as your new friend, I'm not going to lie. Your whole deal," she let out a long, melodramatic breath, "*way* crazier than mine. And I'm now somehow dating a Sietinen, so that's saying something."

"Well, Kali is Lower Dynasty, too, so there's that…"

"Dude."

He smiled. "Kinda wild when your life gets put into perspective, huh?"

"That's for sure. I've had a lot of that, recently."

"Any tips on how to settle in around here?"

Lexi raised an eyebrow. "Oh, you're going to be hanging around?"

"For the time being, I think. They…" He faded out. "I don't think they trust me."

Jason had indicated as much to Lexi, but she didn't want to discourage Mika by confirming his perception of his somewhat low standing at the moment. She knew all too well how easily confidence could be shaken when there was only a questionable past to fall back on. "Trust is earned," Lexi said. "From what I've heard, you've helped save the day on more than one occasion recently. I'd say you're off to a pretty good start."

"Yeah, I guess so." He paused. "May I ask you a personal question?"

"Sure."

"Are you happy?"

The question caught her off-guard. "Yeah, I am."

"So, you've put your past behind you?"

She shrugged. "As much as I can."

Mika got a distant look in his eyes. "How?"

"By focusing on the present and future instead."

"There's this weight, you know? Sometimes I'm fine, but then it… it's suffocating."

"Yeah, I get it. But when you have someone who loves you, that weight gets to be a little less every day."

"I guess."

She leaned forward slightly. "Has anyone been harassing you?"

He shook his head. "No, it's not that. There are all of these people who are willing to give me another chance, but how do I forgive myself?"

"The first step is to recognize that you did what you had to do to survive. What you do now is up to you. Is it in Kali's best interest for you to wallow in self-pity about the shite hand you were dealt earlier in life?"

"I hear you." Mika pulled out a handheld from his pocket

and checked the time. "Ah, shite, sorry, I've gotta go. I'm meeting with the High Commander."

"Oh boy, yeah, don't want to be late for that."

He winced. "I have no idea what to expect."

"He's fair," Lexi said. "Just don't try to hide anything and you'll be fine."

"Yeah, thanks." He stood up, and Lexi rose to face him. "I guess I'll see you around?"

"Definitely. And hey, thanks for what you did on Antaris, helping people get out safely. They were there because of my training program, so…"

"Sure, anytime. I'm glad I could help."

Lexi could hear the sincerity in his tone. Despite his insecurities and tarnished past, he had a good heart. With a little time and healing, she was confident he would be just fine.

— — —

It had been a busy three days of interviews and discussion, but there was one conversation Wil had intentionally put off to the end. In his head, he'd run through what he could say to Mika, and he came up short every time. Their last conversation had been an interrogation more than anything, but now he needed to figure out Mika's future; it was a lot of responsibility.

Wil knew better than most what a burden it was to have been born as a tool for someone else's designs. Though their masters' ambitions were on different scales, there had been a similar result in that the first twenty-so years of their lives had been following orders to do objectionable things. It took a toll on a person in a profound way.

He didn't know if he might be able to offer Mika the kind of words of wisdom he'd wished someone would have shared with him when he was a young man, but he wanted to try.

Wil arrived at the conference room a few minutes early and sat down at the far end of the table while he waited for Mika. A couple minutes after the scheduled start time, the door finally opened.

"Sorry I'm late," Mika said as he entered.

"It's okay. Please, have a seat." Wil motioned to the chair across from him.

Mika kept his eyes downcast as he sat down, and his shoulders were rounded forward. There was no resemblance to the Priests of his lineage. This was just a scared young man looking to find his place after his life had been upended.

"How are you settling in?" Wil asked, hoping to ease the young man's nerves.

"Everyone has been great, thanks." The reply was barely above a whisper.

"This isn't an interrogation this time. You can relax."

Mika chuckled a little. "Sure."

Right, like a person can relax on demand when facing an authority figure. Wil leaned back in a casual position in his seat to lead by example. "You've been through a lot since we last spoke. I was pleased to hear about many of the things you've done, and others…"

"I've done what's been needed to help correct wrongs. I know I've bent the rules, but it was never without a reason."

Wil caught his gaze. "I want you to know, I always make a point to look at each individual and their actions. You were in difficult circumstances for a long time, and that can force a person to do things they wouldn't have otherwise."

"Yeah."

"That doesn't give you a free pass going forward, though."

"I know. I understand what's expected of me, and I'll try to do better." His tone was sincere, but Mika had made those promises before and broken them.

I wish they hadn't already bonded. Wil trusted his Agents, but from a professional standpoint, he couldn't extend that faith to Agents' partners without each person having proven their reliability. Yet, Wil knew firsthand how a bond eclipsed everything else. Essentially, Kali had to be considered compromised until Mika had demonstrated he could adhere to the Agent code of conduct. The pair would have to be put to the test sooner than later.

"Kali is a good Agent," Wil said at last. "I think you'll make a nice team."

"A team?"

"It's inevitable, isn't it? That is, if you'd like to work together."

Mika seemed surprised by the suggestion. "We have a good track record so far. I'd like to see what else we can do."

"I would, as well. I believe you two are a good test case for TSS Agents and civilians working together in a partnership. With the new civilian training initiative, those graduates may look to us for career opportunities, and it'd be nice to know if that kind of arrangement might be viable."

"Doesn't that defeat the purpose of going through the Agent training program if you can just do that?"

"It'll be different roles and responsibilities, but I'd like to show that we can collaborate in a productive way."

"Yeah, that'd be good."

Time to find out in what way that might be. Wil sent out a subtle questioning probe. "I was surprised to learn you have your own starship at such a young age. The *Sepiantia* is quite an interesting vessel." He decided that 'interesting' was a nicer word than 'odd', though he found the vessel to be rather grotesque—almost to the point of being visually offensive. Nonetheless, it did possess intriguing functionality not usually found on private vessels, and especially not the combination of elements.

Mika brightened. "Yeah, she's my baby. I designed her myself."

Wil bit back a gasp of horror. The ship was so contrary to his own design aesthetic that there was no way the two of them would see eye-to-eye. "It's… creative."

"I started working on it as a kid. Tregaren helped get it constructed."

"Nice." The story wasn't too dissimilar from Wil's own experience as a teenager, only his secretive design was co-opted by the TSS and eventually turned into the *Conquest*—by his estimation, the most perfect ship ever built. He decided it wise to change the subject. "So, what is it you'd like to do with your life moving forward?" *Please don't say ship design.*

"Really, I don't care what I do so long as it's with Kali." He paused, searching for the words. "I… don't know what my life would have become without her."

Wil smiled. "The right person can change everything. I'm glad you found each other when you did."

"Me too. I can't imagine a future without her in it."

There was no doubt the young man loved Kali, that was clear. But Wil could detect something wasn't quite right deeper down—like Mika was somehow detached from himself and was holding onto his relationship with Kali like a lifeline.

"Is everything okay, Mika?" Wil asked.

Mika tensed, only perceptible to Wil's trained eyes. "It's great."

I see what Jason meant. There's something off. He didn't want to call attention to the suspicion, so Wil smiled. "Well, let's see what we can do to get you and Kali a posting together."

— — —

Hanek tensed when he saw the incoming transmission marked with TSS credentials. *Have they found us?*

He glanced around the office, unsure whether to answer or ignore the message. Tentatively, he reached out and accepted the incoming vidcall.

Hanek nearly fell out of his seat when he saw Mika's image appear. Tregaren's son. A traitor to the Coalition's cause. "How did you get this number?" Hanek demanded.

"Easy now, Hanek. Where is my mother?"

"Your mother?"

Mika looked down at himself. "Oh, not his. Maggie."

"What?" Hanek froze in his seat.

Mika sighed. "I'm Andrei, I'm using this body. You wanted an 'in' to the TSS, now you have it."

"But you… ascended."

"You're her assistant, aren't you? Well start assisting!"

Hanek finally broke free from his shock and transferred the video feed to Magdalena's office, running up to her door as the connection moved over.

"Oh, my stars!" Magdalena exclaimed just as Hanek entered her office.

"Don't be dramatic, Mother. I have no intention of remaining in this vessel."

"How did…?" she faded out, reaching toward the screen as though trying to cup her son's face.

"He tried to destroy me, but I linked myself to him instead," Mika-Andrei explained. "I've been exerting control when I can for little bursts, then backing away so they can't detect me. The TSS truly is full of idiots, no different than when I trained here."

"We thought you were dead," Magdalena whispered.

"Far from it. I'm more alive than ever—no more restrictions."

Proof that ascension is possible. Hanek hadn't fully believed it. But unless Mika was deranged and also an excellent actor, this was Andrei's mind speaking through the other man's body. The fact alone that he knew how to reach out to this secure, private line was proof.

"How do we get you back in a body of your own?" Magdalena asked.

"Why would I want that?" Mika-Andrei replied. "I can be much more useful this way. In fact, I have a plan."

CHAPTER 23

"Yeah, I've heard the name," Raena told her mother. "May I ask what's the sudden interest in a random Lower Dynasty?"

"Not random," Saera said. "A close associate of Monsari."

Raena caught on. "Probably worth me feeling out a potential business relationship, then?"

"As a TSS officer, it's not my place to make recommendations related to business or political dealings."

"Of course. I was just thinking out loud." Raena flashed an innocent smile. "I should get to work."

"I appreciate your dedication. Love you."

"Love you, too." Raena ended the vidcall.

It was rare for her mother to reach out on TSS business, but perhaps her father wanted to distance himself from this particular request. The message had clearly been meant as a tip for a line of investigation the TSS couldn't conduct itself without drawing unwanted attention. Given her own interest in the topic, Raena was happy to help them out off the books.

However, this wasn't something to look into on her own. She checked Ryan's calendar and saw that he had some free time for the next hour, so she headed over to his office.

"Hey," she greeted him behind his desk, "got a few minutes?"

"Sure. What's up?"

She closed the door. "Do you know Reva Calrosi?" she asked while taking a seat in one of the visitor chairs.

Ryan's brow pinched together. "The name is familiar, but I can't place it off the top of my head. Why?"

"Word has it they're close associates of a certain other dynasty we'd like to know better."

He nodded his understanding. "And might they link to external activities?"

"Perhaps the very link we've hoped to find." The office was supposed to be secure, but it was always better to err on the side of caution by speaking vaguely.

"Have you run a search on them yet?" he asked.

"No, I thought it might be best to do that together."

"Okay, let's see…" Ryan adjusted the controls on the glass walls facing the rest of the DGE administrative center so they were in opaque privacy. He then brought up a search for the name on the holodisplay.

The results didn't take long to load, but the information wasn't at all what Raena had expected.

Her eyes widened. "What's a media company doing in a partnership with a power supplier?"

"That is an excellent question."

It was very common throughout the High Dynasties for select Lower Dynasties to fall under one of the larger corporations. For instance, Hyttinen's Apex brand served as a dealer for DGE ships. In almost all cases, those smaller companies match the general scope of work of whichever High Dynasty corporation they supported. But Calrosi Enterprises was a media firm working under the umbrella of a company in an unrelated technical field, which meant they must have a different sort of relationship.

Why didn't Mom mention this? Perhaps she hadn't wanted to taint Raena's read of it. "If a company has done something bad or isn't performing well, it's not uncommon to hire a PR firm."

"Yes. I suppose the next question is, how long has this relationship existed?"

"Is there an easy way to find out?"

"Ask. But I suspect an investigation is in order." Ryan returned his attention to the computer to see if there were any historical news reports about the working relationship between the two corporate entities. "Huh, that's interesting," he said after a minute. He pointed to an article. "This indicates they started working together several months after the Erebus showed up."

"You mean, at the same time we started getting all the bad press out of the blue?"

He let out a long breath. "Yep."

"It *is* all connected, isn't it?" Raena shook her head.

"Looks that way." Ryan leaned back in his seat, pensively reviewing the information.

She scoffed. "No wonder the media has been pushing that narrative—they're being directed."

"That makes me feel better, honestly."

"Yeah, it's messed up, but I agree." She crossed her arms.

"Do you think anyone else has made the connection? It's not like it's well-hidden."

"There's no reason for others to be suspicious. It's only standing out to us now because of external factors others won't be thinking about."

"What can we do about it?"

"I don't know. The media angle is annoying, but I'm more concerned about what they've been using that relationship to hide."

"Like funding the Coalition," he said in her mind.

"Exactly. But that *relationship is buried behind layers and layers of protection. I doubt we'd be able to prove they're funding those activities in a timely manner."*

"True," he continued out loud, "but they've opened themselves up for scrutiny by making accusations against us and DGE. We'll fight this."

Raena combed her fingers through her ponytail. "I want to do what's right. Is there any way to gain trust and avoid this kind of further conflict?"

He shrugged. "Some people will always look for fault. We can only try to make ourselves a little better every day."

"Still, the continued targeting of DGE, no matter what we do, just doesn't make sense. A move against Dainetris is a move against Sietinen. All of the other dynastic corporations rely on the SiNavTech network. Why would they…" She faded out as a disturbing thought flashed through her mind. "Oh, my stars."

"What, Raena?"

"What if they try to make the case to push SiNavTech into public control?"

"No, that…" Ryan started to protest before fading out. His brows knitted. "The High Dynasty corporations were already reclassified as public services after the Priesthood fell. What more could be done?"

"That reclassification changed the businesses to be subject to public approval," she clarified. "However, they remain for-profit private entities from a financial standpoint. If the case were made that it should be *truly* public… Well, that would change everything."

"It would set a precedent the other dynasties would never agree to," Ryan said.

"SiNavTech is different, though. *Everyone* relies on the beacon network for interstellar travel." Raena's head spun with the implications of the scenario. "You can plant a garden to grow your own food or go mine your own ore, but there's no feasible alternative to maintain interstellar society without nav beacons."

"That's true," Ryan agreed.

While independent jump drives were capable of performing the necessary calculations for safe travel without the galaxy-spanning SiNavTech infrastructure, the civilian version of the drives still used the nav beacons as reference points whenever possible to increase safety and reliability. There was no denying that SiNavTech was the lynchpin of galactic society.

"We need to talk to Cris. Right away," Ryan said.

Raena nodded. *Stars, should we have seen this coming sooner?*

The morning had quickly spiraled into worrisome territory. Hopefully her grandfather would be able to offer some much-needed perspective and reassurance.

She initiated a connection to Cris' office with an invitation to the holoconference. A 'busy' notification popped up on her desktop.

>>Emergency,<< she wrote. >>Monsari strategy ASAP.<< Not her most elegant message, but it would get the point across.

>>Give me a minute,<< Cris typed back.

Raena's leg shook with nervous energy while she waited for him to get on the call.

As soon as the image materialized and he saw their concerned faces, Cris' brows drew together. "What happened?"

"Not an event, but rather something we learned," Raena replied. "Well, more like may have figured out."

She gave him a quick recap of the lead from her mother and the media connection before going into the potential motivations behind the targeted messaging. "Do you think it's possible?" she asked when it had all been laid out.

Cris sat in silence for several seconds, thinking. "I would like to dismiss the possibility, but I can't," he said at last.

Raena's heart dropped. Even though it had been her idea, she'd hoped it was wild speculation and cooler minds would prevail. For her grandfather of all people to be entertaining the hypothesis painted an alarming picture. "Where do we go from here?"

"You're right about this kind of move setting an unappealing precedent for the other High Dynasties' corporations, so getting support for any legislation will be an uphill battle. I'm not sure that there's an urgent risk here."

"Except for the fact that Monsari has been relentless in their messaging, so they might have something lined up already," Ryan pointed out.

"True. And if this is a last-ditch bid for survival, they very well may have called in every favor and bought off everyone they can to rally support." Cris sighed. "I'm going to need to think on this and consult with Kate. Without hard evidence, it's difficult to strategize."

"Of course, take your time," Raena said. "I mean, as much time as—"

"We'll make it quick, don't worry. I'll get back to you soon."

Raena wished she could be in the room to hear their

discussion, but there were other matters where her time would be better spent at the moment. Her grandparents were the right people to strategize about this; she could have them walk her through their thinking for educational purposes at a later time. "We'll be standing by," she said.

He nodded. "In the meantime, I suggest keeping a low profile. Keep it business as usual."

"Will do," Ryan acknowledged.

As soon as the call ended, Raena leaned back in her seat. "This is a mess."

Ryan shrugged. "On the bright side, this is the most sense anything has made in months."

"That's true."

He paused in consideration. "It's funny about that media connection. Didn't even occur to me to check."

"It's always like that, isn't it? Something seems so obvious the moment it's pointed out."

"For sure. What else aren't we thinking about that we should be?"

"A very good question." She rapped her fingers on her crossed forearms. "If they have a media company in their pocket, I'd wager they've also bought off someone on the financial side."

Ryan nodded. "That would make a lot of sense. And what about legal counsel?"

"Yeah, someone like that would have to be in on it. The councilmembers aren't infallible." Raena and Ryan had come face-to-face with corruption several years back during the legal proceedings to reinstate the Dainetris Dynasty. While they'd tried to root out any other compromised individuals in the time since, there was no way to know others weren't well-hidden within the ranks of the Taran legal system.

"I trust your grandparents, and your Vaenetri family members are fairly trustworthy, but beyond that…"

"I'd draw the line of 'full trust' only with my parents, grandparents, and Jason," Raena said. "We'll need to tread carefully with everyone else."

"Okay." He took a slow breath. "I know we must have other allies. We'll figure this out."

"If not for personal reasons, then there will be other highborn who side with us because the notion of Sietinen losing its power over a legal technicality is too disconcerting to stomach."

"Ahh, the motivational force of greed and ambition."

"What does it say about us for wanting to hold onto our power?" Raena asked.

"That we care—we're passionate enough to fight for it. But I'd gladly hand over the reins."

"Yeah, me too." Raena smoothed her dress. "But we can't walk away—not with so many people counting on us." She stood and began pacing. "The best countermove to the negative press remains to get the public on our side. No matter what other leaders say or do, if our people want us around, the rest is just noise."

"How are we supposed to do that?" Ryan asked.

"By listening to the will of the people."

"Right now, that seems to be splitting up the Empire. I'm not sure we can grant that."

She shook her head. "No, but there are other ways we can show we're listening to them. We as leaders need to remember, and put into action, that the government answers to its people, not the other way around. It's our job to find a way to fulfill the public's wishes while still looking out for the Empire's best interests."

"An eternal struggle."

"One which other civilizations have failed to navigate. Those trials often don't end well for anyone."

"We're in a shitestorm either way now. How do you follow the will of the people when they're fundamentally divided?"

"By finding common ground. It's a narrow sliver, but it exists."

He examined her. "I'm continually impressed by your endless optimism."

"There's a fine line between optimism and desperate dreaming these days." She sighed. "There are moments when giving up is tempting."

"Never an option."

"Exactly. So, I'll pull out my pom-poms and rah-rah us to success."

He stared at her, head tilted. "I think something was lost in translation there, but sure."

She chuckled. "The point is, fake it until you make it."

"That'll be the title of my biography."

"I was going to say the same thing." She laughed.

"Well, let's figure out how to write that story together."

Raena nodded. "Chapter One: How to Prevent a Full-on Civil War."

— — —

Good workers were hard to come by, and with a potential galactic civil war and transdimensional alien invasion both potentially on the horizon, the TSS needed all the help it could get. In particular, Jason knew he needed to have a team ready to face those challenges. Whether it was the Coalition investigation or a future threat, he was in a leadership position now. Just like his father had formed the Primus Elites as a young man and those team members remained close friends and colleagues to this day, it was time for Jason to begin establishing a group of his own in earnest.

He would have scooped up Kira if she wasn't already subscribed to the TUF. Another name had quickly risen to the top of his list, though. Kali had proved herself to be a courageous and capable field Agent, and since she was currently between assignments, this was as good a time as any to see if she was interested in working together. He also recognized that she was a package deal, and Mika was still an unknown. Before anything else, Jason needed to test Mika's loyalties.

A knock at Jason's office door called his attention from his desktop. Kali gave him a little wave when he looked up.

"Hey, thanks for coming," he greeted. "Have a seat."

She sat down in one of the visitor chairs across from his desk. "So, what can I do for you?" she asked.

"A very good question. What is it you'd like to do with your career going forward?"

Her brows raised with surprise. "I haven't thought about it too much."

"You must have some aspirations."

"Well, sure. I can say this: I like being out in the field. I think I'd go crazy behind a desk… no offense."

He smiled. "Believe me, I get out whenever I get the chance. What aspects did you like the most about your last assignment?"

"Not the part where I had to perform with the band, that's for sure!" She shuddered. "I guess my favorite part was trying to track down clues and put the pieces together."

That's the answer I was hoping for. He folded his hands on his desktop. "What would you say to revisiting one of those planets from your last investigation."

"I'm going to have to give Red Ghost a hard pass, sorry."

"Not that one. Zeron."

"That lifeless shithole? Why is it of interest?"

"It's come to my attention that their archaeological efforts might be a lead worth pursuing."

She tilted her head. "Is this by any chance related to the ancient alien tech discovered on Earth?"

"Perhaps. That's what I'd like for you to definitively determine."

Kali nodded, her eyes gleaming with the spark of interest. "Is this a solo assignment?"

"Naturally, it would make sense for Mika to accompany you as a second set of eyes."

"I appreciate that," she said after a slight delay.

"This job is difficult enough without needing to find ways to get in quality time together."

"It's nice to see someone else making it work."

"There's no other choice once you jump in." Jason hesitated. "I'm willing to give Mika a chance. My parents are, too. I can't vouch for every Agent, though."

"I know. I'm no stranger to stigma." She crossed her arms in reflexive defense. The fall of the Priesthood had been so well-publicized that it had gotten out that she had been one of their captives. No doubt, shaking off the 'victim' label had been difficult. Only time would tell if Mika could rise above the brand of 'traitor's son'.

"You're not alone," Jason said. "I'll do what I can to help you start your lives together." *Assuming he proves himself.*

"Thanks, I appreciate it."

"So, what do you think? You want to give the task force a try?"

She smiled. "Best offer I've had in a long time. Yeah, I'm game."

"All right. Laura will help coordinate the logistics of your transit to Zeron. Check in as soon as you get settled."

"Will do. Thank you for the opportunity. I'm excited to be a part of the team."

CHAPTER 24

WIL HAD BEEN over the possibilities dozens of times, but he kept coming back to the same option. *Stars help us if I'm wrong.*

The technology hidden on Earth was part of the answer, he was certain. Too many indicators pointed toward it—too many to pass off as coincidence.

There were risks no matter what he did. He'd delayed making decisions in favor of gathering more information, but that approach hadn't gotten them anywhere. Now, he had one last clue to go on. Though it required taking a risk, at least this way there would be proactive *action*.

His mind made up, he called a meeting for the TSS senior officers to convene in the C-1 conference room next to his office. If there were going to be objections, he may as well get them out of the way as soon as possible.

Saera was the first to arrive in the meeting space. She took one look at him and knew his mind. *"Are you sure?"* she asked.

"We can't refine how to use the technology to our advantage until we understand how it operates."

She nodded and took a seat.

Jason and Michael were next in, followed by Ian and Ethan.

"Thank you for coming on such short notice," Wil said when they all were seated. "I've decided to do something you may not agree with, but I believe it's the best course of action."

"It wouldn't be the first time we've supported a crazy plan of yours," Ian said with a slight smile.

"Very true," Wil acknowledged. "And I'll ask you to trust me again now. I want to activate the device on Earth—with Darin."

"Darin Suro?" Jason clarified.

Wil nodded. "The Aesir indicated that his apparent precognitive abilities might have something to do with a higher-dimensional connection. My hope is that latent link will focus the device's interface."

Michael frowned. "That's a big leap."

"Not for me based on what I've experienced firsthand. We're dealing with matters outside our conventional reality here. Call it a... feeling that this will work."

The officers exchanged glances.

"What do you need from us?" Michael asked.

"For you to keep a close watch on what happens when that device activates. If there is, in fact, an alien element working with the people behind the Coalition, they very well may be monitoring the device and react when we access it."

"You do realize we're completely screwed if the Erebus take this as an act of aggression?" Ian asked.

"And we're equally screwed if we sit back and do nothing until they decide to make a move against us," Wil replied. "At least this way, the fight would be on our terms."

Michael gave Wil the look he did when he had objections but knew he'd end up agreeing after a long, circular argument and had resolved to save them both the trouble. "Okay, I'll notify the appropriate people in the field."

"We'll take care of everything at Headquarters," Ethan added. "Good luck."

I suspect we're going to need it. Wil looked up to meet Saera's gaze. "I trust all of you to take appropriate action if things go sideways and I'm unable to provide instruction."

"We'll be standing by," Saera said.

"All right, no need to drag this out further." Wil stood up and nodded to the group.

As the other officers dispersed, Saera hung back. She telekinetically swung the door closed when everyone else had departed.

"What was that?" she asked.

"What do you mean?"

"That meeting was a joke. Why gather everyone like that to say all of two sentences?"

"It was more like a dozen."

She cast him a stern look. "You know what I mean."

He sat on the edge of the conference table. "It didn't feel right to try this without saying… something. There's a lot of risk here."

"Do you want me to talk you out of it? Because I can think of at least twenty good reasons why it's a bad idea."

"And how many of those would only result in delaying the inevitable?"

"Most."

He nodded. "If you tell me not to do this, I won't."

She didn't reply at first, standing with her arms crossed while staring through the floor, deep in thought. "We've been backed into a corner, and this is a chance to leap past our aggressors. I don't like it, but I agree it's ultimately the best course of action."

"Okay."

Saera let her arms fall to her sides and stepped up to Wil. "At the first sign of trouble, you drop everything and come back here. Agreed?"

"Yes." He took her hands in his. "I'll be as careful as I can be, I promise."

"All right." She wrapped her arms around him, hugging him close. "Come home soon."

He returned her hug. "I will. Hopefully with answers and a better plan."

All that remained was to gather Darin and head down to Earth. Under normal circumstances, he would contact Darin, explain the situation, and then give him time to decide if he wanted to participate. However, in this matter, there wasn't really an option; he needed Darin, and he needed him now.

Wil didn't like to throw around his authority, but there was an undeniable convenience in being able to interrupt any meeting within TSS Headquarters and extract someone for a side project. He sent a summons to Darin for him to leave class on Level 7 and to meet Wil in his office.

Several minutes later, there was a knock on the frame of the cracked-open door, and Darin peeked inside. "You wanted to see me, sir?"

"Yes, thank you for coming on short notice."

"How can I help?" The kid had a great attitude, there was no denying that.

"I'd like to see if we can put this precognizant ability of yours to use in a new way. You've no doubt heard about the ancient device we've been investigating on Earth, correct?"

"Yeah, a little."

"Well, I was able to interface with it recently. It appears to have some kind of higher-dimensional link, which isn't dissimilar from your own connection that grants you the flashes outside present time."

Darin nodded hesitantly. "Okay…"

"In short, I'd like to see if we can work together to interface with the device and focus its power."

"Sorry, sir, I just don't see how I'd be able to help with that."

"I hope you'll humor me and give it a shot."

"Yeah, I guess. I mean, yes, sir."

Wil didn't want to make it an order. He understood the young man's reluctance; it showed good sense. Clearly, though, he was a good soldier and would do whatever his commander asked.

Nonetheless, Wil had resolved to always be upfront with his subordinates. He needed Darin, but it had to be support on the right terms.

Wil leaned forward and looked Darin in his eyes. "I won't lie, Darin. This might be dangerous."

"What could happen?"

"Honestly? Anything." Wil shrugged. "My hope is that we'll be able to glean critical information that will give us a lot more options for dealing with the Erebus than we have right now. However, you know how powerful and unpredictable they are. Accessing this technology might be taken as an act of aggression."

"Oh." Darin swallowed hard.

"I wouldn't ask if it wasn't important. Will you help me?"

He nodded. "I don't care about the risks. I want answers. These things killed my family, and I'll do anything to stop them."

"Okay. Let's go."

Wil escorted the young man to the transport room, where

they took the TSD arch to the site in Belize. Darin took the bizarre transit method in stride, seemingly more intrigued by the prospect of being on Earth than anything to do with the unique technology.

"I've been curious about this place," Darin said as they exited the tent housing the arch on the planet's surface. "A lot of people around Headquarters have been talking about what's going on down here."

"We know much less than we should by this stage," Wil said. "I hope you can help change that."

"I'll do what I can," he said.

The two ventured through the little camp and down the well-trodden path toward the ancient pit. Workers around the camp looked on with surprised expressions as Wil passed, since he hadn't given any advance notice of his intentions. Seeing all the people now, though, he realized his mistake; he'd given Darin a choice about being here but none of these people. Really, the entire planet should be warned if he wanted to be equitable about it, but that was impractical on many levels.

He stopped in the central walkway and looked around. After several moments of consideration, he addressed them. "I'm going to activate the device again. If you would rather not be here for that, I suggest you depart immediately."

The onlookers stopped what they were doing and stared at him.

"Welcome back, sir," a familiar voice said from behind Wil.

He turned to see Trevor emerging from one of the work tents.

"What's this, now?" Trevor asked.

"I intend to tap into the device again," Wil repeated. "I have no idea what might happen, so clearing the area might not be a bad idea."

Trevor frowned. "That's not really an option. There are tours going on above," he indicated the floating platform supporting the ruins, "and dozens of people are working here. What kind of radius are we talking about?"

Wil didn't have a good answer for him, so he shrugged. "Honestly, if this goes wrong, I doubt there would be a safe place anywhere in the galaxy."

There were several concerned gasps at that and wide eyes all around the camp.

"I guess we may as well stay put, then," Trevor said with an uncomfortable chuckle.

"But please clear the site so we don't have distractions," Wil replied.

"Yes, sir." Trevor pulled out his handheld and started making entries.

Darin looked rather dour as he walked alongside Wil toward the excavated pit.

"Go ahead and speak freely," Wil told him.

Darin glanced at him before looking straight ahead again. "It's not really fair to give people the illusion of a choice when there isn't one at all."

"Welcome to my life."

Wil continued forward without further commentary for several meters before adding, "I know it's not fair to warn some people but not others. In some cases, the best I can do is look out for the people closest to me in the TSS. It's what anyone would do for their family."

Darin paled. "Do you think we're all about to die?"

"I always assume the worst so I can be pleasantly surprised."

The young man considered the statement. "I guess I'd

rather know I might be facing the end, so I have a chance to say goodbye. Not that I have anyone now."

"Select people know what we're about to do—those in positions to act if there's an interruption in the conventional chain of authority. The people in this camp are the early alert system."

Darin nodded with understanding. "So, it wasn't about giving them a choice, just priming them to sound the alarm."

"Fear isn't my preferred motivator, but it's effective at making a population hyper-aware. I want to know if there's any shift, however subtle."

"I can see why everyone considers you the best."

"I've just been through enough to have a reasonable sense of what works and what doesn't."

"Since you're suggesting we do this, I'll trust your experience."

Wil only nodded in response. He didn't have the heart to tell him that he was making up the strategy as he went along. Nothing about the Gatekeeper tech or the Erebus followed conventional wisdom. He could only hope that he wasn't leading all of his people astray.

Several workers hurried past them in the opposite direction along the path, heading back toward the camp. Their brows were pinched with concern as they looked Wil over, no doubt having received word from Trevor that something of significance was about to happen. There would be plenty of watchers monitoring the situation, just as Wil intended.

Wil paused at the top of the pit when they reached the site, gazing down into it as he assessed the strange energy which still emanated from the place. As requested, the site had been vacated.

"Do you feel anything here?" he asked Darin.

The young man stood still and quiet for several seconds. "Yeah, there's something strange here, but I can't put my finger on it."

"Keep ahold of that feeling and try to trace it. That's the connection we're here for."

"I'll try."

They descended the entry ramp curving around the edge of the ruins. The musty air and humidity closed around Wil, making it difficult to breathe. Part of it was certainly nerves, which he refused to show in front of this young Militia trainee.

The energy intensified closer to the bottom—even more than Wil remembered from his previous visit. At the base of the ramp, he sensed the device's interface reaching out to his mind.

"There's something here," Darin whispered, a slight waver to his voice.

"That's the device. It has a telepathic interface, though you're the first non-Gifted person who's been able to detect it. The first person other than me, in fact."

The young man's eyes went wide. "Really?"

"I chose you for a reason. Let's see what we can learn together."

"What do I do?" Darin asked. His eyes darted nervously from side to side, scanning every surface within the chamber.

"That's going to be a bit of trial and error, I'm afraid," Wil replied. "Clear your mind and do whatever you do when you try to control the visions."

"It's so random…" Darin started to say before fading out.

"Nothing is truly random. You just haven't identified the pattern yet. Don't overthink it; relax and be in the moment."

The young man furrowed his brows and stared at the pedestal in the center of the chamber. "This place feels so weird."

"That's a good start."

"It's old, isn't it?"

"Very."

Darin took several slow breaths. "Other places where I've gotten this feeling, I've been able to get a vague sense of where its history started. I can't here."

"You just have to go back further. Try to trace it back to the beginning. Who built it, and why?"

"The visions don't work like that."

"Then what *can* you tell me?"

Darin squeezed his eyes closed, taking slow, deliberate breaths. After a minute, he opened his eyes and shook his head. "There is something here, but I can't touch it. It's like it doesn't want me to."

No, that would be too easy. Wil nodded. "I wanted to start simple, but I figured we'd have to get creative. You've mentally linked before when they were testing your ability, right?"

"Yeah. And in some interviews."

"That's right, with Jason."

He nodded.

"Okay, good. With me, it will be similar to how it was with him." Wil indicated for Darin to sit down on the ground with him near the pedestal. "Relax. Let me direct your thoughts."

When they were settled, Wil initiated a telepathic link, hovering at the edge of Darin's consciousness until he was allowed in. He could tell that Darin was uncomfortable with the link, but he complied.

"We're going to try to speak with the device, together now," Wil said in his mind. *"I'll take the lead."*

"Okay."

Wil reached for the device like he'd done previously. It was waiting for him.

"Specify request," it stated.

Direct communication with the device wasn't Wil's objective. Instead, he focused on the presence of the entity on the other end of the link. It felt closer to him now than it had when Wil had come alone. Somehow, Darin served as a more direct connection. He tried to trace that link to the entity's location in space.

"Display record of this device's last full activation," Wil requested.

"Invalid parameter."

An overwhelming sense of immensity exploded in Wil's mind. Darin cried out in pain and fell limp on the ground where he'd been seated. Wil felt like he'd been gripped in a vise, unable to move and barely able to breathe.

A new presence filled his mind. *"We are nowhere and everywhere. You are one. You will submit."*

Wil recoiled from the sudden assault, but like his first time connecting to the device, it held onto his mind. He fought against it, desperate to check on Darin and get out of there. *This was a mistake.*

The ground began to tremble and the energy in the pit intensified. Rivulets of light around the sphere atop the pedestal started to move faster and glow more brightly.

"What do you want from me?" Wil asked.

"Submit."

There was zero chance of that happening.

"No!" Wil sent a powerful energy wave at the presence pressing in around his consciousness. It loosened its grasp just enough for him to pull free.

He hastily severed the connection. The trembling stopped and the lights returned to their leisurely pace of movement.

That power... This device was a connection, all right. But whatever was on the other side wasn't something he could face right now, alone and unprepared. He'd hoped to bypass the higher-dimensional entities to use the device to read the pattern, but that wasn't an option.

What else can we do? It might already be too late for Tarans. It was clear the Erebus weren't going to keep up their façade of being generous benefactors to the Taran race any longer. *Do we keep pretending or make our stand?*

Darin had yet to move from where he fell, though his pulse was still strong and steady.

Wil took several calming breaths, realizing his heart was racing. As soon as he'd collected himself enough to move without feeling like he was about to pass out, he knelt next to Darin and checked his vitals.

Though Darin was still unconscious, Wil could sense the thoughts within his mind, much like those of someone dreaming. He gently reached out to him telepathically. *"Darin, wake up."*

The young man stirred. "What... What happened?"

"I'm not sure. How do you feel?"

"My head hurts." He massaged his temple with one hand as he sat up. "Did you talk to it?"

"It wasn't open to discussion, I'm afraid."

"So, it didn't work?"

"No. But on a positive note, we're still alive and the galaxy wasn't instantly destroyed."

Darin flashed a weak smile. "Pretty good day, then."

"Yeah." Wil extended his hand to Darin to help him up. "Let's get back to Headquarters."

The mission had been an utter failure, but it had offered confirmation for a reality Wil had been reluctant to accept. *We can't fight them like this.*

He'd been avoiding that truth for the better part of a year now, but the cold reality of it closed in around him. No matter what they did from this dimension, it would never be enough. They would need to fight the Erebus on their level.

He knew the thought of that should terrify him, but instead he felt a sense of peace he'd rarely experienced in his life. Ever since he was a boy, he'd been running from problem to problem, trying to find solutions for issues others created centuries, or more, before his own birth. He'd been told time and again about his purpose—who he was meant to be and what he was meant to do. Now, though, he understood. Everything had been leading to this crossroads. His path was clear, and he knew what he had to do.

— — —

"They've accessed the device again."

The fact that the report wasn't from an operative on Earth but rather directly from Carjen sent a cold chill down Hanek's spine. That meant the information had come directly from the Erebus.

"This will all be over soon," Magdalena said, tapping her fingers pensively on the conference table. "Is everyone in position?"

"We're making the final arrangements now," Carjen replied.

Magdalena looked around the faces at the conference table, both in person and holographic representations. "It will happen quickly once the word is given."

"Even faster than you realize," Felina said.

The knot in Hanek's stomach tightened. Felina's distaste for Tarans had been evident since their first meeting, despite her hybrid form. Yet, that was merely a vessel. If Hanek had access to the being's full power, he imagined he'd hate the constraints, too.

"We await your word," Magdalena said with a bow of her head.

Hanek's heart pounded in his ears. Everything had come down to this. Soon, the Taran civilization was about to change forever.

— — —

Mika had been to Zeron once before as part of the band's music tour, but he looked at the place differently now with Andrei's presence in his mind. Andrei's wonder came through via their link, revering the place like he was on a religious pilgrimage and had just stepped into an ancient temple.

What's so significant about this place? Mika didn't see it.

His assignment with Kali was to keep a low profile and gather information about anything that seemed out of place. So far, the only notable aspect of the planet was that the population was awfully large for a place where habitation was restricted to underground. There were plenty of worlds in the Outer Colonies where biodomes were the norm, but Zeron was downright inhospitable on the surface, its population forced to reside in carved out caves. People didn't choose to live in a place without natural light unless there was no other choice, and there didn't seem to be anything compelling enough on the planet to warrant that sacrifice.

"*What do they do here?*" Mika asked in Kali's mind.

"*They dig.*"

"*Right, but dig* what?"

"*That's what we need to find out.*" Kali took his hand,

sending a happy tingle up Mika's arm.

He still couldn't believe she'd chosen him, especially after everything they'd been through together. She'd seen him at his worst, and yet she'd grown to love him.

She's in love with Mika. Am I still him, or am I Andrei? He didn't know for certain. At times, he felt fully like himself, and then he would be trapped back in the darkness, watching his actions through another's eyes, unable to resist. He kept waiting for Kali to feel that something was wrong, but Andrei was crafty with how he exerted control, never coming to the forefront at a time when others might notice.

"You're not supposed to be here," the Andrei-voice suddenly said in Mika's mind.

"Why? What is this place?" Mika asked.

He got no reply.

Kali looked around at the workers. "Do the people here seem strange to you?"

"How so?"

"They're kinda…" she scrunched up her nose, "glazed over, or something."

There was an odd sheen to their eyes, as though they were operating on auto-pilot. "Maybe it's a lack of sunlight. Prolonged living underground can't be great for a person."

"No, it's something else."

Mika sensed her reach out to glean the surface of a passerby's mind. "I thought you weren't supposed to do that?"

"It's non-invasive." Her eyes went wide. "Oh, my stars." She glanced around, spotting another person and initiating another probe. "No, it can't be." She did another. And another.

"What?" Mika asked.

"All of these people have had their memories altered—or, more like wiped," she replied in his mind.

"Deny it," Andrei instructed.

"That's crazy. You must be mistaken," Mika said in spite of his real thoughts on the matter.

"No, it's true. Can't you see it?" She looked at him like he was missing the most obvious thing in the universe. "I can't believe I missed it before."

"You had no reason to read their minds then, and you shouldn't now," he said per Andrei's instruction.

"That's not like you, Mika."

"I was wrong before. I shouldn't have done those things."

"Point out the decoy ship," Andrei instructed.

"What ship?"

Andrei puppeteered Mika over to a communications console.

"Where are you going?" Kali asked, jogging to catch up with him.

"We should check the transit logs," Andrei told him to say.

Andrei wanted him to move through slowly and methodically, acting as one would when examining something for the first time. However, Andrei had already communicated what he was looking for—and that was his mistake. Mika might not be able to tell Kali that he was under an outside influence, but he might be able to carry out Andrei's orders in a way that would tip her off that something was wrong.

Rather than the careful perusal of the ship transit logs, Mika's hands raced over the controls. Before Andrei could realize what he was doing, he skipped to the records for a week back, going straight to the ship in question—something he should have had absolutely no way of knowing. "This one seems strange."

"Fool, don't!" Andrei protested.

"What makes you say that?" Kali asked, casting him a

suspicious glance.

"It's just like the ship they spotted leaving Glaendor at the time. A ship can't be two places at once."

"How did you find this so quickly?" She took a step back.

Mika could feel Andrei's fury in the background, but it didn't matter. Kali had finally seen through the ruse, and that gave Mika a fighting chance.

Andrei started to panic. "I wasn't honest before," he told Mika to say in a desperate attempt to salvage his cover. "I saw a little bit of how the Coalition operates. They have a command ship and a decoy. You can never be sure which is which."

"Okay…" She sounded unsure.

"Just tell TSS Command, okay?" Mika-Andrei said. "I don't want them to get caught off-guard."

"All right, I'll pass on the message."

Mika relaxed. He could see in her eyes that the message would be more than the tip about the Coalition vessel. *Maybe I'll soon be free again.*

CHAPTER 25

"BOMAXED STARS ALIVE, we found it!" Laura declared, bursting into Jason's office.

"Found what?"

"The foking Coalition mothership!" She excitedly cast information from her handheld to Jason's desk.

A stellar map sprang to life on the holoprojector, illustrating several star systems with planets and an icon for a ship in a seemingly random location away from other notable cosmic features.

"I don't know what magic strings you pulled behind the scenes, but it worked like a charm!" Laura grinned. "Looks like the ship just jumped to here in no man's land."

"Great work. Do we have eyes on it yet?" Jason asked.

"The initial report from the long-range scans is coming in now. Looks like a large cruiser, probably well-armed given the Coalition's track record."

"No doubt about that." Jason's chest tensed with anticipation. *We have a location. We need to go in before they move.*

They'd been making strategic plans for how to prospectively mount an assault on a vessel since the revelation that they were dealing with a command ship rather than a planet- or asteroid-based facility. The results of this scan didn't reveal anything they hadn't already accounted for, so it was just a matter of putting the plan into action.

"Keep the details coming," Jason instructed. "I'll run this up the chain. Let's get these fokers."

Laura gave an enthusiastic nod. "Yes, sir. We're on it!"

Jason sent a telepathic alert to his father and then rushed down the hall to the High Commander's office. He found the door open when he arrived and stepped inside.

"Thanks for the tracking help. We're ready to go on your word," Jason said.

"Show me the scan," Wil requested.

Jason displayed the information on his father's desktop. "This is what we know so far. We're getting higher resolution imaging to get the specifics on the ship. Based on what I see here, it'll be no contest for the *Conquest*."

"Agreed, but there's more to consider than just this ship."

"Like what?"

"These are the leaders. They answer to beings beyond our understanding. We don't know how they'll take this aggression."

"Yeah, I suppose we don't take it too kindly when enemies come after our representatives, either."

"I don't think these are 'representatives'—more like spies," Wil said. "They're the eyes and ears for what happens in this dimension, filtering information and processing it into terms the Erebus can understand. I think that's the only reason they're willing to work with the Gatekeepers, because they offer a perceptual bridge."

Jason shook his head. "Okay. Where does that leave us?"

He'd walked into the office expecting an enthusiastic endorsement to seize the ship, but now it seemed like his father was trying to talk him out of taking any action.

"I need to think." Wil turned away and started pacing.

If we take too long, we may lose our chance. There was no way to tell how long the ship would remain in its current position, and they were two hours of transit away from reaching it. Sure, they could likely track it down again using the same method, but the conditions at this intercept point were ideal—far away from civilians and structures.

His father turned back toward him. "All right, we need to go after them now, as you've suggested. But I suspect it will set in motion a chain of events we may not be prepared to face."

"Did you learn something when you went to Earth?"

"Not in the way I'd hoped. As I told your mom when I got back, I'm sure now that they've been biding their time to eliminate us—meaning, the Taran race. *Why* they are waiting, I don't know. They're executing a plan; that much is certain. When we take out their envoys, they may be forced to act, whether they're ready or not. My hope is that they have enough of their preparations in place to move forward with their plan but aren't yet at full strength, which could give us a fighting chance."

Jason nodded slowly, processing the situation. "And they could make that attack immediately, or… months, even years, from now?"

"The Erebus can't perceive time on a scale like we do. The only constraint they have right now is the perception of their spies. Once they're gone, they'll no longer have that frame of reference."

"Okay, so we could make sure they still have it," Jason said. "How so?"

"We keep them alive, thinking everything is okay. The TSS is full of powerful telepaths. If these envoys really are the eyes and ears for the Erebus in this dimension, then we can shape what they perceive to be whatever we want the Erebus to believe is happening."

Wil considered the suggestion. "That's an interesting approach." He raised his eyebrows and smiled slightly, clearly impressed.

"It might not work, but with enough Agents, I think we could make a compelling alternative reality in the minds of everyone on that vessel."

"A big unknown is the Gatekeeper hybrids. I doubt they'll be as easy to deceive as a normal Taran."

Jason nodded. "I thought of that. But what I'm thinking is that we only need to do enough to temporarily cast doubt about what's going on."

"What's the goal, then?"

"To gather every bit of information we can from that ship. We find out who's on it, what race they are, who they've been talking to, where they travel, and if we're lucky, find a treasure-trove of information in the ship's database about all the alien tech they use. And we'll get all of that information without anyone on the ship realizing there's been an infiltration, because we'll be in their minds controlling their sensory inputs while we're there."

"And then let them go?"

"That's the idea. Except now they're our spies, too."

Wil leaned against his desk. "It's extremely risky because they could see right through the telepathic manipulation. But if it does work… that information would be invaluable."

"Worst case, if they see through it, we take any prisoners we can and shoot the rest," Jason said. "Either way, we're taking control of this situation rather than allowing the Coalition to continue scheming in the shadows. I think this might be our only chance to get ahead of whatever big move they're planning."

"I agree." Wil stood in silence for several more seconds, staring through the floor. He finally met Jason's eyes. "Okay, do it. Take whoever and as many people as you need."

"You would be an asset."

Wil shook his head. "That kind of mental manipulation isn't my strength. You'd be better off with a team of specialists. Besides, this requires an exception to our normal conduct around telepathy, so the person granting that authorization shouldn't be involved in the act."

While Jason would have liked to have his father along on the mission, given his exceptional abilities, he couldn't argue that his true strength did lie in other areas. The Agents who'd trained in therapy and interrogation would be a better fit for the mission, even if they weren't as innately strong.

"We're a go, then?" Jason confirmed.

"Yes. And you're authorized to use any means necessary to gather any and all information from the ship and its inhabitants."

"Okay. I'll assemble a team and take the *Conquest* as soon as possible."

"I suggest taking more than one ship. If it turns into a firefight, you'll want the backup."

"Will do. I'll keep you apprised."

He quickly left his father's office, already thinking through who to recruit for the spur of the moment mission. The kind of people he'd need for this type of operation weren't the sort they'd prepared in the previous scenario analyses.

Unfortunately, telepathy specialists were one of the rarer

focus areas among Agents since the sovereignty of the mind was held so sacred. True mental invasions were a rarity, so there were only a select few trained in the nuances. A quick scroll through the TSS roster revealed the short list of those with the requisite skills. To Jason's disappointment, they didn't have a lot of field experience.

Those Agents alone wouldn't get the job done, but they could lead the charge with the telepathic network to form the illusory perception of those on board the ship. Beyond that, he needed powerful Agents to bolster the overall strength of the field and who knew how to handle themselves in combat.

In the end, he had four telepathic specialists and three dozen other Agents on the list, plus a hundred Militia soldiers, as well as Kira—true to his promise to include her. He sent instructions for everyone to immediately report to the spacedock, where they'd divide up on five ships.

With the orders sent, he swung by Lexi's office to give her the news. "We have a location for the Coalition's operations base. Storming in there is going to be a gamble."

She searched his face. "You want me to sit this one out, don't you?"

"Is that okay?"

She let out a deep breath. "I got Melisa back from the Coalition—that was my personal mission. As long as they're taken out, I don't need to be there for it."

He nodded. "It's not a question of your capabilities."

"I know. I have my own job to do. Leave the baddie takedown to the Agents."

"Exactly."

"Be safe out there."

"I have a lot of incentive to come home, don't worry." He kissed her. "I'll see you soon."

Jason wished he could tell her more and say a proper goodbye, but there wasn't time. He headed straight for the *Conquest*, determined to finally turn the tide in the fight against the Coalition.

— — —

"Five ships just departed the spacedock at TSS Headquarters," Hanek reported. He'd been keeping a close eye on the scanners monitoring the TSS moon base, and these were the only vessels to depart that packed any firepower. It couldn't be a coincidence since the bait ship had dropped into position merely forty minutes before.

"What's the estimated transit time?" Magdalena asked.

"Two hours."

She nodded. "Good, that will work perfectly."

Creating a dummy drive signature to match the *Horizon* had taken some creative finagling, but it had been a necessary step after it'd become clear that the TSS was tracking them. There wasn't much point in having a secret base of operations when it wasn't secret.

The rest of the plan was a matter of educated guesswork. The Coalition's leadership had learned that Jason Sietinen was in charge of the TSS' task force investigating the organization, so it made logical sense that he would lead the effort to apprehend the Coalition's lead ship. If not him, then another senior Agent would certainly be in the field for the mission. That's all they'd need to put their plan in motion.

The entire ploy was a lot of effort to throw the TSS off the trail of a single planet, but Zeron was worth protecting. This diversion would open the door for the final stage of the plan. They were ready.

Hanek settled in at his desk, focused on the screen. *Now we wait.*

— — —

Is it almost over? Though Lexi wanted to be excited about Jason leading an assault on the Coalition's main base, she could tell he hadn't given her the full story about their intentions.

Lexi replayed their brief conversation in her mind and the emotion he'd shared with her through their bond. Nothing about it read like 'take out the baddies once and for all'. *If not that, then what are they planning?*

She could drive herself crazy all day thinking through the possibilities. Instead, she tried to turn her thoughts to more productive endeavors, like figuring out the next phase for the civilian training program. Since the Antaris base was destroyed, the students had been meeting instead at a temporary facility on Crydael. The intention was to rebuild the Antaris training center at a new, less city-central site, but these things took time.

For now, they needed another way to connect with people. *A mobile training center.*

The Coalition's base ship was a brilliant idea, she had to admit. Any stationary place was inherently vulnerable, but a mobile training center would serve multiple purposes. They could get greater exposure for the program by allowing potential students to see the training up close, and it would also make it more difficult for critics to hit. Never stopping at a port, always maintaining an open perimeter around it for good visibility.

Like a prison ship. No, that wouldn't make for a good sales pitch. There had to be a decent balance between security and accessibility.

Her thoughts were interrupted by an incoming vidcall. The caller specifics were blocked, but it was tagged with Agent credentials. She answered it.

Kali's face appeared on the screen. "Hey, Lexi. Sorry to bother you. Do you happen to know where Jason is?"

"Somewhere in subspace right now, I expect. He's off on a mission."

Kali paled. "What kind of mission?"

"Going after the Coalition's leadership."

"Shite!" Kali's eyes widened in panic. "It may be a trap."

"What? How do you know that?"

"Is the High Commander there?" Kali asked, ignoring her question.

"Yes, as far as I know."

"Thanks."

The vidcall terminated before Lexi could ask anything else. *What's going on?*

It wasn't her place to get involved, since she wasn't an Agent and had no authority within the TSS beyond her role as a training advisor, but Jason was the single most important person to her in the universe. Any potential threat to him directly impacted her.

Against her better judgment, she headed toward the High Commander's office at the far end of the administrative wing. When she arrived, the door was closed. She hesitated, not sure whether to knock or leave.

Before she'd made up her mind, the door opened and Saera rushed out. The woman stuttered in her step when she noticed Lexi lurking in the hall.

"Why are you here?" Saera asked.

"Sorry, I got a weird call from Kali, and—"

"We know. We're working on it."

"Can I do anything—"

"Not right now." Saera patted Lexi's shoulder as she passed by. "Don't worry."

In Lexi's experience, when someone said *not* to worry, that was precisely when there was the greatest risk. As soon as Saera was further down the hallway, Lexi continued toward the door to the High Commander's office, which was still open. She peeked inside.

Wil noticed her right away. "There's nothing to report. I've passed the message on to Jason."

"Telepathically?" she asked.

"Yes, and a text relay to the ship."

"Is the mission scrubbed?"

"No."

She tilted her head questioningly. "But she said it's a trap."

"We have a trap of our own in mind," Wil replied. "It was Jason's idea, in fact. If we're successful, it won't matter that they were waiting for us. Though, I don't know how or why they're using Mika to relay that message."

Lexi's eyes widened. "What do you mean?"

"It seems he's been compromised in some fashion, though we're not sure to the extent of it yet."

"Shite." Lexi had genuinely enjoyed her conversation with him. He hadn't seemed traitorous to her eye.

"It sounds like something may have happened on Glaendor," Wil explained. "Nothing for you to worry about."

"No offense, but I'm concerned about Jason heading toward an enemy trap that we had originally planned to be us ambushing them."

"Knowing about the trap is the first step toward diffusing it."

"I'd like to know how you take a disaster of a situation like that and turn it into a plan."

"You would, huh?" Wil evaluated her.

She'd meant it as a flippant remark, but he was looking at her with genuine interest. She went with it, staring him squarely in his eyes, unwilling to back down. She might not be an Agent, but she plainly saw the dynamic between Wil and Saera. They were a team and could bounce ideas off each other. She wanted to have that with Jason, too, and this seemed like a prime opportunity to learn. "Yes."

"All right," Wil said at last. "I wouldn't call this a conventional strategy, but it's a good example of how we can be adaptable. Let me walk you through it."

CHAPTER 26

"WHAT KIND OF trap?" Kira asked from across the conference table in the *Conquest*'s Strategy Room.

Jason shook his head, not sure where to start. The information he'd received from Kali via his father had called into question all of his conversations with Mika over the past several days. He was proud to have picked up on the subtle clues that something had changed in Mika on Glaendor, but he was sad those concerns had been founded. What was very strange, though, was how quickly Mika's façade had cracked once he and Kali got to Zeron. There was, indeed, something strange about that world, but not in the way he'd thought. The planet definitely warranted further investigation.

"It appears Mika was either never working with us or has been turned," Jason said. "As soon as Mika and Kali got to Zeron, he pointed her toward information he shouldn't have been able to locate in such short order. Information that revealed a ship matching the description of the one we're tracking. However, the time it was there corresponds with the sighting at Glaendor, which means we're dealing with two craft that have identical signatures."

"They're using a decoy," Kira surmised.

"Quite possibly. Which leads to the question of *why* they would want to lure us to this remote location of their choosing."

"A very good question. Any ideas?" Gil asked. He'd been Jason's first pick for the assignment after the telepathic specialists, both as a trusted friend and fellow Primus Elite.

"Only a hypothesis without any concrete evidence," Jason continued. "Kali noticed something strange about the population on Zeron. The workers' memories have been altered. Like, whatever they do during their shift, someone doesn't want them to remember."

Kira frowned. "Oh, that's never good."

"So, there's obviously some kind of mind-control situation going on, which would also explain Mika's sudden change in behavior. Now, that wouldn't indicate much except for the fact that this isn't the first Gatekeeper connection involving memory manipulation."

"That's right. One of our Agents was captured by Victor Arvonen, who was a known collaborator," Agent Locklan explained. "I treated him once he got back to Headquarters. He was a mess. Whatever tech did that to him isn't like anything we have. They were viewing and rewriting memories."

"And what does that have to do with this trap?" Kira asked.

"Maybe nothing, or maybe everything," Jason said. "What if they want to breach the TSS from the top? Lure us in and program some sleeper agents of their own?"

She shook her head. "Would that work though? That wouldn't be a very good plan."

"Well, they're not setting a trap for a firefight—that's the most obvious reason for a ploy like this. They might be arranging a sacrificial offering to the Erebus, but there's no reason to have that be in a remote location. I think it's far more likely that they want to mask their true actions, just like we intend to do. And there's no greater deception than altering the mind."

Kira tapped her fingers on the table. "It's a guarantee someone senior will be on the mission, so there would be a reasonable target. But how would they single out that person? They must assume we'd send multiple, well-armed vessels. You can't brainwash someone without everyone around them knowing something's off."

"I haven't worked out that part yet," Jason said.

She shook her head. "I'm not convinced that's what the trap is about."

"We could call it off," Gil said; he was one of the few in a position to make the suggestion.

"What good would that do?" Jason replied. "We're never going to get answers if we keep playing it safe."

"You're right," Kira said. "It's either a trap, or it isn't. And the trap could be anything. Those conditions could be true for any encounter. In that sense, we may as well get it over with."

"Even going into a trap, that doesn't mean we won't succeed," Jason added. "Between our ships' firepower and the talent on board, we're well-equipped for a fight—or for our original plan."

Everyone around the table fell silent, mulling over the possible courses of action.

"I say we go forward," Kira said. "When we drop out at the site, we can reassess. If we get new information, we can adjust accordingly."

"I support that," Agent Locklan agreed.

Gil nodded. "As do I."

Jason spread his hands on the table. "Okay. Let's go over Plan A one more time."

—

They were as prepared as they were going to get. Jason sat in the *Conquest*'s Command Center, eyes fixed on the forward portion of the wraparound screen. They were moments from dropping out of subspace and seeing exactly what kind of mess they were flying into.

He activated the bioelectronic interface using a telepathic command. The hand-grip for the central command seat rose from its compartment in the deck, stopping at waist-height in front of Jason. He placed his hands on it preemptively, wanting to be ready to use the onboard telekinetic weapon in case they came under attack.

Gil sat next to him as second-in-command. *"This is probably a bad time to say I regret agreeing to this crazy plan."*

"Me too." He reached out telepathically to Agents on other ships, the only way to coordinate in real-time while in subspace, *"Bring up the telepathic net."*

He sensed the dozens of minds link into one clear mesh— the most he'd ever joined with at one time. Though he was by far the strongest individual, their joint power was a marvel. He lent his strength to the network but allowed the weaving of the mesh to be led by Locklan and the other Agents specializing in matters of the mind.

An alternative mental reality began to take shape, a purely telepathic virtual world for the target ship's crew to occupy. It was identical to the present reality with the exception that there was only one TSS ship and it wasn't yet prepared for battle.

Meanwhile, the tech specialists stood by to hack into the

enemy ship's sensors and make sure the vessel only perceived a reality that would match the telepathic version.

The *Conquest* dropped into normal space first, and the tech specialists got to work. As soon as they had control of the target, the other ships would follow.

As the ship entered normal space, the telepathic net enveloped the Coalition ship. Only, rather than finding a hundred or more minds within their target, Jason detected fewer than a dozen, most on the flight deck and a few more in Engineering.

He sensed confusion and concern from the other Agents.

"Why aren't there more?" Gil asked on behalf of the group.

"I don't know."

They were already committed, so they continued to put the mental net in place. Each person on the Coalition ship fell under the influence of the artificial reality being implanted in their minds. They wouldn't know what they were facing until the boarding teams got over there.

— — —

Hanek's perception shuddered, only for a moment. He blinked rapidly several times; everything was as it should be on the *Horizon*'s flight deck.

"The TSS hasn't taken action," the captain was reporting to Magdalena. "Would you like to open a commlink?"

Magdalena studied the on-screen image of the TSS vessel, designated the *Conquest*. There'd been stories about that ship. They'd sent their best, as the Coalition's leadership had hoped.

"No, let's see what they do," she instructed. "Any sign of the other four vessels?"

"None," the captain replied.

Hanek waited at the back of the flight deck, awaiting instruction from Magdalena. The TSS had clearly sent five ships based on the reports from Headquarters, which meant the others were likely nearby. No doubt, they were figuring out the best way to seize the *Horizon*, which was the point. They'd already offloaded most of the ship's crew, leaving only enough people on board to make it appear to be a fully functioning ship.

Why aren't they doing anything? Hanek tried to hold back his impatience. The sooner the TSS acted, the sooner he could be off the doomed vessel and get to safety.

A shudder rocked the ship, followed immediately by an alarm.

"We're under attack!" the helm officer exclaimed.

That's not how this was supposed to go! Hanek watched two more TSS ships become visible on the front viewscreen, weapons aimed at the Coalition ship.

The TSS fired again, and the flight deck lit up with alerts reporting weakening shields.

Hanek's pulse pounded in his ears. He hadn't expected them to take aggressive action like this. All of the intelligence had suggested that the TSS would board and capture the vessel, not destroy it.

"We need to go," he whispered to Magdalena. Keeping her safe was his priority as her assistant, and this ship wasn't the place to be. They needed to get to the exit.

"No, if the ship is destroyed, we'll lose our chance. We need to get away." She shoved him aside to speak with the captain. "Is the jump drive operational?"

"We're having a lock issue," the captain replied. "It's going to take some time to sort out."

"We don't have time!" Magdalena assessed the reports.

There hadn't been any damage to the ship yet, but the shields were getting dangerously weak.

"Ma'am, we need to get to a safe place," Hanek urged. "If we go now—"

He cut off abruptly when the flight deck's door slid open. Felina and Carjen entered. Hanek had never seen them outside the conference room, so he froze with surprise.

"It's not real," Felina stated.

Carjen looked directly at Magdalena. "We are not under attack."

"I can see it with my own eyes!" Magdalena protested.

Felina shook her head beneath the hood of her dark-blue robe. "It's only what they want you to see."

Magdalena faltered. "What…?"

"They are manipulating all of your minds, telling you the ship is under attack to cover their true plans for infiltration. We will handle it. Stay here."

Hanek gasped, his gaze darting around the flight deck. *None of this is real?* It certainly *felt* real, with every jolt of the ship lurching his stomach.

"Let them proceed. Play along," Carjen said. "This is exactly what we wanted."

— — —

"We have control of the ship," Rianne reported to Jason.

"Good. Time to head over." Jason turned to Gil. "Keep an eye on things from here."

"Will do. Good hunting."

The energy draw of the telepathic net was starting to give Jason a headache. He was used to using his abilities in short bursts, not this kind of prolonged exertion at a strong intensity.

The other Agents were very powerful by normal measures, but he was shouldering the brunt of it—serving as a conduit for the raw energy, which the skilled telepaths were then weaving into the complex alternate reality for those on board the Coalition ship.

With the net now fully in place and still no sign of detection, the TSS infiltration teams were clear to board so they could extract as much information as possible. As far as Jason knew, no operation like it had ever been attempted on this scale.

He rushed down to the hangar, where he boarded a large shuttle with the other members of the primary infiltration team. Additional teams would come from the four other TSS ships.

The shuttle departed the *Conquest* and quickly traversed the space between the vessels. The Coalition ship's hangar was open, thanks to the TSS' control of the ship's systems, and protected only by a standard electrostatic barrier. Once inside, the shuttle set down next to two other TSS shuttles, which had already arrived. The remaining two were close behind.

"Let's get to work," Jason instructed telepathically.

Agents and Militia soldiers flooded out from the shuttles, invisible to everyone on board the Coalition ship. If all went well, they'd be able to jog past any crew, who would remain unaware there'd been any sort of breach.

Jason led his team toward the central lift, with the intention of going to the flight deck. Unfortunately, the lift was small enough that they could only fit eight people in it at a time. He motioned to seven of his companions to join him; the rest could follow.

Based on the ship's schematic, the lift should open in a corridor right outside the flight deck, providing centralized access to hardwire connections into all the ship's systems. Once they were in, it'd be easy from here on out.

The lift's door slid open at the destination level. Only, rather than an empty corridor, Jason found himself face-to-face with a man and a woman dressed in dark-blue robes. Everything about them felt foreign to Jason's senses, though they looked normal enough. The strange tingle along his spine and pressure in his head revealed their true form, though.

Gatekeeper hybrids. Jason struggled to maintain his hold on the telepathic net. There was no way he could fight these two entities while maintaining that telepathic connection. *Fok, so much for not being detected.*

"What are you doing on our ship?" the male hybrid demanded, his gray eyes hard beneath the hood of his robe.

"This vessel has been implicated in illegal activity and is subject to a search in accordance with Taran law," Jason said with as much authority as he could muster.

"We will not stand in the way of you executing your rights. The ship is yours to search." The female hybrid and her companion stepped aside.

Oh, no no no. The fact that the Gatekeepers *wanted* them to search the ship told Jason everything he needed to know. The ship itself was the trap. *But in what way?*

He was about to give a telepathic order to abort the mission, but then he remembered his father's words. Though it was risky, there was still an opportunity to salvage the mission—but only if they stuck together. *"I have confirmation we're in a trap,"* he telepathically relayed to the other Agents on the team.

"If you're staying, so are we," Ron replied, with echoes of agreement from the others.

"Then search the ship. Carefully."

"On it," Ron acknowledged.

The entire exchange took less than a second with telepathic efficiency, all while the two Gatekeeper hybrids observed with cool, calculating gazes.

Since the ruse was up, Jason gave the instruction to drop the telepathic net so everyone could re-channel their energy. Once it was released, Jason brought up a shield around himself and his team.

"No need to be defensive," the male hybrid said.

"That depends on if you resist. You're under arrest." The words sounded hollow when spoken to these powerful beings. Jason didn't think for a second that they would comply.

"We do not acknowledge Taran authority over us," the female hybrid stated.

Then, she and the man turned to walk away.

"Stop!" Jason threw up a telekinetic shield in front of their path.

They walked right through it.

"A little help here!" Jason pleaded to the other Agents.

All the TSS officers in the hall simultaneously reached out to grip the two Gatekeeper hybrids, but they may as well have been grasping at air. The two hybrids rushed down the corridor, uninhibited, and into a room. The door snapped closed behind them.

"Your orders?" one of the Agents asked.

Jason considered following his own instruction to get off the ship, but he wasn't content to let dangerous enemy operatives get away without a fight. *Not that I know how to fight them. But they're not the Erebus. There* has *to be a way.*

He ran after them down the hall, and the other Agents followed. The five Militia officers who'd come up in the elevator took up guard positions outside the flight deck, awaiting the arrival of the second half of the team. Jason sent telepathic instructions to the Agents waiting for the lift below to capture the flight deck as soon as they made it up. The former mission was scrubbed, but they could still gain control of the vessel and then scour it for information, as planned—at least, that was his thinking in the moment. Or, he might be condemning everyone on board to death by not insisting they evacuate immediately.

He burst into the room where the hybrids had gone. It appeared to be some kind of conference room with a round table at the center and communications equipment throughout. There was a strong electromagnetic signature in the place, but there were no signs of people.

"Where did they go?" Jason asked.

"I saw them come in here, too," Gina said, coming in behind him. The other Agent assessed the space. "I don't see another door."

They began searching the room, not finding anything obvious.

"Flight deck is secure," another woman said from the doorway.

Jason whipped around, recognizing Kira's voice. "Thank you."

"Why are you investigating an empty room?" She looked around.

"Two Gatekeeper hybrids ran in here and disappeared."

"Were they actually ever here?" Kira asked. "I mean, like, physically on the ship, or was it just a projection?"

"I'm not sure." Jason frowned. "I *think* so. The Gatekeepers are hybrid Tarans, so they do have a defined physical form."

"Then *how* did they get away?"

"There's clearly some kind of back door."

They continued examining the area around where the conspirators had last been seen. There was no obvious way out of the space, just a wall.

Unless... Jason sent out a telekinetic probe to pinpoint energy signatures around the space. Sure enough, he detected the residue of a spatial distortion. "Stars, there's a TSD arch here!"

"Andrei Steyn used one to get away to Red Ghost, too, right?" Kira said. "Where does this one lead?"

"It can't be far." However, that was a conundrum, since there didn't appear to be anything nearby. Jason made a telekinetic assessment of the arch. It had a strong energy signature, but there was no way for him to trace its path using his Gifts alone. "We need to interface with it."

He called over Anya, the tech specialist on his team, to interface a specialized handheld with the arch controls. Since the transport device was integrated into the wall, it wasn't immediately apparent where the system was hidden.

I wish I'd paid more attention when Dad offered to explain the tech to me. The technology was generally used for short distances, like space-to-planet; he knew that much for certain. *But where could it go from the middle of nowhere in space...*

"The other ship!" Jason exclaimed. "The decoy. They might be holding it in subspace right on top of us."

"How didn't we see it coming in?" Kira asked.

"I'm on it," Gina said.

Tracking vessels in subspace was notoriously difficult but not impossible if they weren't moving much. Minutes had already passed, though. It might be long gone.

"We can't go through the arch," Kira said to Jason. "That might be what they intended with the trap. You'd be a good prize."

She's not wrong. Still, that seemed too obvious. The Coalition played smart, and there was no doubt something much craftier was going on.

"Sir, we have a situation on the flight deck," one of the Militia soldiers called from the hallway.

Since there was nothing Jason could do now with the escapees, he abandoned the TSD arch investigation and ran to the flight deck to see what was going on.

The 'situation', as it turned out, were two men pointing handguns at the Militia officers while an older woman was yelling at everyone to stop acting like children.

"You have no right to be here!" she shouted. "This is a private ship with—"

"You're Magdalena Steyn, correct?" Jason asked her.

She set her jaw, looking him over. "Oh, it's you."

"Contrary to your insistence, this is a sanctioned TSS operation, lawfully conducted based on evidence connecting this ship to criminal enterprises and acts of terrorism. Like it or not, you're under arrest."

— — —

We missed our chance to escape. Hanek had made the unnerving realization the moment the TSS forces had swarmed the flight deck.

He had stayed with Magdalena because Felina and Carjen had told them that they would take care of the situation, but what had they done? As far as Hanek could tell, they'd stepped aside and allowed the TSS to capture the vessel, unhindered. The order to stay had cost them their escape window, and now there was nothing they could do.

"You can't let them take her," a voice suddenly said in

Hanek's mind. *"She knows too much."*

No, he'd sworn to protect Magdalena. There had to be a way out of this. His mind raced, desperate for a solution to get himself and Magdalena safely off the ship.

We have to get to the TSD arch. Unfortunately, there were now a dozen TSS personnel standing in between their present location and the arch, including one of the most powerful Gifted people alive. Nonetheless, Jason Sietinen hadn't been able to stop Felina or Carjen from getting to the arch, so perhaps he wasn't as strong as rumors had indicated.

"She can't be captured," the voice said again. Hanek didn't know how he was receiving the instructions, but he felt the power and authority of it. He must comply.

There would be no talking his way out of this. So, Hanek did the only thing he could. He fired at Jason.

The ballistic round flew through the air directly toward the Sietinen heir's head. Two centimeters from his face, it bounced off an invisible barrier.

What happened next, though, defied any sense of conventional physics. It ricocheted at an impossible angle and accelerated back toward Magdalena, striking between her eyes.

No!

— — —

Magdalena's lifeless body dropped to the deck.

One of the Agents had telekinetically wrenched the firearm from the man's hand by the time Jason processed what had happened.

The bullet had bounced harmlessly off his shield, losing all its kinetic energy. But it had somehow then been propelled backward to strike Magdalena. None of the Agents present would have used telekinesis in that way, but who had done it?

Jason looked around the room at the mystified faces.

They must have wanted her dead so we couldn't interrogate her. But who 'they' were, precisely, still remained a mystery.

The man who'd fired the gun dropped to his knees next to Magdalena's body, raising his hands above his head. The ship's captain did the same.

"You won't make it off the ship alive," the gunman said.

"Why?" Jason asked him, stepping forward.

The man only got a mirthless smile on his face in response.

"*Why?*" Jason repeated, both out loud and in his mind.

The man—who's name appeared to be Hanek, based on his thoughts—recoiled from the force of the question. "The w-weapon," he stammered.

"*What weapon?*"

"A-Another Pesta."

Shite, like the weapon on Quel and Glaendor? Jason sent an immediate telepathic warning to the team searching the ship.

"*Yes, we just encountered an area marked as a biolab,*" Ron replied. "*But here's the thing… it's empty.*"

"*I've been told the weapon is invisible,*" Jason warned. "*Look for the handler.*"

"*Yeah, I see her through the window. She's dead.*"

That didn't make any sense. Based on everything they'd learned about the strange transdimensional weapon, it required a person to keep it anchored. Kill that person, and the weapon would be released. The moment it was released, everything would start coming apart. If they weren't dead already, that meant the room was somehow containing the weapon—though, nothing on Quel had seemed to stop it.

"*Don't open that door,*" Jason said. "*The weapon may have been released already.*"

"They wanted us to take this ship intact," he added privately to Kira. *"Did they want us to fall victim to a Pesta?"*

"I don't like this at all," she replied.

"Your weapon's handler is dead," Jason told Hanek and the captain.

"No, that's impossible!" Hanek paled. He caught himself. "But we're…"

"It's contained in the lab," Jason said.

"No, that wouldn't stop it. Nothing can."

If it wasn't trapped in the lab, that left only one other possibility: there wasn't ever actually another Pesta; it'd be easy enough to fake the presence of something invisible. *But why lie to the crew?*

Then, it all came together in Jason's mind. *The* Taran *crew.* He looked down at the frightened man and captain. "Your bosses set you up."

Hanek and the captain exchanged glances, realization dawning on their faces.

Jason shook his head. "It's time we have an honest chat about what you've been up to."

CHAPTER 27

TWO TSS MILITIA soldiers thrust Hanek into a chair inside the metal-lined interrogation room aboard the TSS *Conquest*. Jason Sietinen stood across from him, arms crossed and with his glowing teal eyes fixed on Hanek in an accusatory gaze.

He thinks I shot her. Of course he would; I pulled the trigger. Hanek had replayed that horrible moment dozens of times in his head, but he still didn't understand what had happened. Had whatever being who'd been speaking in his mind altered the bullet's course? But why? Why kill Magdalena rather than using that power to help them get free?

"Your own people abandoned you," Jason stated. He tossed a mobile holoprojector in front of Hanek and activated it. "See for yourself."

Text appeared midair above the projector. It clearly laid out plans for another iteration of Pesta, but it was all dummy files to make a convincing cover for a project that had, in fact, never existed.

Did Carjen and Felina plan this? No, it wouldn't have been just them, Hanek realized. They were working with the Erebus.

The aliens had used all the Taran members of the Coalition and then served them up to the TSS—taking out Magdalena, the one person who'd truly been on the inside.

Hanek had pretended he was an insider, but he knew next to nothing compared to her. He knew just enough that the TSS would interrogate him for weeks yet not enough to give them anything which would compromise the aliens' longer-term ambitions.

He couldn't help but laugh. *They wanted me to suffer.*

Jason raised an eyebrow at Hanek's apparent amusement. "You find this funny?"

"Don't you? You've been chasing us for over a year now, and yet the only thing you've gotten is what they *wanted* you to get. I'm merely a pawn."

"You worked for Magdalena, correct?"

"Yes."

"Then you must know what she'd been working on with the Coalition," Jason said.

"I thought I did. Then again, I was told that we were luring you to the *Horizon* to kill you with a new Pesta, with the plan to escape through the TSD arch. We all know how that worked out in reality."

"Who were those two hybrids?"

"What does it matter?"

"You can tell me, or I can make you tell me," Jason said.

Hanek shrugged. "Carjen and Felina. They were on the Coalition's leadership council." He could resist, but he didn't see any point to it. Since he'd been left as a sacrifice, whatever information he had to offer was something the Gatekeepers and Erebus wanted the TSS to know. In that way, he was doing his duty by divulging those details.

"And who else was involved?"

Hanek got comfortable in the chair. "Well, that will require some explanation."

— — —

"How are we supposed to trust any of this information?" Wil asked his son, brushing aside the report fanned out on the holoprojector above his desk.

"I don't like it either," Saera agreed.

"I'm just passing on what I've learned," Jason said. "It gives us the money trail directly to MPS, though. It's what we need to bring them down."

"Why would the Gatekeepers and Erebus want us to do that?" Saera asked.

Wil was willing to believe that the information might be accurate, but the nature of the Coalition's trap still didn't make sense. The trail was too clean, too perfect. They had set up their Taran collaborators to be exposed. All of the information in their possession had been carefully curated. "There's only one explanation that makes sense to me."

Jason tilted his head. "Which is?"

"The Gatekeepers and Erebus want to throw the Taran government into chaos."

Saera's brows knitted. "Why?"

"Because when people are scared and disorganized, they don't work together. Whatever invasion—or extermination— they have planned, they want us at our weakest."

Jason crossed his arms. "That means our best counter-move is to strive for unity."

"Much easier said than done, given the current political climate," Saera muttered.

"Tarans need to collectively face the truth that we're not

alone in this galaxy," Wil said. "If we can't get along with our own race, how are we expected to interact with others?"

Jason shook his head. "You'd think facing an interdimensional invasion would bring people together."

"It was like this during the Bakzen War, too. Some people do seek kinship in the face of adversity, but others think only of themselves and will turn the smallest divide into a chasm. But we'll never find others more alike than we are to each other."

Saera nodded. "If we can't heal those divides between Tarans, there's not a lot of chance to coexist with other races."

"Precisely."

"How do we fix it?" Jason asked. "Everything we do seems to make matters worse, not better."

Maybe real peace isn't possible. Wil had seen enough conflict to understand that it was the nature of any society to change over time. Peace required contentment, and to be content would mean to no longer have ambition. That spark, the desire for 'more', was as engrained in biology as the impulse to breathe. People always striving to evolve, never content, never truly at peace.

Yet, Wil couldn't admit defeat. His own motivation for change and bettering the circumstances of his loved ones demanded that he keep fighting for a utopian future he knew would never truly be achieved. Still, he held onto that dream, because otherwise, all the sacrifice would be without meaning. They needed to try.

"There is something we should keep in mind," Wil said at last. "We have divides within the Taran sphere, so it's possible the Gatekeepers and Erebus have internal conflicts of their own. I can't forget the fact that when we spoke with the Gatekeepers, they said they were taking their technology and leaving—we saw evidence of that. It's possible that the hybrids who were working with the Coalition are as much a rogue faction within the Gatekeepers as the Coalition's members are to us Tarans."

Saera nodded with consideration. "That's a very good point. Should we try to reach out to their central government, then—assuming they have such a thing?"

"I'm not sure yet. But we certainly can't allow this group of hybrids to continue operating within the Taran Empire."

"I tried to stop those two hybrids," Jason said. "They're incredibly powerful. They walked right through my shield, like I wasn't doing anything at all."

"I know that power," Wil said. "I felt it when I met with them. They're formidable, but they're not an unfathomable power like the Erebus."

"Do we try to fight them, then?" Jason asked.

"I don't want us going after this group of hybrids to reignite the larger conflict with the Gatekeepers as a whole, but we can't let these individuals run unchecked."

"Not everyone on the High Council might agree with that approach," Saera cautioned, no doubt referencing Monsari's influence.

"This is a matter of security, not politics. I'll deal with the political fallout if it comes to it."

"There are only so many bridges we can burn, Wil. There aren't many places we can turn now," Saera said, her arms crossed and brows drawn together with concern.

"We do have another card to play, but it's a one-time deal," he replied. "I don't know if we're there yet."

"Either we let things continue to spiral or we head it off now. With the former, things might get beyond the point of salvage. If we have a move that will allow us to stay ahead, then we need to make it," she insisted.

"I'm inclined to agree," Jason chimed in.

Wil shrugged. "It's never too late. There's always an opportunity to rebuild."

"Sure, but with which players? If we're all dead, then the Coalition gets to shape the new Taran society. Are you really okay with that?" Saera fixed him in a firm stare.

The tension was mounting. It wasn't often he and Saera disagreed, but their son didn't need to see them divided.

"Jason, can you give us a minute?" Wil asked.

"Yeah, sure." Jason reluctantly got up to leave the office.

Wil waited for the door to close before continuing. "If the Taran people no longer want us involved in the military or government, so be it."

Saera shook her head. "That's giving people too much credit. There is no 'general public' that peacefully and unanimously decides what they're going to collectively think or who they're going to listen to. There's always someone behind the curtain shaping the narrative. Question is, do we want to leave it up to the faceless 'someone' behind the current chaos, or do we take control?"

Wil swallowed. "It'd be an abuse of power for us to unilaterally step in like that."

"Like no one else has overstepped those bounds." She let out a long breath, leaning forward so her elbows rested on her knees. "I respect that you want to do things the 'right' way, through legal channels with all the correct checks and balances, but we're way beyond that. Legal and the 'right thing' to do aren't always the same thing."

"Like when we stood up to the Priesthood."

She nodded. "Just like that."

"I swore I'd never do it again."

"We didn't know about these new enemies at the time. You talk often about how we must adapt. Well, here we are."

He thought for a long while. "If I do this, it's going to start a war within the Empire."

"The war has already begun, Wil. We're simply taking a stand."

Is it really the right thing to do, though? He'd asked himself that question countless times in regard to his role in the Bakzen War. He hadn't walked away then, and he couldn't imagine walking away now. Nonetheless, it felt wrong to have the futures of so many once again in his hands. No singular person should have that much influence. *At least I recognize that. Must count for something, right?*

Wil rubbed his hands down his face. "Okay, I'll make the call."

Saera stood up and squeezed his shoulder. "I trust you more than anyone."

He gave a faint nod in response before she left him alone in the office.

I should have retired when I had the chance. He didn't mean it, but in that moment he could see the appeal.

The decades of political manipulation combined with ongoing bodily threat had worn him down—it'd get to anyone. No matter what he did, there was always a new crisis threatening to unravel the little corner of happiness he'd been able to carve out for himself. He'd been in this place enough times that he didn't have any expectations for it to be his last. As before, he'd act now because it was the most sensible thing to do under the present circumstances. His only hope was that he wouldn't one day look back on this moment with regrets.

Steeling himself, he made the one call he could that had any prospect of making a difference. He watched the emblem swirl on the screen while he waited for the vidcall to connect.

Admiral Mathaen appeared on the screen, seated at his desk. "Hi, Wil. What can I do for you?"

"Have you been tracking the recent political developments?" Wil asked the head of the Tararian Guard, not seeing a point to a preamble.

"Peripherally."

"Well, I've just learned some new information. We once found ourselves on the opposite sides of a standoff with significant implications for the future of the Taran Empire. In the spirit of the TUF, I'd like to avoid that kind of division again."

Mathaen folded his hands on his desktop. "What information?"

"The Gatekeepers never left. They've been working with a shadow faction within the Empire to spark a civil war with the hope of seizing control. The Monsari Dynasty has been funding them, and I suspect other influential families are involved."

"Fok." The admiral groaned and leaned back in his seat, shaking his head. "I knew something about this didn't feel right."

"The tricky thing is that the proof of these actions is… difficult to quantify. You'll just have to trust me when I say it's been verified."

The older man sat in silence for several seconds, tapping his fingers on the desk while he stared off in the distance. "Okay," he said at last. "What do we do?"

Wil smiled in spite of the somber mood. "I expected I'd have to convince you."

"Were you anyone else, we wouldn't be having this conversation. You've proven yourself, Wil Sietinen. You say jump, I'll jump and command my troops to follow suit."

"We can issue commands, but that doesn't mean everyone will follow through. This could turn ugly fast."

"War is never pretty."

"They'll call us monsters for trying to maintain control, say we're standing in the way of freedom, even though their supposed leaders would bind them in new ways we can't begin to fathom."

"The court of public opinion doesn't bother me. I swore to protect the Taran people, and I will fight to my last breath to keep our Empire from falling under the influence of outsiders."

"As will I," Wil agreed. *They made me to fight the Bakzen, but the Gatekeepers and Erebus will be my real test.*

"I suppose we'll have to wait to see what the history books say about us to know if we're rebels or the real patriots."

Wil nodded. "If there are people left to write those books, that's good enough for me."

CHAPTER 28

FOR ONCE, MIKA was happy to be at TSS Headquarters. He'd realized on Zeron he'd be okay the moment Kali ended her call with TSS Command. She'd looked at him with concern—finally, a sign that she knew something was wrong, as he'd been so desperate for her to see.

I'm not myself, he'd thought when he first saw her worry, *just like I wasn't when Tregaren made me do all those awful things. I want to be me so I can be there for her.*

He still wasn't able to explain what was happening with the voice in his head, but sitting in an official TSS psychologist's office, he was confident that the trained Agents would root out the problem. There had to be a trace of Andrei in there *somewhere.*

"You know why you're here, Mika?" Agent Locklan asked.

He nodded; he could do that much.

"Can you tell me what's wrong?"

"No."

The Agent got to work. The invasion of Mika's mind sent a searing pain down to his fingers and toes. Andrei, not wanting his presence detected, burrowed deeper and deeper in his bid to escape the expert mental probe. Locklan followed.

Mika detached from himself as much as he could. Any amount of pain now was worth it to regain his autonomy. He'd had a short taste of what it could be like to be loved and be a part of something bigger and better than himself. His past didn't control his future—not when he had the freedom to choose his own path. He would rise above it, just as he would break free from Andrei's unbidden influence. He would be free.

Faced with the agony of his mind ripping apart, Mika separated from his senses, drifting in a calm sea of nothingness. He didn't know how long he was there, only that eventually the pain in the distance lessened, and then it was gone.

When he opened his eyes, he found himself lying on a bed in guest quarters with Kali sitting by his side.

"Hey, you," she greeted with a warm smile. "How do you feel?"

"Like my brain was just split open."

"Probably because it was." She brushed her hand gently over his forehead. "You're going to be okay."

Mika searched in his mind for any indication of Andrei's presence but found nothing. "Is he gone?" He sat up with excitement. It was the first time he'd been able to make any mention of the mental presence.

"Was it Andrei?" she asked.

Relief flooded through him. "Yes. I don't know how…"

"All this higher-dimensional stuff is beyond me," she said. "It took half a dozen Agents rooting around in there to finally figure out what was going on."

"I went somewhere else. It hurt so much."

"I'm so sorry you had to go through that, Mika." Her

warm, soft hands took his. "I'm sorry I didn't realize sooner."

"He hid. He wouldn't let me say anything."

"But *I* should have known, through our bond."

"I'd hoped." He looked down.

"Is that why you did it?"

"It wasn't the only reason." He gazed into her eyes. "You're the first person who's looked at me like I'm not a monster. With you, I knew I could be better. Andrei tried to take that away, but now I want it more than ever."

She suddenly leaned forward and kissed him, slowly and deep. "We will."

They lay together for a while, processing everything that had happened and what it meant for their future. Eventually, they got up with the intention of getting something to eat in the mess hall. However, as soon as they walked out into the living room, there was a buzz at the door.

"Expecting company?" Mika asked.

"No." Kali went to answer the door. "Oh, hi." She straightened at the sight of Jason. "What can I do for you?"

"I wanted to check in on Mika," he replied before spotting Mika deeper in the living room. "How are you?"

"Feeling a lot more like myself," Mika said.

"You're welcome to come in." Kali stepped aside.

"Thanks. I won't keep you long." Jason stopped in the middle of the room, his attention still on Mika.

He could feel the Agent's telepathic assessment, searching for any lingering signs of Andrei or any other outside influence. "He's gone," Mika confirmed.

Jason nodded. "Good to have you back with us."

"Yeah, thank you." He paused. "May I ask you a question?"

"Sure."

"On Zeron, I didn't understand the message Andrei made

me give, about the ship. Were you able to figure out why he'd want you to track down that ship?"

"Depends on who you ask," Jason replied with a shrug. "The Tarans within the Coalition thought it was an assassination trap, which I think is what Andrei was driving at. However, the Gatekeepers and Erebus... I believe they were just toying with us."

"But why? What happened to everyone on the ship?"

"Magdalena is dead, a few other Taran collaborators are in custody, and the rest are still in the wind."

Mika's heart dropped. "So, it's not over."

"No, but it will be soon. They wanted a war, and it looks like they're going to get it."

— — —

Just when Lexi had started to feel like order was returning to her life, she was back to feeling like it was all about to fall apart.

From losing Melisa, to her time in the Alliance, to meeting Jason, and then the attack on the Antaris training facility, she'd been on a rollercoaster of highs and lows. Getting Melisa back had seemed like the start of a bright, new chapter, but now, with the Coalition's leaders still lurking out there, she didn't know how she could ever feel secure—not after Andrei had seemingly ascended and then taken control of Mika without anyone knowing.

Her ruminations were interrupted by Jason returning to their quarters. She rose from the couch to greet him. "Hey. Is Mika going to be okay?"

"Yeah, I think so. He's more resilient than most." Jason pulled her in for a hug and kiss.

"Still…"

"I'm sure your friendship would help with his recovery. This was more psychological than anything physical." He kicked off his shoes.

She shook her head sadly. "He spent all those years under Tregaren's influence only to have the same thing happen again. Poor guy."

"Unfortunately, the specialists believe that Tregaren's programmed backdoors into Mika's mind are what made it possible for Andrei to link with him in the first place."

"Bomax. Does that mean he'll always be susceptible to control?"

"They're working on a solution to heal those pathways. I'm hopeful for him."

She cuddled up onto the couch with Jason. "Me too. I'm glad we can make a positive impact on people's lives."

"For sure."

Lexi leaned her head against his chest. "I spent my life looking for a place where I could belong and feel normal. That shouldn't have needed to be anywhere special. Anyone should be able to be themselves in regular, everyday life. But people like me and Mika just don't fit in."

"We're trying to change that," Jason said, giving her a squeeze.

"I know, but there's such a long way to go."

"The kind of change my family set out to lead will take time. The Priesthood made a mess of things, spending generations spreading propaganda about abilities being a dangerous abomination. It's no wonder Gifted people are still forced into awful situations."

"No one should have to hide an innate part of themselves."

"I agree." He stroked the side of her face. "The work you're doing with the training initiative is going to bring people together—give them a community where they'll always belong. That's an amazing thing."

"It's a start."

"Little steps every day make a difference."

She snuggled into the crook of his arm. "Especially when you're with the right person."

— — —

We can't afford to be divided. Wil had espoused the virtues of unity and setting bygones aside in the interest of the greater good, yet he'd allowed conflicting philosophies to damage his own relationships. He couldn't afford to let those conflicts persist, not when the entire civilization was on the line.

Before he could lose his nerve, he initiated a long overdue vidcall.

Dahl's image appeared on his viewscreen, looking pleasantly surprised to hear from Wil. "Hello again. Have you found what you are looking for?"

"I'm getting there. I have a sense of what's to come, and we're going to need each other."

"I don't disagree."

"Let's hash this out," Wil said. "A truly open conversation, just the two of us."

"Do you not think I share information?" Dahl asked.

"In fact, I don't. Not in the way I would with my close, trusted friends. I believe we've known each other for long enough now to be more than casual acquaintances."

"Indeed."

"Why, even after we've known each other for more than three decades, do we never speak frankly?"

"Some things cannot be revealed."

"Yes, but I've done what you've asked. I've started to read the patterns, and I believe I now have a new understanding of the nature of our existence. I'd like some straight answers."

Dahl studied him. "Yes, I can see you are open to those truths now."

"I'd like to start with something close to home. Did the Aesir construct the facility we now use as TSS Headquarters in Earth's moon?"

Dahl didn't reply.

"Are you really going to keep dodging my questions? If so, we may as well—"

"No, you are right. It is time we explain."

Wil folded his hands. "Please."

"It predates the Aesir, but we have only existed as an independent organization since our split from the Priesthood. I do not know for certain, but my understanding is that it was constructed by our former parent organization, several thousand years before my time."

"So, it *is* Taran-made."

"That is where it becomes more complicated. The Aesir learned how to transition structures into subspace by studying the containment shell housing TSS Headquarters, as well as other places like it; I do not know where those designs originated."

"Either ancient Taran techniques that were lost, or they were working with another race. The Gatekeepers?"

"Perhaps. What we do know for certain is that the builders were aware of sentient life beyond our spacetime reality. They knew that constructing a refuge within subspace was the only way to stay safe."

"Suggesting that they may have been familiar with the

Erebus."

"Or any number of other entities as yet unknown to us." Dahl took a slow breath. "The question is, how did our ancestors go from knowledge of the treaty to building hidden subspace bases across the galaxy?"

"I was hoping you had an answer," Wil said.

"I have insights regarding many matters, but not this. I apologize for not stating that sooner."

"Why didn't you just say that you weren't involved in TSS Headquarters' construction?"

"But we were. It was just a… renovation."

"And when did that happen?"

"The existing structure was repurposed approximately one hundred years before the Aesir and Priesthood split. It was founded as a research facility in Gifted abilities, because of the dampening properties of subspace."

"And once it was under the Priesthood's control, they decided it would work as a military installation when the Bakzen War began."

"An apt summary."

Wil folded his arms. "Now I regret pulling it out from subspace."

"We could help you restore it, if you wish, but I'm not sure it would make much of a difference. It is one facility. We need a solution for Tarans across the galaxy."

"Will you help me figure out how to use the device we found on Earth?"

Dahl studied him. "Do you know where that path leads?"

"I believe I do."

He nodded. "Yes, I will help you. You are already on your way to becoming a Seer."

— — —

Raena had been called into enough secret meetings to know she probably wasn't about to receive good news. "What do you think it is now?" she asked Ryan as they settled into the conference room.

He sat down in the chair next to her. "I've learned better than to guess."

The lights in the room dimmed, and the other empty chairs were then filled with holographic representations of her grandparents and father, so realistic that it almost seemed like they were in the room with her.

Her father was the first to speak. "Thank you for meeting. We need to talk about the Monsari situation."

Cris nodded. "Yes, I suppose we do."

Raena swallowed. She'd been anticipating what the next steps might be.

"I never expected to have one of these meetings again, let alone so soon." Wil looked around the attentive faces of his family seated at the simulated holoconference table. "This situation isn't going to resolve on its own. Once more, we need to take action."

"You mean remove Monsari from its standing?" Kate asked.

"Unless anyone has a better suggestion."

Cris and Kate exchanged glances. "We can't—and shouldn't—approach this on our own."

"I can't get involved," Wil stated. "Whatever you have to do from a political standpoint is your business. I am here from a purely military perspective, and my professional advice is that Monsari poses an extreme security risk to the Taran Empire. They've been conspiring with, and funding, terrorists as well as engaging in unsanctioned negotiations with alien adversaries. We have enough evidence to make several arrests, but I don't believe that would get to the root of the problem."

"They deserve to fall," Raena murmured.

"This is almost as delicate a situation as when we brought down the Priesthood," Cris cautioned.

"I know," she said. "But isn't it our duty to ensure the stability of the Taran government? If we don't address this situation, no one else will."

"Sietinen and Dainetris can't do this alone," Ryan said.

Cris nodded. "We'll gather support from the other High Dynasties, just like we did with bringing down the Priesthood."

"There's another complicating factor. Do we bring someone in to replace Monsari?" Kate asked.

"Maybe that's the entirely wrong tactic," Raena said. "We're facing a civil war because of centralized rule on Tararia. Adding a new High Dynasty would likely only strengthen that dissent."

"Then what do you suggest?" Cris asked.

"We give the people what they want."

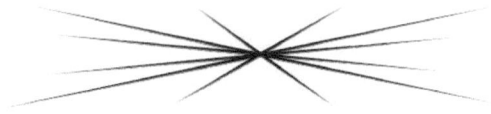

THE STORY CONTINUES *EMPIRE UNITED…*

They had a plan all along…

As the Taran Empire teeters on the brink of all-out civil war, the TSS prepares to take decisive action. Jason and his family still hold hope for a swift resolution to the conflict, but they're rapidly running out of options.

Meanwhile, the standoff with the Erebus and Gatekeepers comes to a head as the enemy's master plans are revealed. But with political tensions high and the enemy's true power still unknown, winning the impending war might come at the ultimate price.

ADDITIONAL READING

Cadicle Space Opera Series by A.K. DuBoff
Book 1: Rumors of War (Vol. 1-3)
Book 2: Web of Truth (Vol. 4)
Book 3: Crossroads of Fate (Vol. 5)
Book 4: Path of Justice (Vol. 6)
Book 5: Scions of Change (Vol. 7)

Mindspace Series by A.K. DuBoff
Book 1: Infiltration
Book 2: Conspiracy
Book 3: Offensive
Book 4: Endgame

Verity Chronicles by T.S. Valmond & A.K. DuBoff
Book 1: Exile
Book 2: Divided Loyalties
Book 3: On the Run

Shadowed Space Series by Lucinda Pebre & A.K. DuBoff
Book 1: Shadow Behind the Stars
Book 2: Shadow Rising
Book 3: Shadow Beyond the Reach

In Darkness Dwells by James Fox & A.K. DuBoff

AUTHORS' NOTES

Thank you for reading *Empire Defied*! This book took a lot longer to write than I'd intended, but I hope it was worth the wait!

A lot happened over the course of writing this novel. Most notably, I got distracted for several months while working on my first feature film. I joined forces with filmmaker and co-author James Fox to write and produce a sci-fi technothriller (working title *Crypto*). I wrote the screenplay and got to serve as script supervisor on set, which was an incredible experience. Though a challenging project, it was a ton of fun and affirmed for me how much I hope to see the Cadicle Universe on the screen one day.

Another reason this book took so long to write is that there were so many threads to track between this novel and the Shadowed Space books. While the previous novel, *Empire Uprising*, required a fair amount of cross-coordination, this book took it to a whole other level. Not only did the timeline and action need to sync, but the character arcs needed to make sense.

Telling two sides of the same story made for some big challenges. For example, I realized toward the end of writing this book that there was far too much "people at TSS Headquarters reacting to stuff" and not enough "on the ground action", so adding the Mika point-of-view scenes into this book was a last-minute change from my original outline. However, since the entire Shadowed Space trilogy was covered in the span of about half of *Empire Defied*, this meant the entire

Kali/Mika relationship story arc was incredibly compressed. If you'd like to know more about these two characters and see more of that relationship development, please check out the Shadowed Space books—they're a great read and provide a lot more background to the side characters and Pesta.

On the whole, though, I'm really proud of how this book came together and how it connects to the other novels in the universe. It's been awesome exploring the higher-dimensional energy possibilities and hypothesizing about the "science" behind the telekinetic and telepathic abilities found throughout the Cadicle Universe.

I owe a huge thank you to my incredible beta readers who always provide the feedback I need to hear to make these books better. Many thanks to John, Gil, Steve, Marc, Leo, Louise, and Liz.

Thank you also to Steve, Diane, Liz, Angel, and my other proofreaders for helping to add the final polish. I appreciate everything you do!

Special thanks to my husband, my parents, and the Fox family for all their love and support during the writing and editing process.

Thank you again for reading this third novel in the Taran Empire Saga. I plan to write up this story arc with the fourth book in the Taran Empire Saga, but there are other projects in the works. Until next time, happy reading!

GLOSSARY

Timeline of Key Events

All dates are adjusted for the standard Earth calendar

~98,000 BC - Ancient war and signing of the peace treaty between Tarans, the Gatekeepers, and the transdimensional aliens

AD ~50 - Priesthood's rise to power as a governing entity on Tararia

AD ~1000 - Taran Revolution period, following the split of the Priesthood when the Aesir left Tararia

AD 1587 - First skirmishes of the Bakzen War

AD 2016 - Invention of the Independent Jump Drive

AD 2025 - Official end of the Bakzen War; destruction of the Bakzen homeworld

AD 2050 - Fall of the Priesthood; transition of Dynasty corporations into public entities

AD 2054 - Reactivation of Gatekeeper tech

AD 2055 - Reopening of the rift/tear and reappearance of the transdimensional aliens

Key Terms

Aesen *(Ay-sen)* - The foundational energy of the universe; pure energy capable of being shaped into any form. *Aesen* energy exists in a higher dimension and can be drawn upon to perform feats of telekinesis.

Aesir *(Ay-seer)* - A group of Tarans who broke away from the Empire around 1000 AD (Earth years) to engage in metaphysical pursuits, such as reading cosmic energy patterns. The founders of the Aesir were all former members of the Priesthood and possess strong telepathic and telekinetic abilities. The Aesir are isolationist and long-lived, possessing advanced technology lost to the rest of the Empire during the Priesthood's corrupt reign.

Agent - A class of officer within the TSS reserved for those with telekinetic and telepathic gifts. There are three levels of Agent based on level of ability: Primus, Sacon and Trion.

Ateron *(at-er-on)* - An element that oscillates between normal space and subspace, facilitating high levels of telekinetic energy transfer.

Baellas *(bAy-las)* - A corporation run by the Baellas Dynasty, producing housewares, clothing, furniture, and other textiles for use across the Taran civilization. Additional specialty lines managed by other smaller corporations are licensed to Baellas for distribution.

Bakzen *(Bak-zen)* - A militaristic race that lived beyond the Outer Colonies. All Bakzen were clones and possessed varying levels of telekinetic capabilities.

Bakzen War - A centuries-long conflict waged primarily by the TSS in a secret spatial rift.

Cadicle *(Kad-i-kl)* - The definition of individual perfection in the Priesthood's founding ideology, with the emergence of the Cadicle heralding the start to the next stage of evolution for the Taran race.

Course Rank (CR) - The official measurement of an Agent's ability level, taken at the end of their training immediately before graduation from Junior Agent to Agent. The Course Rank Test is a multi-phase examination, including direct focusing of telekinetic energy into a testing sphere. The magnitude of energy focused during the exercise is the primary factor dictating the Agent's CR.

Dainetris Dynasty *(Dayn-ee-tris)* - One of the seven High Dynasties, the Dainetris Dynasty was considered lost for nearly two hundred years. After members of the family spoke out against the Priesthood's corruption, the Priesthood destroyed the family and buried the city that served as their seat of power. The Dynasty's status was restored in 2050, and a new seat of power was established on the Priesthood's former administrative island, renamed Morningstar Isle after the flower in the Dainetris crest.

Earth - A planet occupied by humans, a divergent race of Tarans. Considered a "lost colony," Earth is not recognized as part of the Taran government.

Enforcers - The police force of the galaxy; a division of the Tararian Guard.

Erebus *(Ayr-eh-bus)* - A race of transdimensional aliens capable of manipulating *aesen* at the foundational level to create and un-make matter within the spacetime dimension. The beings can reach down into spacetime through dimensional rifts and are capable of telepathic manipulation.

Gatekeepers - An ancient alien race with advanced portal tech. Little is known about their native form beyond that they are higher-dimensional beings and create hybrid versions of themselves to interact with spacetime reality, including Taran hybrid vessels.

Generation Cycle - Also known as the Twelve Generation Cycle. A genetic mutation in Tarans where seven generations will express no telepathic or telekinetic abilities, followed by five with those Gifts—the strongest expression being 10th Generation. It is believed that the genetic line descending from the Cadicle may hold the key to developing a genetic patch to fix the mutation. The Aesir left the Empire before the dissemination of the gene therapy that resulted in the Generation Cycle, so they do not suffer from the mutation; they do not intermingle with other Tarans for this reason.

Gifts - The colloquial term used to describe a variety of telepathic and telekinetic abilities, ranging from simple mind-reading, to object levitation, to manipulating energy fields on small or large scales. These Gifts typically emerge between the age of sixteen to eighteen. Before the Priesthood's fall, all but telepathy were illegal; since then, telekinesis has been legalized for non-violent applications. The TSS remains the foremost training institution for those with abilities.

High Commander - The officer responsible for the administration of the TSS. Always an Agent from the Primus class.

High Dynasties - Seven families on Tararia that control the corporations critical to the functioning of Taran society. Each have a designated Region on Tararia, which is the seat of their power. The Dynasties in aggregate form A High Council oligarchical government for the Taran Empire.

Independent Jump Drive - A jump drive that does not rely on the SiNavTech beacon network for navigation, instead using a mathematical formula to calculate jump positions through normal space and the Rift.

Initiate - The second stage of the TSS training program for Agents. A trainee will typically remain at the Initiate stage for two or three years.

Jump Drive - The engine system for travel through subspace. Conventional jump drives require an interface with the SiNavTech navigation system and subspace navigation beacons.

Junior Agent - The third stage of the TSS training program for Agents. A trainee will typically remain at the Junior Agent stage for three to five years.

Lead Agent - The highest-ranking Agent and second-in-command to the High Commander. The Lead Agent is responsible for overseeing the Agent training program and frequently serves as a liaison for TSS business with Taran colonies.

Lower Dynasties - There are 247 recognized Lower Dynasties in Taran society. Many of these families have a presence on Tararia, but some are residents of the other inner colonies.

Makaris Corp *(Mak-ayr-is)* - A corporation run by the Makaris High Dynasty responsible for the distribution of food, water filters, and other necessary supplies to Taran colonies without diverse natural resources.

Monsari Power Solutions (MPS) *(Mon-sayr-ee)* - A corporation run by the Monsari Dynasty, responsible for power generation systems for the Taran worlds, including geothermal generators, portable generators, and reactors to power spacecraft. Their foremost product are the Perpetual Energy Modules (PEMs) that function in the most critical systems.

Rift - A habitable pocket between normal space and subspace. The largest rift—specifically known as *the* Rift—is located at the site of the former Bakzen homeworld, a wound left by the destruction of the planet at the end of the Bakzen War. It is thought to be a place where the veil between dimensions is thinner.

Sacon *(Sak-on)* - The middle tier of TSS Agents. Typically, Sacon Agents will score a CR between 6 and 7.9.

Sietinen Dynasty *(sIgh-tin-en)* - High Dynasty overseeing the Third Region of Tararia, responsible for the SiNavTech navigation network. Considered the most influential of the Taran dynasties due to the family's ties to the TSS and responsibility for the Empire's transportation infrastructure.

SiNavTech - A corporation run by the Sietinen High Dynasty, which controls and maintains the subspace navigation network used by Taran civilians and the TSS.

Spatial Dislocation - The act of physically transitioning from normal space to the brink of subspace, either by means of a jump drive or telekinetic abilities.

TalEx - A corporation run by the Talsari Dynasty, managing mining operations and ore processing across Taran territories.

Tarans *(tayr-ans)* - The general term for all individuals with genetic relation to Tararian ancestry. Several divergent races are recognized by their planet or system. Humans are of Taran descent.

Tararia *(Tayr-ayr-ee-a)* - The home planet for the Taran race and seat of the central government.

Tararian *(Tayr-ayr-ee-an)* - Someone from or residing on the planet Tararia.

Tararian Guard - The military and peacekeeping arm of the Taran Empire. The military side is known colloquially as the Guard, and the personnel on the policing side are known as Enforcers.

Tararian Selective Service (TSS) - A quasi-military organization with two divisions: (1) Agent Class, and (2) Militia Class. Agents possess telekinetic and telepathic abilities; the TSS is the only place where individuals with such gifts can gain official training. The Militia class offers a formal training program for those without telekinetic abilities, providing tactical and administrative support to Agents. TSS Headquarters is located inside the moon of the planet Earth. Additional Militia training facilities are located throughout the Taran worlds and there are numerous TSS bases throughout the Empire. Since the end of the Bakzen War, the TSS has also engaged in more academic pursuits so many Agents can pursue careers related to the sciences rather than being 'soldiers'.

Trainee - The generic term for a student of the TSS, and also the term for first-year Agent students (when capitalized Trainee). Students are not fully "initiated" into the TSS until their second year.

Trion *(Try-on)* - The lowest tier of TSS Agents. Typically, Trion Agents will score a CR below 5.9.

Priesthood of the Cadicle - The institution formerly responsible for oversight of all governmental affairs and the flow of information throughout the Taran colonies. During its rule until 2050 AD, the Priesthood had jurisdiction over even the High Dynasties and provided a tiebreaking vote on new initiatives. The organization perpetrated many secret experimentations on Taran citizens and was voted out of power by the High Council. All known associates have been arrested or were killed in the fall.

Primus *(Pree-mus)* - The highest of three Agent classes within the TSS, reserved for those with the strongest telekinetic abilities. Typically, Primus Agents will score a CR above 8.

Primus Elite - A special classification of Agent above Primus signifying an exceptional level of ability.

Vaenetri Dynasty *(Vayn-E-tree)* - High Dynasty overseeing the First Region of Tararia. The family operates VComm, a corporation specializing in telecommunications.

VComm - A telecommunications corporation owned and operated by the Vaenetri Dynasty.

Voydite - A unique crystalline substance used to make the nanotube casings for PEMs. The Monsari Dynasty holds a complete monopoly on the secret source of the material.

ABOUT THE AUTHOR

A.K. (Amy) DuBoff has always loved science fiction in all its forms—books, movies, shows, and games. If it involves outer space, even better! She is a Nebula Award finalist and *USA Today* bestselling author most known for her Cadicle Universe, but she's also written a variety of space fantasy and comedic sci-fi. Now a full-time author, Amy can frequently be found traveling the world. When she's not writing, she enjoys wine tasting, binge-watching TV series, and playing epic strategy board games.

www.amyduboff.com